ABOARD CABRILLO'S GALLEON

Christine Echeverria Bender

CAXTON PRESS
Caldwell, Idaho
2013

ISBN 978-087004-525-7

Library of Congress Cataloging-in-Publication Data

Bender, Christine Echeverria.
  Aboard Cabrillo's Galleon / Christine Echeverria Bender.
    pages cm
  Summary: An historical fiction novel depicting Juan Rodriguez Cabrillo's 1542 voyage of discovery to North America on his ship, the San Salvador.
  ISBN 978-0-87004-525-7
  1. Cabrillo, Juan Rodr?guez, -1543--Fiction. 2. Explorers--Fiction.
I. Title.

  PS3602.E6614A26 2013
  813'.6--dc23

                    2013005355

Other novels by Christine Echeverria Bender:
Challenge The Wind
Sails of Fortune
The Whaler's Forge

Sarah Pilar Echeverria artistically created the maps within these pages.

Lithographed and bound in the United States of America

CAXTON PRESS
Caldwell, Idaho
184125

This book is dedicated with immeasurable love to my siblings, who have taught me a thousand lessons and brought me a million smiles: John Echeverria, Teresa Townsend, Debra Geraghty, Mark Echeverria, Felisa Wood, and Diana Echeverria. For each of you, I will always be grateful.

Acknowledgements

The conception of this story occurred amid towering shadows of historical ships gathered from around the world for San Diego's annual Festival of Sail. As I signed books and chatted with readers, the staff and volunteers from the hosting Maritime Museum began to mention with great enthusiasm their plans to construct a replica of Juan Rodriguez Cabrillo's galleon *San Salvador*. Later that afternoon the museum's president Dr. Raymond Ashley asked if I might be interested in writing a novel about the 1542 voyage that unveiled California's mysteries to the world. Considering such an enticing subject, and given my earlier work related to whaling galleons of this era found in Red Bay, Labrador, I was captivated, and my research began almost immediately.

After studying maps, accounts, and analyses for months, as is my practice, I began to investigate how I might retrace this ever more intriguing protagonist's voyage in order to gain first-hand knowledge of his experience. Good fortune provided just such an opportunity when Dr. Ashley organized a crew for the tall ship *Californian* and allowed me to join them on a sailing expedition up the California coast as far as Santa Barbara and, with special permission from the U.S. Navy, to all eight of the Channel Islands.

The days and nights spent aboard that ship, working, talking, exploring, eating, and sleeping in close quarters with the other hands, fostered tight friendships and countless impressions and memories. I was able to land upon beaches very little changed from when Cabrillo set his feet upon them, and on other shores he'd have found unspeakably changed, but with each landing and every crossing of ocean stretches in between, I learned to appreciate the man and his mission more highly. This voyage aboard the *Californian* undoubtedly allowed me to capture Cabrillo's tale with greater clarity than would have been possible otherwise. To Captain Ashley and the other officers, and to each of the crewmembers who offered their kind, patient instruction as generously as their camaraderie, I am deeply grateful.

Much thanks is also owed to Robert Munson, Historian at the Cabrillo National Monument in San Diego, who met with me during my visits to that lovely city (and my former home), sharing his wealth of knowledge and insight about Cabrillo and his age, and remaining available throughout the writing and reviewing of my book. Of him and his associates at the monument, lovers of history have much to be proud.

To the wonderful Cabrillo scholars and writers, including Harry Kelsey, Henry R. Wagner, Thomas E. Case, Paul A. Myers, Bruce Linder, and those involved in the Cabrillo Historical Association (now the Cabrillo National Monument Foundation), and to Pablo E. Pérez-Mallaína for his works related to early Spanish men of the sea, I offer my admiration and appreciation. Through the studies and teachings of past and present tribal leaders, university professors, and so many other educators, the publications by R. F. Heizer, M. A. Whipple, Ramón A. Gutiérrez, Richard J. Orsi, Robert F. Heizer and Albert B. Elsasser, and the tireless dedication of those employed at fine regional museums such as John Johnson at the Santa Barbara Museum of Natural History, a greater understanding of California's native people is being fostered daily, and a debt is owed to them all.

I am also much obliged to Fr. Dennis Gallagher, the University Archivist at Villanova University, for sending me the insightful article on Fray Julian Lezcano, without which it would have been much more difficult to gain insight into his personality.

My husband Doug Bender, sister Teresa Townsend, and friends Alice Tracy, Sally Mendive, and Helen Berria are the treasured reviewers and proofreaders who saw to it that this book was well polished before my admirable and much appreciated editor, Scott Gipson at Caxton Press, took over its guardianship. Each of you, please accept my sincerest thanks.

Author's Notes

Both singularly tantalizing and frustratingly concise, Cabrillo's files allow glimpses of fabulous discoveries while leaving persistent mysteries unsolved. A full autobiographic account of his experiences does not appear to have withstood the passage of centuries. However, notes, maps, and Andrés de Urdaneta's invaluable summary of the voyage (originally produced by notary Juan León from the testimonies of the newly returned voyagers in 1543) have survived. These and the short description published by royal historian Antonio de Herrera y Tordesillas in 1601, along with limited court records, represent much of Cabrillo's source material. A complete crew list also remains elusive, but the ancient record does permit Julian Lezcano, Bartolomé Ferrelo, Gerónimo de San Remón, Lorenzo Hernandez Barreda, and Antonio Correa to live on in this story. Although most of the tribal characters depicted in my novel are found in historical documentation, Taya and her family are literary creations based on my study of her people.

Since conflicting evidence raises doubt that the debate over Cabrillo's nationality will ever be settled fully, my description implies that he shares Spanish and Portuguese heritages.

Another area of conjecture is whether horses were indeed aboard these ships, and if so, how many. Spanish horses were certainly brought along on many ocean crossings, but the record of this particular voyage is unable to answer this and other questions about what was actually loaded. Considering Cabrillo's highly prized right to own horses and his war history, and that he had been ordered to seek settlement opportunities, which would have greatly benefited from the presence of horses, it seems likely that he would have wanted mounts with him. Also, he believed that throughout most of the voyage they would be sailing along a coastline that might well provide adequate feed and exercise for a small number of horses. For these reasons I chose to bring a select few into this story.

Fascinating substantiation is still being found that gives witness to the arrival of early Spanish explorers. Opposite is the image of a petroglyph found in southern California's Jacumba National Wilderness. Based on scientific analyses, these could well have been created around the time of Cabrillo's voyage.

~Christine Echeverria Bender

vii

x

TABLE OF CONTENTS

Chapter 1

MARKS OF THE LASH

January 29, 1542

If fate whispered one of its rare and subtle warnings along that reckless ride, not a single cautioning word reached the young messenger. Deaf and blind to the repercussions ahead, he spurred his mount on through the pelting rain over roads pocked with puddles and sliced by gullies, flinging mud with every pounding footfall. Snapping his quirt sharply against the horse's wet flank, his elbow clutched the pouch sheltered beneath his cloak in an effort to keep the contents dry until he could surrender them to their legitimate owner. Yet each thoughtless and impatient lash of that short whip would soon inextricably bind its wielder to a stranger who would shadow the rest of his life.

Lifting his head and squinting into the assaulting wetness, the rider took a sweeping glance at the devastation he flew toward. He thought he'd prepared himself, but a tight exhale of, "Our Lady, save us," escaped him as he pushed on. There ahead were the remains of what four months earlier had been the blossoming village of Santiago, Guatemala. Today it looked like the mutilated victim of a vengeful god, and perhaps it was.

A massive wide-based volcano, its peak diminished and marred by a collapsed cone, loomed ever larger as he rode. The natives called it Hunaphu after the god that had so recently exposed his self-destructive tendencies in order to demonstrate an undeniable might. Preceded by many days of downpour, a tremor had jolted the volcano's rain-filled crater so viciously that it had burst outward with a roar heard miles away, unleashing floodwaters upon the town and burying hundreds of inhabitants in moments.

1

Like most people in Guatemala and Mexico, the rider had received word of the mountain-rattling quake and its grim aftermath, but today he was gripped by the immeasurable difference between the senses of hearing and sight. The vivid outcome, though so many days had passed since the original disaster, tightened the stomach of the uninitiated. He steadied his breathing and let his eyes take it in.

Due to recurring rains, water still flowed from the caldera's torn lip like blood from an unstaunched wound: a painful reminder for the humans below of the impermanence of life. Dark earthen mounds scarred the southern hem of the volcano, divulging the presence of dozens of mass graves. Here and there scavenger-picked body parts of cattle, sheep, goats, and horses protruded from the silt. The latest rain had somehow stirred to life a lingering stench that now probed the air in search of vulnerable nostrils.

As the messenger rode swiftly on, he began to parallel intermittent lines of bent figures toiling amid broken tools, spoiled crops, bent trees, and crumbled adobe. These curving human chords of filthy peasants and slaves pointed toward the heart of town where the wealthier citizens had resided. Shortly after the quake, most local workers had taken up the task of constructing a new town four miles to the north. The laborers who still toiled under the silhouette of the volatile volcano could only be clinging to the hope, for themselves or their owners, of salvaging what lay unclaimed beneath the ruins.

The horseman slowed only slightly when the city's center came into clear view. There, he could see that the once dignified stone cathedral and bishop's house now lay in crude chunks and fallen timbers, half-submerged in wandering brown pools. On the northern side of the plaza, the public buildings and governor's residence had fared little better. A small number of ragged huts had been newly erected from salvaged planks and beams, and near one of these structures several soldiers guarded their unimpressive post. The rider drew his horse to an unsteady halt before the men and called out, "Where can I find Captain Juan Rodriguez Cabrillo?"

"Who asks to see him?"

The messenger stated his name and business.

"There, sir," said the guard, cocking his head and pointing southward, "with that group standing beside the foundation of his old home."

2

Giving a quick nod and spurring his horse toward that destination, the rider soon skirted the boulder-strewn town square and spotted a man matching the description he'd heard many times.

At this newcomer's approach several slaves paused in their digging. Some raised their gazes toward the courier, but any expressions of curiosity were dulled by a bleakness chiseled from the hammering of repeated tragedies. Two young pages looked on as each held a feed bucket to the muzzle of a horse tethered beside the open-walled shelter. A short, heavyset gentleman standing under the roof beside Cabrillo lowered a map they'd been studying. Cabrillo lifted his face, took in the horse and rider at a glance, and tightened his jaw.

At forty-two years of age, Juan Rodriguez Cabrillo had the facial features, shoulder breadth, and corporal bearing of one who had survived countless trials, at least in part, by sheer strength. A wild mane of black, curly hair and closely trimmed beard framed his dark, narrow face. The quality of his shirt, doublet, and boots would have distinguished him as a gentleman even without the presence of the exquisitely crafted sword at his belt. As the messenger nudged his horse close enough to observe the captain's face plainly, he saw that the scar from an old wound trailed down his jaw line from right ear to chin. A shallower scar, roughly the size of a one-real coin, rested high on his left cheek. Any man with such a past might carry similar scars, but what surprised the rider enough to momentarily hold his stare were the deep-set and pensive eyes now aimed at him, eyes that seemed more fittingly possessed by a wizened scholar than this distinguished leader of warriors.

The messenger was so struck by Cabrillo's piercing gaze that he failed to notice the set of his jaw. Leaping from his mount, the youth stated officially, "I have a message for Captain Juan Rodriguez Cabrillo. Do I have the pleasure of addressing that gentleman?"

The messenger paused with the expectation of being invited into the shelter, his hand resting protectively on the pouch as rain sputtered down to drip from his hair and clothes, but he was given not a crumb of attention. Instead, all heads turned as Cabrillo stepped from his shelter into the heavy drizzle and took possession of the winded horse's reins. One of his pages hurried forward to assume the stallion's care, but Cabrillo waved him back. Slowly, Cabrillo smoothed his right hand over the horse's wet-darkened bay coat and murmured unintelligible phrases. At this soft touch and calm voice the animal's legs, all the way down to one white and three dark stockings, gradually relaxed and grew still. Coming to the horse's head, Cabrillo took gentle hold of both sides of the bridle and peered into the great brown eyes. Through his face and body, through means too delicate to specify, Cabrillo appeared to communicate a worthiness of trust and an offer of benevolence. The horse's nose inched forward with each slowing breath, and after taking in Cabrillo's scent its breathing eased even more. With a soft whicker, the stallion brought its ears forward and nudged Cabrillo's offered hand. Still unhurriedly, and seemingly unaware of the drenching he was receiving, Cabrillo circled the mount a second time and finally paused beside its right flank.

The rider betrayed his building restlessness by taking a step forward. "Sir, the message I bring—"

"Come here," Cabrillo ordered in a voice made more compelling by its tightly controlled faintness. The messenger obeyed.

For the first time Cabrillo faced him directly. The slender courier was handsome, almost fair, and could be no more than twenty years of age. "What is your name?"

Under this intense and evidently displeased scrutiny, the messenger's expression lost a portion of its certainty. "I am Julian de Lezcano, acting as messenger for our most illustrious viceroy, Don Antonio de Mendoza."

Without taking his eyes from Lezcano, Cabrillo said in a more conversational tone to his companion in the hut, "Diego, the men may return to work."

That gentleman nodded, the overseer barked the diggers back into action, and the pages locked their eyes on the feed buckets. All ears, however, strained toward the coming exchange.

Noting a lessening in the rain, Lezcano began to undo the pouch's ties but Cabrillo stilled his hand with a question. "Tell me, messenger Lezcano, what have you heard of me?"

"Sir? Well, sir, I have heard that you served the Crown with great distinction in the conquests of Tenochtitlán, Oaxaca, and Tututepec under General Cortés." Cabrillo waited in silence so the messenger went on, gaining a little momentum as he spoke. "More recently you commanded companies under General Alvarado and won many battles in lands to the south. Also, you have overseen the construction of ships, which you then commendably captained. Your achievements have been recognized and rewarded through gifts of several valuable properties." Cabrillo stood fixedly, obviously unimpressed by this flattering recital and apparently awaiting something of a wholly different nature, so Lezcano tried again. "Your success has earned you the right to own horses and —"

Cabrillo stopped him there. "Yes, I maintain the right to own horses, an honor I hold very dear." The steel in his voice had begun to reveal its edge. "Any man fortunate enough to ride so proud an animal should understand its worth. Do you own this horse, Lezcano?"

He hesitated for an instant. "No, sir. It is the property of Viceroy Mendoza."

"Look at his flank and belly. Tell me what you see?"

The quickest of glimpses revealed the swelling welts, but rather than answering directly Lezcano made the mistake of trying to explain. "As ordered, sir, I rode first to your home in New Santiago. You were not there, so I came south in all haste. I was certain you would want the message with little more delay."

"Did you whip this horse along the entire length of that final distance, nearly two leagues?"

Lezcano's voice barely managed to hide his growing discomfort. "I meant only to deliver Viceroy Mendoza's message with the speed he bade me to maintain, sir."

The next words were conveyed like sword strokes. "Then deliver your message."

Cabrillo grasped the oilskin wrapped papers from Lezcano's outstretched glove and immediately handed them to Diego within the shelter. "Now you may leave."

"May... sir, may I take your response to the viceroy?"

"I will send it with another messenger."

Weary, hungry, heavily weighted by water and mud, and frustrated by this dismissive rebuff, Lezcano could see no possibility of mercy in the disapproving eyes that held him. He darted a glance at the other gentleman, but Diego Sánchez de Ortega merely studied his notes more closely. Now grimly resolved that no courtesies would be extended, Lezcano reached for the reins still held by Cabrillo.

"No. You will walk."

Lezcano asked in disbelief, "Walk, sir?"

"All the way back to the garrison at Iximché. Your returning those twenty-some leagues without a mount will give your horse time to recover, and you time to reflect."

Lezcano's body had stiffened more tautly with each word, and he now just managed to hold his voice level. "Sir, today I act as a mere messenger, as a special favor to our viceroy, but I must inform you that I am of noble blood. My family and that of our viceroy have lived near one another in Castile for hundreds of years."

Cabrillo restrained his own anger to momentarily disarm the defensiveness rising before him. "A man's family can not always teach him what must be learned. Sometimes the most essential instructions are left to others, so hear me. In this land one horse can save the lives of ten men, twenty, if a battle is raging. You have abused a fine horse over miles of roads harsh enough to kill you both. That animal," he said, pointing to the exhausted mount, "has the best heart among us all. If you lack the capacity to see such things for yourself, you had better learn how before speaking again of noble blood. Nobility is more than a birthright."

As these words cascaded down upon Lezcano, causing far greater discomfort than the drops descending from the clouds, the breath left his pride-expanded chest. Yet an air of defiance remained. "Perhaps I do have much to learn, sir. My destiny has not led me to serve in His Majesty's mounted military, so some lessons are new to me. I have been trained to give service of another kind. However, on this occasion I have been especially entrusted to deliver this message and return directly to the viceroy with your response. I ask you once again, sir, if I may be allowed to fulfill that mission. I promise to heed your words and to never again misuse a horse, but I entreat you to devise another means of satisfying yourself that I will keep this commitment."

Cabrillo considered the request as his hand gently glided around the welts on the horse's flank. At last, he said, "Very well. Count these lash marks."

Lezcano's heart began to sink and it grew heavier with each welt he counted. After numbering them twice he said clearly, "Seventeen marks, sir."

"Yes. Here, then, is your choice. Rather than immediately retracing your miles to Iximché on foot, you may rest and eat, and I will give you my response to the viceroy's message. You may then return riding a horse I will provide. However, if you choose to leave mounted you will be accompanied by two of my men, and at a quiet place outside of town you will halt long enough for them to mark your back with seventeen lash strokes. No one but my men will witness this punishment, and they will not recount what takes place. What you tell Viceroy Mendoza of the event will be your choice. In time, the evidence of the lash will fade, but I trust the lesson will not."

Watching Lezcano closely as he issued this alternative, Cabrillo guessed the thoughts that were passing through the youth's mind. He was likely imagining the pain of the lash, fearing that his courage would weaken in front of his guards, and dreading the scars that would mar his back the rest of his life. He will refuse this option.

Seldom did Cabrillo misread men, yet today his perception missed its mark. He was surprised by the grave smile that drew itself across Lezcano's face, and the answer he gave.

"I thank you for allowing me to choose, sir. I will take the lash."

Cabrillo took a moment to reassess young Lezcano. "I see now that there is strength in you, messenger, and courage. Once you learn to use both wisely, you may fare well."

Giving orders for his pages to see to the horse and motioning Lezcano into the shelter, Cabrillo unwrapped the papers that came from the municipality he'd first known as Tenochtitlán but was now called Mexico City. Within the protective sheets he found a letter and a printed pamphlet. After scanning the pamphlet's cover, he lifted his eyebrows in question towards Lezcano.

The messenger spoke as if little unpleasantness had previously passed between them, saying, "The viceroy was pleased with your account of the earthquake, sir. Because of its clarity and thoroughness, he had it printed. He bid me to tell you that it is the first secular document to be so honored in our new lands. Copies have already been sent to Spain."

Still more taken aback by this news, Cabrillo set the pamphlet aside, broke the seal of the letter, and silently read. When he'd finished, he let out a sigh and asked Lezcano, "Do you know its contents?"

"Yes, sir. I acted as scribe for the viceroy. He wishes for me to serve you in that role as well, if you wish."

Scanning the letter again, Cabrillo passed it to Ortega and explained before he had a chance to read its content, "I am to return to Puerto de Navidad with all haste. The Bolaños fleet was stranded off the southern tip of California and needed immediate aid. Villalobos has already been sent to rescue Bolaños and his men, but I am to oversee the completion of the fleet that Villalobos will sail to the Spice Islands upon his return." His expression grew more meaningful as he added, "I must also see that the fleet Pedro de Alvarado was to lead northward is speedily finished, only now *I* am to take command."

Ortega said with concern, "After so many crewmen were killed with Alvarado at Nochistlán, and still others taken by the earthquake, it will be difficult gathering enough men."

Cabrillo nodded his head wearily and then addressed Lezcano. "You need not write down my reply. It is brief. Tell Viceroy Mendoza that I will set out toward Navidad immediately after my family is settled in our new home. I hope to be there within a month."

"Very well, Captain-General."

Cabrillo said softly, more to himself than the others, "Captain-General, yes, I am to bear that title once more." Giving Lezcano another assessing look, he asked, "Has your decision concerning your return held firm? Do you still choose to ride and to bear the bite of the whip?"

"I do, sir."

Cabrillo's expression revealed a measure of grudging approval before he sent a page off to collect two guards. Lezcano was given food and drink while three horses were quickly made ready for their journey. When the guards appeared Cabrillo gave his strange but explicit orders regarding Lezcano. Neither by word or sign did his men question these commands, but he had the most senior of the pair repeat them to be certain they were understood precisely.

Just as Ortega was handing one of the guards a small package to deliver to his wife in New Santiago, the horses near the hut suddenly tossed their heads and shifted their feet. The men tensed, holding their bodies in strained suspension. Watching, listening, his nerves as taut as full sails, Cabrillo abruptly snatched up the papers from the table and shoved them under his doublet as he shouted, "Out of the hut!"

Lezcano hesitated in confusion, so Cabrillo grabbed his arm and yanked him forcefully from beneath the shelter. While dogs barked and women and children shrieked, Lezcano perceived the first tremblings beneath his feet, which swiftly strengthened to a ground-rumbling shaking. Feeling as if he'd been tossed aboard a madly rocking ship, he just managed to keep from toppling over by grabbing hold of the nearest guard's shoulder. He righted himself and stood swaying precariously, his legs and arms spread wide. The tremor intensified for several seconds, increasing the growling emanating from the earth's depths and causing Lezcano's heart to beat at a previously unknown cadence. The support posts of the hut they'd just left swayed until three of them snapped, causing the roof to slide several feet off center, but it refused to fully collapse. At this, one of Cabrillo's horses broke free of its staked tether and fled at a stumbling trot down the broken road. Without awaiting orders, a page set off in unsteady pursuit.

People of the town had raised their eyes toward the volcano as they scurried from ditches and shelters, slipping and falling in the mud, scrambling to higher ground well away from the path of the previous flood, hauling small children with them, and crying out for others to follow. When Lezcano's sweeping gaze fell upon Cabrillo's back, he saw the captain-general standing like a stone. He too was facing the volcano and staring at its crater. Remaining motionless until the shaking of the earth had ceased, he then said without alarm, "It would be wise to leave soon." His men wasted no time in preparing for a swift departure. Noticing Lezcano's paleness, Cabrillo asked, "Your first earthquake?"

Lezcano gathered his rattled fortitude and calmed his features, yet he answered with candor, "Yes, Captain-General, and hopefully my last. It was an experience I do not hope to repeat."

"Only a fool would. Go now. Do not fail to treat my horse, or any other, as a blessing." At these words a subtle smile betrayed Lezcano's discretion. Although restrained, something in the expression, something keen and shielded, made Cabrillo wonder if he'd unintentionally struck upon a secret known to no man but the messenger.

But Lezcano said only, "You need not concern yourself about the care of your horse, Captain-General Cabrillo. I swear that the lesson you impose on me today will never be forgotten. After so impressive a first meeting, I sense that we will meet again one day."

Gauging the potential menace behind Lezcano's features and words, Cabrillo responded evenly with, "So we shall, if God wills it."

Now Lezcano could not hold back a clipped laugh. "Indeed, Captain-General, if God himself wills it."

In an icy tone, Cabrillo said, "One last thing, Lezcano. Be grateful you were lighter with your spurs than your whip today. If not, my guards would soon be inflicting their spurs on you as well."

The smile disappeared from the messenger's face. "I do not doubt that you would have given such an order, sir."

At Cabrillo's command the three riders mounted and rode slowly out of town. Lezcano could feel the captain-general's eyes lingering on him as they headed northward, and the skin on his back began to prickle. He wondered but did not allow himself to ask where they would make their short but painful halt before going on.

Chapter 2

CALAFIA'S CALL

Señora Beatriz Cabrillo stood before the open window dressed in a long linen chemise and wrapped protectively in her naked husband's arms. She gazed over the tile roof of the cookhouse and watched dawn's golden fingers reach outward along the edges of the eastern horizon. Too soon the cool breeze that lightly brushed her body would withdraw its touch, just as her man would shortly take his leave. But unlike the breeze, it was to be two long years before he caressed her again.

She began to hear the first stirrings of the servants and slaves, confirming that their large household was again coming to life with the rising sun. In moments the cooks would be cackling over their pots as conscientiously as hens over chicks. The mason would call out orders to organize the men raising the south wall of the new horse stalls. The slaves, a few Africans shipped as prisoners of war but mostly Indians captured during battles in Mexico and Guatemala, would head for the fields with hoes and shovels resting on their shoulders.

Cabrillo sat down upon the window ledge and lifted Beatriz' small frame onto his lap. He picked up her hand and ran his rough thumb, a swordsman's thumb, across the softness of her skin. "I have always loved your hands," he murmured, "so long and graceful. I shall miss them." He lifted the hand to his lips and held it there, then lowered it slowly and met her eyes. "And I shall miss the way your cheeks brighten and pale with every emotion, and the smile that touches your mouth when you look upon our children. But, most of all, I shall long for your nearness."

She brushed back the dark hair parted above the center of his forehead, tucked half neatly behind each ear, and then tucked both sides again. Her fingers trailed to the deep, curved scar on his left shoulder, the remembrance of a wound that occasionally caused him pain even after so many years.

"When we first spoke of your going," she said in a tone of admission, "I hoped we might start another child before you left, a new one to greet you when you return."

"Perhaps we have started one this very morning."

"No, Juan, it was a foolish hope. It has been many years since I last conceived. My body seems to have grown too old for bearing children."

"Too old?" he protested. "You are but a single year older than I." He could detect few signs of age on the small face before him, a face in which his imagination found the same airy qualities possessed by angels depicted on walls and ceilings of Spanish churches. He perceived this goodness even during the rare times when Beatriz bristled with anger. Her smooth skin was lighter in shade than that of most Spanish women. Her eyebrows were the same color as shelled almonds, and the depths of her long hair hid strands of deep copper. From these signs, Cabrillo suspected that at some time in the past a member of the Ortega family had mated with a Hapsburg, perhaps even a distant relative of Spain's royalty.

"Yes, I am too old," she insisted, "so I will be content with our fine sons." She was silent for a moment and then revealed her musings by asking, "As you have been preparing to leave, Juan, have you paused to realize that your daughters may bear their own children before your return?"

He nodded a bit ruefully. "Yes, although I struggle to accept that two have indeed reached an age for marriage. Lucia showed me her list of suitable husbands yesterday, all former conquistadors, I noticed. Her selection of men seemed especially shrewd, perhaps because of some help from you?"

Beatriz affirmed, "We worked on the list together."

It seemed almost strange, looking back, how painfully she'd resented Lucia at first, even though Juan had told her about the Indian woman and his daughters before he'd proposed. In those early days of their marriage it had helped little to know that taking a common-law wife was quietly accepted and fairly widespread here, a youthful union recognized for what it was by the law if not by the Church. No, her jealousy of Lucia's exotic beauty and Juan's past affections had burned with the heat of an oil-doused fire. For many months Beatriz had dreaded losing her new husband to his previous love. She would have been devastated if he'd ever returned to Lucia's bed, but from every sign she could read he had not.

Fortunately those old embers of envy had cooled with the passage of time. Today, not for the first time, Beatriz asked herself what she would have done without Lucia to help guide her along the way. The older woman had taught her many things about this land and its people, as well as how to bring children into the world and raise them to be strong and proud.

Still referring to the list of suitors for his daughters, Cabrillo said, "That was kind of you to help her, my dear."

She gave him a look that held gratitude as much as fondness. "It was a small thing. Even now my heart seems unable to completely relinquish my jealously of her, yet she has been a great comfort to me at times. I can admit that now."

Cabrillo's was mildly surprised by this acknowledgment, and he rightly guessed that Beatriz had come to recognize how his approaching voyage would oblige the two women to rely on one another more than ever before. He breathed in Beatriz' scent and said softly, "As always during my absences, she and my daughters will aid you and our sons."

"That is true. She hides any resentment she might feel for me, treating me with politeness always, but I am not blind to the feelings she still holds for you." Her glance touched his. "With what little wisdom age has brought me, I am learning to hold her emotions against her less and less."

As the moments remaining to them dwindled, Beatriz studied his scarred but still attractive face and eased all thoughts and words of Lucia aside. She thought back to the day after her thirteenth birthday when he'd come to her to say he was sailing for Cuba to make his fortune. When he'd left Seville she'd been inconsolable for months. Then, after nearly two decades had passed, he returned to her at last.

She reached toward him now and cradled his face between her hands, holding his eyes with the intensity of her gaze. "I have loved you since I was nine years old, ever since you brought me that tiny kitten wrapped in the only good shirt you owned." They both smiled, remembering, and she gently released him. Her features clouded as she eased away enough to face him more squarely. "Today I must accept that you are going far away for two years, perhaps longer." She tried to keep her voice steady. "You will make landings in many unknown lands before you join Villalobos in the eastern lands, and you will likely find wonders at every harbor, some in the forms of women." Her voice lowered and her words came with an effort. "I am not inexperienced enough to think that in all that time there will be no other female to give you comfort."

"Beatriz, my lady and my wife, I will never find another such as you. That I know without looking at others. Wherever I am, I will carry you in my thoughts." Drawing her close, he kissed her deeply, lingeringly.

She almost surrendered again to his questing mouth and hands and to the desires of her own body, but she gradually drew back. With a sigh, she said, "There is not much time, and I must speak to you." Reluctantly standing, she moved slowly from his side.

"Please do not scold me for asking this, Juan, because I must." She took a steadying breath. "If you find the island of Calafia, will you go ashore?"

He smiled and shook his head. "Where did you hear that name?"

"Diego told me about her and her land."

"Your brother is a dreamer."

"He said the island is inhabited by women with gleaming black skin and great stature, who guard mountains of gold and pearls. He claimed that the women will kill any man who comes near unless he impresses them with his looks and intelligence, and even such a man is permitted to live only long enough to mate." Cabrillo tried to forestall her with another shake of his head, but she pushed on with rising emotion. "Any male infants born from their couplings are also killed, Juan. Only female babies are permitted to live."

"My dear wife," said Cabrillo, trying not to grin, "you sound as susceptible to myths and superstitions as my sailors. Those tales of Calafia come from a novel written long ago. There are no giant women, no mountains of gold."

"But Cortés himself named the land you will sail to *California*, after Calafia."

"His fleet found pearls in the bay where they anchored, and he probably recalled the novel's descriptions. Believe me, Beatriz, Cala-

14

fia is no more than a legendary creature. She poses no threat to either of us."

"Very well," she said, slightly less than convinced, "but the dangers you have encountered in the past were not based on legends. What if you meet warriors like the Aztecs or the Maya, people who cut the hearts from living men?" She momentarily stilled her words, trying to reign in her fears. "Please forgive my lack of courage, Juan, but that thought chills me to my soul. I need to believe that this fate does not await you."

"Beatriz, what brings such things to your mind now? You know those practices were stopped long ago."

She bit her lower lip as she read his face, knowing she was about to stretch his tolerance, and then admitted hurriedly, "Yesterday Diego told me what you and he saw after the battle of Tenochtitlán. He described the inner chamber of the pyramid you entered with Cortés, and what it was like to stand before the altars of their gods."

At the mention of that dreadful place Cabrillo instinctively worked to suppress his memory but failed. "Those altars have been torn down. Those days are gone."

"Are they, Juan? Everywhere? I pray that is so, but do you truly believe it?"

"I do, Beatriz, and you must not dwell on dangers that cannot be predicted."

"I try desperately not to think of those frightful things, but you have never spoken of that day, or about any of your battles. I needed to know, and Diego told me many things."

She didn't confess that her brother had disclosed enough to chill her soul and begin to regret her questioning. She now knew that Cortés' army had been helpless to change the fate of the Spanish soldiers taken by Montezuma's warriors, some of them Juan's own crossbow-men. The captives had been marched up the pyramid steps to the sound of drums, and her husband and the others could only watch from a distant hill as their men were butchered one by one, and each terrible death was triumphantly cheered by the Aztec crowd below. Picturing Juan meeting a similar doom fed the trepidation now reflected in Beatriz' eyes.

Seeing the intensity of her apprehension, Cabrillo growled inwardly at his brother-in-law's foolishness. He was thankful, however, that even if Diego tried he could never have fully disclosed what it had been like to stand in that accursed chamber the day after the final battle had been won: how the ears rang with the buzzing of a million flies, the stomach churned from the smell of putrefying blood that had accumulated on stone floors and walls from hundreds of thousands massacred there, or how the mind revolted at the sight of the freshest of the human hearts, Spanish hearts, still obscenely exposed within the limestone basin, left there to placate their insatiable deity. He forced aside these images and relaxed his tensing features, fervently hoping that Diego had stilled his thoughtless tongue before telling his sister of the avenging slaughters conducted by their own conquistadors. During the dozen years that followed, too many battles, too many horrors had been inflicted by both sides.

This time Cabrillo took hold of both Beatriz' hands and said sternly, "Diego should never have shared anything that could have troubled your heart." His words tightened slightly as he added with more sincerity than his wife guessed, "If I did not need him here to look after you, I would take the time to find him and beat the breath out of him."

"Do not be angry with him, Juan. Diego is not the only one who has revealed a little of your past hardships. I seldom mention the nights you cry out in your sleep or the times you rise and wander about the room, never waking but always on guard against some threat."

Apologetically, he said, "I have never been a restful sleeper."

"You have faced many enemies, and you fight them still in your dreams. I just pray you meet no more at sea." At sea, she thought. She was well aware of Juan's capabilities as a commander, but could even he keep a crew under control during so long and uncertain a voyage? She unwillingly recalled the Becerra voyage, and how a mutineer named Jiménez had killed Captain Becerra and others. Other voyages too had set out from Mexico, all meeting terrible trials and all failing to reach the East. And even if Juan's fleet reached the Spice Islands safely, what of the Portuguese? Did they not seize any Spanish ship sailing near their waters? Giving herself a sharp mental shake, Beatriz managed to keep at least these last fears to herself.

Cabrillo watched her fight to withhold unanswerable questions. Releasing her hands, he held her shoulders at arms' length. "Listen to me now, Beatriz. While I am away I will be cautious. You must

16

trust that I will lead these ships and these men well regardless of what comes. I want nothing more than to return to you, to our home."

"Yes, I know that. I know you do not wish to leave at all."

"If we had not lost so much in the earthquake, or if Alvarado had lived long enough to settle his debts with me, perhaps another man could have taken my place on the voyage. As things are, I have little choice but to sail."

"You do this for me and the children, for all who depend on you."

"And for my own honor."

To hide the sudden welling of traitorous tears, Beatriz locked her arms around his waist and pressed her cheek to his chest. She said hoarsely, "I will trust that you will return to us, sound and whole."

It took a moment to loosen his own throat enough to say, "Do you think I would leave that rascal Diego to take my place with our boys, to teach them how to become men? They might grow up knowing no better than to frighten their wives and sisters with ghastly stories." He heard Beatriz try unsuccessfully to muster a laugh. She was only able to lift her face and offer him a wobbly smile as she said, "Oh, Juan, I will miss coaxing you from your dark moods, and steering you back to bed when bad dreams haunt you. And who will be nearby to see that you do not work yourself to the edge of illness?"

"Paulo and Manuel will be with me, and all my men."

She huffed softly. "Men. Men have not an ounce of skill at such things." She pulled him close again and held on tightly, memorizing the feel of him. "Just come home to me again."

The squeal of young voices and the scampering of small feet reached them from another room. These sounds were followed by a shushing, scolding female voice that reduced the level of joyful noise only briefly.

Gently, Cabrillo said, "Come now, the boys will be in to greet us soon. This morning, madam, as soon as I am clothed I will serve as your maid." Beatriz brightened somewhat at this uncommon offer, and her eyes followed his every move as she brushed the lengths of her dark auburn hair.

By the time he had washed, shaved, and dressed Cabrillo had abandoned all previous intentions of discussing his will and how to settle their accounts in the improbable event of his not returning to Santiago. Beatriz was obviously in no state of mind to deal with the practical side of the unforeseen. Besides, all the required papers had been properly drawn up and witnessed. Now they must depend on destiny as God designed it and on his own abilities. These had been tested too many times for him to lack confidence in both.

While tying the laces at the back of Beatriz' pale green bodice, he said, "With our share of the voyage's profits, there should be enough for the girls' dowries as well as to replenish our needed stores, and complete our home and outbuildings. With luck, we may even be able to take the boys to visit Seville and Narváez. It would be wonderful for our families to meet them. I want you to imagine such a trip while I am away. Will you do that?"

"It *would* be wonderful to see them all." With her bodice now laced, Beatriz turned to him and asked, "Juan, will you reconsider your decision and allow your daughters to see you off?"

"Lucia thinks it will be easier on them this way. They were very upset when I left them last night."

Beatriz accepted this decision under the influence of her own memories. "When we are young our emotions are very raw. The girls are not much older than I was when you left me for the first time. It was your letters that sustained my hopes enough to turn away other suitors. Juan, you must write to us as often as you can."

"I shall."

There was a knock at the door. "Señora, the sun is rising."

Beatriz smoothed her skirt as Cabrillo stepped to the door. He pulled it wide open and pretended to be surprised when his two sons leaped from hiding behind Lucia's plump body, shouting, "Good morning, Papa! Good morning, Mother!"

Lucia, standing with evident composure in the doorway, said something to the boys in her Indian dialect and they both chirped, "Breakfast is ready!"

Cabrillo spread his arms wide and the boys, small male images of their mother, ran to him. He scooped them up, demanding, "Who are these young pirates?"

The boys laughed with delight. Juan, six years of age and just 11 months older than his brother, said, "I am captain of the pirate ship. Diego can be shipmaster."

"*I* want to be captain!"

18

Grinning, Cabrillo said, "You must follow the orders of the more experienced pirate, Diego."

"I may not be as tall as Juan, sir, but I am *fierce*."

"Diego, you sound more like your uncle every day," their father accused. Beatriz raised an eyebrow at the charge, but her expression was warm and approving. "Well, my sons," said Cabrillo, "shall we accompany your mother to the table?"

Although white streaks peeked from Lucia's braided and coiled black hair and the years had added breadth to her bosom and waist, her beauty had not fully faded. Revealing no sign of either longing or grief, she acknowledged the morning greetings of Cabrillo and Beatriz with a familiar nod and stood back so the family would precede her down the hallway to the dining room. Once there, she seated the boys and slipped quietly from the room.

When a bare-footed Indian girl placed dishes of food before the family, the three males ate heartily. Cabrillo soon noticed that Beatriz was merely pretending to eat the eggs, beans, and maize on her plate, but she never lifted the fork to her mouth. When he cast her a searching glance she forced a weak smile, and he didn't question her. This new attempt at courage from his wife struck Cabrillo once more with how deeply he hated the necessity to leave, and his own appetite waned along with the already limited conversation. The boys, beginning to sense their parent's growing sadness, became quieter too, and their stillness only added to the melancholy in the room.

Suddenly the imminence of Cabrillo's departure was undeniably announced by the sound of approaching riders. He rose from the table and was met at the door by Francisco de Vargas, the sergeant major of his guards, who would not only accompany him to the coast but would also act as leader of the fleet's marines.

"We have been given a fine day, Captain-General," said Vargas in a voice as big and burly as the man himself.

"Welcome, Vargas." Cabrillo pointed to a chest nearby. "There are the last of my things."

Vargas waved two of his men in that direction and the chest was picked up and moved toward one of the packhorses. "I have rechecked our weapons and supplies, Captain-General. All is ready."

All is ready. Cabrillo had overseen every preparation, given every instruction, and his men had carried them out. Now he had only

19

to go. He turned back to find Beatriz and the boys close behind him. Lucia stood at the far corner of the room, her eyes expressing what her voice could not, asking nothing from him but the knowing glance he now gave her in farewell.

Little Juan's face had turned a shade paler than usual and Diego's lower lip began to quiver.

Understanding that it took every bit of his wife's will to keep her expression reassuring, Cabrillo soaked in the steady smile she now shone upon him. Without taking her gaze from his, she said to her boys, "Wish your father well, and show him what brave sons will await his homecoming."

They ran to him then, saying, "Farewell, Papa!" and threw their small arms around his waist. Cabrillo crouched down and pulled them closer still, all the while speaking to his wife with shining eyes. Finally, releasing the boys, he stood and went to Beatriz. He held her hands and touched his forehead to hers. "You will be in my prayers, every day and night."

"And you in mine. Go with God."

He looked toward the corner of the room and said as his throat tightened, "Take care of them, Lucia."

Speaking so softly that no sound reached him, she said, "As I always have."

When Diego began to sniffle Beatriz picked him up and pressed his head to her shoulder. Young Juan snuggled his small body into the folds of her full skirt. Cabrillo kissed Beatriz softly on her flushed cheek and then pivoted away. Striding to the doorway, he lifted his sword from its stand and his cape from its peg. Without looking back, he let Vargas open the door and pull it gently closed behind him.

Rooted in place, Beatriz stood clutching her sons and warring with the urge to follow her husband out the door. But she did not go after him. She would not shame him by exhibiting such weakness before his men.

Diego whimpered into her ear but she hushed him with one quick, "shh!" She strained to listen, relying on the last of her five senses able to confirm her husband's closeness. She stared at the door as she labored to hear each clink of metal and creak of leather. Then the sudden beating of hooves reached her as horses responded to spurs, and their rolling cadence increased as it escaped farther and farther into the distance. She barely breathed until her ears could no longer perceive the slightest reverberation of the earth.

Chapter 3

THE DOUBLE ANCHOR TAVERN

Captain Antonio Correa impatiently banged his pottery tankard on the rough wooden table and proclaimed, "We should start without them, Captain-General. Any man who fails to appear at the stated time for such an important meeting deserves to miss what comes. The noon hour has long since passed."

Accustomed as Cabrillo was to the man's crusty character, such intermittent outbursts caused little uneasiness. Cabrillo gave a nod of acknowledgement but offered no sign of acquiescence.

Scholar and navigator Andrés de Urdaneta, Captain-General Villalobos, Captain Bolaños, and Captain Ferrelo of Cabrillo's own fleet also sat close by on long wooden benches in a private chamber just off the Double Anchor Tavern's main room. The year-old pub had been constructed of adobe, posts, and beams, and thatched with palm leaves, and the inspired owner had symbolically proclaimed its name by mounting a pair of crossed anchors above the entry. In the smaller room now occupied by the seamen a single window provided the only entry for an occasional breath of breeze, which seemed to be forever accompanied by a handful of whining mosquitoes. The warm, muggy air was beginning to make the room feel more crowded than it already was as the six men awaited the appearance of the two late arrivals.

"With your permission, gentlemen," said Cabrillo, bowing his head toward Villalobos, Bolaños, and Urdaneta, and then returning his attention to Correa, "we shall give my men a little longer, Captain." At the use of his title, Correa's irritation eased a bit, just as Cabrillo had hoped.

The captain-general valued this short-tempered Portuguese for many reasons, including his commendable skill as a pilot and significant experience as a captain. Correa had even sailed with Francisco de

Bolaños, who had just returned from his ill-fated voyage over the first stretch of water Cabrillo's fleet intended to navigate. Under Bolaños, Correa had journeyed as far as Abreojos, which lay roughly 300 miles up the western coast from the tip of California's baja. At that point they had been forced to turn back and ultimately await a rescue from Captain Ruy López de Villalobos, the viceroy's own cousin. Cabrillo knew that Correa was anxious to erase the unpleasant taste of failure left by that futile attempt.

Cabrillo had given Correa command of his bergantine *San Miguel* and planned to consult him frequently about the land and sea he had already explored. In addition to the *San Miguel's* sails, thirteen pairs of oars would power Correa's small ship, and he would need every ounce of his obvious toughness to control that crew of rowers, several of whom had been condemned to such hard labor because of their crimes.

Directly across the table from Cabrillo sat Bartolomé Ferrelo, captain of their mid-sized ship *La Victoria*. Ferrelo's ability to steer a vessel under any conditions was so acknowledged that the captain-general had also given him the title of chief pilot. Cabrillo knew him well and held him in unusually high regard. They'd sailed together before aboard the *Santiago*, a ship Cabrillo had constructed but General Alvarado had later commandeered. Several times in the past Cabrillo had seen Ferrelo bring a group of unruly sailors under control with nothing more than a word or an icy stare, and his current crewmen already recognized him as a strict but fair leader. Cabrillo felt confident that those aboard *La Victoria* would be in proficient hands.

At the moment, Ferrelo was smiling with leniency into his tankard of wine, silent as usual. Observing Ferrelo's gentle expression, Cabrillo could not help reflecting on how his two subordinate captains were as dissimilar from one another as snow differs from mud.

While Ferrelo's appearance was neat to the point of fastidiousness, it was evident that Correa could not be troubled about his at all. The cost of Ferrelo's finely tailored wardrobe must have totaled ten times the outlay made for Correa's sturdy clothing. Ferrelo's moustache, with its long tapered ends curling upward to form perfectly balanced arches, was nothing short of a work of art. Correa, on the other hand, seldom remembered to keep his beard or moustache trimmed until it began to itch from the stirrings of small, unwanted denizens. Ferrelo was the fittest, most graceful man in the fleet while Correa sported the beginnings of a gut and moved with the finesse of a lame bull. Beyond appearances, Ferrelo was soft-spoken, thoughtful, and deliberate. Correa spoke loudly and often, his words punctuated by a slight lisp issuing from the gap where two front teeth had once resided.

Fortunately for Cabrillo and his fleet, the two seemed so amused by the extremes of his peer that they got along considerably well. Cabrillo believed that their acceptance of one another was even more due to the fact that, despite their conspicuous differences, the most needed traits to be found in a ship Captains Correa and Ferrelo held in common: loyalty, intelligence, and courage.

Turning again toward the three gentlemen seated to Ferrelo's left, Cabrillo addressed Villalobos, Urdaneta, and Bolaños. "I apologize for Pilot San Remón and Master Uribe's tardiness, gentlemen. They are generally most reliable. I can only presume that something serious has distracted them."

"Please do not concern yourself, Captain-General Cabrillo," said Villalobos. "The viceroy's instruction can wait a little longer."

Urdaneta said, "Such hearty fare as our inn keeper continues to offer has made the waiting enjoyable, sir."

Bolaños added, "I must add, it is seldom that I have a chance to share such esteemed company, Captain-General."

They briefly let their attention be diverted by the thin middle-aged serving woman who quietly entered and placed a small bowl of olives and a platter piled high with sheep cheese and flat bread on the table. Cabrillo gave her a nod that said they needed nothing more. Just turning to leave, she let out a startled cry and leaped back to avoid being knocked down by the precipitate arrival of young Pilot Gerónimo de San Remón. A breathless Master Uribe immediately followed his entry but did so with slightly more dignity.

The two men bowed low to the group and the pilot said with his head still down, "Captain Cabrillo, gentlemen, please forgive us for being so late to appear." He held his bow a little longer than seemed necessary but when he straightened, Captain Correa let out a howl of laughter and Señor Urdaneta slid a hand over his mouth to hide a smile. Cabrillo was so surprised he rose to his feet and addressed his pilot with a highly irregular lack of formality, demanding, "Gerónimo! Explain yourself." Now that they could all see Pilot San Remón's clean-shaven face clearly, they took a moment to study the bleeding lip, reddened jaw, and puffy left eye marring the youthful virtue his face usually portrayed.

"Captain-General," he reported in his most official tone, "we were delayed when a fight broke out among the crew of the *San Miguel.*" This abruptly silenced Captain Correa's laughter and expunged his grin. Pilot San Remón went on hurriedly, "Pilot Barreda had requested that I come aboard to check their binnacle compass, sir. I was doing so when the first punch was thrown and, I am ashamed to admit it, sir, but while trying to stop the brawl I was thrown into it, bodily."

Cabrillo's brow furrowed deeper. "Bodily?" He let out a clipped curse. "What of the other officers?"

San Remón cast his eyes toward Captain Correa and hesitated an instant before confessing, "Pilot Barreda's right arm is being looked after by the surgeon, sir. It might be broken. He also lost a tooth, but he felled three men before he was deprived of the use of his arm. It took the help of the boatswain and some trustworthy rowers, but we soon got all six of the bast—" He swallowed and swept a glance over the distinguished assembly, letting it settle again on Cabrillo. "I mean, sir, that the responsible crewmembers have now been securely chained to the *San Miguel's* oar locks."

When Cabrillo's scrutiny rotated to Shipmaster Uribe, who stood noticeably unscathed, Pilot San Remón added quickly, "Master Uribe tried to come to our assistance, Captain-General, but he was at a storehouse by the dock when the trouble started. It was nearly over by the time he could arrive."

"I apologize, sir," said Uribe, "for noticing the fight too late to give the aid I would have liked."

Cabrillo accepted this and then asked his pilot, "Do you know what started it?"

"Not yet, sir."

"Were any knives drawn, pilot?"

"None, Captain-General Cabrillo, thank God."

Looking about to erupt from the pressure of holding back a reaction to the conduct of his men, Correa shouted, "Why, that pack of criminals!" Despite this outburst, however, there was a barely discernable hint of pride behind the condemnation. Still, he knew what was required under such circumstances. "Every man involved will feel his share of the lash, sir, and they'll all be kept in chains until we sail."

Cabrillo had not yet finished his questioning. "Who were the instigators, pilot?"

"Gaspar seems to have started things by—"

Correa exploded again. "That devil! He gives more trouble than the rest locked together."

To Correa, Cabrillo said, "Considering this new misconduct, Captain, I ask you to reflect on whether Gaspar should be left behind."

Correa actually did pause to reflect, but only for a moment. "He is a robber and a scoundrel, Captain-General, but he is young, and I feel there is hope for him still."

All gazes swung to Cabrillo, who sat down again and closed his eyes while running a hand twice across the back of his neck. At last he said, "Very well, Captain Correa, I will allow you to decide the sentence since it is your crew, but I will have the entire fleet witness both the pronouncement of the judgment and its execution."

"Of course, Captain-General," said Correa. "After the guilty have been dealt with, sir, if any of them value what is left of their hides, they will not repeat such behavior."

"See that your boatswain bears in mind that we sail in two weeks, Captain," Cabrillo cautioned. "The punished men must be seaworthy by then."

"Yes, sir."

Cabrillo signaled for San Remón and Uribe to take seats to his right, his pilot next to him. As they were doing so, Cabrillo bent his head close to San Remón and said in an undertone, "Any real damage done to you, pilot?"

San Remón managed a painful smile, "Only to my pride, sir."

Despite being the youngest of his officers, San Remón had skills Cabrillo held in such esteem that he had chosen him above several others to pilot his flagship. Uribe, wizened by experience and time, and calm as an oak in any crisis, had also been chosen with care to act as shipmaster. It disturbed Cabrillo more than he revealed that these two men had been pulled into a scuffle aboard the bergantine. Things had been going relatively smoothly during the preparation of his fleet, as well as with the construction of Villalobos' ships, until this. Cabrillo tried to reassure himself by remembering that a mishap or two always arose prior to embarking. He just hoped this would be the only such occurrence before they sailed, or afterward for that matter.

Cabrillo said with a touch of chagrin, "Captain-General Villalobos, now that my men are all gathered, would you be kind enough to review the final directives of Viceroy Mendoza?"

Possessing an unmistakable resemblance to his powerful cousin, Villalobos nodded courteously. He was prepared to make considerable allowances for Cabrillo's crews.

Cabrillo had been working diligently to oversee the construction of not only his own ships but Villalobos' as well. Both fleets were to be completed or nearly so before Cabrillo's sailing in late June, although Villalobos intended to remain in Navidad until the end of October or beginning of November. The difference in timing took into consideration Cabrillo's longer northern course versus Villalobos' more direct southern route, and the two captain-generals hoped to rendezvous in the Molucca or San Lázaro Islands at around the same time in the first months of the new year.

Villalobos addressed them all. "Gentlemen, some of you are familiar with the viceroy's orders given to Domingo López de Zuñiga last year. The orders for our voyages mirror them closely." He then began to read the commands, which first stated the names of the ships and the chief officers, and which required a detailed listing of every hand and weapon aboard each ship. The document then described the appropriate handling and storing of goods for barter and the terms of all trading activities. Next, Captain-General Villalobos read the viceroy's words requiring officers to hold the morality of their men to the highest standard. He paused here and glanced pointedly at Captain Correa, then resumed by adding that blasphemy was not to be tolerated and that the two priests accompanying the armada must be treated with great respect.

"Captain-General Cabrillo has told me that an Augustinian friar by the name of Izar Gamboa has arrived in Navidad to sail with you," Villalobos said, "but you are still waiting for your second priest. The viceroy has instructed me to tell you that he personally selected your other priest, who should arrive within the week."

Hearing this news, Cabrillo, Ferrelo, and even Correa kept their expressions composed, but they were all gripped by the same suspicion: anyone personally selected by the viceroy, who happened to be a part-owner in the fleet, would keep a watchful eye and report back on any activities that might have harmed potential profits.

"Now, gentlemen," said Villalobos, "the following rules concern your intended route, so please draw near enough to gain a clear view of Domingo del Castillo's new map."

As the men at the ends of the table moved in to hover over those seated closer to the map, Villalobos unrolled the chart and weighted down its sides with the platter and bowl. "As you can see," he said, "Señor Castillo has done an admirable job of combining charts from the voyages of Captains Ulloa, Alarcón, and Bolaños. He has drawn their entire routes, of course, but he did not neglect the details of the western coast of the California peninsula up to Cabo del Engaño, here, where Captain Ulloa landed two years ago. Unfortunately Captain Ulloa's untimely death has robbed you of his unrecorded insights, which might have been most valuable. Captain Alarcón, as you know, could have shed little light on what you will face since he traveled only on the eastern side of the peninsula. Luck has, however, allowed us the presence of Captain Bolaños who will be good enough to describe his experiences."

They took their time over the map, questioning and speculating, with Captain Bolaños frequently and Captain Correa occasionally sharing their memories of their earlier voyage. At last Captain-General Villalobos said, "Let us now turn, gentlemen, to Viceroy Mendoza's remaining instructions."

The listed mandates made it unmistakable that Cabrillo and his men were to maintain welcoming but wary relations with Indians. In lands inhabited by friendly natives, the expedition was to keep records of their speech, their beliefs and customs, dwellings, crops, consumable game, fresh water supplies, and anything else that would enlighten the prospect of establishing a Spanish settlement in the area.

After a brief discussion delving into these matters, Villalobos went on, "The viceroy strongly wishes a constant watch to be kept for any sign of the Coronado expedition. The reports he has received indicate that Captain Coronado has traveled far into the heart of the northern lands, and he has met with great resistance from the natives. It is conceivable that he will be forced or inclined to head to the western coast at some point. If so, he could well use your aid. Without definite word of him, however, you are not to divert from your orders to conduct a search. His Royal Majesty's goal of locating the cities of Cibola may prove to be more easily obtained through your route than Coronado's. To our king, the gold to be found in Cibola is no mere legend, and he desires it for Spain.

"In addition to this, I cannot state strongly enough how anxious His Majesty and the viceroy are to discover the location of the Strait of Anián. If you are able to find the waterway that traverses the lands of New Spain from the Pacific Ocean to the Atlantic, you will have done much to prevent the English and Dutch from claiming that passage as their own. The importance of this discovery to Spain is immeasurable."

The conversation moved on to analyzing Cabrillo's quest to reach Asia by his northwestern route. Again their discussion broadened and contracted until some concerns had been offered possible solutions, but the vast majority of their questions hung in the air as little more than food for insatiable supposition. After nearly three hours, Villalobos and Cabrillo agreed that it was time to conclude the meeting.

Rolling the official papers and map, and handing them to Cabrillo, Villalobos said, "I will pray daily, Captain-General, that nothing will prevent us from a timely meeting in the Asian Sea. With God's blessing, the waters around the Molucca or Lázaro islands will be empty of Portuguese war ships, and we will be able to trade without conflict."

"Yes, may we be granted that favor," said Cabrillo.

Tilting his head toward Cabrillo's officers, Villalobos said, "It is gratifying to know that you have fine pilots to assist in recording the winds and currents, as do I. When your charts and notes are added to mine, they should be most helpful in establishing a westward passage to Asia as well as an eastward route of return. As our good Señor Urdaneta can confirm, a means of safe homecoming has escaped us for far too long."

Standing up with Villalobos, Cabrillo said, "I thank you, Captain-General, for conveying the viceroy's orders to my officers. Do you still plan an immediate return to Mexico City?"

"Those are my instructions," he said, his expression communicating that even a cousin must be obeyed if he wears the mantle of Mexico's viceroy.

"Then I wish you the greatest success on your own voyage, and I look forward with much pleasure to seeing you again in the land of spices."

"You and your spices," Villalobos said with a smile. "I have heard that your personal servant has learned to be a magician with them."

"I admit that enjoying good food is a vice I have a dreadful time eradicating," said Cabrillo without a hint of shame, and both men chuckled.

Addressing his own men more soberly, Cabrillo said, "You may return to the ships, gentlemen. I will remain a little longer, if Señor Urdaneta will be kind enough to speak with me further."

"With pleasure," said Urdaneta as Cabrillo's men bowed and took their leave.

Before departing, Villalobos gave Cabrillo a rueful look and admitted, "In a way, I envy you, Captain-General. You will sail into the complete unknown, with the possibility of discoveries almost beyond imaginings. My own voyage, following a route already traveled by others," he cast his gaze upon Urdaneta, "will likely yield stories that sound tame when heard after yours."

"I trust that both voyages will hold opportunities for few wild tales, sir."

Offering words of farewell, Villalobos clasped Cabrillo's hand and bowed, as did Captain Bolaños in turn, and the two men left the tavern.

When only he and Urdaneta remained in the room, Cabrillo called for the serving woman, ordered that their wine cups be refilled, and settled once more on the bench. He picked an olive from the bowl and tossed it into his mouth. "Well, Andrés, how on God's good earth have you avoided the viceroy's attempts to convince you to sail with Villalobos? Surely, he has tried many times."

The thin, ruddy-skinned man sitting across the table let amusement enter eyes as wise as those of any owl as he fingered the edge of his thick beard. Both the beard and his shoulder-length hair were heavily streaked with gray, though he had yet to reach the age of thirty-five. "Yes, there have been quite a few opportunities to accept. I was only able to avoid his entreaties by matching my determination against his persistence," he said. "I can be very hard-headed."

"You simply outlasted him?" Cabrillo asked, then spat the olive pit into the seldom-used fireplace.

Urdaneta smiled gently. "That, and I promised to compile the results of both voyages."

Cabrillo laughed. "I thought it must be something like that. You are such a rarity, my friend: a Spaniard who has seen the Moluccas and lived to tell about them. The viceroy will certainly keep after you to sail again, probably long after his cousin's ships have left port. There will always be another fleet."

"Undoubtedly, Juan, but I must correct you again on a point you seem determined to forget. I am a Basque, not a Spaniard. As you too are by now quite aware, we are known for our tenacity."

Cabrillo said with mock severity, "You are a citizen of the king's realm. Being Basque is a mere technicality."

"Not to a Basque."

"I know, I know," Cabrillo said, smiling broadly now. "Because your people are talented sailors you all think you can claim your coastal seas right along with the fish. And you believe you have as much right to your mountains as the oaks that give birth to your ships."

"Is that not natural? They *are* our seas, our mountains after living there for thousands of years."

"Forgive me, Andrés, but His Majesty is not likely to agree that you are entitled to more authority over that piece of the world than he is."

Now Urdaneta let his own grin widen a little with each word. "It takes more than a king to convince a Basque he is wrong on this subject."

"Ha, and many other subjects! But you are far from alone in the possession of such leanings." Cabrillo became thoughtful as he picked up another olive, and he said, "I have asked you before about the generalities of your travels, but since those events were dreadful for you and the other survivors I have not pushed to learn more. Would you mind telling me now?"

Urdaneta kept his eyes on Cabrillo's face for several moments, his thoughts drifting back. "Yes, perhaps the time is right. As the months pass, it becomes less difficult to speak of the voyage. Even so, it was an experience I could never survive a second time. Never. What do you want to know?"

"Everything."

He took a deep breath and began, his lids half-closing in reflective contemplation. "When I was seventeen I signed up to sail with the

Loaísa expedition as the assistant to our ship's scribe. Quite soon, old though I was, I became Juan Sebastian de Elcano's cabin boy. Just as most young men, I was familiar with the fame of the man who had completed Magellan's voyage, but I did not meet him until a week before departure. My admiration for that man quickly grew into a great fondness." Cabrillo merely nodded, encouraging Urdaneta to continue.

"He had an extraordinary ability to accurately read the character of a man, and this made him a very skillful leader. With him as the fleet's pilot-major and captain over all six of the flagship's consort vessels, things went well enough as we crossed the Atlantic and descended the coast of South America. Captain Elcano led us through Magellan's strait, which many thought impossible once we were there, fighting for every mile against its treacheries. We did reach the Pacific Ocean, however, but only after scurvy had claimed Captain-General Loaísa's life. Captain Elcano became our commander, though he was also beginning to show signs of illness. Not long afterward, to my horror and grief, he grew too weak to stand."

Urdaneta raised his eyes to Cabrillo, and they still reflected the pain of that loss. "I acted as a witness when he signed his will. By then, he barely had strength enough to lift the quill. He had already suffered through scurvy during his voyage with Magellan, and he had no more reserve to defeat it. I was with him at the very last. That cursed disease took him from us when we needed him so badly, even more badly than we knew at the time."

Cabrillo pushed Urdaneta's cup closer to his elbow, encouraging him to drink. His friend wrapped a hand around the vessel but did not lift it from the table as he went on. "Scurvy ruthlessly killed many more men and badly weakened those of us who dared to hold onto our lives. All the while we tried to hold off starvation with nothing more than spoiled food and tainted drinking water, and there was very little of either. When the storms hit, those endless storms, we had no choice but to work the pumps night and day in order to remain afloat. Many more men died laboring at those pumps. When they fell, we merely rolled their bodies aside, stepped into their places, and kept pumping. Ship after ship went down despite our pitiful efforts; their men sinking under the waves without the strength even to scream."

At these words, these terrible memories, Urdaneta's head lowered for a moment. When it lifted slowly he seemed to notice the cup in his hand, and he took a couple of swallows of wine. Setting the cup down and bracing himself with a deep breath, his tongue forced the words from his mouth. "Only one of our seven ships reached the Moluccas, and I shall always wonder why ours alone was spared. And yet, once there, rather than finding the rest and pure food we longed and prayed for, we few survivors were captured by the Portuguese.

"I was their prisoner for seven years before I was finally able to escape. Seven eternal years. Please do not ask me to describe how they treated us, Juan. That, I cannot do. Not yet."

He paused for another drink. "Afterward, for several more years I sailed at length around those islands in boats too small for the Portuguese to bother. I learned the Malay language and I traded. In the end, six years ago now, I managed to return to Lisbon aboard a Portuguese ship. I slipped away from them again and got back into Spain in February of 1537. Shortly following my return, I met your old commander, Alvarado. Did he tell you that it took him over a year to convince me to face the sea again, so I could accompany him back to Mexico?" His expression became poignant as he said, "And then Alvarado allowed himself to be killed by rebellious natives."

He met Cabrillo's sympathetic gaze. "Well, Juan, that is my story."

"I thank you for telling me. Andrés, I was wrong to tease you about the tenacity of your people. You needed every bit of it to endure those trials, and no small amount of courage." After a pause, he said without accusation, "You must hate the Portuguese."

"*Those* Portuguese, yes, at least I did for many years. Now I try to forgive even them."

Cabrillo paused and then said, "What would you think if I told you I had some Portuguese blood myself?"

"That is not a very well kept a secret, my friend. I have known for some time. But I learned long ago that a man's nationality does not dictate his integrity, or his choices. There are doubtless as many fine Portuguese as Spaniards and as many wicked Spaniards as Portuguese."

In a lighter tone, Cabrillo asked, "Even as many wicked Basques?"

Urdaneta gave him a surrendering smile as his only answer.

They grew silent for another breath or two, and Cabrillo asked softly, "Do you intend never to set sail again, then?"

"Truthfully, I am not certain. Despite everything, at times I actually consider returning to the Moluccas. For now, however, I will try to make myself useful to the viceroy as he directs the voyages of others."

"I understand, and yet I cannot help greatly wishing that you would be standing beside me when we sail. Ah, but since that is not to be, I will accept things as they are if you agree to tell me more about the people of the East. Yes?"

Urdaneta nodded, and their conversation carried him back to the Molucca Islands of his fonder memories. He possessed a wealth of knowledge, which Cabrillo began to explore with the methodical thoroughness of a miner digging into a rich vein.

The afternoon had well matured when the captain-general asked him at last, "Can you give me any last pieces of advice that might prove helpful?"

Urdaneta's face clouded for a moment before answering with a question of his own. "Do you know much about the nature of poisons?"

"Not a thing. Why?"

With concentrated gravity he said, "I suggest you learn enough to discover one that is as painless and quick as possible." At Cabrillo's uneasy expression, Urdaneta explained, "You are a Christian and a good man, Juan, but if in the year to come you find yourself about to be captured, it would be useful to have such an aid close at hand."

Stunned, Cabrillo said, "Take poison willingly! Could you do such a thing?"

Urdaneta placed his hand on Cabrillo's shoulder. "While under torture and enduring the pain afterwards, I wished a hundred times I could have done so. Yes, under the same threat I would do exactly what I am proposing. If you are caught in waters they consider their own, sailing under a Spanish flag, any Portuguese blood may make things even worse for you. You will likely be looked upon as a traitor. Please, if you spot a Portuguese ship, beware."

Chapter 4

BLESSING OR CURSE

The beach of Navidad clamored so raucously with bellowing seamen, squealing pigs, chopping axes, barking dogs, haggling vendors, squawking chickens, clanking hammers, and bellering cows that fishermen a half-mile offshore glanced at one another and shook their heads in disapproval. If the harbor had been astir throughout the last few weeks, it was frenzied this morning, and Cabrillo strode along the sand scrutinizing the whirlwind of activity with pensive satisfaction.

As the captain-general and supply officer Lope Sánchez passed by the pigpen, a particularly loud and fretful chorus of squeals burst from its occupants, announcing that the four-legged creatures sensed high anticipation in the air as acutely as their bipedal masters. Though the animals would not be loaded until tomorrow Cabrillo had ordered them corralled near the seaside to avoid last-minute delays.

At first light boats ashore had begun skimming the water toward the fleet where men, yards, blocks, and tackle awaited their arrival. With long-practiced agility they raised heavy armaments, gunpowder, ropes, canvas, metal fastenings, pitch, and firewood, as well as barrels of wine, water, and dried and salted food to the ship's waists. Chests, crates, and bundles of trade goods had already been carefully stowed below decks. Cabrillo glanced toward his flagship and spotted Pilot San Remón with his back to the *San Salvador's* railing, personally supervising her loading while Sánchez carried out his related duties on land.

Sánchez was easily distinguished as a maritime supply officer by the set of formidable keys that hung from his belt and jangled dully with each step. These keys kept the bulk of their food stores and weaponry securely locked behind iron bars, thereby reducing the temptation of any sailors inclined to opportune pilfering.

Not far beyond the pigpen, he and Cabrillo paused to observe the transfer of a seven-foot breech-loaded great gun fashioned of wrought iron, known as a bombardeta, from a solidly-built wagon to one of the *San Salvador's* launches. Because each of these guns was so precious, only a single such weapon was permitted to be transported at a time. Three other bombardetas and their two-wheeled carriages had previously been taken aboard the flagship and stowed in the bilges, joining their supply of five-pound balls as ballast. This last big gun alone would be positioned on its waiting carriage beneath the starboard gunwale, where it could be used to hold off any attack until the other bombardetas were mounted. Although neither the *San Miguel* nor *La Victoria* carried bombardetas, they had each received an allotment of smaller swivel guns called bercos that nearly equaled the sixteen assigned to the *San Salvador*. Three bercos were already mounted at both side rails of each ship. These along with their other assorted armaments were capable of causing great damage to any enemy within close range, especially when trying to board.

As two brothers with startlingly bright reddish hair eased the heavy bombardeta from its wagon braces, Cabrillo nodded approvingly and said to Sánchez, "I would willingly wager that we have the only two Irish gunners on this side of New Spain."

"And they are good men, sir, though the younger brother speaks not a word of Castilian."

"One of many who will learn quickly enough. What is the condition of our weaponry, Lope?"

"Beautiful, Captain-General," Sánchez answered with pride, though he knew that Cabrillo was as aware of the state of the fleets' armaments as he was himself. "With every piece in complete readiness, sir, we will not be caught unprepared. The viceroy has been generous."

"Has anything yet to be brought to the beach?"

"After this last gun, every bombardeta, berco, crossbow, javelin, pike, shield, musket, ball, and keg will be aboard, sir. We await only the few fighting blades still being sharpened and oiled, and they will be delivered within the hour."

With frequent glances at myriad other loading activities around them, Cabrillo and Lope noted how ably the hands performed the ticklish task of settling the great gun onto its bed in the launch. When at last the weighty artillery piece rested serenely, the now low-riding launch eased away from shore and pulled gently toward the flagship. Upon the gun's safe arrival, Lope let his breath out in a soft sigh of relief, then smiled. "May I say, sir, how lovely our ships look today? So shining and proud, as if they too are pleased to be sailing with the dawn."

"Yes, Lope, they are lovely," Cabrillo said, and his voice carried the sincerity of a man who had overseen the birth of all three ships, who had planned, watched, corrected, worried, and occasionally bellowed and cursed, from their inception to the threading of the last sheet of sail. Though he had built other ships before these, his earlier attempts had not caused his heart to swell as it did now. The *San Salvador*, his masterpiece, dominated the small fleet as she floated restfully at anchor. Here was a vessel about which Spain and its subjects could rightfully boast.

Measuring 74 feet in length and 24 feet abeam at the waterline, her distinct design exhibiting the marvelous technology of her age, she was a galleon built to sail undauntedly into wild open seas. Her trim had been painted red and blue, highlighting the deep browns of her pitch-treated hull and masts. Every line and knot aboard was rightly placed, and every plank and block was smoothly scrubbed.

Fluttering now and again from her main masthead, a bright cloth emblem honored the royal oversight of King Charles I, who held the additional august title of Holy Roman Emperor Charles V. This particular standard was much simpler than the king's extravagantly crowded coat of arms, however, and reflected none of his holdings in the lands of Aragon, Navarre, Sicily, Naples, Granada, Flanders, Austria, Brabant, Tyrol, and both old and new Burgundy. Instead, this flag displayed New Spain's particular approbation for his grandmother Queen Isabella I by bearing only the red and yellow castles of Castile and lions of León. The viceroy's banner, adopted from the red and white Burgundy cross, decorated the flagship's foremast, as did the fluted crimson cross of Santiago. From the top of the mizzenmast astern, Cabrillo's own pennant depicted the simple yet stylishly arrayed initials JRC in dark blue upon a golden field.

Though the sails were furled at the moment, both levels of main and fore yards would carry precisely cut rectangular planes of canvas. Only the mizzenmast would sport a triangular lateen sail. In addition to her sails and lines, the *San Salvador* would be steered by a whipstaff that attached perpendicularly to her tiller and rose up through the planks of the main deck to extend its nearly six-foot height into steerage. She was capable of carrying 200 *toneladas* of cargo, equivalent to 400 barrels of about 117 gallons each.

Cabrillo's flagship had proven herself commendably during her maiden voyage to Peru over a year ago, and he had made small improvements to her since then. Even during that first sailing, there had been times while braving a storm or flying before a bold wind and current when she'd seemed to possess a daring soul of her own. She had responded to his wishes as if she'd discerned them before her whipstaff or lines had been touched.

Today she rode a little lower in the water with each new load of cargo she accepted, but her forward, quarter, and upper stern decks continued to stand tall and willing. Ah yes, she was a lady of the very finest order. With this affectionate and satisfying thought, Cabrillo turned his gaze to his other ships.

La Victoria had nearly equal total square footage to that of the *San Salvador*, but her somewhat broader beam and deeper body sacrificed a measure of mobility for cargo capacity. Cabrillo looked upon her as the mother duckling of the fleet: sure, steady, and protective of the greatest share of their supplies. The spry, dependant bergantine *San Miguel* was significantly smaller and sleeker than the sister ships. Her oars and shallow draft provided fine maneuverability, and she had repeatedly confirmed her usefulness during the earlier transportation of goods to the larger ships.

This was his fleet. As he looked upon it, the tide continued to tease each prow toward the beckoning sea, making the ships appear more than ready to sail whenever he commanded. Under the heat of the strengthening morning sun he wiped his sweating brow and smiled at his imagining that the vessels were as impatient as he to be off. A priest would almost certainly deem such personifications of a fleet heretical in nature.

He turned away and wove his way slowly along the beach, letting his thoughts turn to the vigorously working crews. With recent injuries being light and few and any with signs of fever being kept far from their activities, the men were in first-rate condition for their departure. Last evening while aboard the *San Miguel*, Cabrillo had noticed with satisfaction that the men who had been involved in the fight two weeks earlier were working with healthy vigor. Their lightly marred backs affirmed that Captain Correa's boatswain had followed his orders to use the lash sparingly.

The same sort of leniency, he uneasily reflected back, had not always been extended to the Indians pressed into labor in order to complete the building of the ships. Much of the heavy equipment and materials had been carried on their bare shoulders from interior provinces over backbreaking terrain to reach this port. Even here the men had nearly revolted due to working and living conditions, so Indian women were gathered from the nearby countryside and marched to Navidad to calm the men by serving them both sexually and domestically. Some of those same Indians would sail with them tomorrow, and a number might even be utilized to build a settlement in the strange lands they would encounter.

Cabrillo was pulled from his reverie when Sánchez pointed back toward the *San Miguel* and said, "Captain Correa is approaching us, sir."

Before his launch reached the sand near their feet, Correa called out, "How goes the morning effort, Captain-General?"

"Well enough, Captain Correa." When Correa dropped from his boat and strode up to them, Cabrillo confided, "There is but one thing that devils my peace of mind, Captain, and it grows worse with every passing hour. Where is our second priest? He should have been here days ago."

"If he fails to arrive, will our sailing be postponed, sir?"

"You know our orders as well as I, Captain," Cabrillo grumbled. "We would have no choice but to wait. We *must* have two priests aboard. To think that the majority of our efforts in preparing for departure could be wasted because of a single individual..." He gave Correa a sidelong glance and lowered his voice to the level of mischief. "If it were left to me I would be tempted to ask Father Gamboa to perform a peremptory ordination, even of your rowers."

Correa choked back his laughter. "One of my men! What a thought, Captain-General! The heavens would weep."

39

The officers swung around at the sudden crash of pottery followed by volleys of accusation between an olive merchant and a sailor, both standing over a three-gallon, pointed-bottomed clay jar that lay in pieces amid its spilled contents.

"Bilbao!" Cabrillo raised his voice toward the nearest sailor. "See that that vessel is replaced. I want no shortage of olives."

"Yes, sir!" the young seaman responded smartly, as aware as every other crewman that the captain-general's weakness for the small salty fruit was nothing to be ignored.

"Since all is going well here, Lope," Cabrillo said to his supply officer, "I will leave things in your hands. Captain Correa, will you join me while I check on the horses?"

"With pleasure, Captain-General. Since my little mare has never been to sea I am anxious to confirm her fitness."

Over the past three weeks Cabrillo had kept the horses stabled a little longer each day and had seen that their feed was gradually changed in order to more closely imitate their future conditions on board. The ships were taking with them what Cabrillo deemed a generous supply of dried carrots, maize, grain, and chopped hay. He was fairly confident that they would be hugging the coastline throughout the voyage to the East, and he looked forward to taking the horses ashore and having wild replacements for their feed collected whenever possible.

He and Correa dodged a small flock of panicking chickens that had just escaped their keeper's wagon, and walked toward the barn located behind a nearby inn and livery. As Cabrillo rounded a corner and the barn's front came into view, a tall dappled stallion lifted his head at the open upper half of his door and called out to him. Pawing the floor of his stall, he continued to whicker as if demanding an immediate conversation.

"That horse of yours seems half human, sir, the way he speaks to you. I have never seen the like."

Cabrillo approached the horse wearing an expression so filled with devotion that it might well have made his wife and children jealous. Even they, however, had learned very early that horses had found the soft regions of his heart long before he'd met any of them.

"Nor will you see his kind again," said Cabrillo. "Viento is the finest of an exceptional Andalusian line." The stud arched his neck, shook his head, and extended his fine muzzle. Except around his eyes and muzzle, his head was a much lighter gray than the rest of his body. Downward and back from his jaw, his mottled coat gradually darkened to nearly black as it approached his tail and hooves. Viento had been dark as pitch at birth but had dappled through his youth and would one day mature to a brilliant white. His black-tipped mane and tail were lavishly thick, and Cabrillo seldom let either be cut, preferring to see them hang long and free.

Reaching out, Cabrillo's hand met the softness of Viento's neck and began to scratch what he knew to be a favorite spot. Viento responded by leaning into the hand of his master and half-closing his eyes. This equine expression of contentment evoked soft chuckles from Cabrillo and Correa.

The captain-general's half-blood nephew, page, and soon to be cabin boy, Mateo, poked his head out of a nearby stall and trotted toward them. "Good morning, Captain-General, Captain Correa."

"Well, Mateo, how are the horses faring?"

"As you see, sir, hearty and willing."

"You have done good work with them, Mateo." Cabrillo seldom was able to keep the fondness from his voice when addressing this young page, which was due only in part to the fact that he was the natural son of his wife's brother and lifelong friend. The boy was quick-witted, hard-working, and shared his uncle's love of horses.

Much to Viento's disappointment, Cabrillo now patted him with the two light slaps that signaled an end to his scratching session. His master eased him back a few steps and then entered the stall to examine him from forelock to tail while Correa went to find his own mare. When Cabrillo had completed his inspection he nodded and proclaimed at last, "Yes, he is as fit as can be." To the eleven-year-old boy, he asked, "And you, Mateo, are you ready to become a man of the sea?"

The slightest hesitation betrayed the lad's uneasiness before he stiffened his lips, pushed back his shoulders slightly, and said, "Very ready, sir, though I have so much to learn."

"Everyone has much to learn on his first voyage. You are a bright lad and you will learn more quickly than some."

To Correa, who had reappeared at the stall door, he said, "Will you be good enough to look over my other two mounts with me, Captain?"

Correa gave an acquiescing bow and they moved to a stall two doors down, where Cabrillo's brood mare was lodged. Correa's horse glanced around the end of the wall that separated the two stalls and whickered at them. "Ah, my Luna," Cabrillo said, "you have become a kind older sister to Captain Correa's filly, eh? You will be a comfort to her on our long voyage." He lifted her left forefoot, muttering softly as he checked the soft tissue of the hoof. "Since Viento must not be tempted by such fine mares while at sea— steady there —he and Seguro will sail with me. Good, good, firm but not too dry. Now this foot up, girl. That's right. You will travel aboard *La Victoria*. Do not worry, she is a fine ship and Captain Ferrelo will take care that no harm comes to you. This one now. Hold there. Yes, yes, it feels fine. One more, my lady. Up, that's it. Ah, again, no sign of trouble. All four hoofs are sound as I could hope. And how are your muscles feeling, Luna? Smooth and strong, just as they should be, and your eyes are as clear as ever. Although Captain Correa may be unwilling to admit it, you are the most excellent mare in all of Mexico. When we reach the East you and Viento will mate again and produce a foal as beautifully as you did last year."

His faithful sedate gelding, Seguro, awaited a portion of his master's attention with a patience gained through fourteen years of life. For his sweet nature and serene acceptance of being visited last, Cabrillo rewarded him with a brief brushing before scrutinizing the many signs of his physical well-being.

The inspection of the horses included particular attention to the animals' hooves for good reason. Three days earlier their forefeet had been vigilantly trimmed to encourage a shifting of weight to their heels in the hope of reducing the risk of hoof fever, which could be fatal. The horses had then been reshod. Muscles, teeth, throats, eyes, noses, ears, and even their droppings were studied for any indication of a pending problem.

After all four horses had been fully examined, Cabrillo pronounced, "They are all in top sailing condition, praise the Lord. Remember, Mateo, allow them no food or water for three to four hours before they are taken aboard. Once they are safely installed they will feel comforted by receiving both."

"Yes, sir. I shall not forget."

While giving Viento a few final pats, Cabrillo was interrupted by a sailor who hurried into the barn, bowed quickly, and announced, "Captain-General, our second priest, he has arrived! He is here, sir!"

"At last," said Cabrillo with heart-felt relief. "Where is he?"

"He is coming directly to you, sir."

These words had barely been spoken before a brown-robed man leading a dusty bay horse rounded the inn and became visible through the barn door. His eyes were aimed quite low so that the top of his head, capped by a round patch of gleaming skin and skirted with a ring of short-cropped hair, was the most visible feature. It was not until the friar lifted his face that Cabrillo recognized him, abruptly stilled his hands, and swallowed back an unholy curse.

They slowly approached one another until they met at the corral's railing. The friar was the first to speak. "Good day, Captain-General."

Cabrillo demanded, "Is this some sort of joke, some mockery?"

"Not in the least, sir. I pronounced my vows as a friar several months ago and have since been ordained a priest. I am fully qualified to celebrate the sacraments."

"Ordained as a priest," Cabrillo echoed, still trying to accept this unexpected and most unwelcome challenge. He stared penetratingly into the young face, discovering little.

Correa, much confused by this exchange, looked from one man to the other but for once found his tongue to be of no use whatsoever. Mateo's eyes had grown huge in anticipation of the calamity that his uncle's manner foretold. He stood very still, his muscles tight.

"Captain-General Cabrillo," the priest said evenly, "I have come to offer you my services. I have ridden far and have taken only what time was needed in getting here. I ask that you observe the condition of my horse. You will find that he is in good spirits and, under the coating of dust that the road has bestowed on both of us, he is in admirable health."

When Cabrillo moved neither his disgruntled gaze nor his body, the young friar continued. "Please allow me to apologize for my late arrival, sir. As you can see, my horse is no longer youthful." The tenor of his voice lowered just enough to deepen the meaning of his next words. "I was recently taught never to mistreat a noble animal."

After a moment Cabrillo allowed his attention to be diverted to the horse, and he eyed the animal critically. At last he said, "I must admit that he appears to have received acceptable care. But this does not keep me from questioning your motives for being here at all."

"A priest goes where he is assigned, sir."

"Assigned? Did you receive this assignment before our first encounter?"

"I did not, sir. When we met in Santiago I had just completed my year as a novice. My vows as a friar in the Order of Hermits of St. Augustine had only newly been pronounced."

"Yet you wore none of the clothing of your order that day, and you said nothing of your true calling. You allowed me to believe you were no more than a messenger."

"For that journey, since it was to be the final personal service I was to perform for the viceroy, he felt I might travel with greater safety and speed if I displayed the visible evidence of his authority, carrying his seal and riding one of his horses. My superiors at the monastery complied with the viceroy's wishes and gave me permission to briefly don the clothing I had so recently set aside rather than wear my friar's robe." An evocative smile, perhaps unwillingly, touched the youthful face. "As you may remember, sir, during our initial interactions I was given little opportunity to discuss any calling I might follow."

Cabrillo chose not to validate this accusation with a direct response. "Did Father Gamboa know of your coming to act as our second priest?"

"No, sir. Even *I* did not know until two days prior to my departure from Mexico City. Any messenger that might have been sent to inform you of my appointment would have failed to reach you much sooner than I. My superiors asked me to deliver their sincere apologies for the delay in sending me to you. They hope you will understand that since the Augustinian order has not been in Mexico long, many of our activities are still being organized and refined, including the assignment of priests." He stepped to his saddlebag and withdrew a paper. "Here is my letter of introduction, sir."

With a notable lack of enthusiasm Cabrillo accepted the letter, unsealed and unrolled it, and scanned the words. Curling the parchment up again, he turned to Correa. "Forgive me, Captain, but I must now speak with our visitor in private."

"Of course, sir," said Correa, failing to hide his disappointed curiosity. He bowed and moved off to resume his duties on the beach.

One quick glance from the captain-general sent Mateo scurrying back to the stalls.

Addressing the priest alone, Cabrillo asked, "Did you request to be assigned to this voyage, or are you here at the viceroy's command?"

"Viceroy Mendoza felt that my abilities with native languages might be of particular service to you, sir."

"My men can tell you that I favor full and direct responses. Did you request this assignment?"

"Very well, sir. I am here at the order of the viceroy, but he did ask me of my own thoughts before the order was made official. I told him I would be most willing to serve you and your men on my first priestly mission."

Cabrillo could find no sign of an absolute lie, yet he felt something being withheld, some undisclosed motivation. "Then tell me, *Father* Lezcano, why you chose to sail under the command of one who has had you soundly whipped?"

The priest answered without pause or preamble. "Even when under the lash a man can admit when he has been wrong, Captain-General."

"Only an exceedingly uncommon man could do such a thing at such a time."

The priest lifted his chin a degree or two. "I have been described by that word on more than one occasion, sir."

A smile heavy with irony now lifted the corners of Cabrillo's mouth. "The cross and robe seem to have done little to curb either your pride or brashness."

"I admit that I am still striving to find my way to humility, sir. It escapes me often."

"Am I to believe that you hold no personal resentment toward me, then?"

"I ask you to believe just that, sir."

"Are you willing to swear before God that no thought of vengeance or sabotage has brought you here?"

"I swear it readily, sir. Before our Heavenly Father, I harbor no such intentions."

The suspicion did not leave Cabrillo's face, but it lessened. "Doubtless, you know that we intend to depart at tomorrow's sunrise, and that we are under orders to sail only if we have two priests with us."

"Yes, sir, I am aware of those orders."

"Simply put, I am cornered." Cabrillo suddenly slapped the nearest corral post so hard it tilted, and then he slapped it back into position with his other hand. Releasing a great huff of exasperation, Cabrillo pronounced, "There is nothing else to be done but to take you aboard."

"Thank you, Captain-General. I will pray for a safe and successful voyage."

Giving him one more visual raking, Cabrillo said, "As will I." He raised his voice and called out, "Mateo, come see to Father Lezcano's horse."

But before the boy had emerged from the barn Father Lezcano spoke up again. "If you would not mind, Captain-General, I would like to tend to him myself. He has served me faithfully."

Surprised, and immediately wondering if this request was some form of posturing, Cabrillo said nevertheless, "Very well. Afterward, Mateo will present you to Father Gamboa, who can introduce you to Captain Correa, the gentleman who was with me when you arrived. When the captain has time he will show you the workings of the *San Miguel*. Tomorrow you will sail aboard her." He did not need to add, *which will keep you well away from me.*

Anticipation greatly lengthened a night that offered no sympathy to ease Cabrillo's restless tossings and mutterings, leaving the fleet's commander to waken with a start and open his eyes on the day of departure hindered by a headache and a foul mood. He had finally fallen asleep only two hours earlier, cursing his luck at being forced to endure Father Lezcano's unreadable motives and blatant audacity during the voyage. But worse than this, he'd dreamed of Beatriz with another man, and the man had been an Aztec warrior. He now sighed as he rubbed his temples and wondered for the hundredth time, *Why am I cursed with such dreams?*

He rolled over in his bunk and sat up, planting his bare feet on the deck. Momentarily remaining quite still, he listened to the rustlings, bumpings, and mutterings of the ship and her crew. Nothing sounded amiss. He said a quick prayer, asking that all would go well today, June 27, 1542. He wondered if this would be a day that men would find worthy of remembering. Fortune, fate, and the sweat of them all would decide.

Pushing himself off his bunk, he stepped to his small desk, examined the tip of his quill, dipped it several times in his inkpot, blotted the excess lightly onto a rag, and began to write his wife a letter. While his quill danced, telling of Lezcano's arrival, of the fleet's final preparations, and of his devotion to her, Cabrillo heard the commotion forward and below increase as the chickens, the horses, and a cow were being boarded. All still sounded as if procedures were flowing smoothly, so he continued to employ his quill and paper to express his dedication to his wife and children. He wrote not a word about his disturbing dream.

By the time he'd finished his letter, he felt better. He was tilting the page to slide the ink-drying sand into its tin when a knock sounded at his door.

"Yes?"

Paulo, Cabrillo's personal servant of several years, opened the door and bowed. "Captain-General, Father Gamboa has sent me to tell you that he and Father Lezcano will be ready to hear confessions soon, about an hour before Mass is to begin."

Paulo was a Spaniard whose slightness of stature had been compensated for by a wiry strength of body and unmovable force of will that even the sailors had come to respect. He was bristly by nature, and his prickliness reached its height whenever he witnessed dishonorable manners displayed in his master's presence. Such an occurrence was only slightly less tolerable than any event that interfered with providing the proper appearance and comforts for Cabrillo. These were Paulo's areas of expertise, and his territorialism could be fierce. On most days he endured a lesser but always nagging frustration that sprang from his master's evident lack of dependency on his valet even after so long an association. Cabrillo seemed to accept his solicitations to avoid displeasing a willing servant rather than in acknowledgment of a needed service. At times Paulo almost suspected that Cabrillo would have relished returning to the privacy and freedom he'd known before his successes had been acknowledged and rewarded. Such a thought was not to be borne for long, however, and it was soon tucked away in his mind.

"With nearly a hundred of us to be heard," said Cabrillo, "we will have to be quick with our confessing. Very well, Paulo, get my dress clothes together and we'll head to town. While I may, I am going to wash ashore one last time."

Pleased as always to attend to Cabrillo's wardrobe, Paulo gathered what was requested with a brisk, attentive airiness. In moments all was ready.

They left the ship in a launch that landed them speedily, but before Cabrillo could head for the inn and a bath Lázaro de Cárdenas met him at the shoreline. This soldier had fought at Cabrillo's side in many campaigns, and he now held the respected and often feared position as handler of the war dogs. It was highly unusual to see Lázaro wearing a concerned expression, but this morning he looked like a mother who had misplaced a favorite child. A large gray-brown mastiff with a white belly and a bandaged left front paw stood beside him, tense and watchful. As Cabrillo neared them the dog danced and pulled against his leash in attempt to welcome his master, but Lázaro yanked him back sharply and shouted a command that the dog obeyed by sitting and keeping still.

"Greetings, Captain-General," said Lázaro, holding the leash tightly.

Less than pleased, Cabrillo asked, "Lázaro, what brings you two here?"

"I came with reluctance, sir. I know you prefer that the dogs be kept away from the men, but his paw is corrupted, sir. I thought you would want to see it before he is brought aboard. The surgeon says it will not heal completely for at least a week."

The dog whined for Cabrillo's attention, but he had been trained to understand that this would gain him nothing unless he complied with Lázaro's handling. He waited for any signal of release.

"Very well, show me."

Lázaro commanded, "Hold!" but with his master so near the dog did not obey until Cabrillo repeated the word.

They bent down and Lázaro removed the bandage. Cabrillo shoved the dog's licking mouth aside, examined the swollen and seeping paw, and said, "He will have to remain behind, Lázaro. Now, there is no need to look so glum. You will have the other three to oversee."

"But, Captain-General, only three dogs? The viceroy sent us more than twice that number. If we should find lands where the natives are dangerous..."

"If so, we have adequate armaments at our disposal. As you well know, the dogs are my last choice as a weapon."

"Yes, Captain-General," he said, his downcast eyes clearly indicating his unsatisfied preference.

"Lázaro, I know that you have heard the name of Nuño de Guzman."

"As have we all, sir. A godless man. Bishop Zumárraga was right to have him arrested and shipped back to Spain. Few men lament his rotting in prison."

"Then you have not forgotten the crimes he committed with his dogs. And you can be certain the Indians will not soon forget how their people were fed to his beasts for sport. Even those who fought against my commanders and me have valid reasons for their hatred for our war dogs, as do many who fought beside us and became accidental victims. I took pains to have these dogs trained to bring down a man without slaying him, but you well know how capable they are of killing. I pray that will not be necessary on this voyage. One fewer dog may reduce our chances of bloody misfortune. Understand me, Lázaro, I will not have my name recalled in the same breath as Guzman's."

"No, sir. Of course not."

"Three dogs only. Leave him here." Over the years Cabrillo had learned to hide his own discomfort around the war dogs, even from the dogs. It was an uneasiness born less from fear than dreaded memories. He had been only ten years old and under the command of Pánfilo de Narváez when he had first seen the animals used in the gory massacres through Cuba. He had long hoped he would forget that horror or at least outgrow his aversion to the brutal, sacrilegious efficiency of the huge dogs, but those old unrelenting images returned again and again to torment him, especially at night.

Cabrillo motioned Paulo forward, and they hurried to the inn where a tub was already waiting. He slowly sank into the water and settled there up to his chin with a smile that stretched his cheeks. He let the near-scalding heat soak into his muscles for several long moments and then began to soap his body from crown to toe. When he could find no patch of skin that had not been rubbed at least three times, he stood and left the tub with pitiful reluctance. For once he showed great patience as Paulo dressed and shaved him before he joined his men heading toward the chapel.

49

Once there, the sailors and soldiers formed two lines according to rank, and when their turns came they stepped behind the two large screens of woven palms that served as partitions for the confessionals. Cabrillo noted that the expressions of the waiting men ranged from reflective, to resigned, to downright rebellious, but every Christian was there except the few left to guard the ships, and they too would be given a chance to confess their sins before anchors were weighed.

The only slave permitted to stand in line was notable, even to those unaware of his status as the captain-general's prized property, due to his powerful six-foot three-inch frame and the blackness of his skin. He had been a gift to Cabrillo from his old commander, Alvarado, and he still bore Alvarado's brand on his right forearm. Several years ago, after this slave had saved Cabrillo's life by deflecting a Mayan war club with his shield, Cabrillo had offered him his freedom. But the man had asked instead to be baptized. The wish had been granted, and he now was called by his Christian name, Manuel, and was privileged to participate in all Christian rites.

Standing first in the confessional line, Cabrillo did not have long to wait before Father Gamboa beckoned. He acted as an example to his men by keeping his confession brief. So brief, in fact, that when he came to the end of his short list of sins, Father Gamboa paused and then encouraged, "Is there anything else, Captain-General?"

A decidedly firm, "No, Father," was the only response.

Father Gamboa possessed the tact to push the matter no further before hearing Cabrillo's prayer of contrition, pronouncing the captain-general's assigned penance, and, with God's blessings, absolving him of his misdeeds. Cabrillo stepped from behind the screen and bowed Captain Ferrelo toward the waiting priest.

After the confession line had dwindled away and, presumably, the penances had been sincerely offered, Mass began. The scripture Father Gamboa chose on this propitious morning was John 6:16. He read of when the disciples had tried to cross the lake toward Capernaum but were caught by a storm three miles from shore. As the storm raged, darkness fell and they began to fear greatly for their lives. Suddenly they spotted Jesus walking toward them upon the surface of the water. When Jesus reached them and they took him into their boat, the winds and waters immediately calmed, and the men soon reached the safety of the shore.

"The message is clear," said the priest. "We have only to accept Our Lord into our lives and let him guide us, and we too will be saved. We must hold this lesson within our hearts as we face the challenges ahead on this great voyage." Father Gamboa bowed his head and asked God to keep their conduct holy and their bodies and minds in good health.

Throughout the service Cabrillo had furtively kept his eyes on Lezcano. He had to admit that the man seemed pious enough. Time, however, would reveal his true character.

When the rite was concluded, Cabrillo ordered his officers to gather the men at the water's edge. Before joining them there he momentarily led Father Gamboa aside, and said in a voice meant for no other ears, "Father, I must ask you to tell me your impressions of Father Lezcano."

The small, gentle priest smiled and answered with, "He gives every sign of being devout and hard-working. Do you have concerns about him, Captain-General?"

Unwilling to disclose his brief but turbulent prior contact with Lezcano, Cabrillo hedged, "He is very young."

"True, sir, but I am only nine years his senior. I believe he will learn quickly."

"Do you sense any rebellion in his nature?"

There was a slight hesitation, and then the tolerant smile reappeared. "Is there not a touch of rebellion in all young men, sir?"

"In all seriousness, Father, I must ask whether you perceive the potential for treachery in him?"

Surprised, Father Gamboa said, "Captain-General Cabrillo, you are a just man. Is it right to suspect such a thing after so short an acquaintance?"

At this Cabrillo was tempted to tell him everything but ultimately shook his head. "The men are waiting, Father. I hope my suspicions are groundless. I only ask that you watch him closely, and come to me if there is any difficulty."

Father Gamboa's face clouded but before he could question Cabrillo further, his commander turned away and hurried to join his officers.

As the wind played with the beaching foam and the morning sun flared to its brightest glow, Captain Ferrelo stood to his right, Correa to his left, and Cabrillo gave strength to his voice. "Men, this is a day to lock in our memories. You all know our goals, but I will state them again to strengthen our resolve to see them attained. We set out to explore and claim the coast of California all the way to the shores of Asia. Along our way, we shall seek to locate the Strait of Anián. Once we reach the San Lázaro or the Molucca Islands we will aid Captain-General Villalobos in his trade efforts, and then return home with our holds filled and our routes proven.

"Whether we will find only wastelands as we voyage, or we discover places such as the Seven Cities of Gold, only God now knows. There is much, however, that we can do to improve our outcome. Each man who gives the full measure of his strength and determination to achieve what we now set out to do increases his chance of survival and reward. Such high efforts must be maintained throughout every challenge the sea and sky may deliver. And on land we must always offer welcoming relations with the Indians we come across, *regardless* of your past encounters with any natives."

At these last words Cabrillo did not miss the slight shifting and muttering that ensued, and he said with an icy bite that left none doubting his seriousness, "Any man who jeopardizes the success of this voyage by not heeding my words will meet a punishment both swift and severe." Silence and stillness instantly followed. He held them there for two breaths.

As he continued, his expression and voice warmed. "I am confident that in the weeks and months to come you will show me, and our viceroy, and our king, the depth of your courage and honor." He scanned the bodies and faces before him, taking in the staunchness of his battle-scared soldiers and seamen. Some wore an eye patch or stood upon a pegged leg. Others displayed the unmarred body and bare cheeks of shining youth. The Indian allies who accompanied them stood erect and calm, their expressions implying an acceptance of whatever came.

Cabrillo felt his chest suddenly swell with pride and affection. He raised his arm and pointed to the northwest. "Out there lies the unknown, and I would rather face it with you than with any other crew in the world. Our time has come, men. Are we ready?"

The shout of a hundred voices confirmed the eagerness of a hundred hearts.

"Then, men of the *San Salvador*, *La Victoria*, and *San Miguel*, say one last farewell to this land and board your ships!"

Chapter 5

TESTING THE SHEETS

Overhead, clinging to ratlines with their feet, Cabrillo's sailors released the ties along the yardarms and the canvas surfaces unfurled with a blending "*whoosh.*" Deckhands on all three ships hauled with gusto, as a stiff possessive wind billowed the spotless sails. The fleet glided proudly forward while men secured the dripping anchors to the bows. Captain-General Cabrillo signaled with a nod to Pilot San Remón, who lifted his face, drew air from deep within his lungs, and shouted, "In the name of the Father, the Son, and the Holy Spirit, we ask for a splendid voyage and a safe return!"

Onshore a small but lusty crowd let loose a high-spirited cheer. When the breeze caught the answering roar from the ships, it blew it toward the northwest, away from Santiago. Even so, Cabrillo imagined their farewells somehow carrying all the way to Beatriz. She would be on her knees this Tuesday morning, praying for their safety. It took much willpower to turn his thoughts from her and his sons, as well as Lucia and his daughters, and to allow the concerns of the fleet to possess him. For now, he belonged to these men and these vessels.

He turned his gaze ahead and studied the responses of his fine flagship under the handling of his chosen men. Although they had made short trial runs to train the newer crewmembers, Cabrillo sorely missed the seasoned hands who had sailed with him to Peru but had been killed by the earthquake. Brief hesitations and slight errors were occurring on the decks below that those men would never have made. Watching his frustrated boatswain bark corrections at the men working the lines in this stiff breeze, his shouts occasionally emphasized by the snap of a stiffly knotted rope across a pair of shoulders, Cabrillo assured himself that they would learn quickly. They had no choice. In a few short days their bellies would stiffen to the rocking of the ship and their hands would toughen with each tug on the lines. Despite the disparity in their languages of Castilian, two Indian dialects, Basque, Galician, and Catalonian, they would soon discover how to be sixty men working with the will of one. In the meantime, the older hands would often preempt the boatswain by yelling at the sailors deemed slow or inept, and the younger men would jump to their tasks a little more spryly, dodging the occasional fist whenever possible. The twenty-four soldiers aboard had been given enough instruction to make them useful at the lines if the need arose, but for now they stood aside and left the duties of departure to the seamen.

At the last moment prior to boarding, Cabrillo had changed his mind about having Father Lezcano sail aboard the *San Miguel*. Better to have the young monk on the *San Salvador* where he could watch him closely, he decided. Both priests on board the flagship were absolute novices when it came to the workings of a tall ship but, so far, both seemed willing to follow the dictates of their captain-general as well as their God.

In spite of the rawness of the newcomers, the ship's officers already had made the three shifts familiar with their assignments. Rotating every four hours, each seaman was designated specific duties in the fore, mid, or aft sections of the ship. Shipmaster Uribe commanded the decks from the hours of twelve to four, day and night. Their pilot took control of the watches from four to eight. Although Cabrillo's active dominion theoretically ran from the hours of eight and twelve, his word was always final and he spent most daylight and many nighttime hours on deck.

Manuel was never far from his side. He stood close by at the moment, staring out at the sea ahead and swaying with the stern deck, a black guardian of the man who owned him.

To Cabrillo there was little interest in the section of nearly treeless coastline along which they were sailing. Others had studied and claimed these shores, and this land was at least somewhat settled. Before long he altered their course slightly westward and let his gaze leave the coast in answer to the beckoning ocean.

Thoughtfully, he asked Manuel, "How does it feel to be at sea again?"

"Steadier than the first time, sir."

A glance at his slave revealed a slight droopiness of the eyes and slackness of the mouth that were unusual to Manuel while on land. "Ah, I remember," said Cabrillo. "We began to wonder if you would ever see Peru. Thankfully, your stomach behaved much better on the return voyage."

"Now I wish to see California, sir. That will keep me well."

A couple of loud thumps came to them from below their feet. "It sounds like Paulo may need some help in my cabin."

With a respectful bow Manuel headed for the stairs, careful to find secure handholds along the way. Cabrillo glanced astern at the closely trailing *La Victoria*, and then at the *San Miguel*. The bergantine sailed with her oars at rest, allowing her crew comparative ease as they adjusted to their new lives upon the waves. As Captain Correa prowled her decks, Cabrillo occasionally caught sight of him or heard one of his bellowed orders. The captain-general's attention swung again to *La Victoria*, and his eyes met those of Captain Ferrelo. Ferrelo bowed from the railing of his quarterdeck in a manner that expressed thanks for this chance to command under sail. Cabrillo returned the bow, understanding all too well.

He was not a man who hungered for the sea, aching to set foot aboard another ship from the very moment he returned ashore. When home Cabrillo found fulfillment and happiness, and his ships were almost forgotten. But each time he made his way back to the ocean's realm and stood upon an upper stern deck, he was swallowed anew by the sensations that possessed him only here.

The unconquerable enormity of the sea never failed to expand his heart and mind. It drew from him an untamed, boundless spirit that the land never could. In times past its beauty and power had come together in a way that had shouted, "Take all of this deep within and rejoice at the glory laid before you!" Yet on other occasions it had murmured, "Beware, for I can crush you and your ship whenever I please." Hearing these whisperings, his daring had risen to defy them, and God had chosen to see him through the sea's mighty trials. After each terrible storm the magnanimity of the ocean had emerged and calmly reclaimed his welcoming soul.

Even the longing he currently suffered for his family could not diminish the countering amplification of himself that the sea both bestowed and demanded. More fully with each mile that separated him from the harbor, he surrendered to the familiar, undeniable pull.

The *San Salvador* had settled well into her canvas sheets and was making good time when Mateo approached Cabrillo, lost his balance, and almost stumbled into him. His captain-general caught him under the arms and yanked him upright.

"Please forgive me, sir," the boy gasped weakly, his eyes glassy as he fought to keep a waving nausea down. He gulped a few breaths before trying again. "Paulo sent me to ask, to ask what..." He swallowed hard.

Taking pity on the boy, Cabrillo grasped his shoulders and turned him to face the bow as he stepped him to the leeward railing. Knowing he would do his nephew no favors by showing him unwarranted leniency in front of the other men, he kept his voice firm as he said, "I told you, Mateo, keep your gaze ahead. Hold onto the rail and inhale deeply. Paulo's question can wait."

Mateo tried to obey but it was too late. Clapping a hand hard to his mouth until he'd leaned over the side, his gut heaved upward in wave after wave until it had emptied its contents overboard. Pale and sweating, his eyes working to focus, Mateo returned to his commander accompanied by the chuckles of several crewmembers.

"Now, Mateo" said Cabrillo, "concentrate on where the sky embraces the sea. Imagine there is an island of gold awaiting you there."

After several minutes had passed a little of the color returned to Mateo's face and he began to breathe more evenly. At last he muttered thoughtfully, "If you do not mind, sir, I will imagine a horse swimming far ahead of us. I would rather have a horse than a whole island of gold."

"Well said, young man. Then dream of a herd of horses, but you will have to wait to own them for some time. You are a sailor at present so stop looking at me and keep your eyes on the horizon."

"Yes, sir, but I was to ask about your choice of wine for dinner."

"Tell Paulo he may choose the wine," he said, "and tell him you are to be relieved of your cabin duties for the time being."

Never were Mateo's next words spoken with more sincerity. "Oh, thank you, sir! Am I to return to the stern deck after I deliver your message?"

"You may report to Pilot San Remón, with my request that he instruct you in the mechanics of reckoning latitude and longitude. A seaman must have the skills to estimate the position of his ship."

"Yes, sir. I thank you, sir." With this, the boy left to make his way to the captain-general's cabin, and Cabrillo was able to solitarily enjoy his ship and the vast waters upon which she sailed. Such periods never lasted long, however, and the flowing consistency with which a ship captain is visited while on deck soon brought Pilot San Remón to his side.

Even if the pilot's face had been able to hide something of his present exhilaration, his voice could not when he said, "Captain-General, with a wind such as this we could sail to Asia in a month!"

"As you are quite aware, pilot, such a wind seldom presents itself for two days running. Still, it is a fine sign." Cabrillo observed that the pilot carried his logbook and astrolabe case, housing the precious instrument that would help them compute their rising latitudes as they ventured farther north of the equator. "Have you seen Mateo? He was to come to you."

"He did, sir. He will help make the reckoning at the turning of the glass. I believe he is staring at the sand at the moment, hoping it will fall a little more quickly under his scrutiny."

The men smiled, recalling the days when they were just as eager for an opportunity to prove themselves. "I will have him read the astrolabe at noon, sir, and begin to teach him the calculations. He is bright enough to learn them."

"Diego said it was very hard on his mother, his leaving with us."

"Is it ever easy for mothers, sir?"

"Perhaps not, but an Indian mother has even less power than most over the life of her son."

Knowing of Cabrillo's half-blood daughters, San Remón treaded softly around this subject. "Mateo is fortunate to be the son of your brother-in-law, sir. He will find his place in the world."

With the turning of the sand glass imminent, Cabrillo said, "Here comes your pupil, pilot." Mateo was quickly moved into position with the astrolabe held in readiness, when from the deck below the oldest of the ship's cabin boys sang out, "The hour of fourteen is upon us. God has granted safe passage thus far. May He give us fair sailing ahead." Mustering impressive volume, many men joined him to end with, "Ahhh-mennn."

Mateo's lesson began at the first utterance of this announcement by his raising the astrolabe and adjusting the arm to mark the sun's position at its zenith.

Lingering close by but giving no outward sign of interest, Cabrillo surreptitiously witnessed Mateo's instruction with satisfaction. He noticed that Mateo seemed to have forgotten his seasickness while focusing his mind to something new. As the pilot explained the basics of their method, the lad took in every word with an expression of almost painful seriousness. Afterward, he asked few but appropriate questions. As San Remón was replacing the astrolabe in its wooden box, he said to the boy just loudly enough for Cabrillo to hear, "Although I bear the title of pilot for our ship, Mateo, our captain-general is recognized as the finest pilot in Mexico."

Cabrillo glanced at him with a raised eyebrow.

"It is quite common knowledge," the pilot went on. "Why, I have seen Captain-General Cabrillo study the sea and wind for only an instant, and somehow their shades and movements, and perhaps even their smells enable him to discern the speed of the ship. It is a wonder indeed."

Mateo turned an enthralled gaze upon Cabrillo. "Sir, can you tell us our speed at this moment?"

With a pointed glance at his pilot, Cabrillo said, "Pilot San Remón greatly overstates my ability, Mateo."

Unruffled, San Remón asked, "Please, sir, will you do us the honor of giving an estimate of our speed? For the boy's education?"

Cabrillo sighed resignedly as he gazed up at the sails and beyond to the sky. He moved to the railing to stare first at the waves breaking from the port bow, then walked over to starboard, and finally strode to the center of the stern rail and eyed the wake of the ship. What other observations had been taken into consideration Mateo could only guess before his uncle squinted at the sails once again and said, "Very well, I believe she is sailing at no less than seven knots. Perhaps a bit more."

"Thank you, sir," said the pilot and the boy in unison.

Now it was their turn. On San Remón's command Mateo tossed the log chip, a rectangular piece of wood tied to a thin but sturdy line, over the stern railing, and counted the evenly spaced knots as they spun from the ship's line reel and cleared the rail. The pilot, holding the thirty-second sandglass, called a halt just as the top half of the glass emptied. Mateo grabbed the line, studied the length from his hand to the nearest knot, and announced the count with amazed pleasure, "Seven and a quarter, sir!" Their pilot didn't bother hiding a smug smile as he entered this reckoning into his log next to the figure recorded a half-hour earlier. Cabrillo ignored the smile entirely.

"There," San Remón said to Mateo, "now you have learned how to use the small sandglass, chip, and reel to judge the pace of the ship."

"Perhaps one day, Pilot San Remón," said the boy as his eyes trailed to his uncle, "I will need only to study the sea flowing around her to tell her speed."

"Perhaps, but today there is still much to learn, so listen closely. You know that the half-hour glass allows us to track the passing of time. Using it and the sun, we count our shifts and our days. We have just gauged our speed. Now, when both time and speed have been recorded, what can be discerned?"

Mateo thought for several moments but his face showed only that the struggle was growing more painful the longer his mind groped for the answer.

"Mateo," the pilot tried to help, "if we know how long and how fast we have been voyaging...?"

Blank brown eyes stared back at him.

Pilot San Remón took an impatient breath to prepare for a lecture, but Mateo suddenly brightened and burst out with, "Will we know how far we have sailed from Navidad, sir?"

Relieved, the pilot said, "Yes, but only roughly." Here he paused long enough to scratch out and explain a sample calculation on a piece of parchment, then he resumed. "We must also consider the changes in our speed between readings, as well as how the cross currents may alter our readings. If we were sailing due west, with a consistent current, we could better approximate our distance and, thereby, our longitudinal position from east to west. The astrolabe tells us how far north we have come."

Confident that the lessons would continue to proceed admirably, the captain-general left the quarterdeck under the watch of his pilot and descended the stairs to check on his horses.

Before his eyes could fully adjust to the dimness below decks he heard the low voice of a man near the horse enclosure. Approaching that area, he saw the robed back of a priest, and the man was too tall to be Father Gamboa. Cabrillo immediately stilled his steps but he had already been heard. Viento lifted his head and gave a short, shrill call to his master.

Tensely watchful, Cabrillo walked up to the stall as Father Lezcano stepped away from the horse, an empty milking pail in his hand. In a voice rigid with restraint, Cabrillo said, "The cow is in the end stall."

"I meant no offense, sir. I came only to admire him. He is a magnificent horse."

Cabrillo's glare pinned the priest as his words bit the still air. "No one touches him but me and his assigned grooms. *No one.* Every member of the crew understands this order."

Manuel, who had been drawing nearer in the shadows, stepped forward carrying a heavy bag of grain. He lowered the canvas sack to the ground and admitted, "It is my fault, sir. Please forgive me. I thought, since it was Father Lezcano, that it would be... but I should have known. I should have told him about Viento."

There was something in the priest's overly innocent expression that flared Cabrillo's suspicions rather than dampening them, and it took a significant effort to temper his tone as he addressed his slave. "Yes, Manuel, you should have told him." To Father Lezcano, Cabrillo said with an acidity that etched his words, "I will make things perfectly clear so there can be no *confusion* in the future, related to my horses or anything else related to this fleet. At sea, even a priest is bound to obey his captain-general. If a man, sailor or priest, is unsure of his commander's wishes, he should ask for permission before he acts. Now, you will stay away from my horses, particularly *this* horse. If any harm should come to him, even the smallest scratch, things would go harshly for whoever was to blame. And you, Father, would be the first man I would search out as the perpetrator."

During this castigation Father Lezcano's cheeks had darkened and his eyes had narrowed. Despite the flash of temper that heightened the urge to defend his affronted character, he managed not to speak until his words held the restrained tenor of warning rather than outright challenge. "One who makes threats of harshness to a man of the cloth appears to hold little fear for his soul, Captain-General Cabrillo."

Cabrillo threw back at him, "My soul is in God's hands, not yours, priest."

Momentarily stunned by so sacrilegious a statement, Father Lezcano said, "Such disregard for his representatives, sir, could be judged an act of blasphemy."

Again Cabrillo rebuffed the priest, saying, "I doubt Father Gamboa would deem it so. I also doubt that he would have the impertinence to show defiance toward me."

"You misunderstand me, sir. I meant only to caution."

"If I ever seek your cautions or any other words of advice, I will make my requests obvious."

Manuel's eyes shifted most uneasily from one man to the other as he held his body motionless. Viento, having sensed the mounting tension in his master, had begun blowing out deep breaths and shifting on his hobbled feet. Cabrillo moved forward to place himself directly between Viento and the priest, and said, "I must calm my horse."

Father Lezcano hesitated, then gave Cabrillo a stiff, shallow bow and left them.

With his voice lowered to a murmur, his touch reassuring, Cabrillo carefully examined every strap of the large sling that supported the horse's body and kept him from harm whenever the ship swayed. He then tested each of the looser tethers that secured Viento's head and hooves to support posts. Without the need of an order, Manuel began conducting the same thorough evaluation of the ties protecting Cabrillo's gelding.

When they both stood together again, satisfied that all was well, Cabrillo noticed Manuel's reluctance to meet his gaze. "What is it?"

Manuel lifted his head but remained silent.

"What is on your mind, Manuel?"

"Sir, you do not trust Father Lezcano. But why would a priest, a man of God, harm Viento?"

"He wears a friar's robes, yes. Whether his intentions are holy, I am uncertain. I fear only time will tell us that." Cabrillo could see that these words only further troubled his pious slave, but he explained nothing more.

Although the strength of the wind was waning somewhat, by late afternoon the beating sun had coaxed most of the men to shed their shirts and hike the hems of their breeches to well above their knees. The officers and Father Lezcano were the only exceptions. Cabrillo had allowed the lightening of attire only after the sun had reached a point he deemed less dangerous. He wanted no sunstroke or serious burns reducing the health of his men. Even Father Gamboa exposed his bony back to the breeze while offering what comfort he could to the many Indians battling appalling seasickness. These first days out were always the worst.

The ships had traveled far and well before the sun became less generous with its light, always keeping to their planned formation with the flagship in the lead. It was, therefore, the *San Salvador's* lookout who shouted out first, "Whales ahead, sir! A point off the starboard bow!" The cry was quickly taken up by the lookouts of the other two ships and dozens of bodies rushed to the starboard railings for a better look. Mateo leaped up and down to get fleeting views from between necks of the others until Manuel grabbed him and lifted the lad to his shoulders. "Ohhhh!" he said. "Look, Manuel! Look at them!"

Excited cries and laughter burst from many others, especially from those new to life upon the ocean. The massive humpbacked whales paid little heed to the fleet, spouting and breaching within their small group, and slowly veering away from the course taken by the sailing vessels. Within the hour, to Mateo's renewed delight, two more whale pods were sighted, and dolphins began to appear almost predictably, skimming and leaping free of the water like acrobats performing at a festival.

As the sun moved farther west and began to sink to the waterline, according to a long maritime routine the three ships drew closer together and the captains of the smaller two vessels saluted their captain-general. Cabrillo returned their greetings and asked how they fared.

"We of *La Victoria* fare as well as can be hoped, sir," reported Captain Ferrelo.

"As do the men of the *San Miguel*, sir!" called Captain Correa.

"Fine, then we shall sail through the night with our headings steady toward Cabo de Corriente."

Even given their brisk pace, the ships did fairly well at remaining close together while Father Gamboa led them in vespers. Cabrillo then dismissed the other ships with, "God keep you all safe through the night!"

One by one lantern wicks kindled to life throughout the ship, and Cabrillo felt warmed by their glow as he headed to steerage. There he reviewed the compass settings and speeds recently recorded within the log book, and the accuracy with which they'd been plotted onto the course-map carved in the top of the binnacle. This wooden box also served as a housing for the ship's main compass, and that precious instrument was set before the vertical whipstaff within easy viewing of the man who controlled the tiller and, by its connection with that device, the rudder. Finding all to be as it should, Cabrillo said to the tillerman firmly embracing the *San Salvador's* whipstaff, "Hold her steady, Tomas, and pray this wind stays with us."

"It is indeed a blessed wind, sir. Brawny yet smooth as a Gernika wine."

Cabrillo took his time as he made his way back to the upper stern deck, observing along the way the mood of his men, his ships, and the sea, all of which gave him reason for contentment. He forced thoughts of Father Lezcano aside, surrendering them to the peacefulness surrounding him. The sky's final traces of deepening blue slowly blackened and the first shy twinkling of early stars grew steadily bolder. The light of the two great lanterns at opposite sides of the stern railing shone merrily out from their ornate metal cages, visually proclaiming the ship's quiet passage. The ocean ahead held nothing but swelling, bending, smoothing waters. The distant shore showed no firelight and issued no call. *In all the world, at least this side of the world,* Cabrillo thought, *there are just these ships and the sea.*

Sleep, he knew, would not come easily tonight, even after he relinquished his command to the second shift at midnight. Though the ship would be in excellent hands under his pilot's watch, the night was too beautiful and too abundantly filled with possibilities to allow for effortless slumber. Without needing to look, he felt Manuel's presence behind him, and he knew this faithful companion wouldn't close his eyes until his master had done so first.

Walking to the port railing, Cabrillo peered over the edge and smiled. After so many sightings such as this he could not be surprised, but neither could he hold back a feeling of delight. Here in the foam was one of so many magnificent mysteries of the sea. He had tried to explain it more than once in Seville to friends who had never sailed, but none had believed him. Yet here in the froth churned up by the ship, tiny lights exploded in blue, green, red, and gold, as if some saintly hand had reached down from the heavens and set the bubbles to multihued glistening. He watched, spellbound and somehow refreshed, for several moments.

When he lifted his face he found Manuel a step away, and said softly, "Send Mateo to me."

The boy soon appeared and Cabrillo motioned him to the railing. "Look there," he said, pointing downward.

Mateo followed the direction of Cabrillo's arm, gaped, and took a step back as he gasped, "Blessed Mother of God!"

With a low chuckle Cabrillo motioned him back to his side. "If it is the work of Our Lady, and it may well be, why should you fear it? Come and look again. Whatever magic it holds, it is not evil, and it was meant only for men of the sea. Savor it, and give thanks."

With considerable trepidation the boy again cast his eyes upon the bursting colors and held his gaze steady. Gradually, but only somewhat, his fears seeped away. He became reflective and said at last, "It was kind of you to share this wonder with me, sir."

"Since you must help stand watch until midnight, Mateo, whenever you feel sleepy glance at these lights and let them keep you awake. As you know, falling asleep during a watch is one of the worst offenses a sailor can make. The lash is put to use to make certain it is not committed twice."

"Yes, Captain-General. I shall remember."

"Well then, join the men at the foredeck for this hour of the watch."

"Yes, sir." He bowed and was gone.

In the quiet that settled after the boy's departure Cabrillo was allowed to reflect back on the first time he had seen the mystifying lights in the foam. He had been a year younger than Mateo, traveling from Spain to Española, then Cuba, then Mexico, lands that would hold terror and enchantment far beyond what he could have imagined.

And now, now, what would California unveil to him and his men? Once seen, would any of them survive to tell of her mysteries?

Chapter 6

A QUESTION OF TRUST

Someone gently shaking his shoulder drew Cabrillo, grumbling and groggy, from the deep slumber he'd fallen into for no more than three turnings of the sandglass. He recognized Manuel's touch before he heard his voice. "Captain-General, Pilot said to wake you. Cabo de Corriente lies four miles ahead."

Cabrillo was now sitting up and reaching for his shirt. He peered at Manuel who stood outlined by the morning light slanting in through the window. "Four miles? What is the hour?"

"Not yet seven, sir."

This news brought him fully awake. "I knew it. May the saints be praised! That blessed wind will have carried us a hundred miles in less than twenty hours!"

As Manuel bent down and began picking up a few sheets of paper scattered across the floor, Cabrillo cast him a puzzled look. Smoothing out the pages on the desk, Manuel said, "You went sleepwalking again, sir. You must have bumped your desk."

Cabrillo shook his head and muttered, "Even during so short a night."

"Maybe you meant to write something, sir, while you were dreaming. I listened close, but you soon settled down again." Without having been instructed to do so, Manuel had taken possession of the floor outside the captain-general's door as his sleeping area, to guard him from harm, certainly, but also to lessen any embarrassment brought on by the nocturnal meanderings that plagued him.

A knock at the door preceded the arrival of Paulo with a bucket of water. He entered and asked Cabrillo, "May I assist you now, sir?"

"I thank you, Paulo, and I know it will take time for you to become accustomed to life at sea, but I need even less help dressing while aboard this ship than I did on land."

Paulo expression grew decidedly pinched.

"I ask you, as I have many times, to accept that I was not raised to be a coddled gentleman."

Paulo's stiffened even more at such a self-inflicted affront. "Forgive me, sir, but you *are* a gentleman of high esteem and captain-general of this fleet. I prize the honor of serving you, and one of my duties is to assist you with your dress."

"Perhaps I should find a servant less educated in his duties and more prone to obedience." Having heard similar threats repeated for two years, Paulo paid these words little heed until Cabrillo said with much more conviction, "Paulo, show me the goodness to be satisfied with confining your duties to my meals, my laundry, and my cabin. While under sail leave me to tend to my dressing and grooming as I will. If necessary, consider this an order."

His servant's haughty expression fell to one of mournful resignation, and he began quietly tidying up the small room while Cabrillo gave Manuel his orders for the day ahead.

After hurrying through breakfast Cabrillo appeared at his usual post on the stern deck to be greeted by a pilot in particularly buoyant spirits. "We have arrived, Captain-General. A sailor can not hope for a day and night better than what we enjoyed."

Cabrillo glanced behind to check the positions and movements of his other two ships as he said, "Agreed, pilot, and the wind holds steady."

Shipmaster Uribe, older than his commander by a handful of years, with a ruddy face already bristling with gray stubble but matched with a body still nimble and a wit still sharp, climbed the stairs to join them. More to spark the morning dialogue than to announce anything unknown to his captain-general, he said, "The decking has been washed and the bilge waters pumped, sir, light work after just setting out."

"Very good, Master Uribe."

"And there lies our first port, Captain-General," Uribe said with a jerk of his chin. "What are your orders, sir?"

"We shall not tarry here but sail on to California. It would be sinful to waste such a breeze."

67

San Remón and Uribe bobbed their heads in harmony. Men standing just below them grinned and slapped each other on the back as if they'd just heard of an unexpected increase in pay.

Enjoying their exuberance, Cabrillo said, "May the men always be this pleased when I order the fleet to ignore an anchorage. Please pass the word to the other ships, Master Uribe." When this order had been obeyed, Cabrillo asked his pilot, "While I slept did you spot any signs of life ashore?"

"Not many, sir. A flash here and there that might have been campfires, nothing more."

Growing thoughtful as he took in the coastline, Cabrillo asked, "What might we have seen, I wonder, if we had sailed here before Bloody Guzman pillaged the land?" The gazes of his officers grew more speculative as they too searched the farther reaches of the shore. "Knowing how swift the Indians' vengeance can be, I would not readily risk a landing in that bay even if the wind was against us. Hurtado should have been more cautious, and I doubt the ten years between now and then have quenched the thirst to repay some of Guzman's devilry."

"Is it true, sir, that Hurtado's mutineers were killed not far from here, at another spot in Bahia de Banderas?" said San Remón.

"That crew was killed at Banderas, yes, but Captain Hurtado and those loyal to him met the same fate farther north, near Rio Fuerte. And the following year, as my wife recently reminded me, Jiménez and his mutinous crew were slain near La Paz. Happily for us, we may avoid facing the natives of both locations. Doubtless we will encounter Indians enough in the lands ahead to keep us attentive."

Uribe's eyes twinkled with mischief. "There is a warning to be learned from these tales, eh, sir? Mutineers beware of natives."

"Indeed there is."

San Remón asked, "One of the Jiménez survivors returned to tell of gold and pearls at La Paz, did he not, sir?"

"There were three survivors to spread that story, which was likely true. Cortes, too, found pearls there. Even so, gold and pearls carry too low a value to recklessly trade for our lives."

"Far too low, sir."

"And our mission does not allow us a delay to hunt for previously claimed treasure."

68

"No, sir," said San Remón. "We had best find treasures not yet claimed, had we not?"

At the turning of the glass the ships drew together for the early prayer services of matins, and Father Gamboa gave humble praise to the Lord for his benevolence. Though Cabrillo's head was bowed, his devotion was significantly diverted by nagging thoughts concerning Father Lezcano, who stood in apparently pious silence beside his senior priest. It was unlike the captain-general to let a potential problem pester him this way, and he wondered if his own reluctance to deal adequately with the matter was bothering him as much as the man. He asked himself if he should have punished the priest for approaching Viento rather than merely warning him? On the other hand, could Lezcano be completely innocent of malicious intent?

At the intonation of the final "amen" the captain-general raised his eyes and found his gaze met by that of the young friar. Cabrillo replaced the velvet hat upon his head and was turning away when Father Lezcano approached him and asked politely, "Captain-General, may I trouble you to spare me a moment of your time, in private?"

"It is my watch, Father," Cabrillo responded. "I do not wish to relinquish it."

"Yes, of course, sir, then may I join you on the quarterdeck for a few words?"

Father Gamboa, noticing the terseness in Cabrillo's voice, glanced between the two wearing a troubled expression.

"If you wish, Father," said Cabrillo. "Please excuse us, Father Gamboa."

Discerning their commander's desire for privacy, the sailors cleared the way as he and the priest passed by, and an area around the aft of the ship grew sparsely populated.

Cabrillo's withheld impatience was nearly as tangible as the heat of the rising sun, so Father Lezcano came quickly to the point. "Captain-General, I ask you to reconsider your opinion of me."

His frankness was a surprise. "My opinion of a man can only be changed by his actions, even if that man is a priest."

"I meant no harm to your horse, sir, and I can imagine no other action that might have caused concern. Can it benefit your men or your mission to show distrust of a priest who only wishes to serve you and God?"

69

Though the question was posed in a humble tone the challenge in the words made Cabrillo's gaze sharpen. "To serve me? You have no worldly ambition beyond that?"

"When I was ordained I spoke my holy vows with sincerity, Captain-General. I will spend my life attempting to obey God's will, and his will has placed me on this ship. I cannot minister to the *San Salvador's* men as I should if they neither respect nor trust me. And they will not, if you do not."

Cabrillo folded his arms over his chest, considering. "That is very likely true. How then, would you gain my trust?"

"Give me the care of your horses, sir."

Cabrillo almost let loose an incredulous bark of laughter but managed to check himself. "My horses?"

"I have given it much thought, sir. That would be the best way to show how I have changed, before the eyes of men and God, since our first meeting."

With his brow knitted, Cabrillo was about to refuse when Father Lezcano hurriedly added, "I accept the fact that you would kill any man, priest or otherwise, if he intentionally harmed Viento."

They studied one another for a long moment until Cabrillo said, "I would be justified in doing so. Are you saying you will gladly risk that?"

"It is no risk at all, sir, since I know my own heart."

Cabrillo still hedged by saying, "I remember your pointing out that you are of noble blood. How does working as a stable-hand fit with your high breeding?"

"It suits my calling if not my breeding to do even the humblest of work, sir."

Faced with this final declaration, Cabrillo felt his defenses waver a bit. "I do not often misjudge men. I would have died very young if I had not learned to read a man quickly, but perhaps with you I have been too abrupt."

"At our first meeting, Captain-General, you said you saw courage in me but that I must learn wisdom. I ask you to be one of my teachers."

Cabrillo weakened further and Father Lezcano noticed, and there it was, a brash though slightly tempered smile that celebrated the realization that his captain-general would yield.

"Cloak that boldness, Father, if you seek my favor." The smile vanished. "And take care in what you ask of me. As you know, some of my lessons are not easily endured."

Father Lezcano heard the warning, but he still said, "I have been told that I too can judge the make of a man. I ask again that you help me learn what a man should know."

Cabrillo turned to face the eastern clouds but found no escape in them. "Then, for the sake of my soul as well as yours, I will grant at least a share of what you ask. Do *not* let either of us come to regret it." Looking around and calling Manuel to them, he said, "In the future Father Lezcano will assist you in the care of my horses."

Manuel tried to mask his astonishment. "Yes, sir."

"You are to be with him at all times when he is near the animals. At all times, Manuel."

"Yes, Captain-General."

Father Lezcano bowed deeply and said, "I am grateful, sir."

Cabrillo offered a short, deliberate bow in return. "Now, Father Lezcano, I must resume duties."

Almost immediately Cabrillo began to question the prudence of his decision, another train of thought relatively unusual to him, yet within minutes he had reassured himself by recalling Manuel's unquestionable loyalty and watchfulness, and he forced his mind to become more engrossed with the command of his ship.

At the southern-most point of the fifteen-mile-wide Bahia de Banderas they sailed past protruding Cabo de Corrientes, where the deep green foliage of the plain reached toward them from the mountains. If this place had held a different history Cabrillo might have been tempted to linger briefly. The rivers here could provide fresh water, which was never passed by lightly, but they had water enough for the present circumstances. The wind still seemed willing to acquiesce to the wishes of the fleet, and it swept them up the coast at a speed almost equal to that of the day before.

That evening, after first obtaining permission from the captain-general, Father Gamboa delighted the men by appearing on the main deck with his bagpipes. Anticipation brightened the faces of men who gathered around him. It took only a moment or two for Father Gamboa's breath to expand the leather bag and for his fingers to find their marks. The priest's eyes glowed as he drew the first notes from the instrument, and he soon produced a melody so poignant that no words were needed to touch the emotions of all who listened. The rising, circling notes expanded out over the waves and into the sky. It carried to the other ships, stilling hands and lifting gazes to the summoning sound. Here and there eyes began to fill and noses to sniffle as the music turned thoughts toward loved ones left behind. The piper played on, and as he finished his first song he immediately began another, and then a third. When he paused, men begged for more, and he complied with a soft smile. If anyone heard the sound from shore, they doubtless look out to sea and were mesmerized by what they saw.

At last the priest's music drew to a gentle close and he tenderly tucked his pipes into their chest. The two Irish gunners had been among those most moved by the music, and the one who spoke Castilian, the taller of the two, said, "Father, I never knew that any but the people of my own land could play the pipes so. That was mighty fine, mighty fine indeed."

"I thank you, my son."

"I heard tell that the Irish were the first to breathe life into a set of pipes, Father. Have you heard the same?"

"Well, I have read that bagpipes were played a thousand years before Our Savior was born, and shortly after Jesus' death Emperor Nero of Rome played them. I was fascinated to also read of a primitive pipe, carved from the leg bone of a bird that was found in Viscaya. That pipe may be thousands of years old." The eyes of the sailor had grown large in amazement. Father Gamboa smiled and said, "Who can say with certainty where the pipes were first played?"

The Irishman offered no supposition, but his expression left little doubt that he was unwilling to surrender his faith in his earlier claim. As the men drifted away toward their sleeping corners, the humming of tunes that the bagpipe had yielded could be heard about the ships.

The following dawn the benevolent wind demonstrated the capricious side of its nature by swinging around 180° and buffeting them from the northwest just as they attempted to nose away from Mexico's mainland and head toward the southern tip of California. They toiled against the gusts and swells for every mile they gained, and the rolling decks worsened the seasickness aboard, further torturing those already weakened by its effects. The next day and the next the fleet fought against contrary winds that swept away the occasional moans of the sufferers. While the ship's surgeon treated the sick bodies by doling out sea biscuits hard enough to chip teeth, Fathers Gamboa and Lezcano ministered to their souls with prayers. Little by little, most of their patients gained the ability to hold down food.

Even his duty to care for the ill didn't prevent Father Lezcano from accompanying Manuel on at least three visits per day to the horses. Initially Cabrillo made unannounced appearances to oversee and add to the equestrian education of the priest. Somewhat to the captain-general's disappointment, Viento didn't seem to object to Father Lezcano's touch.

On Sunday, shortly after the morning prayers and as if by divine intervention, the wind shifted to a more favorable direction. Weary faces began to illuminate, reflecting their excitement at leaving the waters off Mexico and nearing the mystifying territory of California. Eyes seeking land now turned eagerly from the east to the northwest.

Just prior to the turning of the glass at the hour of twenty, the *San Salvador's* lookout shouted, "Land, Captain-General! Land dead ahead!" The cry of "California! California!" swept through the ships. Many of the hands peered and gaped as if they half expected to see Queen Calafia waiting on shore to greet them. Cabrillo also felt the thrill and wonder at this long-anticipated sight, yet he kept his emotions contained for the sake of his excitable men. His young pilot revealed a struggle with his own anticipation by asking, "Sir, may I volunteer to be among the foremost landing party?"

"A landing is not yet assured, pilot. We must first study the situation from the ships to determine the advisability of sending out a scouting party."

Subtle though it was, Pilot San Remón understood the admonishment for his impetuosity. "Of course, Captain-General."

Quietly, Cabrillo said, "However, if there is to be a scouting party, I know I need not look far to find the right man to lead it." With that, Cabrillo headed to the foredeck and began to examine the approaching coast. Here, at the most southeastern cape of the Californian peninsula, the barren rocky hills seemed to have shoved their unwanted offspring into the sea, leaving the boulders to protrude from the waves like so many overgrown fingers and knobs.

Morning prayers were curtailed as they entered the cape. Even their cold breakfast of cheese and hard bread was postponed until the

73

ships, settling as gently as three swans tucking their wings, came to a full rest in the brilliantly blue water. When the food was quickly set out the men were so captivated by the features of the land, they hardly noticed what they ate.

One sailor swallowed a mouthful and voiced with disappointment, "Why, it needs trees to look anything like the paradise we heard so much of."

"And women," said another. "There's not a creature in sight, man nor beast, male nor female."

"Be grateful there are none here looking to cut out your heart and eat it," said a third. "As for me, I can wait awhile longer before I face that kind of enemy." His comment was met with head nodding and general mutterings of agreement.

While the crew hurried through their breakfast Cabrillo sent Manuel to his cabin for writing material and continued to scrutinize the beach. When his slave reappeared, the captain-general dipped his writing quill and began to make notes and sketches of the geography at hand. After several minutes, he handed Manuel his papers, cupped a hand to his mouth, and called to his lookout, "Bilbao, any movement?"

"None but from the birds, Captain-General!"

"Very well." He faced his shipmaster and said, "Master Uribe, have both launches lowered but keep one tied alongside."

"Yes, sir."

"Pilot, take four sailors, Vargas, and three other soldiers to scout for water. If you are challenged, withdraw at once. If you need assistance fire a signal shot. *Do not* fire upon an enemy unless your lives are clearly at risk. And if all seems safe, send a man back to the beach bearing a white cloth, and I will come ashore with the next barrel crew."

"Very good, sir. Thank you, sir," the pilot said as he hurried away to collect his men.

Master Uribe descended to the main deck and passed along similar landing instructions to the captains from the other two ships, and it took little time before the keels of three small boats slid onto the golden sands of the California peninsula. The men remaining on board the ships felt pangs of envy as the landing parties leaped from their boats, hauled their crafts ashore, hefted their weapons, and watchfully moved inland.

Neither Cabrillo nor Mateo were immune to the same yearnings as the others, but Mateo had neither the experience nor the passage of years to keep his from showing. Noting the boy's drooping mouth and sad eyes, Cabrillo said, "How many landings do you suppose there will be before we reach the San Lázaro Islands, Mateo?"

"I can not guess, sir. Will there be very many?"

"Dozens at least, perhaps a hundred."

"A hundred, sir?"

"Perhaps more. We shall see. If things remain quiet here, you shall have your turn ashore by nightfall."

"Oh, thank you, sir!"

"But for now, you must have duties in need of attention. Such as scrubbing barrels."

"Yes, sir, I will go at once." Casting one last glance toward land, Mateo went in search of the ship's cook.

"Master Uribe," Cabrillo called down, "unless the scouting party encounters trouble, all on board will be allowed time ashore at the end of their watch." At this announcement, a grateful cheer burst from the men. "And, Master Uribe, set some men to fishing. These waters seem to be begging for hooks and nets."

"Right away, sir."

Cabrillo's two priests approached him with a respectful bow, and Father Gamboa said happily, "This is a fine precedent, Captain-General. I, too, look forward to a cool swim in the river."

Father Lezcano added, "It will be good to rinse our clothes as well as our bodies, sir. The clothing will last longer if it is kept cleaner."

"That is my hope," said Cabrillo. "When the weather becomes cooler in the north, every article of clothing will be needed."

"May I ask if you intend to take the horses ashore, Captain-General?"

During the last few days Cabrillo had watched every movement made by Father Lezcano as he helped tend to Viento. The priest had shown nothing but a gentle touch and growing affection for the horse. Still, this question struck a slightly uneasy chord in Cabrillo.

"I will await the report of the landing parties before deciding," he said, "but at the moment I will check on how the horses are faring below. Please excuse me."

Within the hour a soldier bearing a white flag appeared on shore and cried out that the area was secure. Although Pilot San Remón was not visible, four other soldiers stood positioned around the landing beach as guards. Cabrillo wasted no time in collecting his journal and several canvas bags from the ship's steward and choosing a group of more than willing men to row him ashore. His heart drummed to an animated beat as he climbed into the *San Salvador's* second boat.

By the time they landed, Pilot San Remón was striding to the shoreline to meet them. He announced as Cabrillo stepped onto the sand, "We found good water just upriver, sir, and a small amount of wood a little farther inland. I saw no fresh traces of Indians but there is a deserted camp nearby where perhaps twenty of them lodged not long ago."

"Can you estimate when?"

"Perhaps three or four days, sir, but it is difficult to know. The fire rings we found over that southern rise are quite cold. Judging by what was left behind, it would take them almost no time to collect what little they own and carry it away. They may move quite often."

"Show me, pilot."

Cabrillo's hungry gaze took in every plant, rock, and bird they passed, and he paused now and then to collect specimens and write notes, setting a pattern for the many landings to come. After he had seen enough to satisfy his concern for the safety of his fleet, he sent back word that they would remain here for at least one more day. The horses were to be prepared for landing.

Relieved from duty by watch, officers and crews of the *San Salvador* and *La Victoria* were allowed ashore, and many were soon swimming and lazing in the shallow waters where the river emptied into the ocean. Only a few of the *San Miguel's* rowers were trusted with such liberty and, for most, their sentences forbade such leniency. So as Captain Correa descended to his boat and his rowers pushed it away, most of his men watched and wished from the confines of the small bergantine, softly cursing their hard fortunes, or their officers, or both.

One of the few sailors shackled to his block glared after the launch with open hostility, then leaned close to the skinny man beside him and snarled under his breath, "If they think we'll stand for anchorages with never a leave to go ashore, our fine officers may feel the bite of a blade or two one of these lonely nights."

Shifting uneasily, his fellow rower muttered, "Here now, Gaspar, such talk can get a man's neck stretched tight."

"Quell your cowardice, Alonso," Gaspar whispered through gapped teeth. "When the time is right, no one with a mind to do any neck stretching will be left alive."

With a dreadful mixture of fear and admiration, Alonso stared at the huge, shaggy man at his side. He noticed how the brawny hands were clamped around the idle handle of his oar, twisting forward and back, as if intent on choking off whatever life the wood might possess. The smaller man wiped a hand across his mouth and said, "Share no such plans with me, Gaspar. Not even in jest. I want no part of them."

Gaspar only sneered at such frailty, but as he shifted away in disgust he spotted the steady, sober eyes of an unchained, pock-faced Indian slave clasped upon him. The stare held a kindred understanding and perhaps the spark of a bond that could be inflamed to meet a mutual goal. *An ally*, thought Gaspar, then he dropped his glance as the boatswain strolled by softly patting the palm of his hand with a wooden billet. Keeping his eyes lowered, Gaspar slowly released his oar and forced his body to relax as he considered the Indian further. *Savage or man, it makes little difference. I will sharpen any tool that will strike at my call.*

Chapter 7

CONTACT

Long ago Cabrillo had learned that sailors treasured visits ashore as much as gluttons treasured feasts, but spending two days at anchor so soon after the outset of their expedition left him and most his men with an agitating desire to push ahead. When he ordered the eager seamen to set the sails, a cooperative wind carried them swiftly south and west to the harbor of San Lucas. Here, too, they were unable to detect a single inhabitant but easily located an abundance of fresh water; so welcoming a watering spot, in fact, that shortly after the bay had been scouted Cabrillo proclaimed, "Master Uribe, give the men time to wash themselves and their clothing. As long as we can prevent lice and fleas from devouring us, we shall."

It took little time before the area resounded with energetic shouts and laughter from the crews splashing near the river's mouth. Most of them wore their clothing only until they considered them well enough rinsed, then shed their false skins like relieved reptiles. The more conscientious among the men used sand to scour their garments thoroughly before tossing them on bushes to dry. While his men washed, Cabrillo, Paulo, Manuel, Mateo, and two guards headed upriver to stretch their legs and explore its banks.

They'd hiked long enough to work up a sweat when a deep pool under a canopy of shade beckoned so strongly, and Mateo flashed his uncle a glance so pleading, that the captain-general gave in with a bob of his head. He and the boy began striding quickly forward, then trotting, then racing full out to reach the water, stripping their clothes and flinging them aside as they went. Manuel grinned after them but Paulo muttered disapprovingly as he collected the strewn belts, shirts, shoes, stockings, and breeches. The guards exchanged furtive glances of amusement at the entire scene.

Mateo let out a great shriek of elation as he ran into the water, his speed launching him forward and thrusting his chest and head under with a splash. Cabrillo's entry was even louder, and his smile even broader when he surfaced and tossed his hair back out of his eyes. He cried to the cloudless sky, "May heaven feel this good, and may we all get there someday to feel it!" Noticing that Manuel and Paulo were already preparing to wash the clothing they'd brought along, most of it his own, he said, "No, no. Let that wait until you two have rinsed yourselves."

Manuel needed no more encouragement before kicking off his shoes, unbuckling his belt, and tugging at his shirt, but he was momentarily stilled by Paulo saying, "Captain-General, it would not be appropriate for us to—"

"Damn your propriety, Paulo. I *order* you to put it aside on this one occasion and get into this water."

With an offended air, Paulo sat on a rock and delicately began to remove his garments. He'd gotten as far as lifting his shirt when Manuel leaped from a large rock into the pool and shot a spouting shower high into the air that splattered Paulo from nose to knee. This set off howls of laughter that Paulo did his best to ignore. Moments later, although he never would have admitted it, he savored the blissfulness of cool water dancing against his bare skin and the smooth current massaging his muscles. None of them hurried to leave their river retreat.

That evening Cabrillo could see that the swimming had done a world of good for everyone who'd taken part, everyone but Paulo. Though he may have enjoyed it at the time, his indignation at being ordered into the water had obviously ripened since returning to the ship, manifesting itself in the stiff manner in which he served dinner to the three captains, pilot San Remón, and Father Gamboa. As Paulo and Manuel cleared the dishes away, Cabrillo said, "That was a meal even the king would have relished, Paulo."

Paulo bowed but remained silent.

Deciding not to humor this rebellious mood, Cabrillo ignored it. "We are ready for our chocolate now."

Again the rigid bow was made, but soon cups of the requested liquid were set before the captain-general and his guests.

After his first sip, Captain Ferrelo said, "I have heard, sir, that you drink chocolate every day."

"I have done so whenever possible since first tasting it," said Cabrillo. "The beans used in our drinks were grown on my own encomienda. With the Mayans cultivating it for centuries, I am happy that Spaniards can also reap its rewards. Mayan holy men once used it in their religious ceremonies and some probably still do. The Aztecs believe it comes from one of their gods, and that it will bestow good health. Perhaps there is some truth to the claim. I suspect that drinking chocolate has helped me keep so many of my teeth."

"Do they not also believe, sir," said Correa with a speculative expression, "that chocolate enhances a man's prowess and potency? Perhaps that is also true."

Cabrillo raised his cup in toast to such a possibility.

As Captain Ferrelo sipped his spicy, bitter drink, he noticed that Father Gamboa was merely making a show of drinking his. He said to the priest, "A thought just came to me, Father, about a rumor I heard recently. I was told that a nun has concocted a formula for chocolate that has removed the bitterness."

Father Gamboa shifted uneasily, but every other diner found this news to be of great interest and they cast their expectant eyes upon him. "Captain Ferrelo," said the priest, "if I knew of such a formula, I hope you would not ask me to divulge such a secret."

In various glances the officers all acclaimed that they would indeed ask such a thing.

"It is not even *our* secret," Father Gamboa tried again. "It belongs to the Dominican order rather than the friars of St. Augustine."

"Well then," proclaimed Correa, "If the Dominicans have already shared it with the Augustinians, just how secret can it be? Besides, our faith surely does not hold chocolate to be sanctified. To put such heavenly value on a victual would be a sacrilege, would it not?"

Father Gamboa decided that his best chance at maintaining discretion lay in attempting a compromise. "Dear gentlemen, I offer to do this much and hope you will be satisfied. I will look into the captain-general's supplies, and if all of the needed ingredients are among them, I will make you the chocolate myself."

"Fine! Fine!"

"Very well, tomorrow evening then?"

"Tomorrow? Why wait, Father?" demanded Correa, standing and stepping behind the priest to pull his chair out for him.

Resignedly, Father Gamboa signaled Paulo to accompany him to the captain-general's stores chest. Within moments Paulo was sent back to the diners while Father Gamboa headed with a pot and an armful of ingredients to the ship's fogon, where he could work his magic in solitude over the glowing embers of the firebox.

The officers continued to chat easily among themselves but now and then the attention of each broke off to listen to the activities of Father Gamboa. Although it seemed longer, in only a few minutes the priest called to Paulo, and both of them reappeared with vessels full of the awaited brew.

As each man savored the thick, sweet richness his eyes brightened with surprise and delight. A round of "Bravo, Father! Well done!" circled the cabin, and Father Gamboa bowed humbly.

"Not a trace of chili peppers, and the bitterness *is* gone!" said Ferrelo.

"Why, this is creamy," said Cabrillo. "Our good cow must have contributed to our cups."

"I taste sugar and vanilla," said Correa, licking his upper lip.

"And cinnamon," said San Remón.

"And even nutmeg," said Cabrillo, taking another drink. "Though I ration such spices dearly this *is* divine, worth every grain of seasoning used."

Cabrillo said to his servant, "Come, Paulo, you must taste this, so you can do your best to recreate it without our extracting the secret from Father Gamboa."

Paulo took Cabrillo's cup and brought it to his lips. With an expression of intense concentration he let the liquid circle his tongue before swallowing. His grumpy, aloof expression gave way to a smile. "I may need another swallow or two, sir, so I will remember."

All of them laughed. "Let it not be said that I withheld my chocolate from a man of science. Let the rest be consigned to your memory."

Disappointment flickered across Manuel and Mateo's faces, who had been hoping for a small sip from the captain-general's cup. But they both brightened when Cabrillo said, "Paulo, why not set to it at once while the original brew is still fresh? Make a thorough study of it, and let Mateo and Manuel help with the tasting of your reproductions." Seldom had so welcome an assignment been issued, and the three were soon out the cabin door.

After the rest of the cups had been emptied to the appreciative smacking of lips, the dinner guests prepared to take their leave. Father Gamboa, however, hung back and asked, "Captain-General, may I have a moment?"

Cabrillo agreed and the two men sat down again, the oil lamps bestowing a soft glow to their sun and wind-burned features. Father Gamboa asked, "May I speak freely, sir?"

"Always, Father."

"It appears to me, sir, that something has caused you to form a poor opinion of Father Lezcano. He was not invited to dine with us this evening, and I have seen disapproval, no, perhaps a better word is distrust, when you speak to or even look upon him. Yet you allow him to groom your most prized horse that very few others are permitted to approach. I am confused and unsettled by it all, as are others. This trouble between you, sir, is it something I can help to repair?"

Cabrillo folded his hands together and laid them on the table. "Did Father Lezcano give you no explanation of what has occurred?"

"None, sir. He has refused to discuss it, and he generally confides in me. I have even suggested that his silence could be sinful if any harm comes from it, and still he says nothing."

Cabrillo had lifted an olive from its bowl but it still rested in his fingers. He said softly, "Truly? The man has the ability to repeatedly surprise me."

"Is it possible, sir, that you are mistaken about him? He shows the deepest dedication to his faith and to his role on this voyage… and to you."

Even more thoughtfully, Cabrillo admitted, "I let him share in Viento's care on the chance that he indeed means well. But you are quite right about my lingering mistrust of him."

"I am willing to stake your benevolence toward me, Captain-General, a thing I value greatly, and to pledge my word on the belief that Father Lezcano is honorable."

Without haste Cabrillo said, "The fact that he has held his tongue about our past encounters tells me much. Very well, Father, if you see such unquestionable good in him, I will surrender my prejudices as far as I am able."

Relieved and pleased, Father said, "God blesses a generous man, sir."

"Do not offer me grace that is undeserved, Father. I merely try to interpret and lead fairly, and in this I may have judged wrongly. If that is all, Father, will you please find Father Lezcano and send him to me?"

Father Gamboa bowed and departed, returned shortly with his brother priest a step behind, ushered him into Cabrillo's cabin, and immediately left them alone.

What exactly was exchanged between the young priest and the captain-general that evening was never revealed to Father Gamboa or anyone else, but from that time forward there was an improvement in the consideration Cabrillo showed toward Lezcano. Perceptive to his master's unspoken permission, Manuel began to more openly display his own growing esteem for the priest. The rest of the crew noticed the change as well, and as with the resolution of any tensions between superiors, it put the men more at ease.

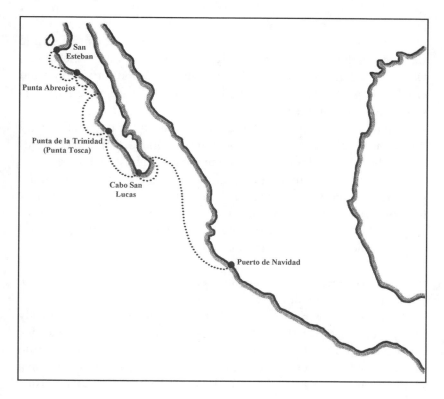

When the fleet left San Lucas on July 8, sailed to Trinidad Point, and was held there for three days by a tight-fisted wind, the two were seen together often. If an occasion arose for Father Gamboa to be invited to the commander's cabin, Father Lezcano's presence was also requested. Once, Cabrillo publicly praised Father Lezcano for his devoted care of Viento. Much to Father Gamboa's gratification, and a little to his surprise, there even seemed to be threads of camaraderie being woven between them.

As they sailed ever farther up the coast, Captain Correa frequently came aboard the *San Salvador* at the captain-general's bidding. Correa had seen this treeless, mountainless shoreline while a part of the Bolaños expedition, and Cabrillo questioned him minutely as they studied the land and their charts and speculated about when they might sight their first Indians.

Heading into Puerta de Madalena, whales numbering in the dozens spouted, rolled, and breached in undaunted proximity to the ships. As far up the beach as the eye could trace skeletons of the great beasts, washed ashore over the ages, now littered the sand. Gulls circled and scolded overhead as the ships drifted gently to this new anchorage. Other birds, feathered beasts of every color, size, and form, flitted and cried amongst the bushes or dove to scoop a prize from the innumerable schools of sardines.

Scanning the scene from the railing, assessing the potential bounty this fauna would provide to any human inhabitants, Cabrillo concluded, "If there are no Indians here, there most certainly should be."

He chose to be among the initial scouting party, and once on the sand he and his men paused beside a monstrous cetacean spine that had long since been washed clean and pitted by the elements. "As I suspected," he said to Vargas as he looked the skeleton over, "several of the smaller ribs have been removed. Likely used to construct shelters."

"They've been taken from the next one, too, sir," Vargas said, pointing to a carcass thirty feet up the beach.

"Keep a sharp eye," Cabrillo said to his soldiers, who were already tautly alert. He gave the area a sweeping glance but other than the birds nothing stirred. With Manuel standing guardedly by, Cabrillo allowed his fascination to be recaptured by the whalebones. He ran a hand over the porous surface of the long skull, and then stepped inside the frame, straddling a gap between two vertebrae and spreading his arms wide between a pair of ribs still attached to the spine. He could just touch their inside edges. Letting his arms fall, he said in wonderment, "This mighty fish could have fed a village for months."

"A big village, sir," said Father Lezcano.

Drawing his men and himself away from the baleen cemetery at last, Cabrillo easily found a path that had been used not long ago by the natives. They searched, expectant and even hopeful, but many minutes and then two hours passed without an Indian sighting. If any were near, they remained artfully hidden. The men of the fleet lingered long enough for Cabrillo to make note of what they'd seen before heading back to the boats.

Setting sails against headwinds, the fleet was forced to channel its way through pod after pod of whales swimming in previously unimagined numbers to reach Puerto de Santiago. After nudging a lane between the massive bodies to reach an anchorage near nightfall, the whales began to bump the ships with such regularity that concern began to build as to whether they might cause significant damage. Faced with the risk of leaving an unfamiliar port during an hour of darkness or dealing with the whales where they lay, Cabrillo called for his pilot and shipmaster and said, "Well, gentlemen, before we become any more like grist under these unrelenting millstones, I must give the unique order to make as much clamor as necessary to keep these cursed whales from the sides of our vessels. Please pass the word along, Master Uribe."

To help, Father Gamboa immediately brought out his bagpipes, but his well-intended music seemed to have the unanticipated effect of drawing the whales closer rather than repel them, and he almost immediately ceased his piping. At a signal from Master Uribe drums of every shape, size, and material—including the temporarily adopted bombardeta, swivel guns, and kegs—were beaten upon amid a chorus of earsplitting yells from the drummers, and the resulting din was loud enough to frighten any whale, bird, or unsuspecting human for miles around. These noise-making activities began with merry, rowdy enthusiasm as a welcome reprieve from the routine of shipboard life, but within an hour the men's arms grew weary and their heads developed a pounding ache that pulsed painfully to the cadence of their drumming.

Cabrillo, too, soon yearned for silence, but every time he ordered the drummers to still their instruments the whales began to draw near and shove the ships anew, so men were ordered to resume beating with their billets, knife hilts, kindling sticks, or whatever else was at hand. It was an exhausting, restless night that made even the most even-tempered of the men growl with longing for their habitual practices. With barely enough light to make their way clear of the bay and with all ears ringing after so prolonged a period of clamor, Cabrillo made sail and aimed his fleet's sterns at Puerto de Santiago.

Up to now Correa's sharp memory had proven to be of great service, recalling the best approaches, anchorages, and springs or rivers of fresh water. But from this point until they reached uncharted waters, the captain-general and his navigators relied heavily on the maps that had been drafted by Ulloa and compiled by Castillo.

Making a brief landing fifty miles up the coast at Bahia Santa Ana, they rejoiced at the sight of an abundance of trees again. Here the whales were blessedly much fewer in number, but there was no shortage of other marine life. Thousands of sea lions basking on the rocky shore and swimming at its edge raised such a riotous barking chorus that human discourse was difficult. Again, Cabrillo chose not to loiter. They reached Puerto Fondo with the intention of leaving the following day, but shortly after departing at dawn they were met head-on by forceful winds that refused to relent. After struggling against them for three additional days, the fleet was driven back to their previous anchorage. At the first easing of the blow, they sailed on.

With similar determination to reach uncharted waters, Cabrillo allowed the fleet to stay no longer than the winds demanded at San Pedro Vincula, San Esteban, Isla de Cedros, Puerto de Santa Clara, Puerto de Mal Abrigo, Isla de San Bernardo, or Punta del Engaño, all visited earlier by Ulloa and his crew. Though a careful watch was kept at each of these landings, Indians were seen only at Puerto de Santa Clara, and those four fled at once to a distant place where they could not be spotted again.

The hunger Cabrillo felt to reach their first unknown, unseen, untrodden land was building in all of the men. When the sails were lifted and the ships eased away from Punta del Engaño, the final landing named by those of another fleet, many eager voices arose with the sails. "Onward, onward!" they cried. "To the heart of California!"

Pilot San Remón stood tall beside his captain-general and breathed in a huge breath, his teeth gleaming at the open sea. It was clear to Cabrillo that it took a significant effort from his young pilot to refrain from committing a breach of protocol by joining the men in their wild cheering. San Remón, however, did allow himself to burst forth with, "We stand at the last point on our map, sir! The last point! Ahead, everything is new."

Cabrillo was not untouched by the contagious exhilaration exhibited on his decks, but his relative age and war experience helped soften the tugging at his nerves. He smiled broadly and said, "Yes, pilot, new to us as well as our country."

Mercifully, they didn't have to endure an extended wait before the opportunity to land arose. Unlike Ulloa, they rounded Punta del Engaño without difficulty, and just twenty-seven miles beyond it the hearts of everyone aboard pounded anxiously as they glided ever-closer and entered an uncharted harbor. Once clear of the mouth, the port seemed to form an irregular horseshoe dominated in the center by a large brown hill. Scrubby trees and bushes thickly covered the rising, curving edges of the land. The eastern arm of the bay appeared to offer the best prospect for a river, and Cabrillo directed the ships in that direction. Within minutes, their anchors rested securely upon the seafloor.

Despite the eagerness of his men and himself, Cabrillo remained cautious. In the deepening dusk he could see no movement of any kind, but the low growing greenery could hide many warriors. He forbade anyone from going ashore other than a few well-armed soldiers assigned to search for needed firewood and water. No more would be permitted to land until daylight provided a better sense of the dangers that might await them.

The midnight watch was exceptionally alert, and this attentiveness brought Pilot San Remón to Cabrillo's cabin and bedside just before the hour of one to awaken his commander.

"Captain-General," he said, "the lookouts have spotted at least one campfire. I would not have disturbed your rest, sir, but for the order to inform you at the first sign of natives."

Clearing his throat and trying to sharpen his sight in the dimly lit cabin, Cabrillo asked, "Did you see the fire, pilot?"

"No, sir, only two lookouts. After they called out, no one saw it again."

"How far from shore?"

"The range of an arquebus shot, Captain-General."

"Very good, pilot. Double the lookouts and keep me informed of any other sighting."

"I will, sir."

He left Cabrillo to ponder the possibility of encountering natives at this newly discovered location, and growing speculation gradually swept all grogginess from his mind and body. Less than an hour later he gave up all attempts to return to sleep, dressed, and went on deck to stand along with the men of the second and third night watch and await the sun's arrival. When the light finally appeared, it shown down on a land that revealed no evidence of ever having supported human life, by neither smoke stream, structure, nor footprint.

Still taking every precaution, Cabrillo ordered three boats to be filled with soldiers and two of the war dogs, and these launches were sent ashore to establish a protective loop around the beach. When a sailor returned to the captain-general with word that all was ready, Cabrillo dismissed the messenger from his cabin and looked thoughtfully over at his slave. After a moment, he said, "Well, Manuel, here we are on the verge of making history. Are you ready?"

Manuel's pride shone on his big-boned face. "Ready as a man can be, sir."

"You may want to say a prayer that we hold onto our lives while we make our mark here."

"I will do that, sir."

Cabrillo, followed by Manuel and together with his officers, priests, and scribe, headed toward shore. Leaping from his boat as it scraped the beach, he took his first steps into the unknown territory.

Because the day was one of such importance, all who landed wore their best ceremonial dress and all were impressively armed. The officers had donned their finest shirts, sleeveless doublets, and loose-fitting breeches that ended above the knee. Plumed velvet hats adorned the heads of Captains Correa and Ferrelo and Pilot San Remón, but Cabrillo had chosen to wear the conquistador helmet that had twice saved his life in battle. Paulo had polished his master's metal chest plate to a high shine, and it flashed brilliantly in the early sunlight.

All followed Cabrillo as he hiked up a slight rise to a spot large enough for twenty men to gather. When everyone stood waiting expectantly, the captain-general said with impressive volume and precision, "I, Juan Rodriguez Cabrillo, on this twenty-second day of August in the year of Our Lord fifteen hundred forty-two, do claim this land located at the latitude of 31 1/2° upon the western coast of California in the name of Charles our king and emperor, and on behalf of Don Antonio de Mendoza as governor of New Spain. This place will henceforth be called Puerto de la Posesión, and I stand ready to defend the claim now made with my sword and my life."

The captain-general moved to a nearby shrub, cut two limbs, and took a leather strap from the pouch at his belt to form a three-foot high cross. He then collected several skull-sized stones and braced the cross upright in the sand. Taking a cup that Paulo had brought ashore for this purpose, Cabrillo strode to the water's edge to fill it and returned to his small monument. As he dripped the water in a circle around stones that supported the cross, he said, "I place a cross upon this new land as a sign that it is now a possession of our homeland, and that we will hold it in the name of Our Father, and His Son, and the Holy Spirit." At a gesture from Cabrillo, Father Gamboa stepped forward and offered a prayer of thanksgiving, and this concluded the ceremony.

As his men drifted down the hill, Cabrillo remained behind. He wanted a few moments of solitude to take in the full substance of this landing and so he had even Manuel leave him, under orders to help unload the horses. Staring down at the small cross, Cabrillo listened to the calls and songs of the birds that seemed to be harshly discussing the arrival of the strangers. He lifted his head and slowly scanned the country all around him. The breeze was gentle, the sun glaring, the greens and blues brilliant, the dark recesses beneath the trees ominous. In the uncommon solitude of his small hilltop, Cabrillo began to wonder if the lookouts had truly spotted a fire the night before. Were there really people here? If so, what must they be thinking, planning as they watch from their hiding places? What weapons did they possess, and were they prone to using them out of fear? Mulling these questions, he grudgingly surrendered his privacy and let his feet take him down to join his crews.

Though the evidence of a recent native presence was slim, he kept the sentries watchful. He also sent the captain, pilot, and gunner of *La Victoria* back to their ship to safeguard the command of at least one vessel, as well as to see that the swivel and great guns were kept aimed at their landing place.

The *San Miguel* was in bad need of caulking, for which she must be brought ashore, and several sails ought to be spread and mended. He had his scouts make a wider search of the area while the horses were landed, and since nothing threatening presented itself he gave the command to have the *San Miguel* unloaded and hauled onto the beach. A few hours later she was resting on her side in the sand and workmen were busy scraping her exposed belly.

Only then did the captain-general set out to explore with Shipmaster Uribe, Manuel, Mateo, half of his soldiers, and one war dog. Manuel carried Cabrillo's crossbow and writing instruments and walked closely enough to keep them within his master's reach. Cabrillo's sword of many years swung at his side. His mood matched that of the men, tense and vigilant as they heightened their senses to pick up any hint of an ambush.

Following the bank of a river, Cabrillo led them deeper and deeper inland until they veered away from the water and began climbing the rise of a hill. At its top they halted to search for any human sign, and discovered that the river had broadened into a three-branched lake. Cabrillo's eyes were tracing the southern edge of the lake as the rest of his men came up through the brush behind him. Suddenly he stiffened, then dropped into a low crouch and sharply signaled for his cohorts to do the same. Silently pointing with his arm, his intense gaze also marked a group of six men fishing from the lakeshore not fifty yards away. But their movements had caught the attention of one of the Indians who was already backing away and fearfully gesturing to the others.

Cabrillo whispered, "Sergeant Major Vargas, Laca, Sanchez, and Manuel come with me. Master Uribe, remain here with the others. Lázaro, do *not* release that dog."

Slowly, his arms held open, Cabrillo stood up.

The fishermen froze.

Cabrillo and his chosen men advanced carefully with arms held open to show they were empty. Their own weapons hung from belts and shoulder straps but they could still see none carried by the natives. The captain-general began to use his hands to communicate that he had gifts for them, but he could see that they were preparing to flee. The only thing that seemed to have held them this long, in mesmerized terror and awe, was the sight of the large black man walking a step behind and to the left of Cabrillo. When the soldiers narrowed the distance between them to little more than twenty paces, even the spectacle of Manuel was not enough to keep them from bolting toward cover, and Cabrillo shouted, "Catch one of them!"

They raced after the slowest man, gaining on him steadily until Manuel was near enough to leap forward, catch the Indian by the shoulders and roll him to the ground. The other fishermen let out a sympathetic cry for their friend but kept running. As they disappeared into the trees, Cabrillo called out, "All right, Master Uribe, come ahead."

"Gently," said Cabrillo, as the Indian was lifted to a sitting position and surrounded by him and his four men, who were quickly joined by Master Uribe and the others. Seeing the horror on the captive's face melt into an expression of fateful acceptance, Cabrillo said in a calm voice, "Disengage your weapons and sit down, men. Keep the dog on watch outside the circle, Lázaro. We are going to trade."

When the men had settled around him, Cabrillo crossed his legs and eyed the Indian in a frank but cordial manner. The fisherman was impressive in stature if not in costume. Although he was perhaps a decade older than Cabrillo he was tall and strongly built, but he wore not a thread of clothing. His long hair hung loose and tangled around a well-shaped skull and raw-boned face. Cabrillo took a moment to mentally scan the different tribes he had encountered during his career, many of whom had later become allies. The thought touched him that in dress and carriage their captive was wholly unlike the proud Aztecs who had followed Montezuma. This Indian, however, was a fisherman and must hold a humbler status among his people than any fighting man. It was probable that his tribe, just like the Aztecs and Maya, had a separate warrior class to protect and distinguish them. Then again, perhaps, just perhaps, these natives felt no need for warriors or the embellishments of war.

Glancing at his slave, he said, "Manuel, give me your knife."

Manuel withdrew the blade from his belt and handed it to Cabrillo, who offered it with reassuring words and nods to the Indian. Almost unwilling to believe that the knife was being offered as a gift rather than used as the instrument of his death, the fisherman very gingerly reached out and accepted the blade. His eyes diffidently sought Manuel's and he made a sign that Cabrillo presumed to be an expression of gratitude. After a moment's consideration, Cabrillo opened the casing that held his crossbow darts, extracted one, and handed it to their captive. The Indian accepted this new gift with enough courage to examine it briefly, momentarily meet Cabrillo's gaze, and then repeat his previous hand gesture.

Wishing their Indian interpreter were with them now, Cabrillo made several attempts to explain who they were. He then tried to discover a few details about the natives, such as their number and the location of their village. The fisherman replied distinctly and gestured fluidly, yet almost nothing was understood between them.

Eventually Cabrillo surrendered with a soft sigh and said, "Men, let him go. The others could be miles away or they could be heading back here with an army. If we are granted a great deal of luck, this man will take a good report of us back to his people. But since luck is a fickle thing we had better return to the beach and warn our men of a possible attack."

Careful to make no threatening moves, Cabrillo and his men got to their feet and backed away from the captive. When the fisherman did not move, Cabrillo reached down and helped him up, then motioned for him to follow after his friends. The Indian's first departing steps were tentative, then quickened but did not break into a run as he glanced repeatedly backward. When Cabrillo and his men turned away and began retracing their steps, the man increased his pace and was soon out of sight.

At the beach where the *San Miguel* still lay under repair, guards kept a tense alertness throughout the night. Even the birds seemed unusually hushed. As morning dawned Cabrillo stood on his stern deck and watched many trails of smoke rising from scattered locations inland, giving him the first indication that the Indian population could be sizable. He went ashore and found Correa before the sun had reached the treetops. The incisive smell of boiling pitch already assaulted the air, and men were scurrying around the bergantine like ants rebuilding a collapsed hill. As he surveyed the work Cabrillo asked, "When can she be seaworthy, Captain Correa?"

"By noon, sir, if need be. But a few more hours to better dry the pitch would be welcome."

"Welcome indeed. I will do what I can to prevent any interruption."

Not long afterward Cabrillo donned his heavily padded leather vest and ordered the men that would accompany him on a second trek inland to wear the same. Over this vest, he and his men of rank pulled on jackets with diagonal slits on each side of the breast, where insets of lighter fabric could be seen as their torsos moved. These layers, Cabrillo decided, should be enough to protect them from arrows lacking the length, thickness, and iron tips of their own. Their armor could be left aboard to prevent them from boiling like crabs in this intense heat.

He had noted earlier that the nearest smoke seemed to be coming from just upriver, and after assuring himself that this was still the case he ordered his companions of the day before, plus an interpreter, to board the rowboats. They loaded quickly, pushed off, and headed directly toward the mouth of the river.

The river's width and current accommodated the two launches without much difficulty and they soon found themselves approaching a small but wandering lake. Slowly, watchfully they rowed almost stem to stern as they entered it and held to its right-hand rim. They advanced around a sharp bend and suddenly spied a large group of Indians fishing from the shore. At Cabrillo's command the sailors stilled their oars. Vargas whispered, "I count thirty of them, sir, some with bows and arrows."

The armed fishermen had clearly seen the boats. They stood their ground, weapons in hands but not raised. Keenly watching the movements of the natives, Cabrillo signaled for his men to row forward cautiously. Just as wary as the captain-general and his men, the Indians gave no indication of potential flight even as the strangers neared. When the boats drew within easy firing range the natives slowly lowered their bows to the ground.

To Cabrillo's hopeful eyes, they now seemed to be awaiting their landing with guarded curiosity. "Keep your weapons down but within grasp," he ordered.

As the distance between the two groups dissipated, the natives left their bows and arrows idle in the sand and walked boldly toward the boats. To the relief of Cabrillo and everyone else, the more advanced European weapons also proved to be unnecessary as the two groups came together. The Indians greeted the strangers with a measure of warmth that amazed and delighted Cabrillo, and he looked from face to face in an unsuccessful search for the older fisherman they had dealt with generously the day before. Though he was nowhere in sight, Cabrillo could only assume that his good word had caused such a reception.

The evident leaders quickly seated themselves close enough together to begin energetically scrutinizing each other and attempting to improve their means of understanding. The two Indians on either side of the captain-general fingered his fabric and stitching with exclamations of approval and awe, indicating that the clothes of the Spaniards held at least as much fascination for the fisherman as their iron weapons did. Touching his jacket and then his shirt, Cabrillo said, "clothing". The natives echoed the word quite clearly, which greatly kindled hopes of gaining intelligence of their lands and ways. It took little time to discover that the locals in fact possessed an uncanny ability to precisely repeat any Castilian word, but real conversation, even with verbal and gestured efforts by the interpreter, proved only a little more successful than the day before.

Today, however, Cabrillo had instructed the scouting party to bring a few trade goods with them, and these were quickly toted ashore and distributed among the fishermen. This method of communication was easily comprehended, and in exchange the native men soon offered Cabrillo small fishing nets and carrying bags that had been cleverly and beautifully woven from a finely twisted thread.

While the presents were being passed around and examined, Cabrillo spotted several women and children hanging back within the nearby greenery but watching and listening closely. Though they were undoubtedly as inquisitive about the strangers as their men, they conducted themselves by look and gesture with notable restraint and modesty. Most of the women, possibly those who had married, were clothed from breast to thigh in animal skins, and many carried both an infant and a toddler in their arms. Intent on recording any new knowledge, Cabrillo took out his writing materials, quickly drew a few small sketches of the natives, and noted examples on their speech and behavior.

Drawn by an overpowering curiosity about what the strange man was doing, a brave lad of about four approached Cabrillo and plopped down in the sand before him for a closer look, unknowingly providing an excellent model for the captain-general's quill. With this development, a few of the women also drew near. One sharp, sweeping glare from Vargas reminded the men to hold their tongues and positions, and things proceeded peacefully.

When at last the captain-general and his men rose to leave, he invited a few of the fishermen to accompany them back to the ships. It was apparent that his offer had been comprehended when the natives began to debate over who was to come, but eventually two young women and a child were brought forward, each wearing nothing but a small piece of deer skin. Understanding only too well the challenges the women might create amongst his crew, Cabrillo nevertheless accepting these three with grace, had them lifted into his boat, and ordered his men to push off.

With the scantily dressed women sitting in such proximity the rowers found it difficult to keep their eyes and minds on their oars. Not missing the stolen glances and the unusual unevenness in the cadence of their boat's progress, Cabrillo barked, "Look sharp, there!" To Manuel he muttered close to his ear, "When we reach the ship, get them clothed immediately. I will not risk an uprising over two naked females."

In no time they reached the *San Salvador* and, coming aboard wide-eyed with apprehension and wonder, the women were seated on the main deck where Father Lezcano was called upon to reassure them. Cabrillo saw at once that though the young priest spoke with soothing sincerity he was at least as distracted by the feminine bodies as his rowers had been, and one of the Indian women seemed instantly attracted to his handsome young priest. Thankfully, Manuel appeared with long shirts that soon covered most of the skin. An Aztec sailor fluent in several Mexican languages was brought to them in the hope of communicating but the speech of these new people was incomprehensible to him. Offering hand signs he hoped would convey friendship, Cabrillo ordered the newcomers be given small gifts and returned to their lakeshore.

After they had left the ship Cabrillo found Father Lezcano gazing off in the direction of the departing boat. "Why, Father, are not priests supposed to be above such worldly enticements?"

Lezcano's guilty discomfort deepened the color of his sun-bronzed face. "I try very hard, sir, but women are temptations I have not fully overcome as yet. I have been a priest only a short time and on occasion I must sharply remind myself of my sacred vows." Under Cabrillo's unrelenting gaze a hint of Father Lezcano's devilish grin came to his assistance. "Perhaps as my youth fades it will become easier."

Cabrillo could not completely veil a smile. "It would be wise, Father, not to depend too much on the passage of years to reduce such desires."

Shortly before noon of the following day Correa interrupted a discussion between Cabrillo and Father Gamboa to report, "Captain-General, I sent a party of men out to gather water and a small group of Indians led them to a spring. After the barrels had been filled, the same Indians guided them to a salt pool, where they collected this." He opened a leather pouch and pulled out a handful of salt crystals.

Testing the salt and finding it to be of high quality, Cabrillo said, "Well, you bring fine news, Captain Correa. We will certainly welcome a few barrels of this." He handed the salt to the priest to try.

Correa went on, "These Indians seem to be from a different tribe than the fisherman who live nearby. If my men understood them right, they come from a large nation farther inland."

"Are they in your camp now?" asked Cabrillo as he went to his window.

"No, sir, they could not be persuaded to visit us. But before they departed, one of my men gave them his dagger as a sign of thanks."

"He did very well, Captain."

Pleased, Correa said, "Ah, sir, even members of my band of rabble have a worthy moment now and again."

"Worthy indeed. They have helped expand the number of natives who may pass along good words about us."

"Your treatment of the locals yesterday likely reached these new Indians before they fell in with our kind, sir, starting things on a good footing."

"That may be." Cabrillo gazed out at the *San Miguel*. "Since we have been left unmolested, I trust the repair work is progressing well."

"Quite well, sir," was the reply, but Captain Correa's brow furrowed as he spoke.

"Is there a problem?"

He hesitated before adding, "It's Gaspar, Captain-General."

"That rogue. What has he done now?"

"That *is* the problem, sir. His behavior has been beyond reproach, as has the conduct of the men he influences. That's what concerns me. All looks *too* calm, and I sense a growing tension among the crewmen not included in his circle of schemers. It feels like a powder keg about to blow, sir, but without proof of trouble I have no good idea how to ease the mood."

The cabin grew quiet as the men considered the problem. "Captain-General," said Father Gamboa softly, "please excuse my intruding, but do you think my presence aboard the *San Miguel* might give some comfort to those men?"

Shifting the question to that ship's commander, Cabrillo asked, "Captain Correa?"

Correa rubbed his stubbly chin with unusual thoughtfulness. "That is a generous offer, Father, but my men are a rough lot."

This brought a tolerant smile to the priest's face. "Your crewmembers are children of God, sir, and they will not be the first rough lot I have served. If the captain-general does not object, I will gladly do what I can to spread Our Holy Father's guidance on your ship."

"I can offer no valid objection, Father," said Cabrillo, "though I will surely miss your company. You are welcome to go with Captain Correa, if you wish."

Correa shook his head and clasped the priest's hand, thinking, *I hope you know what you're doing.* Aloud, he muttered, "Thank you, Father, and may God protect you."

Not an hour after Correa's morning visit to the *San Salvador* he returned with five native men, warriors of the newly arrived tribe, judging from their distinctive appearance and the bows and flint-tipped arrows they carried, who were brought to the ship at the request of their own leader. Cabrillo welcomed them and had a rug spread upon the deck in order to sit more officially with his guests where all could be seen and heard.

To the fascination and concealed amusement of the sailors, each native had painted his body in an attempt to imitate the clothing of the

Spaniards. Though their waists were lightly belted and their shoulders draped with deerskins, their torsos and arms had been carefully dyed to produce a darker background. Their blackened chests and thighs bore white diagonal slash marks meant to imitate the jackets and breeches that the local natives had seen the sailors wearing. Much more intriguing to Cabrillo than their adornment, however, was how cleverly these men were able to exchange ideas through no more than body language and hand signals.

After preliminary greetings had been extended, their chief addressed Cabrillo and explained through signs that his home lay to the northeast and was rich with parrots and maize. Cabrillo nodded encouragingly to the chief so he continued, using smooth gestures and his rhythmic aboriginal language to deliver a message that astonished his audience. "Chief of the great canoes, you are not the first of your kind to enter these lands."

Cabrillo worked to keep his features calm as he again prompted the chief to tell more.

The Indian said and signed unhurriedly, "Men with beards, crossbows, swords, and dogs have been seen inland at a distance of a five-day march from the sea."

Speculative mutterings broke out and circled them, causing Cabrillo's boatswain to issue a tightly whispered threat to hush the crew.

Over the next half-hour the captain-general tried repeatedly to determine just when and where the bearded men had been seen, but the exceedingly dissimilar languages made it impossible to discover anything specific. Turning aside to Correa and San Remón, Cabrillo tried to hide his frustration as he said, "Who knows how long ago the Spaniards were seen. He could be referring to Alarcón. The mouth of the Colorado River lies only a hundred and fifty miles or so from here. I would wager the Indian runners could easily make such a distance in five days."

"Could he be talking about Captain Ulloa's expedition, sir?"

"Yes, that is possible. Or Coronado's or Diaz's, or some new expedition of which we have no knowledge at all."

Addressing the chief once more, Cabrillo's hands asked if he would deliver a small gift to the Spaniards in the northeast. He then repeated his request to make certain it was understood. After a moment's pause the Indian leader agreed, intimating that it could actually be delivered to a group of Spaniards still present in his land. Cabrillo told himself that this could well be a false assertion, but the possibility of meeting with a group of his own countrymen farther up the coast was gripping indeed.

After presenting his visitors with presents of beads, metal bells, and clothing, Cabrillo turned over his hosting duties to Pilot San Remón and Father Lezcano while he went to his cabin to hurriedly compose a short letter.

Whoever the other Spaniards were, he must tell them where his fleet was headed and offer his aid if it was needed. He could only hope his message would reach them given so untested a means of delivery.

Chapter 8

A PRIEST WORTH BEATING

With the sails mended and the *San Miguel* repaired, and with at least a stone of groundwork laid for agreeable future encounters with regional Indians, the fleet departed from Puerto de la Posesión immediately after the celebration of Sunday Mass.

Twenty-seven hours later they landed on a sizeable island, which Cabrillo christened San Agustin as he stood amid a graveyard of driftwood rather than whalebones. The once living trees must have been of unimaginable size, with these mere remnants of their full trunks still measured more than sixty feet in length. Signs of only occasional human habitation encouraged Cabrillo to take a group deeper into the island's interior. They set off exploring, and Mateo, spotting a massive hulk of driftwood ahead, ran and stood before it with mouth agape as Cabrillo, Manuel, and the others caught up to him. "Will you look at that, sir," said Manuel. "A mighty storm must have tossed it here and wedged it upright as a post." Two of their larger men handed their weapons to a companion and stood on opposite sides of the twisted hulk. Stretching their arms as far as they could reach, they were still unable to span its girth.

"It puzzles me," said Cabrillo, "that natives come here so seldom when they could take full advantage of this magnificent wood. Good Lord above, imagine the forest where these giants had first sprouted."

Mateo piped up, "Do you think we will see the forest, sir, up the coast?"

"I dearly hope we do, Mateo," said Cabrillo. "We may find a tree big enough to sail through." As they walked on he envisioned such a forest of titans shading a landing somewhere not far ahead of them,

100

and he mused deeply on how it would feel to stand beneath the towering heights of those proud trees. It would be, he decided, like standing inside a living cathedral, the most magnificent house of worship ever constructed. But for now, he must be content with this new and welcome supply of firewood for the fleet.

Although they had no intention of lingering on the island, after setting sail their plans were changed by an authoritative wind that forced the fleet to return and shelter in its lee. Three more anxious days were spent waiting out the gale before they successfully left their refuge, and by then August had aged into September. Tacking often against the northeast wind and maneuvering with aggression against a newly opposing current, they made their way up kelp-strewn coastal waters whose shore displayed greater and greater promise of richly fertile land.

Early on September 8 they entered a cape so breathtaking that it struck Cabrillo as having been blessed from above. He asked Father Gamboa to choose a fit name, so the priest gave it the title of Santa Maria on the very day the church celebrated their holy lady's birth. Located at the outlet of a wide, quiet river, their anchorage was indeed lovely, framed by mountains large and small to form a verdant valley that ran far away into the interior beyond their view. An abundance of deep green trees and shrubs spread out before them, cheering the spirits of the men and encouraging them to draw deep breaths of the sweet scents wafting from shore.

Leaning on the gunwale as all three ships' anchors lowered, Cabrillo wished that the lush scene before him could be enjoyed by all of his men. A recently erupted fever had taken possession of three of them, including Manuel, and it was strengthening. The illnesses shadowed the allure of even this place, and Cabrillo acutely felt the absence of Manuel's silent frame that for years had seldom left his side. Offering what relief was possible to the afflicted seamen, all portals and hatches had been opened wide so that the breeze could reach them where they lay below decks.

The scouts were ordered ashore and soon returned with the judgment that the beach was safe for Cabrillo and a full entourage to land. Flanked by the fleet's other leaders, its priests, and soldiers, the captain-general performed his second formal claiming of a new region for Spain's king. This time, with palo verde trees readily at hand, he had his carpenter construct a much more impressive cross to plant on the beach. The exertions of the rite dismayed myriad thin, striped lizards and ring-necked snakes, sending them skittering and slithering to the hidden edges of their site, and causing the men to place their feet with uncommon care whenever they moved. Perhaps because of this caution, no bites were inflicted on the unwary.

Shortly after the ceremony's conclusion the captain-general returned to the ship, drawn back by his growing apprehension over Manuel.

He entered his cabin and found Father Lezcano and the ship's physician, Dr. Fuentes, bending over the pallet set up for Manuel. These two men stepped aside as Cabrillo came near and knelt on one knee beside his slave. The black skin of Manuel's face and chest was beaded with sweat, the whites of his eyes dulled. His eyelids flickered open at his master's approach.

Cabrillo glanced up at the doctor, who avoided meeting his captain-general's eyes. Father Lezcano's gaze held a frightful mixture of sadness, acquiescence, and sympathy. Through a suddenly tightened throat, Cabrillo said, "Manuel, I will not hear of this. You must get well. Do you understand? I will not lose you."

"I am at peace, sir."

Cabrillo's throat closed completely for a moment, then he burst out with, "Well, *I* am not at peace, damn you!" He struggled to calm his voice. "I have lost far too many men over far too many years to these cursed fevers. Not you, Manuel. I will *not* lose you!"

Held as he was in the clutches of the fever, Manuel tried to smile. "Father Lezcano has already given me last rites, sir."

"Damn Father Lezcano!"

The doctor gasped at such outrageous blasphemy. Men had been burned at the stake for less. Father Lezcano's eyes were huge but he held his tongue.

Cabrillo ignored them both. "Manuel, you must refuse to submit to death. Do you hear me? Fight it with all your strength. Stay with us, with me."

For a moment Manuel was able to meet his master's eyes and then he managed a feeble nod. "I will try, sir."

Unconvinced, and suspecting Manuel's unspoken thoughts, Cabrillo said with building anger, "When I offered you freedom you chose baptism in its place. I tell you now that if you surrender to this fever without a fight, if you let it take you away under the delusion that your death is God's will, I will regret ever giving you that choice. God *can not* condone abandoning our lives at the first opportunity merely because we hope to gain heaven."

Manuel lay very still, and then nodded.

"I offer you freedom again today, Manuel, but you must live to gain it. Just live. Wrestle this bastard of a fever for all its worth."

Manuel whispered, "If I am free, will I still serve you, Captain-General?"

Bowing his head to hide his face, Cabrillo said, "Only if that is what you want."

Manuel's voice diminished until the last words were inaudible, saying, "Then, sir, I will fight the best I can." He closed his eyes, and Cabrillo watched Manuel's weak breath lift his chest in small, shallow rises.

Staring at the dark, damp face until his vision began to blur, Cabrillo leaned his forehead onto the edge of the cot as the patient drifted back to sleep. Moments passed in silence before the captain-general got to his feet and gave two words of command to Dr. Fuentes. "Save him."

Descending to the main deck and then the steps leading below, Cabrillo went to the horse stalls. Right now, he needed their company more than human interaction. Seguro lifted his face and brought his ears forward in greeting. Viento nickered lowly as Cabrillo neared, and the stallion's forehead met that of his master to share a moment of comfort, even empathy. "You know, Viento, do you not? Yes, of course you do, and you miss him also."

Hearing someone's approach, Cabrillo turned to find Father Lezcano standing behind him. Expecting a reproach or a warning for cursing of the priest, Cabrillo was surprised when Father Lezcano said, "I have noticed, sir, that the slings have begun to wear slightly on the horses recently. Since we will remain at anchor for a few days, I will be happy to care for them ashore."

Cabrillo moved to Viento's side and ran his hand gently over the raised lines caused by the border of the sling. "It will do them much good to breathe fresh air and stretch their legs again." Still, he hesitated. He had not yet let Father Lezcano care for Viento without

Manuel's or his own oversight. Perhaps it was time to fully release his old suspicions.

"Very well, I accept your offer, father. Mateo is a capable groom and he will assist you. Take whatever men you need to build a couple of enclosures before moving the horses ashore. The mares should be disembarked from *La Victoria* first. Please see that they and Viento are separated at all times. Once ashore, you must not allow any of them to roam, not even if they are tethered and hobbled. Only if I give permission are they to be exercised outside of their corrals."

Aware that Cabrillo was offering something far beyond permission to perform a requested task, Father Lezcano said, "They will be treated with utmost care, sir."

He got to work at once and in little more than an hour two wooden pens stood open and waiting just off the beach. While making a show of confidence in Father Lezcano, Cabrillo often stole glances to check his progress, especially as the horses were lifted one by one from the deck, lowered into the water, and steadily guided ashore. The captain-general waited for the next launch to carry him to the beach.

The two small corrals had been occupied only briefly and the horses just watered when Captain Ferrelo appeared at Viento's gate with unwelcome news for Cabrillo. Bowing quickly, Ferrelo said, "Sir, an exploring party has spotted a large group of Indians at a nearby lake."

"Warriors?"

"About half carry bows and arrows, sir."

"How many?"

"Perhaps forty, sir."

"Were your men seen?"

"I do not believe so, Captain-General."

"In which direction were they moving?"

"At the time we noticed them, sir, they were merely fishing."

"Very well, Captain Ferrelo." Seeing in his officer's face that something had been left unsaid, Cabrillo asked, "What else?"

"Sir, although you have far greater experience than I, I would greatly welcome this opportunity to communicate with the natives."

"I see," said Cabrillo. This was evidently going to be a day ripe with opportunities for delegation. He gazed inland and silently analyzed the risks of allowing the captain of *La Victoria* to head this outing. Weighing heavily in Ferrelo's favor were not only his many leadership capabilities but also Cabrillo's desire to remain close by the flagship while Manuel battled his fever. It was clear that Ferrelo wanted this chance badly, and he'd earned it. Most importantly, he was levelheaded enough to avoid any conflict they couldn't get out of. After another moment, he asked, "Is it your best judgment that there will be no need to engage these Indians in battle?"

"That is my judgment, sir, and I will do everything in my power to maintain tranquility."

Satisfied, Cabrillo said, "Take with you some trade goods and my interpreter, whose signing skills are improving daily, and have Vargas and at least a dozen soldiers join your party. Also, take no more than one dog, and keep him leashed unless absolutely necessary. If you encounter hostility, withdraw if you can and send a messenger back to me at once. We will be prepared to assist you."

"Thank you, sir," said Captain Ferrelo, and even his parting bow expressed appreciation.

Pilot San Remón had been standing close enough to hear the conversation and observe Captain Ferrelo's leave taking. He had also witnessed the transfer of the horses from the ships to the corrals under Father Lezcano's untested yet seemingly capable supervision. Cabrillo glanced at him and guessed his thoughts, "Well, pilot? Do you have something you wish to say?"

"Me, sir? Not a word."

In an undertone, Cabrillo confided, "We should both be praying that my trust in men has not been overly stretched today."

His pilot replied with no more than a slight bow. Though young in years, he was far too intelligent to make any affirming comment.

The sun was arcing toward the west and Cabrillo was just pulling on his shirt after a swim in the river when Captain Ferrelo appeared and abundantly affirmed the confidence that had been placed in him by the procession that followed. Rather than sending a runner back to plead for reinforcements, *La Victoria's* captain strode into the open with full water kegs being carried and rolled by his men as well as some of the Indians he'd encountered. Cabrillo buckled his belt as he awaited the group and upon their arrival was immediately and quite heartily embraced by the native leader. The captain-general was released, however, with a suddenness that almost knocked him off balance as the chief got his first glimpse of the horses around the curve in the beach. He let out a startled exclamation that was immediately joined by shouts and grunts from his men. Barrels were dropped in the sand and several hands reached for bows. Cabrillo stood back a step and addressed them all with a tone and gestures of reassurance, saying, "Easy, easy, now. The horses are our friends, our *friends*. They will not harm you." Still smiling, still in the same voice, he added, "Leave your bloody weapons alone and come sit down with us. Yes, just so, good, good, this way." He ushered them to a shady area where they were seated; the natives finding positions from which they could keep their eyes on the horses. And as the Indians made their equestrian study Cabrillo mentally noted the physical similarities of his new guests to the natives of Puerto de la Posesión. This was easily done given their complete absence of clothing.

He began their discussions with amiable vigor, and the chief pulled his glance away from Viento to respond in kind, each attempting to question and explain, but, again, the lack of a common verbalism allowed them to convey extremely limited details. As before, the art of trade provided a universal translator.

At Father Gamboa's discreet suggestion, the captain-general ordered yards of cloth to be rowed ashore and added to the small gifts already bestowed by Ferrelo at his first encounter, and the Indians joyously tied pieces of the brightly colored fabric around their waists or draped them over their shoulders. Cabrillo had previously explained what he wished in return, and runners draped in crimson, violet, and emerald were now sent racing inland.

Soon more natives began to appear carrying baskets of food for both men and horses. Trading continued and the exchanges delighted the natives, and that delighted Cabrillo almost as much as his somewhat replenished consumables.

The afternoon evolved into an impressive feast, abundant with fish and roasted maguey, which the natives had made from the plump leaves of agave plants. Having witnessed many times how unrestrainedly wine could affect a man new to its influences, Cabrillo had allowed only a taste to each of his native visitors. Fortunately, none of them showed any desire to consume more of what seemed only a bitter and unpleasant liquid. The wine rations of the men were also strictly monitored, regardless of amounts they might have consumed in the past.

If the guests were unimpressed by the drinks and food offered by the Spaniards, including the captain-general's prized olives, the same could not be said when they observed the black men, horses, guns, and other weapons that the Spaniards allowed them to inspect closely. After checking for the second time to confirm the health of Viento's legs and hooves Cabrillo threw his leg over the back of his bridled but unsaddled stallion and rode him slowly along a short stretch of the beach, much to the awe of his new audience.

As the sun began to reach toward a cloud-streaked horizon, the Indians displayed many signs of friendship while they prepared to leave, and they drifted back into the interior bearing many images of the wonders they'd witnessed that day. By the time the last of them had disappeared, though Cabrillo had received regular updates during their visit of, "No change to report, sir," he was anxious to return to the ship to see for himself how Manuel and his other ailing men were faring.

Once onboard the *San Salvador* the captain-general was heartened to learn that the conditions of two of the sailors were improving. But back in his cabin, as he approached closely and studied Manuel's face, Cabrillo could discern little variation in him. Again he knelt beside the cot but this time Father Lezcano added his voice to the prayers. Despite their hopes and efforts throughout the night and into the next dawn, Manuel's fever only gathered strength.

Father Lezcano was sent ashore to care for the horses. Dr. Fuentes suggested removing Manuel from Cabrillo's cabin to reduce the risk of the captain-general falling ill from exhaustion, but he refused to allow it.

By mid-morning their commander's draining worry and need for sleep finally became so apparent to Fuentes and San Remón as they stood beside him exchanging concerned glances that at last his pilot said, "Captain-General, please, you must sleep."

Cabrillo merely shook his head.

"If you will not rest, sir, perhaps some time ashore will help, even if only for a short time."

"The crisis is likely to be hours away, sir," said the doctor. "We will send word of any development."

No response came.

Pilot San Remón, knowing his captain-general's softest spots, offered a last attempt at persuasion. "Father Lezcano may need guidance with the horses, sir. He is new to that role."

The captain-general stared at Manuel, who slept restlessly under the torture inflicted by his burning body. After several moments Cabrillo rose stiffly to his feet and turned toward the doctor and pilot. Flexing his tightened shoulders and then rubbing his tired neck, he acquiesced, "A short visit, then. I will return within the hour."

Captain Ferrelo and his men, who had just returned from another scouting mission, greeted the captain-general as he landed. "All is quiet, sir. No natives in sight today."

"Fine, Captain."

He walked among the men for a while, quietly encouraging their work on the sails or their own clothing, or gazing inland with the sentries from their hilltops. When he rejoined Ferrelo, his captain asked, "How is Manuel, sir?" Every man in the fleet knew what this companion meant to their commander.

"There is little change for the better."

"Perhaps soon, sir."

"I will ask Father Lezcano to offer a Mass for him."

"Very good, sir."

Cabrillo returned Ferrelo's parting bow and headed around the outcropping of trees that blocked his view of the corrals. As he drew nearer to the wooden barriers he heard no acknowledging neigh from Viento, but his mind was so preoccupied that he barely noticed. It wasn't until he looked up and scanned the other three horses without seeing Viento that his heart began to increase its pace. He walked more hurriedly around the enclosures toward the trees that served as posts on the inland side and gazed searching in that direction. Nothing.

"Father Lezcano," he called out, telling himself that there was a simple explanation for Viento's absence. Yet he remembered with painful clarity his telling the priest to keep his horses contained at all times unless given permission to do otherwise. "Mateo!" he cried, circling the corrals completely and this time eyeing the sand. Though human prints marred the smoothness all around the enclosure, on the far side of the corral where Seguro was contained Cabrillo spotted a set of Viento's tracks. They led off toward the mountains, and were mingled with more human footprints. He started trotting along the line of the prints, and then loping at an increasing speed, and then running so fast that his chest burned, his anger gathering momentum right along with his legs. As he crashed into the forest curses and threats burst from his lips like bees from a beaten hive. His breathing grew ragged and his legs tight but he pushed on through the slapping branches and grabbing undergrowth. He reached a small clearing and suddenly spotted Father Lezcano. The priest was leading Viento back toward him but Cabrillo slowed his pace only slightly. He could see that Viento was heavily lathered and his eyes were wild. There was a bleeding cut on his left shoulder. He was hurt.

When Cabrillo reached them Father Lezcano tried to speak but Cabrillo grabbed the rope of Viento's halter and shouted into the priest's face, "You bastard!"

Again the priest tried to make himself heard, but Cabrillo yelled, "You sneaking bastard! I was right about you!"

Under this verbal assault the face of the priest darkened to crimson and his teeth gritted tight, and Viento danced and snorted, but Cabrillo was beyond noticing.

"I was a damned fool to listen to Father Gamboa. He claimed you were trustworthy, that you—"

Father Lezcano drew back his right fist and smashed Cabrillo in the mouth with enough force to knock him off his feet. Viento tried to rear but Cabrillo never loosened his grip on the halter rope. When the captain-general jerked his gaze up he saw that the priest was even more stunned than he. Paralyzed and speechless for a moment, Father Lezcano gaped at his fist as if trying to discover how it had so abruptly developed such a destructive mind of its own.

Cabrillo touched his split bottom lip and drew away fingers reddened with blood.

"Captain-General..." Father Lezcano wheezed in a strangled voice.

Still sitting where he'd fallen, Cabrillo thrust out the flat of his hand to silence him. He spat the blood from his mouth and ran his tongue over his teeth. Out of the corner of his eye he saw Mateo cringing amongst the trees. His gaze found the priest again, and he spat once more. A moment later the captain-general's shoulders began to agitate at the same cadence of a deep rumbling that was rising in his chest.

Father Lezcano would never have guessed that he could be more shocked than he'd been by his own incredible action, but it actually seemed that the commander he had just struck, a crime for which he could lawfully be put to death, was starting to chuckle. In fact the laughter grew steadily within Cabrillo until it burst from him so loudly that birds took flight in screeching protest from the branches of a nearby tree.

Father Lezcano fell to his knees, too stunned to stand, wondering if a temporary madness had claimed the fleet's master, and watched without a word as Cabrillo gradually regained his breath.

Mateo stepped from the greenery and cautiously approached them. He knelt courageously beside the priest, yet faced Cabrillo with utmost respect.

A little wobbly, Cabrillo got to his feet and patted his skittish stallion. He walked up close to the priest and the boy, and took in their sweat-stained clothes, their worn faces. He sighed and said softly, "Will you please forgive me, Father?"

"Forgive *you*, sir?" This time Father Lezcano feared that his punch had done lasting damage.

"Yes. If I had been in my right mind I would have realized that Viento had escaped, and that you were merely retrieving him. Your footprints were made after his, were they not?" He glanced at the braid rope in his hand and then at the horse's head. "And he is wearing his corral halter rather than his bridle. You were not riding him." Cabrillo's bleeding mouth stretched into a painful smile. "If these things, which my mind should have grasped sooner, were not enough to convince me of your innocence," he said, lifting a hand to massage his aching jaw, "your punch certainly was."

Struggling against both wariness and shame, Father Lezcano could make no response.

"Did he jump the fence?"

"Yes, Captain-General," whispered the priest.

Mateo now roused his own small voice. "A snake as thick as my arm crawled into the corral, sir. Viento killed it, but then he fled. We chased him for miles."

"I see."

Father Lezcano offered nothing more. He stood awaiting a sentence that surely must come despite the captain-general's confused request for forgiveness. He was not prepared for Cabrillo's next command.

"We will never speak of this again. None of us."

"Sir..."

"Not to anyone, Father." He glanced intently at his nephew. "No one, Mateo."

"No, sir!"

He held the boy with his eyes, his expression growing firmer. He knew a permanent impression must be made. "If word were to get out, Mateo, I would have no choice but to order this good priest drawn and quartered."

"Oh, no, no, sir! Never will a single word about this day come from my lips!"

Above the boy's head, Cabrillo cast another weary smile at the priest, revealing that the threat of drawing and quartering had been an idle one. He touched his bleeding mouth again, this time thoughtfully. "I must come up with some explanation to give the men for my fat lip and loose teeth. Perhaps God will forgive such a small lie, eh, Father?"

Father Lezcano swallowed hard and said in a voice that fell to a mumble. "I believe He will, sir. I thank you, Captain-General Cabrillo."

A slight twinkle appeared in Cabrillo's eyes. "I hope I prove as worthy a student at learning from my beating as you have from yours, Father."

Understanding and gratitude swelled until it overwhelmed Father Lezcano, and he turned his face toward the sea to conceal this tide of emotions.

Cabrillo turned his attention to Viento's cut and determined with great relief that it was superficial. The birds overhead and the waves on the shore did the talking as he led them slowly back to the camp. Once there, the men and boy groomed and pampered the fine horse together.

Late that evening, with Cabrillo and Dr. Fuentes watching over the patient, Manuel's fever broke. When the physician finally finished his ministrations and left the room, Cabrillo remained close by slumped in his chair, his head lowered in prayer.

With all that had happened during the day and despite the lateness of the hour, he had allowed Mateo to remain in his cabin and help tend to Manuel. In the cooling, still night air the boy looked up and said with quiet earnestness, "Captain-General, I am very happy you did not have Father Lezcano punished a second time."

Cabrillo tried to lift his concentration from Manuel, and said through puffy lips that made his words less distinct, "A second time?"

"He didn't tell me, sir. Not a word, but I was there, in Santiago, when you first met Father Lezcano and—"

"Ah, yes. So you were."

"Now, he... he is so good to Viento and the other horses, sir." His words trailed away, and then he muttered, "I wanted to tell you of his kindness to them."

"You need not be concerned for our young priest, Mateo. I harbor no ill will toward him."

"Even after he—forgive me, sir, but after he struck you?"

"I was wrong to berate him as I did, Mateo. I was tired, and I was worried about Manuel and frightened for Viento, but I was wrong to take these things out on another. Father Lezcano, perhaps with God's own help, has shown me that a man should recognize his mistakes even while being punished for them."

Amazed, Mateo said, "But you are Captain-General, sir."

"Is a captain-general allowed no mistakes?"

"Oh, yes, sir. Ever so many as you like."

Cabrillo smiled with his eyes. "No, Mateo, I should be allowed no more than other men. Someday you may become an officer yourself, or lead men in other ways. If you or anyone else wishes to be worthy of leadership, he too must strive to face his wrongs honestly and learn from them."

Mateo's brows furrowed deeply as he considered these words, and his mind found a special berth within his memory where he could tuck them away, a place from which he could easily retrieve them in the years ahead. He lifted a smile up to his uncle.

After resting peacefully for a little while and drinking some weak wine that Cabrillo held to his dry lips, Manuel felt strong enough to turn his head and eye his master's swollen mouth and purple-green jaw with perplexity.

In answer to this quizzical gaze, the captain-general cleared his throat and explained with wondrous specifics that he'd gone riding that afternoon and a cursed snake had spooked Viento. Before he could rein Viento in, Cabrillo had been carried into the forest where he collided with a tree branch that slammed into his mouth and knocked him flat on the ground. Thankfully, Father Lezcano and Mateo had come to his assistance and they'd tracked Viento down together before the spooked stallion could do anything worse than cut his shoulder, which was doing fine now.

Foggy as his mind was, Manuel found it a highly curious tale, considering the horse and rider involved, and he puzzled on it hazily as he drifted into an undisturbed sleep.

Throughout and after the telling of Cabrillo's imaginary account, Mateo sat listening from the corner of the cabin, as silent and still as a hare burrowed beneath the shadow of an eagle.

Chapter 9

ATTACK

The strength of Manuel and the two other sickened men
returned steadily as the fleet maneuvered mile after well-
earned mile against a capricious breeze. And by the time
they made a landing at a place they named Cabo de la Cruz, Cabrillo
dared to breathe a sigh that celebrated the end of this relatively mild
rampage of fever. Since this newest site offered no extraordinary enticements and since no Indians could be spotted, the captain-general
decided not to tarry here. On the morning of their departure, Cabrillo
stood on the foredeck as the cape slid away behind them and said to
his pilot, "I wonder how long the nature of the land, both its fruitful-
ness and beauty, will continue to improve as we advance northward.
See, there, how the beaches are giving way to occasional bluffs of
reddish soil, and the trees are becoming wonderfully large, with some
groves so thick they hide whatever lies within them. I keep thinking
of the giant driftwood we found on Isla San Agustin. How I would
love to walk in that forest."

"As would I, sir. But, do you imagine that the animals living there
are as extraordinarily large as those trees?"

Cabrillo smiled. "If so, we had better hope they dislike the taste
of red meat."

As they stood leaning on bent elbows atop the railing, absorbed
in their conversation, both men suddenly caught sight of movement
up the coastline a moment before their lookout shouted, "Indians in
boats, Captain-General! Heading ashore a quarter-league ahead, sir!"

There were seven canoes now being drawn from the sea and far
onto the beach, each craft large enough to carry only two men. Cabrillo watched the Indians as his ships quickly drew nearer, and the

natives stared back, their bodies tight with apprehension. They did not flee, but neither did they attempt to set their canoes back in the water.

"Shall we approach them, sir?" asked Pilot San Remón.

Cabrillo observed them a moment longer, then shook his head. "No, pilot, regrettably. Not in this unpredictable wind. We must sail on."

The men of each culture continued to lock gazes until they'd completely lost sight of one another, and Cabrillo's curiosity about these people nagged at him as the fleet nosed ahead.

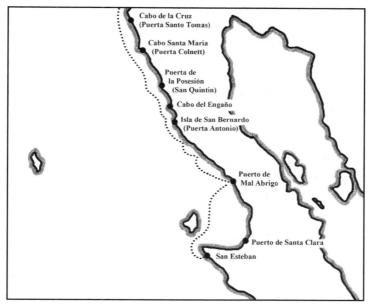

Not more than fifteen miles out of Cabo de la Cruz, though it felt more like ninety against the wind's bullying, they passed an island too small to coax them nearer and headed for a significantly larger, more promising harbor that beckoned from the mainland just beyond. They turned to the east and soon, lowering the sounding weights continuously and finding more than adequate depths, entered the mouth of a wide port that seemed to draw them in like an embrace. As always, they approached the anchorage site with care but saw nothing to cause concern. On the contrary, this harbor brought delight to the hearts of every man and boy who looked up from his tasks long enough to take in his surroundings.

They furled their sails, and at the northeast edge of the bay the command was given to release their anchors. With three crashing splashes the heavy iron weights hit the water, and their ships came to rest. The men readied their decks in high anticipation of going ashore, and even as hands moved and muscles strained the crews let their eyes devour this protected spot in quick, hungry bites.

Cabrillo's flat, oversized cap shaded his eyes as they skimmed the features of the beach and hills, his face breaking into a smile. With a deep-throated rumble of satisfaction, he said to San Remón, "I do like the look of that land, pilot. In fact, this place reminds me just a little of Spain. Look at those trees," he said, pointing to a specific grove. "They resemble the floss-silk trees of home. And the colors blooming, have you ever seen such variety? This soil seems able to produce every imaginable form of vegetation. My fingers are itching to record them all." He paused, his eyes still absorbing, and then said, "I wonder what breathing life awaits us here."

Since no natives were visible Cabrillo had two launches quickly lowered, and he was among the first group of his men to head toward shore. Within the hour most of the rest of the crews had also landed and arrangements were already underway for the captain-general to officially claim the new port. While waiting for a felled tree to be shaped into a cross, and with soldiers forming a moving ring around them, Cabrillo hiked with Father Lezcano, Father Gamboa, Mateo, and Manuel up the slope of a hill overlooking the site chosen for the ceremony. He paused at a height of about sixty feet and turned to survey their port. A mild breeze cooled them where they stood gazing over the sun-kissed sea and coast. Cabrillo's eyes were shining when he said, "Such a perfect day. It makes the heart swell, does it not?"

All agreed, the priests giving praise to God.

After several moments Cabrillo drew his attention closer in to share a conspiratorial glance with Father Lezcano, and then asked his cabin boy, "Do you know what saint's feast arrives on Sunday, Mateo?"

"Why no, sir. I do not even know what day this is today."

"It is Monday, the seventeenth of September, and you should know that in four days it will be the feast of the apostle San Mateo." The boy's face lit up and Cabrillo satisfied his hopes by saying, "Fathers Gamboa and Lezcano believe it would only be right to name this harbor after him."

116

"Truly, sir? It will be called San Mateo?"

"Truly, and you must remember everything about it so you can tell your family its characteristics when we return home."

"Oh, I will, sir!"

"Now, off with you. The ceremony is about to begin."

The rite of possession varied little from those that had come before, but anyone who happened to glance at Mateo during the ritual could read from his glowing face that this particular occasion would be recalled many times over the course of his life.

With the final words spoken and the cross resting securely on the very spot where Cabrillo had stood not long before, he sent the water gatherers out on their search and had the horses brought ashore. Upon the scouting party's successful return he allowed himself the pleasure of gathering a small company together intent on striking a different path from which to investigate the interior. As armaments and small packs were being lifted to shoulders Manuel approached his commander and asked, "Captain-General, will you allow me to come with you?"

Cabrillo could see that the thought of being left behind was painful to his former slave and newest sailor, but he said, "Less than a week ago you lay at death's gate, Manuel."

"Yes, sir, but it would make me stronger to walk awhile."

"I have noticed over the last few days," Cabrillo said, considering, "that you have been eating enough for two men. You have gained back a little of the flesh the fever stole. Perhaps it would do you good to stretch your legs a bit. Very well, but carry nothing heavier than a shield, and if you start to tire return to camp at once."

"At once, sir," Manuel promised, letting his expression reveal how heartbreaking it would be to hold him to such a vow. Cabrillo cast him a glare affirming his intention to do just that, and then let it pass to set the party in motion.

They had advanced perhaps a mile and a half northeastward when Manuel slowly crouched down ahead of Cabrillo and said with hushed excitement, "Captain-General, strange animals straight ahead."

They all hunched lower as word was passed back along the line, and they inched forward to scan the grassy savanna until they'd each spied the alien creatures. "Vargas," Cabrillo called softly over his shoulder to the sergeant-major, known for his keen far-sightedness, "can you guess what they are?"

"From this distance, sir, they look something like the long-necked sheep of Peru, except for those dark, pronged horns."

"Yes, and their different coloring." To Cabrillo, the gleaming white of their rumps and bellies handsomely set off their rich tan backs and black throats and noses. "Come, we must get closer."

Creeping nearer, however, was not quite as readily accomplished as he had hoped. The moment the men stepped into the open the herd of at least a hundred animals skittered several yards farther away and continued to show a frustrating talent for maintaining a distance of just beyond crossbow range. After several more increasingly exasperating attempts to reduce the expanse between them, Cabrillo said, "Perhaps we can approach them with more success from horseback."

He left a handful of men behind to keep the four-legged beasts in sight while he and the others trotted back to the encampment. His men cleared a path for them when he returned riding his young mare, Luna, accompanied by Captain Ferrelo on Seguro.

"There," Cabrillo said, pointing Ferrelo toward the herd of deer. The horses saw them too, and began to blow and sidle in eagerness, making their riders tighten their knees and firm their grips to hold them to a measured walk. Cabrillo ordered his men to hang back as the riders slowly advanced.

For this hunt Cabrillo had chosen to carry a long bow, as did Ferrelo, and they each already held an arrow with its iron tip pointed downward across the center of his bow. Ferrelo's horse breathed a short, anxious nicker and the heads of several grazing deer jerked up. Ferrelo leaned down slightly and whispered cautions to the gelding, and they proceeded deliberately forward.

The deer stared alertly but none moved. One of the herd's leaders took a tentative step toward the riders, and then another. Cabrillo and Ferrelo exchanged a subtle glance and brought their bows up in a careful, protracted movement.

As if warned by an abrupt cry of alarm the herd exploded. Needing nothing beyond instinct and anticipation of her master's wishes, Luna bolted after their prey. Cabrillo's mind and body screamed to let her run but, knowing that all-out exertion would be unwise for his mare after her recent periods of confinement, he held her to a swift gallop, and Ferrelo kept Segura to a similar pace. The deer had no such restraints and they flew as if weightless before them. "Look at them run!" breathed Cabrillo with both admiration and regret.

With incredible agility the deer sprang, shifted, and raced ahead. Cabrillo quickly realized they could not lessen the distance between them unless the horses were given their heads, and he refused to risk it. He suspected that the deer were beyond the range of his bow but decided to take at least one quick, desperate shot. Nocking his arrow, he pulled back on the bowstring, held his breath as he steadied his aim, and freed the shaft. Somehow the arrow flew as far as the last of the disappearing deer, but it missed its rapidly shifting mark by at least ten feet. Ferrelo too let loose an arrow but achieved the same disappointing result.

With his voice and knees Cabrillo signaled Luna to lessen her gait, but the mare hesitated to obey. It had been long enough since she'd felt the stretch and pull of her muscles, the expansion of her heart and lungs that she would have willingly raced for miles. All of this Cabrillo knew, but for her own good he grasped the reins and gently but firmly let her know that the decision was final. This time, Luna complied.

Over the next five days several more brief attempts were made to bring down one of the elusive deer, but the only mementos the men were able to take away from San Mateo were sketches and, to Cabrillo, less than adequate descriptions. Even so, the grass and exercise enjoyed by the horses had given them much vigor. Viento's shoulder wound was very nearly healed and it would not leave a lasting scar. Aside from some lingering yellowish bruising, Cabrillo's jaw and lip looked almost normal. The appearance, mood, and physical condition of the crews and ships had also improved during their stay. It was time to sail on.

To the wonder and appreciation of Cabrillo and his men the land became even more appealing as they progressed northward. Palm trees began to appear in vibrant groves, and valleys grew thick with wide-leafed and flowering shrubs in an array of colors almost beyond belief. They journeyed past three islands that, after seeing no sign of life, they named Islas Desiertas. The presence of natives became evident, however, when great clouds of smoke became visible over the mainland, but since this stretch of rocky coastline looked less than hospitable for his three ships Cabrillo pushed on in search of a safer refuge.

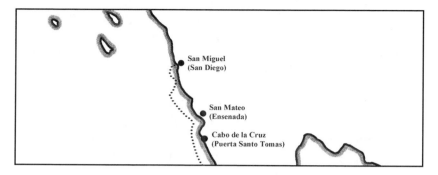

From all initial signs, the last day of September's fourth week could not have presented a better answer to his wishes. The coastal fog had lifted entirely when they sighted a harbor opening so promising that Cabrillo said with relish to Manuel, "This may well be a worthy place to celebrate surviving three long months at sea. May heaven be praised, we have much to be thankful for."

"We do indeed, sir. That tall point ahead seems to mark the place especially for us."

The high spit of land they were quickly approaching pointed directly at them and looked to be at least 400 feet high, and it did seem to welcome them like the curved arm of a waiting friend. They let it usher the ships into its possession as they followed the 5-mile eastward rounding boundary. Drawing deeper into the harbor, the smiles evolved into expressions of attentiveness as men sounded the depths and called the fathom count on both sides of the ship.

When they reached an angle at which much of the bay became visible, they spotted the threat at once. On the shore a group of seventeen Indians stared at the ships in astonishment. They hung in stunned paralysis for only a moment before most of them suddenly pivoted and fled. Yet three stalwart men remained behind, armed only with lowered bows, and these few stood rooted bravely to the sand even after the ships had settled into their anchor lines.

Cabrillo watched them with building admiration as he ordered a boat lowered. Father Lezcano appeared at his side and asked, "Please, sir, will you allow me to accompany you to act as your interpreter?"

Taking his eyes from shore, Cabrillo said, "It may be dangerous, Father."

Father Lezcano's eyes shown with a youthful excitement and daring that his religious training had not successfully quelled, "Yes, Captain-General."

Hungry young pup, wants to risk getting himself killed, he thought, but aloud he said, "Very well, you may come."

The natives were still waiting when the launch rowed ashore with the captain-general at its stern. As he drew close enough for a more minute inspection, Cabrillo perceived that these natives were from a culture further advanced than those the fleet had encountered during the last few weeks. They dressed in more finely tanned and sewn animal skins, wore elaborately beaded decorations around their necks, and bound their long hair back with headbands or in braids. With proud facial features and robust bodies, Cabrillo found them to be a handsome people.

As the captain-general took in the measure of the Indians he was highly aware of their arrow-nocked but lowered bows, yet when he leaped from his launch he chose to leave his crossbow behind. Manuel, Vargas, and the four guards accompanying him, however, did not, and Cabrillo knew his soldiers would keep eyes and weapons trained on him as well as the direction taken by the Indians who had abandoned the beach.

As he gradually approached the three men Cabrillo extended his arms out to his sides, his hands open, and then gestured to express a desire for accord. He strode slowly to within twenty feet before halting, spread the small rug Manuel brought to him, and laid out a collection of metal and glass goods from a small chest. He then drew back several paces and beckoned the natives to accept his offering.

Cautiously, a middle-aged Indian with a deep scar on his left forearm stepped forward and ventured close to the articles on the rug, all the while shifting his eyes to and from the strangers. As this man allowed his fascination to be temporarily captured by the items presented, Cabrillo gradually approached and sat down beside the rug. Only a yard apart now, the two studied one another with open fascination that each tried to keep within the bounds of universal politeness. From head to foot and back up again their eyes took in the look and measure of the man from another world. Cabrillo was struck by the directness and honesty of the Indian's gaze, and appreciated the rich craftsmanship of his necklace that displayed fanning, light-colored shells and dark stones. When the native tentatively reached out and touched the Spanish flat cap, Cabrillo ran extended fingers lightly over the central black beading of the necklace. Both arms lowered, and it was clear that even this subtle, momentary physical contact had been enough to create a small tacit bond between them. Their mutual perusal now generated enough confidence in the native to allow his attention to return to the trade goods.

The other two Indians, seeing that their friend seemed to be growing more comfortable with the stranger and further encouraged when Cabrillo motioned them nearer, came to join them. The captain-general allowed this outnumbered ratio to last long enough for the Indians to gain a higher level of assurance, and then he called Manuel to his side. As hoped, this closer sighting of Manuel also claimed the natives' fascination. In moments all five diplomats sat cross-legged in a small ring exchanging glances, and the captain-general beckoned Father Lezcano forward.

"Father, please tell them we mean their people no harm," said Cabrillo.

Through gestures for the natives and words for the sailors, this was communicated well enough to offer an evident level of reassurance to all three of the Indians. But the trepidation they attempted to hide, and almost succeeded, was still there. Cabrillo and Father Lezcano tried to calm them further by repeating their peaceful intentions and placing gifts into brown hands. These were accepted with unveiled awe.

Slowly, the man who had first permitted Cabrillo's proximity and who continued to act as leader for his small band began to speak. Through signing, he asked Cabrillo, "What do you call yourself?"

The captain-general dispensed with formalities and answered simply, "Cabrillo."

Wondering what this might mean, the Indian repeated the word, testing the sound. Evidently coming to a conclusion of some kind, he signed and Father Lezcano translated aloud, "Our relatives live far inland. They tell us that men of your kind, warriors with great weapons, came to their land. Those men killed many. They treated women badly. My people see you here and they are afraid."

Silently cursing Coronado or whoever it was who had inflicted these wounds, Cabrillo said through his priest, "We are not those men. We have no wish to hurt your people. We come in the name of a great chief and in the name of our God. Today, we will place a symbol of our God on this beach, which will show his great love for all people. We want to stay only a few days. We will trade and then depart in our ships that will take us far to the north and west."

The greatest attentiveness was paid to his words, and the Indian leader said in reply, "I will tell these things to my people." With that, Cabrillo wrapped the presents in a length of light blue cloth, handed the bundle to the natives, and watched as they disappeared into the surrounding trees.

In a brief, vigilant ceremony Cabrillo named the new harbor *San Miguel*, primarily because the feast of that saint would fall on the next day but also in order to greatly please the crew of his ship bearing that same name. To mollify his other two crews, however, he promised that the next couple of landfalls would be duly named after their faithful ships.

Throughout and after the claiming rite Cabrillo keenly sensed that they were being watched, but no Indians showed themselves during the rest of the day. Considering the fears of the natives, and though he kept his most attentive lookouts on watch and his swivel guns ready, he was deeply thankful for the absence of hostilities, which left them to make small repairs in restful peace.

That evening the sunset fanned its brilliance like a peacock's mating array, darkness reached gently into their harbor, and a nearly full moon shone down on the tranquil water like a blessing. Father Lezcano mentally greeted the lunar company as he climbed to the quarterdeck and found Cabrillo. "Have you ever seen a more beautiful night, sir?"

"I wish my wife were here to see it."

"Perhaps, sir, she is gazing into just such a night sky."

"I imagine her at our window, looking out at the moon." He didn't mention how he ached to hold her, as he had held her the last time he'd stood at that window. Wanting to turn aside his thoughts of yearning, he asked, "How many such nights have you seen, Father? You could not have been very old when you entered training for the priesthood."

"My parents died within months of each other when I was eight years old. An uncle delivered me to the nearest monastery."

"You, an orphan? I would not have guessed that." Cabrillo studied the young face as he mulled over this revelation.

"It is not a fact I share with many, captain-general. My family's circumstances were far from exceptional; we were of the nobility but had very little wealth. One of my uncles thought I had a promising mind, and he knew the monastery would offer an education that he could never provide." The priest smiled ruefully as he said, "I doubt it will surprise you to hear that the good friars beat me often, hoping to defeat my rebelliousness. They must have been relieved when I sailed to New Spain." Cabrillo smiled too but said nothing, and Father Lezcano continued. "Once here I served as a page for the viceroy while I continued my studies. As I mentioned before, shortly after that first meeting between you and me—" he paused and they exchanged a meaningful look— "I was ordained."

"Then, before your ordination, you felt called by God?"

"Not as some men have, perhaps, not suddenly or profoundly, but, yes. I do believe this is the path He has chosen for me."

Their voices grew still as they watched the *San Salvador's* boatswain climb the stairs, approach them, and bow respectfully. "Excuse me, Captain-General, but several of the men have requested the chance to toss a net or two from shore. That moon is shining rightly for a good catch, and fresh fish would be welcome fare, sir."

Cabrillo took a moment to observe the bushes, trees, shadows, and hills beyond the beach. "All seems quiet, but that may mean little. I will give permission for no more than five men to fish at a time, and they must be guarded by Vargas and at least four of our soldiers."

"Thank you, sir."

"And keep the men quiet. These natives are already uneasy and it would take little to push their fears into action."

"Yes, Captain-General."

As the boat was loaded and rowed toward a promising spot, the priest and Cabrillo speculated softly about their potential catch and how it should be cooked. Vargas was perched upright and dutiful in the stern of the small craft, with two other soldiers sitting to port and starboard and one in the bow. They landed and pulled the boat above the tidemark, speaking seldom and only in hushed tones. Five sailors gathered up their large net and formed a line in ankle-deep water as their guards took up positions.

To coordinate the toss one man counted, "One...two...three..." and they let the weighted net fly out over the water, hissing *ssstt*. The weights made a rapid syncopated popping as they hit the surface, settled and rested for several minutes before the fishermen, anxious to discover what riches the bay would surrender, began to draw the net back in with practiced efficiency. As they strained against the increasing burden their excitement built, and their voices rose along with their emotions.

From his position at the rail Cabrillo tensed at the increase in noise, but he heard Vargas shush the men sharply. Thankfully, the night air grew quiet once more as the fishermen resumed their work. Under their strong, deft hands the net eased closer to shore. When it was near enough for the moon to confirm the fantastic bounty of leaping, flapping, glistening fish, one of the fishermen let loose a "Hahaaaah!" loud enough to reach the other end of the harbor.

Vargas strode into the water up to the guilty man and slapped him so hard across the mouth that he nearly tumbled into the fish. Struggling to keep his balance as well as his hold on the net, and knowing he had committed a punishable transgression, the fisherman clamped his stinging mouth shut.

Expecting it, yet intending to take over if necessary, Cabrillo heard Vargas order, "Get the boat into the water. This load of fish will be the only one taken tonight."

The soldiers pushed off and rowed close to the net, steadying the boat until the fishermen could board while balancing their load alongside. When all had settled in, the soldiers began to pull at their oars and slowly set the heavily loaded launch in motion toward the *San Salvador*.

They'd rowed only a few strokes when Father Lezcano espied movement in the trees; it was bodies heading toward the boat. "Captain-General, look there!"

Seeing them at once, Cabrillo called in an undertone, "Natives approaching, sergeant-major." But Vargas, watching from the launch's bow, was already aware of the Indians. His and two other arquebuses were now lifting and aiming as the two remaining soldiers kept rowing and four of the sailors grabbed for the free oars. With a steady voice that carried across the water, Cabrillo commanded, "At the first sign of trouble, men, let loose that net." Glancing from his advancing boat to the shore, he headed toward his second launch. Fully knowing that Manuel would meet him there with his weapons, he hurried along signaling to several men who had lined up and in readiness to accompany him. He reached the railing of his main deck and shot a glance toward *La Victoria*, seeing that Captain Ferrelo was already sending men over the side. Captain Correa's boat was also being boarded.

Without further warning, the unmistakable hiss of arrows in flight issued from the trees, and Cabrillo heard the cries of at least two of his fishermen as arrows found them in the boat. Vargas and his men instantly lit their guns and released a volley that lacerated the brush concealing the archers. Cursing under his breath, Cabrillo ordered his master gunner to load the swivel guns and bombardeta and stand by. One sharp nod at Pilot San Remón shifted his command of the ship and hastened men already heading toward battle stations. The captains of *La Victoria* and the *San Miguel* followed these actions in quick succession.

Cabrillo threw himself over the railing, clung to the rigging to steady his landing, and dropped into his launch with a thud. Manuel, his arms loaded with his master's helmet, weapons, and leather breast-plate, boarded two steps behind him. Eight more men soon found their seats near them, shoved off, and sailors sawed at the oars while soldiers aimed their weapons. Scanning the beach and straining to hear any sound from shore as Manuel deftly secured the side straps of his breastplate, Cabrillo then raised his own crossbow. His eyes could detect no movement, and all his ears could perceive were the sharp rustlings of foliage caused by men in retreat.

The three ship's boats met the launch of the fishermen at nearly the same time. Vargas tugged at an arrow protruding from his leather armor two inches below the position of his heart. He gritted his teeth and with one powerful yank he pulled the arrow free, let loose an obscene curse, gulped back a couple of breaths, and lied before Cabrillo could ask, "Nothing but a scratch, sir, thanks to this thick bull hide."

The fishermen had had no body protection other than their linen shirts and cotton vests. Fortunately for them the arrows had managed to strike nothing more critical than a thigh and a shoulder. With gazes still scraping the shore, the crew of the other boats closed ranks around the fishing launch, and they all returned to their ships.

With double watches posted and extra lamps lit that night, the two remaining arrows were removed and awarded to the wounded sailors as trophies. Dr. Fuentes assured the captain-general that the fishermen's gashes had been neatly sewn and should heal quickly, adding his always-anticipated caveat, "barring any putrefaction." Vargas, much to Dr. Fuentes' loud disapproval, had refused medical treatment, preferring to bathe his hurt in seawater and fresh air and to bear the relatively small wound with pride. Although released from the rest of his watch, Vargas remained on the main deck and graciously retold the story of the attack to those who had been below decks when the short burst of excitement took place. Since the wounded had received an extra ration of wine, the sergeant major's tale proved a lively diversion for the healthy, but the two wounded sailors were soon fast asleep.

Well after midnight the knot in Cabrillo's stomach began to loosen at last. He had endured this twisting sensation many times before, whenever one of his men had been hurt in battle. Though this encounter had been extremely mild compared to his past campaigns, tonight the injuries to his sailors and the potential for more pain or death tomorrow made him feel old. He felt the weight of too many battles, too many men lost. Staring at the shoreline still, he heard Manuel step to the rail beside him and saw his large dark hands wrap around the wood. He felt him studying his mood, reading his mind, so he wasn't surprised when he heard him say, "Dr. Fuentes said they will be fine, sir."

"He did, yes."

"What will you do, sir, when the sun comes?"

Cabrillo shook his head, and his words came slowly. "What will I do? The answer would be much simpler if I wanted to fight them, or if I did not understand why they fired upon us tonight. None of our men were lost, so the harm they inflicted was not severe. Even so, we must protect ourselves, and we should make a stand for the sake of those who may come after us. Word spreads far and quick among these people, and if we appear weak or cowardly it will only increase the risk of other attacks along our route." He lifted his face, listening, as if the answer resided with the moon and stars. After a little time had passed, he said, "Vengeance alone is an unworthy excuse for a war. I

127

will strive for patience, Manuel, and hope that dawn sheds a calming light on their warriors. If they do not attack again, we may be given the chance to change their opinions of us. I will try to offer proof that I meant what I said yesterday about intending these people no harm."

"Then, sir," said Manuel, "I will pray they can see what you offer."

Pilot San Remón strolled over to join them and Cabrillo straightened. "Is all well, pilot?"

"Everything is quiet, sir. I take comfort in seeing no canoes near the water."

"Well, then, I have been too long on this deck during your watch. I leave the *San Salvador* in your able hands." He descended to his cabin without hurry, knowing he would sleep little, if at all. Manuel took up his place by the door, wrapped himself in his woolen blanket, and breathed deeply until each inhale had become a gravelly snore.

Sitting at his writing desk with a sharpened quill poised in his hand, Cabrillo heard the snoring only as a soothing hum. At the edge of his lamplight's glow he noticed the impressive thickness of the stacked letters he'd written to Beatriz. He mused about how tall that stack might grow by the time he returned to her. Lifting the lid of his bronze inkpot, dipping his quill, and tapping the tip against the inner edge of the pot, he reflected on the happenings of this day. What would he write to Beatriz about, and what would he chose to withhold so she would not worry overly? At this thought he smiled at himself, realizing how foolish it was to imagine his wife reading a letter and growing afraid for his safety before he could reassure her in person. What chance was there of encountering a homebound ship willing to deliver his written words in these far-off waters?

Chapter 10

TRADE AND TOLERANCE

Red-eyed and heavy-lidded, Cabrillo met the rising sun, and its light revealed that not a soul stirred ashore. Summoning the captains of his other ships, Cabrillo communicated his intention to maintain peaceful ties with these natives. No aggressive action would be inflicted without further provocation. So the men of the fleet waited and watched, their armaments sharpened and primed, but minutes accumulated into an hour and still no Indian showed himself. Nonetheless, Cabrillo did not doubt that their every motion was being observed.

Since all remained quiet around their anchorage the officers met again in Cabrillo's cabin and agreed upon the desirability of learning more about this lush, protective port. "The governor will be hungry to learn all we can gather." He bent over a rough map he and his pilot had already begun sketching. "The far end appears to lie at least five leagues away, and though we have seen little smoke there may be villages hidden along the length of it. Captain Correa, the *San Miguel* is best suited to tour the harbor."

"That she is, Captain-General. And she's ready and willing."

"If nothing delays you, report back to me before noon. Fire a bercos volley if you need aid, but Captain, try diligently to avoid any violence with these natives. We walk a delicate plank here. I want to strengthen it. God willing, while you are gone Captain Ferrelo and I will be approached by Indians more interested in trade than war."

"I shall hope so, sir," Correa said. His bow was returned, concluding their discussion.

Cabrillo watched the *San Miguel* lift her sails and nose southeastward into the depths of the gently arcing harbor, then grow smaller and smaller until she was completely lost from view. His inability to mark her further progress generated a feeling of uneasiness, and as the hours of her absence accumulated he had to make an ever greater effort to conceal his apprehension for her welfare. This calm façade became nearly impossible to maintain, however, when noon came and went and shadows on land and ships grew to half their full length. At last, minutes after the hour of four had been hailed, the lookout in the maintop shouted, "There she is, sir, just rounding the spit!"

Now working to hide his relief just as he had veiled his concern, Cabrillo scanned the bergantine for any signs of attack but found none. He grew even more anxious to learn what had delayed the *San Miguel's* return, and Captain Correa wasted no time in presenting himself to the captain-general. He didn't come alone. As he set foot on the flagship he presented Cabrillo with two wide-eyed Indian boys.

Correa said, "Some of my men came upon these young whelps while filling water barrels, sir. I thought they might be a means of fostering good will, just as our treatment of the women and child at Puerto de la Posesión produced friendly fruit. So here they are."

Cabrillo eyed his captain with displeasure. How the hell would this new development play out with the locals?

He asked Captain Correa, "Did you see anyone else, there or elsewhere?"

"Not one, sir."

"All right, Captain, we will discuss this later. First we must see to your young captives."

He studied his new charges more closely and guessed them to be eight and ten years old. Even so young they stood uncowering before him. Calling Father Lezcano nearer and using signs and words he tried to put the boys at ease by saying, "You are welcome on my ship."

To the surprise of all, and making it obvious that Correa had already taken steps toward détente, the older boy pointed to himself and then his brother and said, "Friend, friend."

Cabrillo's grin couldn't have been more genuine. "Fine!" He tapped his own chest and said, "I am your friend too."

Both boys' faces lit up with toothy smiles of their own.

"Manuel, find these young fellows some clothing. They are to be fed and treated as dignitaries. Father Lezcano, your assistance with communication would be welcome."

In moments the boys sat upon the deck amid officers and crew almost lost in shirts far too large for such juvenile frames and wearing expressions of happy bewilderment. Cabrillo kindly presented them each with a small pouch of glass beads and a few metal fishhooks. These simple gifts delighted the youngsters enough to extract repeated gestures of gratitude. The captain-general then questioned them gently for some time about their people, but he learned little. The boys' glances toward shore were becoming more frequent, their apprehension growing.

To Father Lezcano, Cabrillo said, "Come, they must be returned to their parents before their absence causes mischief. The light is fading."

"Captain Correa, please return the boys to the place you found them. And do not tarry. I am anxious to hear every aspect about what you saw while exploring."

"I will return shortly, sir," Correa promised.

Turning to the boys, Cabrillo said, "My young friends, you likely will not understand this, but I want you to take our greetings to your parents." Father Lezcano signed these last words again and the boys bowed just as they'd seen Cabrillo's men do.

Within two hours Correa proved to be as good as his word. Upon the second reunion with the *San Miguel*, with darkness claiming its transitory right to earth and sky, Cabrillo and Correa met on the flagship, cloistered themselves in the commander's cabin, and talked into the depths of the night. Only after the captain-general had heard and recorded all that Correa could remember of that day did he bid him a good night, drag himself to his own bunk, and allow his exhausted body and mind to surrender to sleep.

Pilot San Remón made it a point, as well as an order to the men of the *San Salvador*, that the captain-general was not to be awakened before dawn. Yet, in the end, it was the pilot himself who called Cabrillo from his dreams at the first sign of light, saying, "I am very sorry to disturb you, sir, but three natives are paddling toward our ship."

Rubbing his eyes and then yawning as he tugged on his doublet, Cabrillo asked, "Only three? This sounds hopeful, pilot. Is it the same three we spoke with on the beach?"

"I believe not, sir."

"Perhaps that is even better. Those two boys, God bless them, spread a kind word last night. Let us greet our new visitors properly, eh, pilot? See what the cook has prepared that we can offer them, and have Manuel choose several finer pieces from our trade merchandise."

"Very good, sir."

Paulo appeared at the cabin door with his master's bucket of water. Beckoning his servant inside, Cabrillo said in parting to their pilot. "I will be on deck shortly."

It took few moments before he joined his pilot, Master Uribe, and Father Lezcano just as the men from the canoe were being helped aboard. From their appearance and manner Cabrillo guessed that these three Indians, each taller and broader-chested than the average Spaniard by a couple of inches, had prepared themselves for this encounter with as much understanding of its potential importance as their hosts.

Their waist-length cloaks, the finest specimens of clothing Cabrillo had seen during the voyage, still brandished the beauty of the animals that had provided skins for their construction. One cloak had been made from the fur of foxes, one from rabbits, and the last had originated from what Cabrillo guessed to be sea otters. From waist to knee they were covered by skirts of woven plant fibers overlain with long eagle feathers. Their hair was also adorned with feathers, the largest array worn by their apparent leader, who also bore the longest cloak. Tied at the throat but spread open across the chest, the cloaks framed wavy horizontal rows of white body paint. Beautifully delicate multicolored shells had been artfully strung to form necklaces and bracelets. Each warrior carried a fur-wrapped bundle secured by a strap slung over his shoulder and resting against his back as he stood before the officers.

Cabrillo bowed cordially, gestured for them to be seated, and soon had them all arranged in a conversational oval upon the deck. Unlike the previous exchanges with coastal Indians, the speaker of this group attempted communication without any encouragement. It was made clear that the villagers on the beach the day before had discussed their first encounter when their leader hailed the fleet's commander with, "We greet Chief Cabrillo."

Cabrillo bowed, returned the gesture of salutation, and said, "Father Lezcano, will you please use your skill to determine his name?"

His priest tried, but he received such a lengthy and confusing verbal reply that he had to make a second attempt, and a third. Even then it was quite impossible to divine which syllables were to be used as a polite address. The chief at last simply moved the dialogue along to the topic uppermost in his mind. Using vocalization sparingly, his hands introduced the story now becoming familiar to the seafarers. Father Lezcano managed to gather the following. "They have heard of men like us, sir, from their people in the east. These bearded men, whom they called Guacamal, wore clothing similar to ours. They were also armed as we are with swords and crossbows." Now the Indian stood and motioned as if he were lifting a lance and thrusting it through an enemy. He then pantomimed a man riding on horseback. Cabrillo nodded his understanding. After sitting down again, the chief observed Cabrillo keenly as he explained through Father Lezcano, "As these warriors made their way inland they kill a great number of our people."

Cabrillo's expression indicated a disapproval of the slayings as he said to Father Lezcano, "Again, I can only guess this was Coronado. Ask him to continue, Father."

The Indian went on signing, "These stories made my people fearful. But I have also heard of your visit with the two boys. You offered gifts rather than war, after my men shot arrows at your men. That is not the way of the other bearded ones."

Cabrillo nodded in appreciation for this distinction. "Tell him, Father, that we seek his friendship. We invite him and his men to eat with us and to accept our gifts as a sign of this new understanding."

These wishes were relayed but the Indian objected, and Father Lezcano explained uncertainly, "He seems to be saying that his people must first make us an acceptable offering."

"For what, Father?"

After several questing exchanges the priest said, "I believe, sir, that he wants to give you something in payment for the men who were wounded last night. He is evidently trying to determine the compensation that must be paid to you. He asks whether the men died."

Concealing his surprise, Cabrillo called forward Vargas and the other two men who had been wounded, and Father Lezcano told the chief who they were. The three Indians stood up and closely inspected each man to confirm that the arrows had not inflicted lasting harm.

Satisfied, the chief now brought forward his bundle and with obvious reverence withdrew the meticulously tanned skin of an albino deer. He held it out and gravely offered it to Cabrillo.

Highly impressed by its beauty and rarity, the captain-general accepted the skin by bowing with a formal grace that needed no word of interpretation. He was about to declare the debt between them fully forgiven, but paused. He perceived something in the native's manner that betrayed an expectation of further bargaining, countering the silent implication that a perfectly adequate compensation had just been offered. This, and the fact that the bundles of the other Indians still rested against their backs, led him to exhibit a look of deep concern. When he spoke, his tone emphasized his wrestling with a dilemma. "Tell him, Father, that we thank him for this uncommon and valuable gift, but the welfare of my men is of greater worth to me than one skin, regardless of its beauty."

It was evident from the accepting, even approving, expression of the chief that Cabrillo's response had been anticipated. Like two duelists the native leader and the captain-general now began to maneuver, making one bartering thrust and parry after another, all the while taking in the character and strength of the other. Their expressions began to warm with mutual respect. When at last Cabrillo paused to make a tally of the furs, shells, flint knives, soapstone bowl, and bow and arrows before him, he said to the chief. "Since my men will live, these gifts make me satisfied. The incident of last night will be forgotten."

Pleased with this conclusion, the chief bowed in perfect imitation of Cabrillo's earlier gesture.

"Now," said Cabrillo, "I ask that you accept the items we offer from one friend to another." Not wanting to disturb the balance of fairness that had been established between them, Cabrillo was careful to select only those articles that might be esteemed in reciprocal measure. He had Father Lezcano hand the goods out and watched the wonder and delight of his guests unfold. In moments the Indians stood draped in bright fabric cheerfully ringing small hawk's bells. The Indian chief approached and embraced Cabrillo, and this well-meaning gesture ignited a round of hugging by his two companions that didn't ease until the shoulders of every officer and many of the men had been warmly clasped. Manuel bore it with tolerance when he was pulled into the affable clutches of native fingers that slapped and rubbed his black skin with particular fascination.

At this time the captains of the other ships were invited to join them on the *San Salvador* for a meal of fried fish flavored with garlic, bean soup, fresh flat bread, and honeyed almonds, all of which the natives seemed to enjoy. During their repast Cabrillo had his scribe record the exchange of basic native words such as "fish," "boy," "wood," "rope," "knife," and "hand." One word, *ikuch*, seemed to mean leader, man, or warrior. When Cabrillo tentatively referred to the Indian chief by this term, he seemed pleased and was thereafter referred to as Ikuch by the captain-general. As the meal progressed, good-natured banter, both verbal and manual, flowed across the deck with increasing frequency.

The cabin boys were just gathering the trenchers and cups when the wind began to rise.

Cabrillo lifted his face and studied the sky. "A devilish storm may not be far off. Father Lezcano, we must induce our guests to return to their village." But the Indians were already getting to their feet without encouragement, eyeing the far-off clouds and sniffing the air in their own evaluation of nature's changing mood. They made their way to the railing where their leader halted and turned back to face Cabrillo. He gestured the "farewell" sign of his people and then bowed to the captain-general in a manner so polished it would have fooled many at the Spanish court. The captain-general returned this salute and said with his hands, voice, and eyes, "Well met, my friend."

When the rain started it fell lightly enough but Cabrillo was not fooled. Although the fleet had been unusually fortunate to avoid facing anything more threatening than strong headwinds during their voyage thus far, the captain-general had been forced to fight storms at sea in previous years. His gut sensed what was to come. As the thunder strengthened from growls to explosions and the rain thickened from sprinkles to torrents, Cabrillo repeatedly gave thanks for this blessedly snug harbor. They felt little more than soft reverberations of the ravaging wind and waves that might have crushed them on the open sea.

Seven hours later, the storm gentled and faded away to the southeast, leaving behind a cleansed and flower-scented evening of stunning, sparkling beauty. Cabrillo stood at his stern rail facing shore and pulled in a doublet-stretching breath, and then another. His pilot joined him, and they looked with admiration at a land that the last two days had enhanced with such promise.

"We must maintain our vigilance," said Cabrillo, "but there is magic in the air tonight, eh, pilot?"

"Be it magic or, as Father Gamboa would maintain, God's majesty, this harbor is magnificent, sir."

"Judging from the health and size of its people, they lack nothing in the way of food or medicine."

"No, indeed, sir. Once we learn their language, perhaps they will share some of their secrets." San Remón added with a grin, "I would not mind adding a few inches to my own stature."

Cabrillo returned his smile, and their conversation wandered from the mysteries of the bay to the needs of the ship and the men, and what lay in the waters and lands ahead. At last they stilled their voices and surrendered to the quiet realm of the sleeping harbor.

Though the following day was a Sunday, Cabrillo didn't want to chance unsettling the natives again by landing a large party, even to attend a Mass. He did allow two small groups to gather firewood, but these men had strict orders to remain very near the shore, and two other boats were kept ready to come to their aid in the event a call was raised. The precaution proved unnecessary and his men returned to their ships without espying a single Indian.

The next day, while the ships awaited an agreeable change in the wind, Cabrillo hoped that peaceful natives would make an appearance, but all remained hidden. Yet the sense of being watched never left him. These people may have moved to what they felt to be a safer distance from their intruders, he thought, but some had remained behind to keep watch over the bay. He longed to visit their village but knew he dared not. Small streams of smoke rose from deep within the lush greenery, greatly tantalizing Cabrillo's curiosity about the ways of these people. Were the customs measurably different from those of the Aztec and Maya? What idols did they worship? What skills did they teach their young? What were their houses like? Were their women attractive? His musings recalled Beatriz' fear that his voyage would lead him to meet the legendary Calafia, and he smiled inwardly before his thoughts were reclaimed by the Indians of this bay. He remembered their favorable impression of Manuel. The blacks aboard his ships must be the first of their kind seen by these natives. He hoped the novelty of the blacks, horses, clothing, weapons, and trade goods would work to their peaceful advantage in the days to come.

When the light of early dawn shone brightly enough to allow one last sweeping gaze over the deserted beach, Cabrillo committed all that he could see to his memory. He delayed no longer the weighing of anchors or setting of sails, and soon the *San Salvador* led the way to the mouth of the harbor. His men were hale and willing after their stay here, and those who had been wounded were healing without complication. Asia and duty beckoned with a renewed will.

Glancing back at the landscape, Cabrillo said, "I leave this place with yearning, Manuel. I hope we will return."

"Perhaps so, Captain-General. Perhaps many times."

"I would dearly love to wander at will in those hills and valleys. Their beauty entices a man to venture closer, with a draw almost as powerful as a striking woman."

Chapter 11

ISLAND ENCOUNTER

Renewing speculations over why men might repeatedly set their world ablaze, the crews watched great billows of smoke rolling upward to mingle with an older, broader layer hanging over the landscape to the east. Since leaving the port of San Miguel they'd been generously favored with three days of fair weather, but as they'd sailed up the coast the fires that generated the gray haze had grown in number and size, signaling a dramatic increase in the number of inhabitants and bringing the seamen to a heightened level of alertness.

As Mateo and Cabrillo also concentrated on the smoke hovering above the coastal hillsides and hollows, the boy asked, "Are they not destroying their land, sir?"

"Fire is not always destructive, Mateo. It can clear and cleanse the earth. Perhaps they are encouraging a crop to grow, but which crop I do not know."

"Then they are farmers, sir?"

"They may not till the land, but they evidently harvest what they can. They hunt too, or they would not have the skins they wear."

"And they fish, sir. There were piles of clamshells on the beach at San Miguel."

"So there were. We have learned a few of their ways, but we still have many questions in need of answers."

La Victoria's lookout cried out, "Land ahead! Five points off the port bow!"

All heads swung to the northwest. The hint of an island was just coming into view. Cabrillo gazed from it to the mainland, estimating the distance at about twenty miles. He immediately ordered their course altered, intent on investigating the island's potential to harbor the ships a safe distance from the populated mainland.

As they drew nearer, another island appeared to the southwest, enticing them farther on, but the wind chose that time to abruptly suspend its force. With little aid given by the current and only an infrequent, ineffective puff of a breeze, the pace of the ships dwindled to a near standstill. For hours they floated, as helpless as three water-soaked logs.

By late afternoon the immobility of his ships was sorely pricking Cabrillo's patience. He'd heard of other ships stagnating in doldrums lasting weeks and eventually costing men their sanities or their lives, and the longer his fleet remained motionless the more these old tales taunted him. He could feel the restiveness growing in his men too. Rather than remain on deck pacing and casting glowers at the inert sails, he headed to his cabin to add notes to his latest map.

He was unhappily surprised to find Father Lezcano sitting in the captain-general's chair and reading aloud to Manuel and Mateo. Upon Cabrillo's entry, these latter two hurriedly rose from the floor. Father Lezcano also swiftly got to his feet, his expression more than a little guilty.

"Please forgive me, sir," he said. "I merely sought a quiet place where I might instruct them for a few minutes."

"And my cabin is the only quiet place on the ship?" Cabrillo demanded in a tone that would have been more aptly pointed at the miserly wind.

"I should have asked your permission to read on the main deck, perhaps, sir. These are words meant to be heard by everyone."

Reining in his testiness somewhat, Cabrillo asked, "What were you reading, Father?"

Father Lezcano handed him the book. "They are new teachings written by a Basque priest called Ignatius de Loyola."

"Ignatius? I have not heard of him."

"Few have, sir. His work has only recently been approved for distribution. You may find him particularly fascinating, Captain-General, since in his youth he was a mounted warrior like yourself."

"A warrior, who became a priest?"

"Indeed, sir. He descended from a noble family and served as a knight until he was badly wounded."

"It is difficult to imagine a knight who is holy enough to write religious works."

"Yes, Captain-General, though, from what I have heard, his earlier life was far from monastic. He discovered the depth of his faith while convalescencing. He has already gained many followers, and not only in Spain. Some call them Jesuits, but they refer to themselves as members of the Society of Jesus."

Eyeing the book and flipping through a few pages, Cabrillo said, "What is the goal of his writings?"

"Helping us and himself to better follow Christ's example."

Cabrillo took his chair and with a gesture offered Father Lezcano the edge of his bunk. "These readings may truly benefit the crew, especially today when our forward progress has been arrested. Although we must not count on miraculous improvements in the overall behavior of seamen, listening to holy teachings might calm them."

"It just might, sir."

"You have my full permission to read on the main deck for a half-hour, Father. But first tell me, does Ignatius recommend any specific means of enhancing faithfulness?"

"Prayers, meditations, and other means of examining our consciences, Captain-General."

"Hmm. Perhaps, Father, you will take me on as one of your students?"

"I would like nothing better, sir."

"Fine. After dinner, then, but before the evening watch. Now, all of you, if you will kindly allow me the private use of my cabin..."

As they were departing Paulo appeared at the door, his arms loaded with plates and utensils with which to set the table. Cabrillo shooed him out with, "Not now, Paulo. The ship lies too calm. I could not eat a bite."

When they had left him with his parchments and ink, he pushed the fatal doldrums from his mind and bent intently over his maps. For a short time he was able to forget the fleet's suspension between two shores and allow memories of the wonders they'd seen to be awakened and recorded. An hour passed, then two, and then his quill suddenly stilled when he felt the ship gently yield as if to a gentle nudge and give a little heave forward.

140

He could anticipate the *San Salvador's* motions as well as Viento's, and he sat alertly as he waited for the soft fluttering of a sail and Master Uribe's orders to adjust the lines. Men's feet beat familiar paths to their positions and strong, eager hands started hauling. By the time Cabrillo reached the stern deck the lines were being tied off. The breeze was weak but he blessed what little there was for giving them enough momentum to advance slowly, slowly toward the nearest island.

The day was growing old and still they were far from an easy rowing distance to the inlet ahead. Even so, expectant looks turned with growing frequency toward Cabrillo. He had no more forgotten his promise to his men than they had, and it was a lovely island, worthy of bearing their ship's name. Scanning the hopeful faces, he said, "We will keep our sails full tonight. God willing, tomorrow our anchors will set in that bay, and at first light I shall go ashore to dub the island *San Salvador.*"

The roar that burst from his crew was loud enough to raise the curious stares of the men aboard nearby *La Victoria*. Cabrillo cupped his hands to his mouth and called out, "Well, Captain Ferrelo, will the farther island be suitable for bearing the name *La Victoria*?"

Having to bellow to be heard above the explosive din raised by his own sailors, Captain Ferrelo shouted back, "Quite suitable, sir!"

Overhearing this exchange and unwilling to omit his crew from the impromptu celebration, especially since his ship had been first to share its name with an island, Captain Correa led his sailors in a robust round of cheers.

Wearing grins, the officers and seamen of the fleet bent their efforts to capturing whatever gust of wind would force the sea to surrender even an inch of distance and bring them closer to land. When stars began to dance overhead the breeze lessened once again, and Cabrillo was forced to accept that any island anchorage was subject to nature's goodwill.

Leaving his boatswain to oversee the watch on this calm evening, Cabrillo dined late with his officers, and Father Lezcano showed up with his book as Manuel and Mateo were clearing the table. "Come in, Father, come in," said Cabrillo. His pilot had been rising to take his leave but quickly found his seat again when the captain-general added,

"I trust you gentlemen do not mind adding to Father Lezcano's group of listeners. Is that agreeable to you, Father?"

"Agreeable, sir? Why, yes. The larger the flock, the happier the shepherd." He opened his pages as the men and boy settled comfortably down to hear the thoughts and recommendations of the priest from Loyola. Father Lezcano began by reading, "Be slow to speak, and do so only after having first listened quietly, so that you may understand the meaning, leanings, and wishes of those who speak to you. Thus you will better know when to speak and when to be silent." At this advice, Cabrillo and his officers carefully avoided eye contact with one another yet managed the rare feat of successfully following this recommendation as Father Lezcano continued on to the next suggestion.

Dawn was just lifting its face above the horizon to reveal the earth in its first gray obscurities when Cabrillo, caught in the throws of another dark dream, rolled from his bunk and hit the deck with a heavy thud. The thump was immediately followed by a loud, angry groan and a clipped obscenity. One step in front of Manuel, Paulo calmly entered as if he'd just received a formal invitation to do so, and set Cabrillo's washing bowl on the table. "Good morning, Captain-General."

Cabrillo gave a curt nod then tossed his blanket back onto his bunk and went to the window. He stood there, his hair in wild disarray and his body clothed in nothing but a linen shirt that hung halfway down his thighs, wordlessly gauging the weather and tide. Allowing his thoughts an additional moment to move from ocean conditions to the shore, he said, "I like the look of that island, Paulo. My feet are itching to wander there."

"Yes, sir. I will bring your breakfast at once."

Cabrillo dressed and ate quickly and within an hour had the fleet lowering its anchors in a lovely cove ringed tightly by steep, rocky hills. Smoke trails rising from a village tucked in with the trees had become visible as they'd neared, and they could now see that the shore was strewn with shells and canoe planks. The captain-general ordered two boats lowered and joined a landing party, as eager as any to explore the bay. A couple of lengths ahead of the other, his launch was twenty yards from shore when Vargas called back from the bow in warning, "Captain-General."

Armed Indians came rushing from the cover of bushes and tall grass, and kept coming. "Still your oars," Cabrillo commanded.

They steadied their boats in place, glancing ashore with heightened consciousness of the capabilities of their own weapons and speculating on the range of the native bows. The beach grew crowded with Indian archers, shouting and gesturing for them to land, but Cabrillo caught glimpses of women and children fleeing farther inland through the greenery and he held his rowers where they were.

Looking back at the ships, Cabrillo affirmed that the other boats were standing by, awaiting his orders. The ships' guns were manned and aimed. Shifting his gaze shoreward again, he spotted several natives nocking arrows to bows, and Vargas and his soldiers raised their guns.

Cabrillo said, "Hold your fire, men. Keep the boat stable."

Standing slowly, he took up an arquebus and a crossbow, held them high above his head and then set them down in the boat with a deliberation that could not be misinterpreted. He instructed his men to lower their armaments as well, and they quickly obeyed. Cabrillo then spread his arms wide open. Speaking in his most calming voice and using words and signs he'd learned from the San Miguel Indians, he said, "Trade. Friend." He repeated this and crossed his arms over his chest. Glances shifted from one warrior to another, and the natives began to lay down their bows and arrows.

As Cabrillo's boats maintained positions of safety a brief discussion took place ashore. Several natives disappeared into the brush and immediately remerged pushing a large, sturdy plank canoe. They launched it into the water and cautiously came abreast of Cabrillo's boat. The men in each vessel eyed one other with tightly controlled curiosity, but Cabrillo broke the impasse by signaling an invitation to accompany them to their ship. To his relief as the boats shifted positions the native canoe fell in line and followed him back to the *San Salvador*.

Nine Indians climbed aboard the flagship, and their trepidation soon gave way to amazement that widened their eyes and heightened the contours of their rich features. Father Lezcano fell in step beside Cabrillo as he showed them his world, highlighting the bercos, bombardetas, capstan, tiller, and whipstaff. Unable to fully conceal his own fascination as they toured the ship, the captain-general took in the powerful naked builds and chevron-shaped facial tattoos of his visitors. He tried to consign to memory the way the hair of several was pinned up with rounded man-shaped splinters of ivory. Their earlobes were also decorated with cylindrical, though much shorter, bones, and their chests displayed artistic arrangements of shells, soapstone, and carved whalebones. Although these Indians had bravely faced them alone, Cabrillo was not yet certain if they were merely warriors or considered chiefs among their people.

When their tour of the ship drew to an end, the guests were seated on the main deck and presented with gifts of beads and cloth, which they received with gracious acknowledgements. Shortly afterward it became evident by their glances ashore that they had no wish to linger. On the contrary, reassured by their welcome the visitors clearly indicated that they were now more than willing to show the men from the sea something of their island. Signing that they would lead the way, they reboarded their canoe, pushed away, and waved for Cabrillo to come along.

This time both of the fleet's boats, now carrying chests of trade goods, landed to a hospitable welcome. A very old man was brought to Cabrillo, and he didn't need Father Lezcano's translation to understand that he too had heard the stories of men like the newcomers arriving east of the mainland shores. He said to his priest, "Word travels faster than the wind among these natives. They will spread news of our coming all along our route to China."

"Then we must hope it is good news they send ahead of us, sir."

Cabrillo questioned the ancient Indian about his people and his neighbors, and the sage seemed happy to candidly share what he knew. While the trading of both information and goods progressed Cabrillo noticed that some native men at the outer rim of the bartering circle had no qualms about letting nimble fingers take possession of any item left unattended, gradually raising the frustration of Cabrillo's sentries. In answer to Vargas's questioning glance, Cabrillo said, "Bring the goods and guards in a little tighter, sergeant-major. There is to be no force used."

Before two hours had passed, Cabrillo had made many notes about his host's culture, which seemed to have advanced a step or two beyond that of their southern neighbors in social complexities, many crafts, and the ability to survive while surrounded by an ever-threatening sea. He had also been able to trade for an impressive collection of shell beads, sea-otter furs, and soapstone vessels.

Spurred by the friendly bartering, and perhaps by the clandestine purloining of a few smaller goods, the native men's sense of comfort with the newcomers soon grew to a level that allowed their women to approach and move freely among them. Initially gladdened by the trust this new development represented, Cabrillo's own comfort became less and less as the intermingling evolved from observing into touching. The women wore nothing more than short, two-piece skirts of woven plants or animal skins. Their hair hung long and loose except where bangs had been cut short above dark brown eyes. A few women bore tattoos similar to those of their men in the shapes of chevrons or wavy lines that ended in arrowheads. Most of the feminine bodies were athletically fine, and this supple attractiveness was proving impossible to ignore.

Within minutes of the interweaving of sexes Cabrillo's sailors began to exhibit a willingness to spread the offspring of Spain among the island maidens with even more enthusiasm than they had extended goodwill to their men, and this eagerness was far from being overlooked by the braves. No one had yet been lured into the bushes, but that could soon change.

Cabrillo noticed that Father Lezcano, with his long dark robe, shaven crown, and manifest good looks, was attracting almost as much attention from the females as Manuel. Although Father Lezcano was trying to maintain a hard-fought forbearance, the women were becoming increasingly curious about the body hidden beneath his robe. As questing hands began to reach for his most intriguing parts Father Lezcano backed away, motioning that he was a holy man and that such activity was forbidden to him. The women did not, or chose not, to understand. One young woman who seemed to be asking something of him with great earnestness now took such a tight hold of his rope belt that he was having difficulty disengaging her. It was clear that his attempts to politely separate himself from her clutches were growing more and more desperate. Highly amusing as it was to see the young priest in such a predicament, Cabrillo took pity on him. Besides, things had gone quite far enough among his crew.

"Father Lezcano," he suddenly ordered in a voice authoritative enough to quell the enthusiasm of both the women and his sailors. "It is time to return to the ships." He stood, bowed and signaled farewell to the old chief, walked over to his priest, presented the woman clinging to him a small hawk's bell, clasped Father Lezcano by the elbow the moment the gift was accepted by the distracted recipient, and steered his priest and crew back toward the boats. Vargas and a couple of soldiers discreetly covered their less than refined retreat, but the Indians showed no sign of anger or intent to pursue them.

Halfway to the ship Father Lezcano mastered his embarrassment sufficiently to mutter under his breath, "I thank you, Captain-General."

Just as quietly, Cabrillo responded with exaggerated seriousness, "I can only sympathize with you, Father. A priest who is irresistible to women carries a heavy burden indeed."

Father Lezcano detected the teasing note in these words and the grin that played at the edge of Cabrillo's mouth. He shook his head and said with as much forbearance as he could gather, "You can have no appreciation for just how heavy, sir."

A sputter of laughter escaped Cabrillo, which he quickly cut off, but he couldn't help adding, "We had better head back toward the mainland. With luck, the women there will be less tempted by your particular charms."

146

Chapter 12

WOCHA'S GREETING

"Armed men approaching in a canoe, Captain-General," Uribe announced as he entered the relative dimness of the steerage compartment.

Cabrillo lifted his eyes from the route chart atop the binnacle. "Thank you, Master Uribe. I will be at the railing in a moment." He finished his postings carefully but quickly and strode to the waist of the ship.

He had had little opportunity to admire the bay they were entering, but the great clouds of smoke that hung above the landscape made it clear that others had found it lovely well before their arrival. He had anticipated interaction with the natives, and now he could see the first visitors coming toward him. These five seemed very little afraid as they paddled up to the ship, and despite their weapons they gave no outward sign of threat. As if to confirm this impression, they lowered their bows and arrows to the bottom of their canoe.

As their craft was being secured to the *San Salvador's* side, Cabrillo noted that the craft was slightly shorter than the one that had come to the ship off San Salvador Island the day before. To Cabrillo's eye, the natives were quite comparable in appearance to the features and dress of the islanders.

"Help them aboard," he ordered.

The first Indian climbed the lower rungs of the ladder and then hesitated, as if having second thoughts about entering the belly of this floating fortress, but two sailors took hold of his arms and lifted him onto the deck with one mighty heave. The other four followed with noticeably more grace, and the group was soon swaying with the roll of the main deck and looking around for a leader with which to deal. Cabrillo and Father Lezcano approached and addressed them as am-

147

bassadors. As had happened with each new Indian encounter, the natives began by signing the story that was now anticipated, that there were men like the strangers roaming inland. This time, however, the story held a significant variation. Cabrillo and Father Lezcano exchanged glances, "Will you please ask him again, Father, where the men were?"

Father Lezcano obeyed, and the leader of the natives signed, "In the lands of the north."

"North?" Cabrillo said more to himself than to anyone else and turned his head in that direction, considering this possibility as his brow furrowed with concern.

More questions were posed but nothing more specific about their claim could be learned. Anticipating many more such visits during their short stay in this harbor, Cabrillo did not attempt to prolong this one. After gifts had been offered and accepted, the Indians reboarded their canoe and turned away from the flagship.

As the officers watched the craft glide swiftly toward the beach, Cabrillo said softly to Pilot Remón and Master Uribe, "Perhaps each new group tells us of the other bearded men merely to gain reassurance that we bear no ill intentions, but I can not help suspecting that they do so to tempt us away from their land to search them out. It is a clever trick. Although the tale may be just such an enticement, if these men to the north *are* real, who might they be? We should have been told if any Spaniards had been sent, by sea or on foot, ahead of us. And if they left Mexico after we did there is very little chance they have outdistanced us."

"Perhaps they are Portuguese, sir," asked Master Uribe, "or the English?"

"Yes, either one. Whoever it is, if indeed it is anyone, we must be prepared to face enemy guns as well as hostile arrows."

"Yes, sir."

Cabrillo's attention drifted upward and was captured by the eastern skies. "By heaven, look at that smoke. It mars these valleys. Doubtless our priests will wish to name this place after a saint, but there is one way to express its appearance. We shall call it Baia de los Fumos."

"Very fitting, sir."

"I hope such smoke does not dog us all the way up this coast to China. When we leave tomorrow, let us hope it does not follow."

148

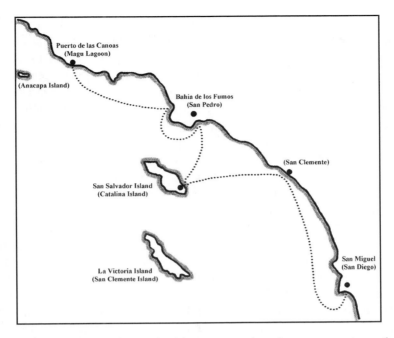

Hugging the coastline and taking care to chart its every contour, the morning allowed Cabrillo to record a shore that swept sharply westward, then to the north, and finally arced northeastward into a huge bay. It was so enticing a harbor that Cabrillo put down his quill and allowed himself to become as enamored as his crew. The breeze had whisked much of the smoke far to the east, refreshing air and men alike. After a moment of pure appreciation, he said with a sigh to his pilot, "If there has ever been an Eden-like place upon which the fable of Calafia was founded, it is surely here."

The light was already dwindling by the time their ships had come to rest within the bay's entrance, but Cabrillo could still discern groves of trees clustering along every feature of the land, greenery beyond description lushly intensifying the valleys and flatlands. He could also see and hear that they were not alone. A sizeable village lay not far down the beach, but no one appeared in the open nearby and no canoe approached the ships. Anxious to discover who lived in so blessed a land, Cabrillo intended to direct the fleet up the harbor in the first light of morning. That night, for a change, he slept in deep peace.

Very early his curiosity was rewarded when the settlement opened up before his approaching ships, made up of large round houses that rivaled many of the impressive Indian dwellings Cabrillo had known in Mexico. He ordered their anchors lowered before the village, which lay within the embrace of a broad valley. The appearance of their ships caused an immediate stirring among the local population, but it was obvious from the lack of panic that their arrival had been anticipated. These people looked anything but unnerved.

As sails were still being furled, Cabrillo began to count the number of plank canoes sliding into the water. Five, ten, fifteen, with more and more coming, and each canoe carried ten to thirteen determined looking men. Although no weapon had been raised Cabrillo was wary of the simultaneous approach of so many natives. "Sergeant-major, have our soldiers armed and standing by. Master gunner, ready the swivel guns. Slow and easy as we go. Make no show of battle." Pilot San Remón, Master Uribe, and Father Lezcano came up to the captain-general, and Cabrillo cast them a look that said, "Brace yourselves."

The Indians paddled straight and fast toward the ships and, as they neared, Cabrillo accurately guessed them to be a nation of people he had never seen. When the first canoe reached the *San Salvador* he addressed the natives in a tone both friendly and commanding. "We welcome you, men of California!" The lead canoe slowed ten feet from the ship, and its fellow crafts drew up and held to a similar distance. Nearly two hundred pairs of cautious, intelligent, inquiring eyes gazed up at him.

Keeping his own glance locked on the oldest man in the first canoe, the one wearing a cape of fox fur intricately decorated with shells, Cabrillo said to his priest, "Father, please translate for us." To the chief, he said, "We greet you in peace. We come from far south to meet the people of this land. We wish to trade as friends."

The old Indian he had addressed, whether official leader or not, responded to Cabrillo with great dignity. He said through signs that his people had heard of their coming from their neighbors, but months before they had learned that people of his kind had arrived at a large river that runs north to south and can be reached by a seven days' journey eastward.

Cabrillo said aside to his pilot, "The river that Ulloa charted, possibly."

Beckoning the man in the fox cape to the outer edge of the ship's railing, Cabrillo selected from the chest of trade goods a metal bell the size of a fist and a flat yellow glass bead suspended from a blue ribbon. These he handed into aged hands, along with signals of goodwill.

The native received them appreciatively, and without delay the captain-general had either small hawk's bells or beads distributed to each man in his canoe. These minor gifts produced such smiles and exclamations of delight that Cabrillo offered a silent prayer of thanks that the fleet had brought along so great a supply.

Before the canoes turned back toward the beach the natives invited their visitors by voice and gesture to follow in their wakes. Glancing ashore and noting the hundreds of villagers gathered, Master Uribe said, "They could wipe out a landing party in a blink, sir."

"Indeed, but they give no indication of aggression." With a hint of a smile, Cabrillo settled the matter by saying, "I had better leave my gunners in the hands of the best shipmaster on this sea. Keep us well covered."

"I shall do just that, sir, but please take care."

Ordering a launch from both the *San Miguel* and *La Victoria* to accompany him ashore, adding the restriction that their captains remain with their ships, Cabrillo, Vargas, Manuel, Father Lezcano, and six soldiers boarded their boat and pushed off.

Amid a great crowd of milling natives, Cabrillo waded ashore where Vargas and his soldiers quickly enclosed him in a protective ring. "Keep your weapons low and your hearts calm, men," commanded Cabrillo, his own heart pumping at a slightly elevated rhythm. Parting the fence-like lines of men one after another, he walked toward an Indian he had not yet seen but whose bearing, dress, and company proclaimed him to be eminent. As Cabrillo neared to take the measure of this chieftain, the word that came foremost to his mind was, "striking." His handsomely distinguished, beardless face was framed by a dense mane of hair as white as milk except the very ends where it darkened to the color of ash. Whatever advancement of age was implied by the whiteness of his hair was completely absent from the taught muscles and skin of his belly, arms, and legs. A small flint knife with a wooden handle inlaid with mother-of-pearl was secured horizontally by a thin, beaded thong against his scalp. A brilliant array of black, copper, white, and red feathers fanned out like a peacock's display from the back of his head. He wore a cape of white fur, tied at the throat and open across the chest, which hung to his ankles. A loincloth painted with geometric images reached nearly to his knees. Simple sandals constructed of hemp-like fibers protected his feet. Coming to a halt in the sand, Cabrillo's concentration rose higher and momentarily fell upon the tiniest shells of pink, orange, and white that had been intricately woven into a breastwork that adorned the chief's chest. When the captain-general's gaze lifted he saw full lips pursed in deep concentration and eyes that stared back intently from beneath thick, black brows: eyes that reflected a sharp and discriminating intelligence.

Under the scrutiny of the chieftain Cabrillo felt suddenly gratified that he had allowed Paulo to have his way when insisting that he wear some of his finer clothing for this meeting. The captain-general, however, had not been willing to relinquish his polished chest plate or trade his helmet for a plumed hat. He hoped his armor now gave a good impression as it flashed brightly in the morning sun.

Allowing an instinctive nudge to compel his feet farther forward, Cabrillo walked up to the Indian, spread his arms wide, and embraced him. Surprised but quickly recovering, the chief returned the stranger's hug. Each man released the other but only to clasp forearms and take a moment longer to evaluate the mind and soul of the man before him. With their close gazes meeting on a level plane, Cabrillo hid nothing of his own curiosity or desire for friendliness. The chief's face became just as open and hopeful as he studied the foreigner.

When at last they relaxed their grips, Cabrillo stepped back and relayed through signs and words, "We greet the people of this land and wish to trade with you in peace."

Father Lezcano interpreted the chief's reply, saying, "We welcome you, men of the sea. Come, and we will trade."

Following the chief's lead, Cabrillo, his men, and the entire village made their way along a sandy path between large dome-shaped houses covered with woven thatch. Knowing his disappearance from the beach would cause uneasiness among his shipboard officers but sensing very little danger and enjoying a great thrill to be entering the village, Cabrillo took in every human, canoe, dwelling, plant, basket, tool, and fire pit he passed. His fingers began to itch for his quill.

152

In front of a house big enough to accommodate fifty people, the chief stopped and signaled for Cabrillo to be seated near the center of an immense rectangular mat that had been placed on the open ground. He complied, with Father Lezcano and Manuel taking flanking positions on each side. The chief sat down facing Cabrillo and his entourage settled around and behind him. Once the shifting of bodies began to still, Cabrillo ordered Vargas' men to bring forward a chest of trade goods and place it nearby. But before the bartering activities commenced, however, the chief raised one of his hands and began to speak.

Listening and watching attentively, Father Lezcano waited for the chief to pause and explained in undertones to Cabrillo, who had already understood much of what had been communicated, "He says his people live on this coast and on the islands that lie northwest of here, sir. I can not be sure, but I believe his name is Wocha."

Since the chief patiently awaited a reply from Cabrillo, the captain-general pointing at the native leader as he asked, "Wocha?"

"Wocha!" he said firmly as he placed a hand upon his chest.

Cabrillo nodded and repeated the name with much respect. Then the captain-general said, "Cabrillo!" using the same tone and patting his own chest.

Wocha pronounced his name accurately, and both men smiled in satisfaction at this small victory.

Now that the initial formalities had been conducted, Wocha, a word Cabrillo would later learn meant only "leader" in the Chumash tongue, told them with evident sincerity that the bearded men who had landed by the big river could be reached in seven days.

Confronted anew by this recurring issue and reminded of his orders to offer aid to Coronado, Cabrillo asked, "Father, can you discover anything more specific, such as the name of their leader or where these men might now be found?"

The priest tried, but the chief had evidently provided them with all that he knew.

Torn between sending a couple of his men on what could well be a fool's errand or worse and failing to attempt a connection with someone that might need their aid, Cabrillo heeded Master Uribe's urgings for caution. He said to his priest, "Tell him, father, that I will write words upon a paper that can be taken to the bearded men. I will tell them of the friendship of Wocha and these people. If I do this, ask if two of his runners will deliver it to the men at the big river?"

The terms "write" and "paper" challenged the priest's translating skills, but soon the idea of their purpose was roughly conveyed.

Fascinated by such wondrous claims, Wocha wished to know more before consenting, and Cabrillo had Manuel pull from his pouch the writing materials he'd brought for his master's use. Wocha learned forward and villagers gathered closer for a better look as Cabrillo spread a parchment sheet atop his writing board, dipped his quill, wrote the word "Wocha" and handed the sheet to the chief. Pointing to the word, Cabrillo pronounced it slowly and then aimed his finger at the chief.

Wocha's brows lifted in wonder as he examined the curling, looping line. Giving the paper back, he said, "Cabrillo," and motioned for that designation to be written. When the new word rested beneath Wocha's title, Cabrillo again presented the sheet to the chief. So impressed was Wocha with this magnificent process that he began to point at people, both red and white, and then inanimate objects, telling Cabrillo the native names and then watching absorbedly as the captain-general wrote each of these down. Whenever he could, Father Lezcano helped provide a Spanish translation to a name, until Cabrillo, nearly as delighted as his host, had filled the first page of a primitive lexicon.

Pleased as he was at this excellent exchange, Cabrillo had not forgotten the issue at hand. After having Manuel carefully store the filled page in his oversized pouch, he again wrote the word Wocha on a clean sheet of parchment. This time, he made the letters as artistically decorative as his talents allowed and handed the page to the chief as a gift.

Wocha took the parchment from Cabrillo with gravest gratitude.

Cabrillo said to Father Lezcano, "Please ask him if he will now agree to send runners with a written message to the bearded men, the ones he calls Taquimine."

Father Lezcano translated this and then conveyed the chief's careful response, "What will your message say?"

Nodding his approval of this query, Cabrillo spoke as he wrote, "I, Juan Rodriguez Cabrillo, on this the tenth day of October in the year of Our Lord 1542, have landed with my ships in a bay along the coast of California that lies at 35 1/3°. Here, we have met native people who have shown us welcome and friendship.

"If you are Spanish, or friendly to the Spanish realm, we are willing to assist you if such aid is within our power and the scope of our mission. Please send us word of your location and intentions." Intentionally omitting specifics about their own mission and course in case the letter was delivered into enemy hands, Cabrillo closed and signed it.

Wocha had attentively observed the creation of the missive and now listened to its translation by the priest. He appeared to find nothing objectionable, so Cabrillo rolled his letter within a waterproof oilskin and tied the bundle securely closed. He then handed the dispatch to Wocha, who accepted it with a satisfied bob of his head. Calling a youth to his side, he ordered the runner to take one companion and carry the message with all haste to the Taquimine who had traveled north up the great river.

As Cabrillo watched the young man choose a friend and the two trot away, he fervently hoped the letter wouldn't fall into English or Portuguese hands. In the unlikely case that it did, he was determined that his ships and men would be ready. Wherever the letter might land, its result would lay far ahead of today.

To repay Wocha's kindness, Cabrillo presented him with two empty sheets of parchment, a quill, and a small, lidded bottle of his ink, all of which pleased the chief immensely. Responding to a small voice from behind, Wocha turned to briefly face the group of seven women, of varying ages but notable beauty, who had been watching the proceedings from a discreet distance. Cabrillo had not failed to notice that the youngest of these had seemed deeply interested in his writing, and she now approached and softly asked Wocha if she could hold the paper with the chief's name upon it, which he allowed her to do.

Facing Cabrillo again, Wocha said with understated pride, "These women are my wives, these and two others. Cabrillo, do your wives travel in your great canoe?"

Withholding any hint of amusement, Cabrillo said, "I have one wife, Wocha, and she is at our home far away."

Visibly concerned by such news, after a moment's thought Wocha gave a quick order to one of his wives that Cabrillo and Father Lezcano did not catch, and the woman moved away to drift quietly among the listening crowd. While Wocha evidently awaited her return, Cabrillo

155

offered him two matching goblets of etched brass. The chief was still expressing his satisfaction when his wife reappeared accompanied by four attractive women, all of them under what Cabrillo guessed to be the age of sixteen. The girls stood in their short skirts with their eyes cast downward and their thick hair draping their chests from shoulders to waists, their manner as demure as any virginal noblewoman of Spain.

As Wocha spoke magnanimously to Cabrillo, Father Lezcano hesitated a second or two in awkward discomfort before finally explaining, "Sir, he says that these women…agree to be your wives." The priest fought to keep his features blank as shuffling and mumbling started circulating among the sailors.

Cabrillo had caught an inkling of Wocha's intentions without the need of his priest's assistance, and he stilled his men's muttering momentarily by saying, "Please thank him for me, father, and explain that it is not our custom to take more than one wife."

But before the priest could comply, Wocha forestalled any declination of his gift with an assertion that Father Lezcano was compelled to convey, "A great man like Cabrillo, a man who comes from faraway lands in great ships and makes magic messages on dried skins, such a man must have many wives."

The insistence in Wocha's voice gave Cabrillo a moment's pause, but in a respectful tone he tried again. "Father Lezcano, please tell Wocha that his women are beautiful and his gift generous, but that this is not our practice."

Recognizing Cabrillo's hesitation, a realization seemed to suddenly cross Wocha's mind. Father Lezcano had barely finished translating before the chief nodded in acceptance and understanding, then he gazed over the crowd, spotted the one for whom he was searching, and beckoned that person forward. A moment later the most spectacular looking man Cabrillo had ever seen stood directly in front of him.

The muttered words, "Holy Mother save us," escaped from Father Lezcano. Several of Cabrillo's men shifted uneasily. Manuel snapped his gaping mouth closed and kept still.

The slender young man's features were stunningly fine and his feet and hands were small to the point of daintiness. His effeminate appearance was greatly enhanced by the fact that he wore the clothing and adornments of their women. His hair feathers were even

156

more flamboyant than those worn by Wocha, and his many strings of tiny shells hung almost to the ground. He was beautiful, and he stood just as the girls had, submissively awaiting the chief's command.

Father Lezcano whispered, "Captain-General, I believe the chief is offering—"

"I know what he is offering, Father," Cabrillo said evenly. "Thank him kindly, but tell him our customs and our God strictly forbid a man from taking pleasure with another man."

Forcing his expression and voice to a calmer state, Father Lezcano relayed this message.

The priest's words were first met with confused disbelief, and then Wocha's friendly manner grew guarded, even suspicious.

Making an attempt to keep things from growing threatening, Cabrillo said quickly, "Your offers are most kind, Wocha. But I must follow the wishes of my king and my God. I must lead my men by my own actions."

Mollified only somewhat by this explanation, the chief let his gaze drift to Manuel, as it had several times during the meeting. He pointed to the black man and asked, "Is this man a leader among you?"

Cabrillo responded with, "He is not, but he is a strong and faithful friend."

Wocha grunted once in acknowledgement and said, again causing Father Lezcano to translate with reluctance. "Since he is no leader, your other men need not follow him. It would please me if he stays in our village tonight. I will give him strong, healthy women. In the new year they will bear his children, and his blood will add life to our people. This will make our friendship strong."

Momentarily amazed, Manuel managed to say a little too readily, "I am willing, sir. For the sake of the fleet."

"The fleet indeed," Cabrillo muttered with an eyebrow cocked. Seeing no other way to avoid offending Wocha and much to the disappointment of his other men for having been excluded from the offer, Cabrillo accepted on behalf of Manuel.

This seemed to satisfy Wocha greatly. He spoke to the girls still standing nearby in a manner that suggested he was bestowing a great privilege. All four of the young women came cautiously forward to sit near to Manuel, occasionally glancing at him as if he were a newly arrived god who had just chosen them as consorts.

Under his breath, Cabrillo said to Manuel, "Just one night. Tomorrow I expect you to be at the beach for the claiming ceremony. And if you value your hide, not a word of your exploits to the other men."

Manuel hoped his tone held the contriteness of a smuggler standing before a hanging judge as he replied, "Of course, sir."

Cabrillo noticed Father Lezcano suddenly stiffen as Wocha's speculative attention moved from Manuel and fell upon him. The priest sat very still and avoided meeting the chief's gaze. Much to Father Lezcano's relief, Cabrillo spoke up and agilely turned everyone's thoughts to the less sensitive practice of trading goods rather than sexual favors.

The next hour was spent exchanging as many ideas as goods, with Cabrillo having Father Lezcano record many of Wocha's words. In addition to a large quantity of fish, the Chumash had maize, furs, nets, thread, shells, fine twisted rope, and seal meat with which to barter. After much lively bargaining that had replenished food stores for his crews and horses, Cabrillo ordered his men to receive what newly acquired merchandise could be gathered quickly. Wocha would have the rest brought to the boats the following morning.

As their negotiations were drawing to a close he asked the chief a question that had been nagging at him for some days, "Why do your people burn the earth?"

To this uneducated question, Wocha replied tolerantly, "We burn the grass so many acorns can be gathered. During the next moon we will find acorns enough to last until the following harvest. Burning also brings animals to eat the new grass and we hunt them."

Both Wocha and Cabrillo posed many other questions, and all were answered to the best of their limited communication skills. As their meeting drew near its conclusion Cabrillo formally introduced Father Lezcano and did his best to explain his role among their people. Wocha grasped the priest's position at once and brought forth his own holy man.

Father Lezcano, showing the shaman diligent respect, explained the basic tenets of the Christian faith. As the descriptions became more clearly understood, the shaman's face revealed cautious fascination. The priest then placed a rosary in Wocha's hand, explaining with the beautiful simplicity of a faith-filled man, "When you pray to Our God, he will hear your words. He loves all people."

Accepting the rosary deferentially, Wocha distinguished this gift from the many others he'd received by placing it around his neck and allowing the crucifix to rest among his shells upon his bare chest.

Not entirely comfortable with so sacred an object being used for personal adornment, especially prior to the baptism of its owner, Father Lezcano had the good sense to keep his misgivings to himself.

Judging that the appropriate moment had come, Cabrillo rose to his feet, followed by his men. With numerous good wishes exchanged they took leave of their host, his people, and Manuel. Before starting back toward their boats Cabrillo said in parting to Manuel, his mouth twitching, "You have your musket but use it only if these women threaten to wear the very life out of you."

Father Lezcano asked uneasily, "Do you think there may be any real danger to him, sir?"

"I do not, or I would not leave him here, but we will keep watch throughout the night." To Manuel, he said, "If we hear a shot, you will have us beside you very quickly."

"Yes, sir. I know I will. Thank you, Captain-General."

"You realize that every man of the fleet will be cursing your name tonight."

He grinned a little ruefully, but only a little. "I know that too, sir."

"You had better be off. Your women are waiting."

As Cabrillo passed the last of the native homes, he said in speculation, "Look at the size of these houses, Father. At least four dozen pairs of eyes will likely watch every move Manuel makes tonight. Somehow, that offers a bit of comfort to the rest of us."

Chapter 13

DELICATE AFFAIRS

Cabrillo's landing party climbed to the flagship's main deck and Pilot San Remón asked with concern, "I do not see Manuel, sir. Is he remaining ashore?"

Motioning his pilot to the less crowded quarterdeck, Cabrillo said, "Their chief wanted him to stay the night."

"Indeed, sir? What for?"

"To add strength to their people, physically as well as spiritually, I believe, in the form of future offspring."

Both surprised and amused, the pilot said, "And he was willing to do his utmost to satisfy this lofty responsibility, I presume?"

"More than willing."

"How good of him to avail himself."

Spotting Father Lezcano surreptitiously watching, Cabrillo said, "Yes, well, our good priest does not wholly approve of the arrangement."

"Well, sir, he is a priest."

They both smiled and soon drifted off to see to their duties.

Word of Manuel's mission ashore spread with the rapidity of the plague from man to man and ship to ship, and throughout the long hours of darkness many a sailor conjectured about his activities. Cabrillo was heartened that no musket shot rang out to disturb the quietness.

The next afternoon just prior to conducting a formal rite of possession in the village the natives called Xucu, and which Cabrillo would christen Pueblo de las Canoas, Father Lezcano entered the captain-general's cabin and asked casually enough, "It has been some time, sir, and I was wondering if you wish to confess prior to claiming this land in the name of Our Lord?"

Cabrillo tossed back a look that implied Father Lezcano was sorely trying his tolerance and said, "I do not relish the position of having a priest aboard my ship, a priest young enough to be my son, whom I have already had flogged, no less, and who has since developed such an admirable nature that his friendship has become quite valuable to me. Yet there you stand, feeling perfectly free to use heavenly authority in an attempt to modify my behavior beyond all appropriate bounds!"

Not the least ruffled, Father Lezcano replied, "It is only my objective, sir, to modify your behavior so that it falls *within* appropriate bounds."

"You are toying with my words, Father."

"Only to serve God, Captain-General, and you. Do you wish to confess now, sir?"

Cabrillo cast an unconvincing glower. "I should say no, to remind you of your place."

Father Lezcano answered him with a saintly smile.

Rolling his eyes and shaking his head, Cabrillo did so with such a degree of helpless acquiescence that it delivered the same response as a nod.

Concealing his satisfaction, the priest said, "We should have just enough time before heading ashore for the ceremony."

"Time enough to confess my sins, perhaps, but far from long enough to save my soul. Oh, very well, you brigand of a priest."

Afterward, not that he would have admitted it to Father Lezcano, Cabrillo discerned a closer sense of peace; a forgiveness he felt he did not deserve but wanted to grasp just the same. The weight of his responsibility to his God, his king, and even his men felt slightly lightened.

Heading ashore, he found Manuel waiting, as previously ordered, and his ex-slave fell into step beside him. His black face and body looked as if he'd been chained to oars in a three-day tempest, but Cabrillo had little time to question him before the ritual began. Manuel stood close by his commander and refrained from glancing toward the crowd of natives.

While presiding over the claiming of Puebla de las Canoas the captain-general was touched by the splendidly mild, sunny morning that wrapped them all in its benevolence. He would have loved to delay leaving, scaling the nearby hills, trekking up the river's course, swimming in the nearby lagoon, and learning more of the Indians' ways. But that was not to be, not now. At the rites' conclusion, he added a silent prayer that the future would allow him to come back and take all the time he wished here.

The others began to disperse, and Cabrillo found a moment to eye Manuel again. "Heaven help you, man. If you were a horse I would say you have been ridden nearly to death."

"That is not so very far from the truth, sir. I'm bone tired."

"You are not trying to say you regret last night?"

"Well, no, sir, I can't say such a thing as that. I *am* sorry if what I did was sinful, but a man could have no pleasanter duty on earth." Glancing up at the group of Indians that seemed unable to shift its attention away from him, Manuel added, "I must admit, sir, being watched by so many while... while a man is... well, it makes things more uneasy than it ought to be."

"Uneasy. Yes, I am sure it would. Still," he nodded toward Manuel's clustered admirers, "all signs point to your having performed admirably under trying conditions." Cabrillo's devilish tone pulled an embarrassed smile from Manuel.

"Come, there will be no rest for anyone today, especially not you. The men must be given no excuse to foster their envy of your exploits. There is work enough for all if we are to finish repairing the ships before we can depart. And, Manuel, do not let the day pass without confessing before Father Lezcano. Our priest particularly desires to perform absolutions today."

Manuel's smile dissolved into an expression of dread. "Yes, sir, I'll confess everything, but that may take quite a little time."

Cabrillo chuckled softly and clapped Manuel on the back as they went to join their men.

The routines of scraping, caulking, washing, sealing, oiling, patching, carving, trimming, and knotting continued in earnest with every hand put to good use. Manuel was so constantly bombarded with prodding and questioning by his fellow crewmen that Cabrillo finally decided he'd had enough. At mid-afternoon he set off with Dr. Fuentes, Father Lezcano, Manuel, two village healers, and a small contingent of guards to scout the surrounding area for native foods and medicinal herbs. As they hiked along well-worn paths Cabrillo listened attentively to the descriptions of a valley many miles inland where maize and game were plentiful. Farther still, he was told, a tall mountain range divided the landscape, and he recorded these along with every other discovery made during their frequent stops to collect plants.

To Dr. Fuentes and Cabrillo's fascination, plant life here was almost limitless in how it provided medicinal benefits to the Indians skilled in their use. They saw only a few species that the natives described along their track, since much of the medicinal flora was acquired by trading with tribes to the north and east. But upon their return to the village, they were shown many more curatives in their dried state. Cabrillo and his physician learned that the leaves of maple trees, wild ginger, giant hyssop, ragweed, columbine, the roots and leaves of yarrow, the twigs of greasewood, the leaves and bark of alder trees, the needles and bark of fir trees, the roots and juice of angelica, the blossoms of cottonweed, the juice of milkweed, the roots of balsam, as well as the parts of seemingly countless other plants held medicinal secrets. By the time they returned to the ships, Cabrillo's notes and drawings filled five pages of his parchment.

Upon his arrival at the beach he could plainly see that the other officers had done a fine job of keeping the men to their tasks. Already the ships presented themselves more respectably. If the work continued at this pace, they should be able to set sail the day after tomorrow.

Espying Cabrillo, Captain Ferrelo approached him and said eagerly, "Captain-General, I have been studying the construction of the native canoes, and I would like to share a discovery. Will you come with me, sir?"

They walked with a few Chumash men to the side of a plank canoe, where Captain Ferrelo crouched down and pointed to the seams. "Look at the sealant, sir. If I understand the natives correctly, they call it *yop* and it is a mixture of pine pitch and an ingredient called *chapopote*. The quality seems extraordinary, sir, much better than pitch alone."

Cabrillo ran his hands over the tightly joined lines, noting with fascination the tough flexibility of the black sealant. "Where does the second ingredient come from, Captain Ferrelo?"

"I will be happy to show you, sir."

They didn't have far to go before stopping beside a pool of smelly, shiny, thick, black goo. Cabrillo asked in amazement, "It just seeps from the ground?"

"It does, sir. There are a number of these springs nearby."

Cabrillo bent down and touched the tip of his fingers at the edge of the pool, then rubbed the warm tar-like substance between them, evaluating its elasticity and strength. "This is a marvel, Captain Ferrelo. A true marvel."

He stood and questioned a native about the durability of the sealant, and the response was enthusiastic gestures meaning, "Strong! Good!"

"I have noticed that they use the yop to seal more than canoes, sir," said Ferrelo. "They turn large abalone shells into bowls and tightly woven baskets into drinking bottles. It seems to be highly serviceable."

"Then it is worth investigating further. Attempt to trade for a number of barrels so we can test it thoroughly, Captain. Use it on a launch first. If it withstands the sea well, as it appears it will, we will seal the ships with it."

To Cabrillo's caulkers' delight, the people of Wocha's village willingly accepted several pairs of scissors in exchange for the asphaltum and helped load two barrels aboard each ship.

Hoping to repay a portion of Wocha's magnanimity, Cabrillo invited the chief and two men of his choosing to dine with him, his captains, and his priests that evening. So large a company crowded the snug cabin and makeshift table but all who gathered proved themselves most congenial, especially his officers after taking up their small glasses of wine. At Wocha's first taste of the deep crimson liquid, Cabrillo could see that the chief was trying politely to hide his unfavorable reaction. Much more to his liking was the salty smoothness of Cabrillo's esteemed olives, as well as the sweet crustiness of a baked dessert filled with spiced ground almonds. Wocha had contributed to the feast by bringing maguey, fresh clams, and fish aboard. And although Cabrillo had noticed that the natives generally ate their fish raw, the chief was cordial enough to allow his catches to be cooked by Paulo. He even made a show of approving of the garlic-flavored outcome. Having no appreciation for how to cook the maguey leaves in anything like an impressive manner, Paulo tactfully placed these out of sight.

More fascinating to the chief than the food were the dishes and trays it was served on. He fingered and eyed each piece of silver, glass, and china within his range, especially his delicate glass wine chalice. Much to the chief's delight, Cabrillo offered him this goblet for his small collection. To reciprocate, Wocha removed the finest of his shell necklaces and handed it to his host.

"Here, now," said Cabrillo, truly moved, "this is something I shall indeed treasure. I shall think of you, Wocha, every time I look at it." Pleasing the chief even more than the sincerity of his words, Cabrillo tied the decoration around his neck and patted it proudly.

Between bites and drinks, the captain-general questioned Wocha further about the surrounding land and people. Wocha responded freely, sharing that many Chumash villages such as his lined the shores to the north. He described the terrain, flora, and fauna that they could expect to find. Tantalizingly, he spoke of the great river to the far north, and Cabrillo prayed that it was actually the mouth of the strait that ran all the way to the Atlantic Ocean, not a mere river.

Having noticed a small nugget that served as a decorative plug in one of Wocha's ears, Cabrillo now asked about the location of any gold in the vicinity.

The chief explained thoughtfully, "My people trade for small pieces of the sun stone but it has little value. It is too soft to make a good knife. Others bring it here from far inland."

This explanation held no real surprise, since very little gold had been seen among Wocha's people.

As the table was being cleared the discussion turned to the topic that evidently most fascinated Wocha. "Tell me more about your one God," he signed. "What are his powers? Why does he wish you to place the cross on the beach? How are men chosen to serve him?"

Fathers Gamboa and Lezcano gladly spent some time answering these and other questions about their faith, providing Wocha with a great deal to contemplate. As the lamp wicks shortened with the evening, Cabrillo drew their conversation to a close. "We have much work tomorrow, Wocha."

The chief asked, "Do you need help with your work, Cabrillo?"

"With the trading, Wocha. We must gather all that is needed so that our ships may leave in two days. Also, you have seen our horses. I wish to bring them ashore, but they must only be handled by my men. Can this be done?"

Wocha said, "My people will only watch. They will not touch your animals." He then looked up at Manuel, who had been among those silently waiting on them. "I have heard that many children may be born to mark the coming of your people. I hope their skin will be the color of the night sky."

Manuel had the grace to remain soundless as he studied the walls of the chamber. When Cabrillo shifted his gaze and noticed the reddening of Mateo's sun bronzed cheeks, he realized that even the boy had understood what Manuel had been up to ashore.

The captain-general rose from his seat and parted cordially from his guests, and after they'd left Mateo was allowed to fall asleep in the corner. Only Manuel, Father Lezcano, and Cabrillo lingered to talk awhile longer.

"I offer my congratulations on such a successful evening, sir," said Father Lezcano.

"Successful? In many respects, yes, but I doubt Governor Mendoza would deem it so. What of the Seven Cities of Gold? How far must we sail before we hear corroborative word of it? And yet, if the river Wocha described to us is the Strait of Anián, its discovery might prove more valuable than mountains of gold."

Cabrillo toyed with the burgundy liquor in his glass, swirling it gently and watching the play of the lamplight within and around it. He took a sip and said to Father Lezcano, "Your interpreting skills are improving greatly, my dear priest. I find myself hoping we meet many more of these Indians along our way."

"Simply because of my interpreting talents, sir?"

Cabrillo smiled, saying, "The abundance of their generosity is very welcome as well. And I appreciate their obvious intelligence."

"They do possess that, sir, but some of their ways are incomprehensible to me. I have been wondering, when we first met Wocha, when you declined accepting one of his women and he offered you the youth instead, you seemed little shocked by his proposal. Was I mistaken?"

"No, Father, I was not surprised. I have read about this custom before. Hernando de Alarcón's reports were quite explicit on the subject, which he observed in a village along the Colorado River."

"It must be widespread if it extends so far."

166

"Evidently so. According to Alarcón, the son of the village chief was one of four men chosen to serve his people by offering himself carnally. These few men were strictly forbidden from having sex with women but had to make themselves available to every marriageable young man of the area. They received no payment but were welcome to take whatever they needed for survival from any house in the village. When one of them died, the next male child born was named as his successor and reared for that specific role. This custom is evidently meant to secure the virginity of their unmarried women, and it may succeed to some extent."

Father Lezcano harrumphed and said, "Their goal is set at a disgraceful price, sir."

"Not to them. Perhaps this tradition so astonishes our own people because it is carried out very openly. And yet, we cannot deny that sexual interactions have occurred between some men of the sea and of our land too, for that matter, since time began."

"But, sir, such activity can not be condoned."

"Trysts of any kind can cause trouble on a ship, and the law in this case is clear. Our faith and our society denounce such a practice, but to these people it is useful, even admirable."

Father Lezcano shook his head and tactfully turned the topic back to the language of the Chumash before a knock sounded at the door.

"Enter," said Cabrillo.

Pilot San Remón closed the door behind him, bowed, and said reluctantly, "Captain-General, a man was just caught sleeping on watch."

Cabrillo's chest sank an inch, but he asked with resignation. "Who was it?"

"Young Battista, sir."

"Curse him, he is a good man."

"Yes, sir, and he has been working like a mule lately. He was exhausted, sir."

"You know as well as I, and as well as he, that the punishment is firmly set for a man who sleeps at his post, even while at anchor-watch in a friendly port."

"I do know it, sir. It is my hope that some flexibility may lie only in the length of his punishment. A man is usually assigned to the bergantine's oars for a month, but in this case…"

167

Sighing heavily, Cabrillo said, "There can be no exceptions, pilot, not for anyone."

Pilot San Remón accepted this judgment with a solemn yet acquiescing bow. "He will be rowed to the *San Miguel* at once, Captain-General." He turned to depart.

"Pilot," Cabrillo said, halting him at the door. "I will not be opposed to Captain Correa being discretely encouraged to spare the lash and the chains on his newest crewmember."

An expression of restrained gratitude and relief accompanied another bow as Pilot San Remón left the cabin to deliver this unusually light sentence.

At dawn, however, the men of the *San Salvador* found themselves ruing Battista's absence and their own added workload due to his assignment to the *San Miguel*. Cabrillo pushed himself as hard as his men, taking little time to rest as he oversaw the final preparations of repair and departure. It didn't help matters that the day turned unseasonably hot, making every exertion more draining. Two men passed out under the dehydrating sun, causing Cabrillo to order water delivered to each man in a timely manner. The sun did not relent until it settled low in its resting place, and the fading light offered the most relief the men had known in days. In Cabrillo's cabin it was almost too hot to eat, and he picked at his food with little interest.

When the evening hour of eight was called out, Cabrillo climbed to the stern deck looking almost as limp as his men. "Get some sleep, pilot," he said to the young officer he relieved, and there was no hesitation in following this command. Cabrillo gazed down upon Mateo standing at the waist of the ship, chatting now and then with Father Lezcano and scanning the water between the island and the railing. He had toiled without complaint right along with the men today. He was a fine boy, a boy to take pride in.

As the darkness deepened and a cooling breeze began to stir, Cabrillo blessed the feel of its breath upon his skin. What a peaceful night, he thought, as serene and gentle as it had been punishingly hot just hours before. As he mused about Wocha and his people, their land and their village, he turned to face the stern rail and let his glance skim his other two ships.

At the sound of a loud splash off the starboard side of the *San Salvador* he hurried to that railing and peered over. Someone had gone overboard and was splashing and sputtering below. He was about to issue an order to those now rushing to investigate, but he saw that Father Lezcano was already lowering the rope ladder. Cabrillo reached the priest as a coughing Mateo grabbed the bottom rung and began to climb. At his captain-general's interrogating stare, Father Lezcano said, "The boy was leaning over the side to check the anchor line, sir. He lost his hold and fell. All is well now, sir."

Cabrillo studied his priest for a moment, then muttered, "Please remain with me, Father. You other men, back to your posts."

As they shuffled away Mateo threw his leg over the railing and landed before Cabrillo looking almost as shamefaced as he was wet. In an undertone not meant for the ears of the rest of the crew, Cabrillo said, "Father Lezcano told me you were leaning over the railing and lost your hold, Mateo." The lad couldn't quite meet his uncle's eyes. This was answer enough. Rather than pressing him further, Cabrillo addressed the priest. "Strange, Father, that a boy would investigate an anchor line at such a time of night and from such a poor angle." He shifted his concentrated gaze from one to the other. "It is fortunate indeed that Mateo is a good swimmer, otherwise such an accident could have proved fatal," he said, his tongue lingering slightly on the word "accident".

Father Lezcano said in a very low tone, "I am certain the boy will be more careful in the future, Captain-General."

"He had better," said Cabrillo, his expression driving home the point. "It is time both of you returned to your watch." He turned aside and made his way back to the stern deck.

Neither Mateo nor Father Lezcano uttered a word for a quarter of an hour. Then Mateo edged closer and whispered, "Thank you, Father. I promise it shall never happen again."

"It must not, Mateo. If you ever feel sleep taking you again, remember tonight. Think of the slap of that water, and if that is not enough, think of the oars you could have been chained to."

"Before God, I will, Father. With all my soul I will."

Chapter 14

CHANGE IN THE AIR

There was barely enough early light to see where to take a step, but this didn't keep Cabrillo from having all hands rousted to prepare for departure. The flurry of activity brought scores of Chumash to the beach and drew Wocha and his small native contingency to the flagship. Cabrillo welcomed and thanked him sincerely for his kindnesses during their stay.

Placing a hand on the captain-general's shoulder, Wocha said, "Chief Cabrillo will stay in my heart until I see him again. We will share stories of this visit for many, many seasons."

"I hope to return, Wocha, but that is in the hands of God."

"It will please me greatly if your God brings you back. If you come again, will you teach me to make the talking marks on skins? This is powerful magic."

"I will teach you, Wocha."

"It would not offend your god?"

"No," Cabrillo said with a slow smile, "you are one of his people."

"Then I will look to the western skies each day and watch for your great canoes."

They embraced in farewell, and the Chumash chief returned to shore with his men.

Overhead, enough sail unfurled to catch the breeze and ease the ships from their anchorage, and Cabrillo's eyes left the activities onboard to seek the shore one last time. Wocha and his people raised their hands in salute. The simple gesture seemed to imply a tribute of honor yet also a sense of sadness at this separation and a yearning to meet again. Cabrillo lifted his own arms, returning these sentiments. The figures slowly diminished and, as the fleet angled out of the harbor and eased northward, were taken from his view.

Although Wocha had told Cabrillo that the two westward islands closest to his village were uninhabited, the captain-general set out toward them in order to better record their locations and features. As they sailed closer, the first of these showed itself to be an elongated stretch of rock where only patchy and meager plant life maintained a hold. Taking in the desolate coastline, Cabrillo decided a landing party wasn't needed to confirm an absence of fresh water and people, and he found little reason to drop anchors. As they headed north around the eastward point of land a nearly flat-topped projection momentarily snagged his attention. Nature had sliced this section of rock away from the main body of the island and carved out an arch that reminded Cabrillo of a monstrous shark, its upper jaw raised high above the water to await an unsuspecting ship.

The sea and weather permitted them to cross a short stretch of water and reach the second and far larger island without difficulty. Cabrillo could see little to imply that this land mass was more habitable than the one they'd just left. The afternoon was aging as they sailed along its curvy northern coast, which he estimated to extend a total of at least twenty miles, and he was quickly concluding that it was time to reverse their course and head northeast across the channel when, rounding an arcing point in the shoreline, the inverted v-shaped mouth of a cave appeared. The men muttered and pointed excitedly, and the temptation to investigate quickly grew too powerful to resist. Upon his orders men scurried to their positions at the lines and brought the ships to rest.

Cabrillo found his shipmaster at the foremast and said, "Bring a number of lamps, Master Uribe. That cavern looks dark as midnight."

The officers of the other ships demonstrated their eagerness to reach the depths of the grotto by casting their boats into the water almost as quickly as the men of the flagship. Once down, their rowers brought their own boats tightly behind Cabrillo's launch.

As the sailors neared the cave, their eyes were drawn upward some ninety feet to the pointed peak of the entrance. Ages of weathering had carved the rough face of the rock into a diverse collection of primordial shapes that included demonic beasts, gaping skulls, and ragged daggers. The haunting realism of these images caused one seaman to mutter, "Them rocky walls could rival the gates of hell itself." Such a comment was enough to set the more superstitious among the men to shifting uneasily. As the cave's shadow began to engulf the boats the rowers peered over their shoulders with increasing frequency, and Cabrillo ordered, "Light the lamps." Wicks were swiftly ignited and lamps held high.

Breaching the mouth of the cavern, a stench hit them with such force that several men coughed as their lungs fought for cleaner air while others cursed under their breaths. And as their noses were being assaulted, their ears picked up a low and indistinct sound, a grumbling that grew louder with each stroke of their oars. This and the intensity of the smell temporarily held the rowers in check, and the limited reach of their lamplight did little to dispel the unknown. Cabrillo ordered them slowly forward and around a pair of opposing curves. A bombardment of roaring and barking suddenly erupted, ricocheted off, and circled the cave walls with such concussiveness that at first it was difficult to determine whether they were surrounded. Ahead, at the point Cabrillo now guessed the roaring of the bull sea lions to be loudest, lay in complete blackness. When the men started voicing their disquiet Captain Correa shouted his sailors to silence with a string of profanity. Captain Ferrelo, true to his own nature, said in a voice just loud enough to be heard, "Steady, men." The captain-general commanded, "Hold here and raise the lamps."

Listening intently and staring into a bleakness little improved by the elevation of the lights, it was impossible for Cabrillo to measure a safe distance from the bulls. "Captains Ferrelo and Correa, two men in each boat are to take up spears, but they are to release them only in defense. Keep your boats in line behind mine."

Oars gently maneuvered them forward, which immediately increased the challenging tone and volume of the sea lion barrage. Very gradually, shiny dull-brown coats could be perceived shifting back and forth along the ledge that fringed the cave. Some of the bulls tossed their heads and necks in ferocious defiance of this intrusion. Both walls and barking drew closer as the cavern narrowed in front of them, and Cabrillo sensed more than saw that forward progress would deliver the boats into the very heart of the sea lion stronghold, well within range of an attack. What lay beyond the beasts guarding the gap was completely concealed by a curtain of black.

He knew that a bull sea lion could weigh up to a ton and had the strength to overturn boats and injure men. Enraged, they could easily kill. There was no choice but to smother his desire to investigate the inner chambers of the cavern and to call over the din, "No farther, men. Ease back."

Perfectly willing hands turned the boats back toward the entrance and pulled hard toward cleaner, quieter air. When they rounded the second curve of the cave its mouth reappeared, and Cabrillo was captivated by the scene before them. Framed by the rough triangular opening their three ships rested on a sea of gray glass beneath a profoundly blue sky, forming as tranquil, proud, and lovely a portrait as he had ever seen. *Ah*, he uttered in silence, *such a view is worth troubling to stop at a hundred caves.*

When they reached the entrance and passed through, each man took great gulps of the fresh sea air, and one or two of the younger hands allowed themselves a tremor of relief. Cabrillo, however, had enjoyed the darkness and the danger, and looked back with a sense of appreciation. That kind of thrill, he believed, never failed to make a man more intensely alive.

Once back aboard the *San Salvador*, he cast a last longing gaze at the cavern, decided they'd seen enough of the island, and ordered the ships to return to the mainland.

The sun had nearly set, with clouds at both horizons brightly afire, when they glided to a snug anchorage that lay about twenty miles up the coast from Pueblo de las Canoas. Seeing few natives, they slept quietly that night, and Cabrillo dreamed of endless caves.

In the morning they'd sailed only a couple of leagues up the coast before coming upon a valley of grand beauty, which the native people had wisely chosen for their settlement ages earlier. The village that spread before them was large and lively, and at the appearance of the ships it burst into a flurry of excitement. Before the fleet had come to rest, native canoes had already reached the vessels. Smiling, gesturing Indians held up fish of every variety to barter as they sought means of climbing onto the decks.

At the sight of the crowd, Master Uribe hurried to his captain-general and asked, "Sir, do we let them board?"

"Yes, Master Uribe. Make them welcome but keep them on the main deck."

"Very good, sir."

Turning to Father Lezcano, Cabrillo said, "They appear to be Chumash, and undoubtedly have heard from Wocha. Bless the man, we shall have no shortage of fresh fish."

It wasn't long before Cabrillo came to question his order to welcome all comers. The new arrivals were so fascinated by every sheet, line, and block that the men had a devil of a time getting the anchors settled and the sails furled. Even after the ships had been secured the Indians kept coming. At last, Cabrillo decided his best alternative was to lead a party ashore in the hope of luring their guests back home. Fortunately this plan proved so successful that only a handful of Indians remained aboard when his boats pushed away from the fleet.

His meeting with the village leaders, though gratifyingly cordial, was kept brief by Cabrillo. With the fall season's advancement he was feeling a stronger sense of urgency to push on, and he told the disappointed chief that they must depart in the morning. Attempting to lessen the sadness that sprang from this announcement, he distributed many outright gifts and generously traded for the goods they desired.

Making true their captain-general's word, his men had sails up before the sun had dispersed the last of the coastal fog. It took little time for the wind to find them and blow the ships northward. As they paralleled a shore reaching sharply westward Cabrillo enjoyed a warm sense of satisfaction watching the Chumash canoes gliding along with them; their occupants waving and crying out now-familiar words in tones of universal salutation. When the first paddlers tired and faded away, others group replaced them, and then others. Sailing on, progressing up nearly twenty-five miles of coastline, their entourage of canoes continued to keep them company.

Often a canoe approached near enough for an Indian to request to board, and Cabrillo had his men lift a paddler or two to the main deck. Sometimes a small gift but more frequently nothing at all was needed to acquire the names of the towns that appeared, such as Casalic, Tucumu, Alloc, and Xocotoc. Their passengers provided descriptions of neighbors living farther inland as well as. When questioning one fellow, Cabrillo and Father Lezcano learned that two villages lay within a three-day journey where the inhabitants harvested great crops of maize and hunted huge animals they called "cae."

Intrigued, Cabrillo said, "Ask him to describe the beasts, Father."

In answer, the native stood tall on his tiptoes and spread his arms wide, then shaped the outline of a four-legged body with his hands. He then lowered his head, with his arms outstretched and arced in a manner suggesting curved horns, and pawed the deck with his feet. Amazed, Cabrillo muttered to Father Lezcano, "Surely he exaggerates the size. What kind of animal could stand so tall?"

When asked for clarification, the Indian precisely and insistently repeated the pantomime indicating the incredible dimensions of the animal.

"Ask if he has seen such a beast with his own eyes, Father."

The inquiry was politely made, and the response delivered with resolve. "Many cae, many times."

Cabrillo and Father Lezcano stared at one another, and then the captain-general concluded, "Perhaps they are some kind of monstrous cattle."

"They may be, sir, and wild as wolves if they roam loose over these vast lands."

As had occurred during so many earlier encounters, their native visitors eagerly shared the rumors of men who wore beards and clothing like Cabrillo and his crewmembers, and they solemnly explained how these travelers had menaced their people farther inland.

Although Cabrillo listened politely to this information, he was suddenly far more interested in learning about the large island that had just appeared some fifteen miles to the southwest. Shifting the topic with care, he was told of several Chumash villages located on the isle. Quickly evaluating the distance, current, and weather conditions, he pointed as he gave the order, "Draw us closer, Master Uribe, perhaps halfway. The hour is late and I have no intention of landing there, but we may still discover something of the lay of her shore and people before nightfall." He shaded his eyes and scrutinized the sky as an artist might study the face of a restless model. "We must keep an eye on the heavens," he added. "I sense a change in the weather, and not for the better."

"Toward the island it is, sir," said Uribe.

The flagship altered course, and her two companions followed with the proficiency gained during months of close proximity. The fleet drew to within several miles of the island but only near enough for Cabrillo, his captains, and pilots to make rough notes of the coastline and to estimate the island's length to be forty-five miles. Since the coast pointed away from them, these recordings were little more than guesses backed by long experience. Briefly holding their position before turning back to gain the protection of the mainland, Cabrillo thought he could detect pathways and dwellings. These he continued to try to bring into focus even as his men turned the ships away, complying with his command to head in for the night.

The sky was growing dim by the time the fleet came to rest at a small mainland harbor, and the heavens were bright with glittering stars when at last Cabrillo ordered the few Indians who had come to meet them back to shore. The final hour of his watch was nearly spent, and he began to look fondly forward to the comfort of his bunk when Father Lezcano approached him on the stern deck. They stood in companionable silence for a bit, content to let the water and shoreline hold their attention. Taking a deep, slow breath, and releasing it even more slowly, Father Lezcano said, "A quiet night, though perhaps our last for awhile? I have heard that you sense a change in the wind."

Taking time to absorb the hush beneath the moon and stars, Cabrillo said, "I hope my eyes and nose are mistaken, and from the look of present conditions, they are. We have been very fortunate thus far, traveling so great a distance without major mishap, but we have learned nothing to dispel the possibility that we are still far from China. We must reach it and take what refuge that land offers before harshly cold weather finds us. Have you felt the bites of chill in the last few dawns?"

"A little perhaps, but I do not have your reputation for reading nature, sir."

He smiled. "I would be much happier to have winter come very late than to see that part of my reputation enhanced. We are only moderately equipped to deal with the cold. I find myself sleeping more fitfully than usual, thinking of the men suffering in light clothes. Before I let that happen, I will have layer upon layer of clothing sewn from our trade goods."

"Surely it will not come to that, sir. Those goods are the property of the governor."

"And there would be hell to pay, I know. I pray it will not be necessary. The condition of our ships must also be considered. These brief landings do not allow for the thorough repairs they will need before long, and need badly."

Father Lezcano said gently, "Forgive me, sir, but have you ever considered that you worry more than necessary?"

Cabrillo let out a short, quiet laugh, "I have been asked that too many times."

"We are in God's hands, sir. We must trust in Him."

Another silent pause held them before Father Lezcano again stirred the stillness. "It is strange, sir, after being at sea for so long now but I still find it hard to forego the celebration of Mass on Sunday."

"I must confess that I had nearly forgotten that today is Sunday."

"It has been a very full day, sir. A good day, despite missing Mass. Still, I must ask God once again to allow us a little extra share of forgiveness, given the ways of seamen."

Cabrillo cast a glance at Father Lezcano and his twitching mouth. "We seamen can never have too many prayers offered on our behalf, Father. Still, have you given thought to the fact that sailors name so many places after Him and his saints? Do we not, in a small way, spread his word? Wicked as we are, perhaps we deserve a little additional forgiveness."

"If so," he said, letting his smile show, "today we have earned a small share of absolution, now that San Lucas has a fine island named in his honor."

Chapter 15

MATIPUYAUT'S SHORE

"Captain-General, they've surrounded us!" cried Mateo, dancing from foot to foot and pointing from the railing. "Thousands and thousands of them!"

The sea itself had erupted with life. Everybody aboard the *San Salvador* stared, shouted, grinned, or hooted as the incredibly massive pod of skimming, leaping, racing forms wrapped the ship within its embrace and vibrantly animated acres of ocean around her. The boisterousness of the flagship's men quickly spread to the two ships trailing behind as they too were entwined within the jubilant upheaval. Glinting in the early sunlight, the glossy gray backs and black dorsal fins streaked across intersecting wakes in every direction, daring any pair of human eyes to keep up with their countless movements. The many acrobats of the throng leaped high enough to flash their white chests at the bedazzled onlookers.

Pilot San Remón now stood with Mateo, Manuel, and Cabrillo, his eyes shining brightly. "I never dreamed a pod could be so large, sir!" He gazed all around and laughed. "They encircle all three ships and could easily ring ten!"

The vast number of dolphins amazed even Cabrillo, momentarily easing years from his weathered face. "At times like this I wish I were a merman so I could see what lies under the waves. What it must look like down there, with the total now visible to us multiplied twenty times or more. Imagine swimming right along with this horde! Fetch me my quill and ink, Manuel. I must record this." Manuel reappeared in moments, and Cabrillo wrote, *"The 16th of October has begun as a day of wonder."*

He allowed most of the duties of the morning to be postponed during the quarter of an hour that the dolphins captured the attention of all. His own joy was heightened by the delight of his men, who would undoubtedly weave tales of this moment many times in the years to come. It soon began to seem to him as if the playful creatures actually intended to provide entertainment for him and his crews. It must be that, he mused, or perhaps the dolphins are enthralled by the novelty of the ships, which they view as gigantic but harmless beasts. His quill was kept busy sketching the scene both pictorially and verbally, capturing it as finely and thoroughly as he was able.

Far too soon, and with many a glance following it windward, the pod slipped away to seek a destination known only to its contingent. But the great pleasure the dolphins had given to their human audience during this brief connection lightened both heart and mind for hours.

Not long after the two species had parted, Chumash canoes appeared and came to glide sociably along with the fleet. The sun had just passed its zenith when Cabrillo spied a thickly inhabited harbor where a considerable river emptied into the sea and he ordered the fleet toward it. Sailing nearer, he could see that the river separated two evidently distinct villages, where each settlement layout and home construction differed, some houses possessing gabled roofs rather than the more common domes. With his curiosity highly piqued, he was impatient to settle into a comfortable anchorage and find an explanation.

By the time the ships floated sedately at rest and before Cabrillo had a chance to take to his launch, visitors from both villages were arriving and being welcomed aboard. And they didn't come empty-handed. Within a quarter-hour so many loads of fine sardines had been offered in trade that Cabrillo decided to name the place Pueblo de las Sardinas.

After assisting with the initial flurry of goodwill trading and gift distribution Father Lezcano stepped closer to Cabrillo and voiced his surprising conclusion, "Sir, the people from each village have their own diverse language."

"It seems so to me also, but I hear remnants of the Chumash dialect from each group."

"Yes, sir, but the words of villagers on the southeastern bank of the river are more familiar to me. Thankfully, their clothing helps to keep them separated for communication."

As the genial tumult continued on deck, Cabrillo gazed ashore and considered the distinction of habitat, dress, and language in fascination. This was certainly not the first time they'd come upon Indians speaking distinctive languages. On the contrary, they seemed to have discovered a different language, or at least a different dialect, in nearly every village between Pueblo de las Canoas and this place but never within such intimate proximity. How *could* each group cling to a cultural uniqueness while living within a stone's throw from one another? Then again, he considered, perhaps it was not so very unlike some ancient towns in Spain where divergent ethnicities coexisted tolerably well.

He remembered natives they'd met in southern locations telling him repeatedly about wars arising, not uncommonly, between sub-tribes. Could violent conflicts have contributed to the history of even these two villages? Carefully observing the posturing of both groups and detecting no tensions between them, he concluded that this was unlikely. However, with even the possibility of underlying discord being roused aboard his ships, he quickly organized boarding parties and headed them for the nearest shore. There, he and his delegation began exercising détente in a more structured manner, on one side of the river and then on the other.

Gifts and hospitality proved to be great equalizers. Chiefs of the same stature were honored in the same measure. Trade was divided equally and fairly. By evening, both villages seemed content to have three Spanish ships afloat in their bay.

Although human relations had been kept adequately balanced, to Cabrillo's growing disappointment he had learned little from either clan of new people beside the assertion that farther to the north the natives used much larger canoes. Sitting in his cabin with just his priest, he mused aloud, "Why would northern tribes need larger canoes, Father? To haul larger goods? Perhaps to transport some of those monstrous trees I have been hoping to come across? Or do they use them to travel longer distances out to sea? I hesitate to voice this hope, but perhaps they are needed to cross a stretch of water that reaches China?"

Father Lezcano said, "I sorely wish, sir, that I had been able to make your questions understandable to the Indians. I have provided you with nothing but speculation and hope."

"The fault is not yours, dear priest. The natives may have no answers to offer even if they understood us well. But this damnable uncertainty of the distance to our goal fires the need to advance without any unnecessary delay." He cleared his gloomy brow and asked with a lighter expression, "How about a stroll on the quarterdeck? I can listen for signs from nature while you speak with God."

As he stared up at the twinkling night lights and then out at the endless sheen of ocean he heard only whispered warnings to push ahead.

The day that followed delivered such amiable weather that Cabrillo mentally chastised himself for brooding over imagined omens. The fleet was making good time before fair winds and the only clouds in the brilliant sky were high and widely scattered. His mood continued to lighten as he took closer note of the natives traveling along with the fleet, paddling tirelessly between the many coastal villages they passed. Those bold enough to come aboard were welcomed and rewarded.

To Cabrillo's fascination, one Indian accepted a handful of beads with great solemnity and then proceeded to unwind his waist-length hair and remove a small wooden dagger that had held it in place. He offered the dagger to Cabrillo in two outstretched hands. The captain-general received it with thanks and asked him to demonstrate how he had bound his hair. Seeming pleased by the request, the man gathered and twisted his thick hair into a large knot, wrapped it round and round with a long stretch of twine, and used the dagger to secure two sides of this bundle to his scalp just above the nape.

Cabrillo was so impressed by this feat that he presented the elated native with a pouch filled with beads of every color.

After the man had returned to his canoe, Cabrillo said to his pilot and his priest, "By heaven, some of our own men have hair long enough to be bound in such a manner. It might prove not only more convenient but safer under some conditions. And, in case of need, a dagger would always be at hand."

Pilot San Remón raised a dubious brow but didn't vocally object to even so wild an idea when it came from his commander while on deck.

Father Lezcano, noting the pilot's hesitation, said, "Why, Captain-General, what a splendid idea. My vows allow me only short hair, of course, but the use of twine and daggers by our men with hair, say, something of the length of our good pilot, would be most advantageous."

San Remón darted a firm stare at Father Lezcano but otherwise refused to acknowledge such taunting, which he felt the ship's priest dispensed too freely and too often in his direction.

Cabrillo successfully hid his amusement at this light dueling between the young men. Yet he didn't seem able to keep from pointing out every new variety of regional dagger he spotted throughout the day. "Look, pilot, this one is so cleverly made of ivory. How finely *this* dagger has been chipped from flint! Did you see the carved images on this wooden blade?" San Remón somehow managed to maintain his diplomatic silence on the subject.

That evening, however, he quietly drew the ship's physician aside and asked him to act as his barber. A short time later the pilot reappeared on deck to reveal that his locks had been shorn to a previously unseen shortness, and Father Lezcano's expression drooped as he muttered, "You have dashed my hopes of ever seeing a Chumash pilot."

Such lighthearted diversions were unwillingly swept from the captain-general's mind by the coolness in the breeze that greeted him near the end of his night watch. This midnight held winter in its breath. He could not disregard its imminence.

At daybreak the ships pushed up the westward curving coast but the chilly wind discouraged any canoes from offering companionship. With Cabrillo pushing his men to exert considerable effort to gain each mile, the hour of ten found them approaching what he judged to be the westernmost point they must conquer. From their present viewpoint several men voiced the opinion that the cape took on the shape of a galleon, so it was named Galera.

With noon came a strengthening of the wind and frustratingly little forward progress, and Cabrillo started silently formulating many less flattering names for the cape that taunted them. The weather grew fouler still as they pushed on, and he finally gave the order to break out the heavy jackets. Bracing their stances against the whipping drafts, Cabrillo and Pilot San Remón took out an astrolabe to read the sun and attempted to calculate their present latitude. Though gauging the elevation of old Sol as it flitted from behind shifting clouds proved difficult, they concluded at last that their location was now 36° north of the equator. "From here," said the captain-general, "some questions become more nagging. How much colder will it grow before we can drop southward again? And, how long will we have to endure whatever winter brings?"

For hours they inched along the cape toiling to clear the point that lay a few miles ahead, but the wind mercilessly blasted them back time and again, and the men were growing exhausted. Grudgingly, bitterly giving up every wave they had just conquered, Cabrillo finally accepted that they had no choice but to bow before nature's insistence and turn their ships in retreat. They must head back in the direction of the island they had named San Lucas. He took a strengthening breath before bellowing the order to alter their course into the face of the wind.

As the gale strengthened and the swells rose higher, the fleet turned and flew to the south. Resigned now, Cabrillo kept his eyes peering forward and altered their course to cut through the waves as smoothly as possible. Now, they must find shelter.

When the lookout from *La Victoria* cried out, "Land ahead, sir!" his young voice blew forward to Cabrillo as a shrill wail, and the captain-general's eyes swept the horizon. There, beneath the low swirling clouds in the distance, it waited. Drawing closer, he discovered that what lay before them were two separate islands rather than the one they had presumed from their earlier remoteness. The larger spread east to west, and he quickly estimated it to be twenty miles long; the lesser one, only half that length. He squinted to see the small island more clearly through the whipping air but could tell little.

"We will sail for the smaller island," Cabrillo shouted to his pilot, shipmaster, and priest. "Pray that she has a snug anchorage."

Whether in answer to their prayers or because of a turn of fortune, that late afternoon Cabrillo led his ships through a defiantly rocky reef, past a high-backed sentry rock large enough to consume several ships, and into a moderately sized but deeply cut harbor on the north side of the island.

Once the ships had drawn well inside and been tucked up close to the western arcing boundary of the port, the men of all three ships wiped their slickened brows, scanned their short-term home, and gave sincere thanks for the protectiveness offered by the 500-foot ridgeline that surrounded them. Their next immediate thoughts turned to whomever might own the many canoes that dotted the shore. For several moments, not a soul could be seen.

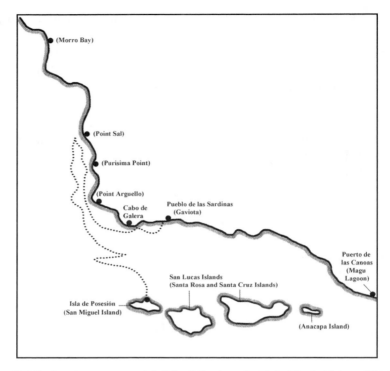

(Morro Bay)

(Point Sal)

(Purisima Point)

(Point Arguello)

Cabo de Galera

Pueblo de las Sardinas
(Gaviota)

Puerto de las Canoas
(Magu Lagoon)

San Lucas Islands
(Santa Rosa and Santa Cruz Islands)

Isla de Posesión
(San Miguel Island)

(Anacapa Island)

While he, too, was watchful of the beach, Cabrillo let himself take another moment to appreciate the qualities of the bay. Here, the bluster of the wind was cut to little more than a huff, and its cry was muffled to a moan. The harbor allowed the three ships to nestle safely enough but provided little room for wasteful maneuvering. With the tightness of their quarters in mind, and eyeing the sentry rock with wariness, Cabrillo issued the order to lower double anchors for the night.

As the ships were being tied down he saw things starting to move ashore. One native appeared from the protection of a sand dune, and then another, and another. The slowly gathering Indians walked to their canoes but didn't slide them into the water. Showing no eagerness to approach the ships, they stood absorbedly assessing their visitors.

Cabrillo could spot no weapon of any kind, yet the manner of the islanders was far from welcoming, and bows and arrows could easily be hidden in the sand or canoes. The situation brought to mind the favorite saying of a tutor who'd instructed him as a restless youth, and

184

he muttered aloud, "Precautions are wise companions." Without giving any sign of hurry or concern, he called out to Vargas, "Sergeant-major."

"Yes, Captain-General." Vargas said, his voice as calm as Cabrillo's.

"Discreetly distribute arms to ten of your men but have them held out of view."

"Yes, sir. Should Cardenas bring up the war dogs?"

"Definitely not." Turning slightly toward the next man he sought, he said, "Master Gunner, quietly ready the swivel guns."

Pilot San Remón, Master Uribe, Father Lezcano, Manuel, and Mateo had joined Cabrillo one by one and had added their eyes to the staring match between the Indians and the men of the fleet. The captain-general surrendered his scrutiny long enough to glance toward his sister ships and happened to catch Captain Ferrelo's eye. His captain's expression showed the same evaluating supposition that tugged at Cabrillo. Then, Ferrelo moved his shoulders in a subtle shrug, and again their attention turned to the island.

Cabrillo began evaluating the turn of the tide, the break of the waves upon the beach, the location of potentially dangerous rocks, and many other variables that might affect landing. The ruggedly descending slopes came nearly to the water's edge, leaving only a short southerly beach that was flanked on its left side by a long sand dune about two fathoms high and on the right by a tightly wedged collection of large boulders. Visually following the curve of the bay around to the right and gazing beyond his prow, Cabrillo beheld the first sentinels of a sizeable sea lion herd that was noisily voicing its displeasure at the intrusion of the fleet. Again he reverted his consideration to the natives, who continued to reveal neither arms nor ill intentions.

"Well," he said, "someone must be the first to offer an outstretched hand. Pilot, the watch is yours."

Vargas, Father Lezcano, and his rowers accompanied Cabrillo as they headed to a fully armed launch. While Manuel handed their commander his helmet and boarded with the others, Vargas said quietly aside to the captain-general, "You have undoubtedly considered this, sir, but that sand dune could hide many warriors. Their arrows could easily reach us on the beach."

"Yes, a perfect opportunity for an ambush."

"The rest of your armor, sir…"

"Judging from the way the surf is breaking, we may have to swim a few strokes to reach the beach. As I have already told Manuel, today we will count on caution rather than armor."

Theirs and two boats from the other ships pushed away together but Cabrillo's launch held the lead position. As was his practice, he had the two captains send chosen officers ashore rather than allowing all of the fleet's commanders exposed to harm at once.

"Watch closely, men," Cabrillo ordered the rowers stroking with their backs to the island, "and pull for the ship if I give any sign."

As the boats neared the beach an apparent leader of the group stepped forward and lifted his arm to slice the air in a cautioning rather than welcoming gesture. Several of his people repeated the signal. Cabrillo read no indication of direct challenge, merely a bold defensive warning, as if to say, "Beware! We can return whatever harm you might inflict."

The captain-general stood slowly in the boat and offered the gesture he had learned for "friend." The islanders lowered their arms but did not reciprocate the sign of goodwill.

Vargas, fearless during the deadliest of times, let his tone convey his mistrust of their circumstances as he muttered, "Captain-General."

"Yes, sergeant-major, just a little closer. Slowly on, men."

Vargas kept his hand on his musket as the boat nudged toward the beach.

Even as the sailors neared, the faces of the Indians revealed none of their intentions and very little of their concerns. But the islanders had held themselves back from the water line, and Cabrillo took this as a positive restraint. He now made his decision and, after ordering the other boats to hold their positions, said to his rowers, "Take me in, men." From the corner of his eye he saw Vargas about to voice an objection, but a subtle gaze stilled it. His boat pulled forward.

Only a few hard strokes were needed to drive his boat within three yards of the sand. Still the Indians did not move. He ordered the men to steady the boat. Leaving his crossbow behind, armed only with the sword at his belt, and protected by no more than his metal helmet and leather breastplate, Cabrillo swung his legs over the side of the launch and fought the chest-high waves to shore. Immediately behind him, Manuel, Vargas, and six soldiers carefully held their firearms above the water as they and Father Lezcano leaped from the boat. The remaining rowers quickly pulled the lightened boat ashore and stood at its side, within an arm's reach of their crossbows.

Cabrillo now could see that light bows and quivers did indeed lie in the sand beside most of the native men. At his approach only two Indians picked up their weapons, but these men set no arrows to their strings. Locking his gaze on the Indian chief while maintaining an awareness of the others, Cabrillo, with Father Lezcano and Manuel a step behind him, walked forward until the space separating him and the natives diminished to fifteen feet.

The chief, flanked by two younger men who were likely his sons, studied Cabrillo keenly. This island leader gave no indication of his emotions, whether amazement, fear, or curiosity, but his natural shrewdness could not be hidden. As were most aboriginal chiefs that Cabrillo had met, this one was past middle age, yet he looked to be far from frail as he stood eye to eye with the captain-general. He wore his gray streaked hair tied up at the back of his head, giving his strong-boned face a roughhewn impression. His long loincloth and fur-skin cape had been decorated with the exquisite care generally shown only to those who are both loved and respected. The elaborate shell and stone beading that fanned his chest was the most beautiful Cabrillo had seen on his entire voyage.

There was palpable tension in the faces and bodies around them, a sharp narrowing of the eyes that gave Cabrillo pause, but he worked to hide his own disquiet. With great respect, and with Father Lezcano's assistance, Cabrillo addressed their ruler. "We greet you and your people, chief. I am Cabrillo, chief of these ships, and I have come in the name of our most honored leader, King Charles of Spain."

After a curt nod of acknowledgment the chieftain said, using widely recognized Indian signs but another dialect unfamiliar to the seamen, "We have heard of you, Chief of the Great Canoes." A few of his warriors shifted uneasily but the chief continued, his face communicating as expressively as his hands and arms. "It is said that you are a friend of the Chumash, but what is said is not always true." There was a marked defensiveness in his voice, the tone of a man determined to protect his people. It suggested the possibility of recent attacks made against them, or of other hardships inflicted by outsiders.

Before Cabrillo could form a response, the young man on the chief's left slowly crouched down and withdrew a spear from the sand at his feet.

Sensing responding movements in his own men, Cabrillo halted any activity behind him by commanding distinctly, "Do not move."

The chief stilled his son with a slight jerk of his hand, and the young man warily returned the wooden spear to the ground.

For several breaths the tension stretched tight as a straining muscle. Then the island leader took a single step forward and signed, "Have you joined with our enemies to war against us?"

"No." Cabrillo signed for himself, his gesture conveying vehement denial.

"Why have you come here?"

"My ships must wait in the harbor until the wind lessens."

The chief considered this and then asked, "What do you want of us while you are here?"

Cabrillo released a breath he hadn't meant to hold. "We will trade for food and water."

After pausing again, the chief asked, "How long will you stay?"

"A few days, only until the wind changes. We bring many gifts and goods to trade." Acting on instinct, Cabrillo added, "While we are here we will help protect you from your enemies."

"Your men will help protect us?"

"Yes, if you will share this harbor."

Perhaps because they perceived a reduction in the misgivings of their leader, discontented mutterings began to rise from his warriors. He silenced them by raising his hand and sweeping it in a wide arc above their heads. When the only thing still rumbling was the wind, the chief announced gravely, "I am called Matipuyaut."

Cabrillo bowed, repeated the name, and said, "I am called Cabrillo."

"Your name is known to me." The Indian leader eyed him as he reached his decision. "If you do not bring war to our island, Cabrillo, you may take shelter here."

Again Cabrillo bowed, this time with gratitude.

Many of Matipuyaut's men glowered with displeasure but he ignored them and let his glance wander to Manuel. With a note of admiration, he said, "We have also heard of your black man who possesses great…" Here, Father Lezcano faltered as he attempted to translate as precisely as he dared, "…potency. Now that my eyes have seen him, it is easier to believe what the storytellers said of his abilities." The speculating gazes of the warriors rested a little too heavily on Manuel for his comfort.

In a voice that warned even as it sought understanding, Matipuyaut said, "So that my people do not fear your coming, your men should stay on the water tonight. At sunrise I will come to talk with you again."

"My men will sleep on the ships, Matipuyaut," Cabrillo promised. Before turning away, he unfastened a silver clasp in the shape of an encircled cross from the neck of his cape. He strode smoothly forward until he had closed half the space to Matipuyaut and held out a hand bearing his brooch.

The chief's pensive expression told Cabrillo he understood that by accepting the gift he would be taking his first step into a new trade relationship. He would also be answering something akin to a diplomatic dare. The slightest flicker of what might have been amusement illuminated the chief's face.

Signaling for his men to remain where they were, Matipuyaut walked up to the bearded man from the sea and solemnly received his offering. The clasp transferred from one strong hand to the other, and as their eyes met again Cabrillo sensed that he and the chief had gained a slight but valuable understanding of the other's tenuous position as the leader of his people.

Gently, Cabrillo and his men withdrew. They returned to his ship bone-tired and grateful for having been granted even a short reprieve from their long day's labors against the elements. Later that evening as the captain-general wandered the stern deck he noticed how unrelentingly Vargas stared at the beach. His sergeant major didn't give up his surveillance until the last of the Indians had climbed the hill that led to their village and disappeared from his sight.

189

Chapter 16

TAYA

Throughout the night the wind showed no willingness to relent, and with the breaking of day the seamen renewed their gratitude for the harbor that kept them shielded from its probing reach. As light spread, Cabrillo stood upon his habitual plank at the railing, the detachment of men chosen and the launch standing by. He waited only for the island chief's entourage just now emerging from the protection of the dune and walking to the open beach. Wasting no more time, he took to his boat, now carrying no fewer armaments but many more trade goods. The two captains again remained aboard their respective ships, with their guns made ready for action.

Even before setting foot ashore Cabrillo sensed a lightening of tensions among the islanders, and it continued to ease reassuringly as the two leaders came together for their first attempts at communication and trade. Within minutes most of the natives were kneeling or sitting in the sand near Cabrillo and Father Lezcano, watching with fascination as goods were brought from the chest and bargaining advanced in rounds. Though both men did a fairly admirable job of concealing it, Cabrillo soon realized that he was enjoying the bartering session as much as Matipuyaut. As promises of fresh water, seal meat, and fish, and immediately delivered furs, stone bowls, and tools piled up for the captain-general, the contents of his large chest steadily dwindled away.

Glancing from the empty chest at last, he saw a fleeting look of desire cross Matipuyaut's face. He looked again at the wooden box, momentarily confused, and then smiled for the first time since their dealings started. He signed to the chief, "The chest is for you," and handed it to him.

At this boon, the chief broke out a smile of his own.

190

Perhaps the most powerful breakthrough came an hour or so after the official trading had ended. They had spoken of other tribes, friendly and otherwise, and Matipuyaut had asked many questions about Cabrillo's people, his voyage, and his home far away. The subject had turned to weaponry when Cabrillo was suddenly inspired to present Matipuyaut with an unplanned but well-chosen gift. From his own belt, the captain-general withdrew an eight-inch knife along with its own small leather scabbard. When he passed it to Matipuyaut with a gesture asking him to accept it, the chief let out an, "Auhh," and raised appreciative eyes. But almost immediately his lips pursed thoughtfully, and Cabrillo guessed that he was puzzling over how best to repay such a gift. After a moment or two his features cleared and he said, "Chief Cabrillo, come to my village, to my house. You may bring," he scanned the gathered sailors and raised six fingers, "six men."

Cabrillo stared lingeringly at the thirty or so braves near Matipuyaut and then said, "Ten men."

Matipuyaut agreed.

This settled, Cabrillo offered a bow and momentarily left the chief to speak with his officers. It was almost noon and the maintenance on the ships must commence at once. Giving the necessary orders, he sent a few men back to their respective ships to set things in motion. He then returned to Matipuyaut, who led him toward the path that meandered up to the village, trailed by Manuel, Vargas, four of his soldiers carrying crossbows against their backs, and two additional men with short swords swaying from their belts and long bows and quivers resting between their shoulder blades. The slim remainder of the landing party was to remain on the beach and watch over the returning launches. All of the native warriors had by now retrieved their shallowly buried spears and fallen in behind Cabrillo's guard.

Just beyond the elongated sand dune the trail turned sharply to the right and began to rise, passing a rocky cistern fed by a cascade that sang in crystallized tones as they climbed. Listening to the sweet music, Cabrillo wondered how many such water sources existed on the island, giving life as well as pleasure to those who drew near. The harsher sounds of saws and hammers reached him from the ships, and these too were comforting.

By the time they'd scaled the precipitous path to a point high above the source of the small waterfall, Cabrillo was sweating heavily and trying to restrain the volume of his breathing. He felt like ages had passed since he'd last trekked uphill. Glancing ahead and then back he saw that his fellow sailors were panting and sweating as profusely as he, but the Indians, even the older Matipuyaut, seemed no more taxed by the climb than a sea lion would be by a dip in the waves.

When the path finally leveled out and the aching in his leg muscles eased, Cabrillo heard one of his rowers mutter between gulps of air, "Sailors was never meant to scale hills steep as this. Give me rigging, any day." A quick snarl from Vargas silenced the speaker.

Now that they'd reached open ground the Indians spread out around the visitors, watchful and wary. Ahead Cabrillo could see that the single village he'd imagined, just as with the islands, was in reality two smaller ones. As they drew near the more substantial of these and the warriors gathered tighter around them, Cabrillo noticed Vargas' growing uneasiness. His sergeant major finally mumbled, "I do not like it, sir. Too many of them."

Just as softly, Cabrillo said, "We are beyond help now. Breathe easy and keep moving."

Matipuyaut led the group up to the most sizeable of the thatched, dome-shaped houses, and ushered Cabrillo and his men through its rectangular entrance. At least a dozen pairs of eyes, belonging to women and children who'd obviously been warned of their arrival and quickly shifted to the outside wall, stared with varying degrees of fear at the guests. One small boy whimpered but was instantly hushed.

The chief motioned Cabrillo's delegation to be seated and then issued brief orders to his wives. Two of the women eased behind the men and out of the house to fulfill the chief's errand. In an effort to avoid offending his host by taking too direct an interest in his family, Cabrillo turned his concentration toward the nonhuman contents of the home.

The interior must have measured fifty feet in diameter and was arranged around a central cooking fire with a smoke hole positioned high above it. Tightly woven mats as well as sea lion and otter skins covered the floors. The arcing wall was framed with whalebones and driftwood, and against it twenty or so raised beds were spaced evenly apart and covered with various furs. On either side of the largest bed, which undoubtedly belonged to Matipuyaut, large woven screens hung suspended from the ceiling to form a semi-private chamber. Baskets of many sizes and shapes, finely decorated with dark geometric patterns, rested near the beds or hung from the poles supporting the walls. A sizeable stone cooking bowl, stacks of abalone and stone bowls, and several other implements were stacked on a raised stone slab near the fire. Also resting beside the firestone was a huge oblong mortar that cradled its grinding pestle.

The undisputable head of this household seated himself upon furs as his two sons and several of his men settled around him. He paused and watched Cabrillo in a relaxed manner that communicated his intention to await something. After several moments had crawled by Cabrillo was about to speak when a short Chumash man in elaborate body paint and head feathers entered and took a place beside the chief, which Matipuyaut's son politely relinquished. The newcomer piercingly gazed upon the leader of the strangers as if attempting to extract hidden motives. His scrutiny then turned upon Father Lezcano, who disarmed him with a sudden and ostensibly innocent smile.

Matipuyaut introduced the man by saying with respect, "This is our *alchuklash*, our shaman. He is called Kipomo."

Cabrillo offered his own name and that of his priest and received only a speculative glare in return.

The chief then drew out a stone pipe measuring four inches in length and three-quarters in diameter, tapered and fluted at one end. With ceremonial gravity the chief filled the pipe with a mixture of tobacco and a plant unfamiliar to Cabrillo. A glance from Matipuyaut toward one of his wives brought her to the fire where she lit a twig, and then demurely brought it to the chief. He kindled the pipe and offered the stem to the captain-general.

Although Cabrillo had smoked tobacco after his young arrival in Mexico, and once or twice since then, he'd never been won over by the activity. Tobacco made his throat burn and the smell was not overly pleasant. Worst of all it dulled his sense of taste, which he valued high enough to protect. Now, caught in the hospitality of a host upon whom his ships' sanctuary depended, he accepted the pipe with as much grace as he could marshal. Nodding at the chief in gratitude, he put the pipe to his lips and inhaled a mouthful of smoke that tasted markedly more pungent than any previously known to his tongue. There was an unusual bitterness and sweetness mixed with the tobacco flavor, and the combination scratched at the back of his gullet so roughly it elicited

one short, quickly swallowed cough. He cleared his throat to ease
the tickle, took a second, smaller puff with more success, and handed
the pipe back to Matipuyaut. The chief passed it to Kipomo, who inhaled languorously, and then conveyed the pipe to Matipuyaut's sons.
Whatever ingredients the smoke contained, they hit Cabrillo's empty
stomach like a hot stone in a cooking pot and set off a burst of hunger.
He shifted noisily to muffle his grumbling stomach.

The sudden sound of muttering from his men and a sharp intake of
breath from Father Lezcano made Cabrillo dart a glance in the same
direction that his men were staring. Just inside the doorway stood
three young women, naked except for their short two-piece skirts and
adornments. Most gazes were pinned to the female closest to the entrance, and Cabrillo understood why.

An astuteness, a potency was there, which by itself would have set
her apart from her peers. But she also possessed a heightened beauty
in her proud face and body. She stood with her chin held high and
her eyes aimed directly, perhaps challengingly at Matipuyaut rather
than shyly at the floor. She appeared to be a few years older than the
others, and her mature breasts and hips made the same features of the
other two girls look disappointingly unripe. Her hair hung loose and
shining to just below her thin belt. Her legs were flawlessly sculpted.
Cabrillo's gaze rose from her feet and settled upon the woven chords
of a necklace that came together between her collarbones to suspend
a single strand, and upon this thread small birds carved from abalone
shells trailed down between her full breasts and shimmered against the
richness of her skin.

At the sight of her, no restraint dictated by diplomacy could hide
the angry glare that darkened Matipuyaut's face or the distaste that
pinched Kipomo's. The chief barked a reprimand at the older wom-
en who'd been sent out at the chief's bidding only to return with a
highly disagreeable choice. The offending wife tried to apologize
but Matipuyaut had already aimed his displeasure back at the younger woman. One biting word that Cabrillo did not comprehend was
snapped at her, but she did not move. A staring battle, his fiery, the
girl's defiant, lasted only a moment before the chief seemed to recall
his duty to his visitors. He calmed his features somewhat and ventured to recapture a less stormy frame of mind.

Father Lezcano interpreted aloud, although by now Cabrillo could understand the Indian signs nearly as well as his priest as Matipuyaut explained, "These women have been brought here to serve Chief Cabrillo during his stay with us. To show my appreciation for his fine weapon, he may choose one or all of them."

"Good Matipuyaut," Cabrillo tried with great solemnity but little hope, "my knife was given in friendship. It is not my wish to deprive you of your women. I have a woman, a wife in my land."

Matipuyaut considered this before asking, "Is your land far away?"

"Yes, far," Cabrillo responded honestly before recognizing his own entrapment.

"A woman who is far away can not care for her man. These women are not my wives so you do not deprive me of them. Just as the knife, they are given in friendship. They are young and strong, and will serve you well. They are the finest gifts I have to offer, Chief Cabrillo."

There it was, the potential for affronting his host's honor and authority, a generous offer set like a snare by which a single misstep could entangle them all. Cabrillo cursed inwardly, dreading what trouble such an arrangement, for the second time, might encourage among his men. They'd been without women for too many months. Trying to conceive some way to keep from wronging either Matipuyaut or his own men, Cabrillo eyed the women. As he sought a solution, he realized that Father Lezcano hadn't attempted to interfere this time. Perhaps he could be of some help, even if only to give Cabrillo more time to think.

"Father Lezcano, please ask Matipuyaut to tell me something about the women."

A bit stiffly the priest complied, and the chief seemed unperturbed as he gestured toward the young girls, "These two were born to families of our nobles who belong to the Brotherhood-of-the-Canoes. They are hard workers and have been trained to be faithful and modest."

"And this one?" Cabrillo asked, referring to the woman who Matipuyaut was clearly trying to avoid mentioning.

Another scowl appeared as he paused, and then admitted to the surprise of the sailors, "This is one of my daughters, but she is a bad woman. She has brought shame to her people. She is unworthy of Chief Cabrillo and should not have come."

Fascinated anew, Cabrillo's men began muttering amongst themselves until Vargas hushed them with one quietly hissed, "Silence, you swine!"

Even under the burden of insults and gawking, the girl neither spoke nor moved any part of her body except her eyes, and these now locked on Cabrillo. They were probing, measuring.

Cabrillo asked, "How has she shamed her people?"

Matipuyaut declared without hesitation, "She is the mother of two children in one birth." The heads of the other females in the room lowered, but not that of the guilty woman. Kipomo glared his condemnation as the chief went on. "Such a curse can be forgiven if one child or both are killed before their first breaths are drawn, but this woman and her husband refused to honor our ways. They even refused to obey the command of Kipomo. By sparing their offspring, they risked the welfare of all of our people. Three years have now passed and both children still live, so the curse still lives. It has already taken the life of her husband. For the last year she has cared for her unlucky children alone."

This was not the first time Cabrillo had heard of a mother of twins being considered the victim of a curse. Perhaps such superstitions had arisen during years of starvation. Even in times of plenty the islanders knew their prosperity could change greatly within a few seasons, so the superstition persisted. But the precautionary measure for survival was merciless and wrong. He let his eyes meet those of the young mother. She and her children undoubtedly lived in harsh ostracism. An idea started to form, and he grew more certain of his next move as it firmly took hold. Here was a case by which his faith could bless these people while peace was maintained.

"Matipuyaut," he said earnestly, "our God is all good and all knowing. He can take away such curses. He can make every child holy, even these children." Matipuyaut attended to his signs with thoughtful vigilance, so Cabrillo went on. "I am happy to choose this woman to serve me. We will teach her the ways of our God. He will wash the curse away from her, and her children, and your people."

This was followed by quiet hopeful gasping from the other women, muttering amongst the warriors, and speculative silence from Matipuyaut. Kipomo shifted impatiently and seemed on the brink of speaking, when Matipuyaut said with genuine concern, "Chief Cabrillo, your words are powerful, but there is more you must know. This woman is not only unholy, she is also disobedient. Our customs allow widows to marry only widowers, and there have been three such men who have come for her. Even with the curse she carries they were willing to take her as a wife, but she refused them all."

To the astonishment of everyone in the room the woman stepped forward, eyeing Cabrillo intensely, and said, "I will not refuse this man."

The quiet, courageous assertiveness of her words and delivery impressed Cabrillo greatly. In the gaze she held unwaveringly upon him, he sensed a plea to protect her children, and in return she offered anything, everything he might ask. As he again took in her exposed beauty, Cabrillo knew he might have asked much if their circumstances had been different.

Matipuyaut glanced at Kipomo, each of his elder sons, and then at the rest of his audience to assess their reactions before saying, "You may take her, Cabrillo. If your god can remove the darkness from her spirit it will do much good. If she does not please you, the others will."

Cabrillo said, "While she is in my care Father Lezcano will also watch over her and teach her the ways of our faith." He hoped his priest's involvement would not only help the woman but also quell the envy of his crews by providing her with a chaperone. It appeared that Father Lezcano sensed his motives when he gave an approving nod, and Cabrillo went on. "She will then teach what she learns to the rest of her people. At dawn we will come to the beach and place this island under the protection of our earthly and heavenly kings. We will mark it with a symbol of the son of our God so that all here may come to honor and love his goodness. Father Lezcano and Father Gamboa will ask our Mighty God to bless this woman and her children."

Matipuyaut took all of this in with an expression of apprehensive hopefulness, evidently willing to ignore the disapproval of his shaman. When Cabrillo had finished, the chief asked in confirmation, "Then, you wish only her to care for you?"

"Only her."

Looking next at Manuel and perhaps recalling the stories that had reached him from the mainland, he asked, "Do you need women for any of your men?"

Cabrillo cut the hopes of his sailors by repeating with finality, "Only her. We will stay just until the wind changes, and my men have much work to do. The land we seek is far across the sea. We must reach it before the cold season comes."

"We will watch for you when the sun awakens," said Matipuyaut. "I wish to learn more of your God and your journey." With a slight hesitation, he added, "Chief Cabrillo, I have heard the strange sounds from your ships. I have also heard that your people ride on the back of a great beast. Do you have such beasts with you?"

"Yes, Matipuyaut. They are called horses."

"*Horses.* Would these horses be harmful to us?"

"They are trained to obey their masters, and if we are with them they will harm no one who is gentle."

"I wish to see these creatures. Will you bring horses tomorrow?"

Subtly sweeping his gaze over the warriors, he found looks of distrust on several faces, yet they seemed willing to follow Matipuyaut's commands. If all went well in the morning, this would be a welcome solution to Cabrillo's ever-present concern over the confinement of his horses. Cabrillo decided to risk landing them under the watchful eyes of his men. "We will bring horses ashore. We will also bring more goods to trade."

"Good!"

"Now, Matipuyaut, we must return to our ships."

The chief rose with the captain-general and his companions. At Cabrillo's signal, Vargas led the men outside and onto the path that would return them to the beach. Cabrillo and Father Lezcano followed them to the entrance but paused before the young woman newly placed under their care. Remembering that the Chumash were hesitant to use their proper names except under very private or official circumstances, Cabrillo asked her only, "What are you called?"

She placed a hand on the abalone birds that decorated the valley between her breasts, and said, "Tasin Taya." Although uncertain whether the sound referred to the abalone or the birds, Cabrillo plainly understood the hope and gratitude that had been expressed with the word. He wondered if everything spoken by the mouth and body of this young female held meaning beyond what was necessary for mere communication. There was something here, something complex, exquisite, and compelling that would have been difficult to mask if she had tried, and she made no attempt to conceal anything from his scrutiny.

Sensing the silent interplay between the woman and his commander, Father Lezcano stepped close to Taya and placed his palms upon the top of her head. She lowered her chin as he quietly prayed, "Heavenly Father, please watch over this girl and keep her from harm. Help her become a blessing and a light among these islanders."

When his hands were drawn away and the woman looked up, her eyes sought and found only Cabrillo. With an effort beyond what he would have comfortably admitted, the captain-general left her and soon joined his men as they marched back toward the waiting boats.

The rowers held their tongues to an unusual stillness as they pulled toward the *San Salvador*, and their hush was severe enough to keep Cabrillo and Father Lezcano from discussing many plans for the ceremony to be held the next day. One telling exception occurred when one of the younger men asked a little too hopefully, "Do you think this wind will hold, Captain-General?"

"We must pray it does not. Our need to reach Asia grows more pressing every day."

With this, the silence of the men became complete.

Chapter 17

CHRISTENING

"Father Lezcano, you look as anxious as I am to get the horses ashore."

The young priest grinned as he said, "Why would I not be, sir, with your promise to let me ride?" He stood at Viento's head scratching the restless stallion's lower jaw.

"Not until after the baptismal ceremony, remember. And, though all looks calm enough, you might ask God to protect them while within reach of the islanders." Cabrillo gave a parting wave as he threw his leg over the railing and boarded one of the two launches that would deliver Viento and Seguro to the beach. The two male horses were being landed before the mares since they had been trained in the art of war and could better protect themselves if the need arose.

He'd already taken the precaution of visiting Matipuyaut at first light to check the mood of the natives. Since no trouble seemed to be brewing, with only a small contingent he'd had a wooden cross constructed and planted and hastily claimed the island, naming it Posesión but intending to find a more unique name in the days to come. He'd then left Vargas and an attachment of soldiers ashore to await his return with the horses.

As if Viento understood that the landing would be hastened by his cooperation, he quieted when the canvas sling was brought under his belly and lifted up his sides. His handlers attached the looped lines of the sling to a connecting line hanging from the cross arm and then carefully swung him up and out over the sea. Cabrillo stood in the bow of a launch and Manuel in the other, each holding one of Viento's long lead lines as the stallion was lowered into the water. His legs began churning before his body was fully buoyant, and the sling was quickly eased free. Encouraged by Cabrillo's voice and bracketed by the pair of launches, Viento swam with powerful strokes through the waving water, lessening the stiffness of his muscles before needing to use them on land. The captain-general's pride swelled at the lack of fear in his great stud as he swam with nostrils flared and ears high, straight toward the sand dune.

Cabrillo and Manuel leaped from the boats and aided Viento out of the waves. To loud exclamations from the Chumash, Viento trotted onto dry sand shaking his head and snorting with gusto. As the captain-general replaced the transport halter with a bridle, he noted that very few natives carried weapons and that their expressions held utter astonishment rather than hostility. Most promising of all, women and children were beginning to trail down the path from the plateau above to the shore. Many of the women turned uneasy eyes toward their leader and shielded their smaller children with their bodies, but Kipomo reassured them by his complete enthrallment with Viento's movements and personality.

Cabrillo handed the reins to Manuel and carefully examined his stud's legs and hooves. Finding them sound, and with Viento impatiently tossing his head and flinging water from his long mane, Cabrillo retook the reins as he stole another glance at the islanders. They were keeping their distance. So with growing pleasure Cabrillo slowly walked his stallion up and down a small stretch of beach as his men rowed back to the *San Salvador* for Seguro. The equestrian landings from *La Victoria* were to begin at Cabrillo's command, but he wanted to weigh the islanders' reactions a little longer before issuing that order.

He spoke softly to his horse as they paced along the sand, and often Viento nickered lowly in response. Patting the sleek neck, Cabrillo said, "There are many watching today. We must be on our best behavior, eh?" After several short trips he stopped in the sand, and when Viento nudged his back Cabrillo faced him with a quiet laugh. "I know what you want, but you must regain your land legs gradually." Viento nosed his master's chest, huffed, and pawed the sand. Cabrillo could not hide his grin. "Very well, but only for a very short distance, and no faster than a walk."

He brought the reins to the top of Viento's withers, threw his right leg over his back, and sat tall and commanding upon the prancing horse. An excited hum arose from the Indians that only encouraged

Viento's restlessness, but Cabrillo kept his stud in place to let his muscles adjust a little longer.

Before the snorting mount and his seemingly supernatural rider, some of the Chumash withdrew a few steps. Most, however, began to inch closer. Having committed to keeping his people at a safe distance, Matipuyaut halted them with a commanding motion.

Cabrillo patted his stallion, bent down low over his neck and whispered, "Well, Viento, are you ready?"

No more than his master's measured tone was needed to set Viento in high-stepping motion but Cabrillo restrained him from surging forward. Commanded by the captain-general's strong hands and legs to maintain a deliberate stroll, Viento cow-hopped to test the firmness of his resolve and then obeyed. Up and back he paraded, with the joy in his master's company, this fresh open space, and even so gentle an exertion reflected over every dappled-gray inch of him. Approaching the crowd for the second time, Cabrillo brought him to a halt seven yards in front of Matipuyaut, whose wonder seemed to have taken years of responsibility from his shoulders. He shouted, "Fine horse! Mighty horse!" which incited cries of approval from all around.

Cabrillo let his eyes skim the cheering islanders, and he spotted Taya standing slightly apart from the rest with two small boys at her sides. He noticed that neither she nor her sons, young as they were, displayed any fear. Their faces revealed only awe and admiration.

When Cabrillo leaped down, patted Viento, and led him to Matipuyaut, the chief found the courage to stand his ground even when his sons took a step or two back. Cabrillo halted and said, "This is my horse, Matipuyaut. He is called *Viento*."

The chief nodded gravely. "Viento, fine horse."

Cabrillo ran a soothing hand over his horse's neck as he beckoned Matipuyaut closer. The chief approached to within inches of Viento as his people looked on with varying degrees of apprehension.

"You may touch him," Cabrillo signed.

With eagerness and hesitation battling for dominance, Matipuyaut asked, "Will your god be offended?"

"Our God will smile." And so did Cabrillo.

This was sufficient encouragement. Matipuyaut reached out, his eyes locked on Viento's, and gently touched the velvety nose of the great stud. His face lightened at the extraordinary newness of this

202

bonding with an animal so enormous and strange, and he muttered a very soft, "Ahhh!" As if trained for such a moment, Viento whickered a deep response that Matipuyaut appeared to understand.

Unfortunately the horse's mild response drew an excited howl from the crowd, and this snapped his head up and set him to prancing again. It took a little more quieting from Cabrillo before Matipuyaut tried to communicate with his horse once again. When he did, Viento shifted his feet and sniffed at the slightly familiar hand, and then allowed the chief stroke him from forelock to muzzle.

When Cabrillo felt that the time had come, he asked Matipuyaut by hand signals, "Would you like to sit on him?"

This question provoked another round of murmuring from the natives, and Matipuyaut took an instant to muster a fresh level of bravery before accepting the invitation.

Glancing skyward and offering a silent prayer to all the saints for Matipuyaut's protection, Cabrillo held Viento's bridle and ordered Manuel to form a makeshift stirrup with his hands. The chief placed his foot within the locked fingers, pushed upward, and lifted his right leg over Viento's back as he had seen Cabrillo do. With his master still standing at his head, Viento took only a step or two as he adjusted to the stranger on his back.

At first Matipuyaut sat low and tense with his eyes locked on the back of Viento's head, yet he accepted with impressive quickness this completely foreign sensation of having a twelve hundred pound animal shifting between his legs. He straightened slowly and looked around from this new vantage point. Cabrillo showed him how to take Viento's mane in his hands, then led his horse forward several strides. As soon as they stopped Matipuyaut motioned his head forward in an obvious request to go farther. Inwardly smiling, the captain-general set off down the beach. The chief clung to the mane, his eyes and teeth gleaming as he punctuated the ride with short outbursts of, "Ayee, ayee."

When they returned at last Matipuyaut bent down and said something to Viento that Cabrillo had no means of comprehending, but the soft, respectful manner in which the chief smoothed his hands over Viento's neck expressed both gratitude and respect. Matipuyaut gazed at Cabrillo, his face betraying that he would have liked his ride to be extended even longer, but he did not ask, and the captain-general chose not to tempt either fate or Viento's tolerance further. Dismounting, Matipuyaut said and signed with emphasis, "He is a friend of high value, Chief Cabrillo. One day horses will be the friends of my people also."

Perhaps so, thought Cabrillo, watching the earnestness of the chief, and he suddenly apprehended that Matipuyaut was voicing some kind of prophetic vision rather than a wish. Yet there was no indication of threat or warning in what the chief had said, so Cabrillo brushed aside his sensation as foolishness. His horses were safe, and men couldn't see beyond today.

By now Seguro had reached shore, and Cabrillo soon gave the order to land the mares as well. At low tide they and Viento would be taken slightly northwest to makeshift corrals at a curve in the rocky embankment where both grooms and soldiers would assure their safekeeping. Any further Chumash and equine interaction would have to wait until after the baptismal ceremonies.

The island men, women, and children followed the sailors as they climbed up and gathered around the knoll near the head of the sand dune. This was where Cabrillo's men had set the five-foot cross and where they had already performed the quiet and sparsely attended claiming ceremony. Now, the mound was as crowded as an anthill, and the wind could reach them with enough force to toss their hair and clothing and carry away their voices.

When all were ready Father Gamboa, with Father Lezcano by his side, called Taya forward. She came with each of her hands tightly gripped by an identically handsome three-year-old. Standing before them, she studied the two priests and the wooden cross.

In a loud, rich voice Father Gamboa said as Father Lezcano signed, "Today, this woman will become a child of our most holy God. He is a loving father, who gave his son to the world so that we could learn how to turn from ways that harm others, so we could better love our brothers and sisters. He gave us his Holy Spirit to help us find the strength to do what is good, so that all of us may one day live in his holy kingdom in heaven above." At these words many of the Chumash followed his uplifted arms and face and glanced speculatively skyward.

Father Gamboa bent down and drew the largest of three linen drapes from the top of a wooden box brought from the ship. He wrapped the cloth around Taya's shoulders and signed for her to tie it closed over her chest. The two boys were then cloaked just as their mother. He took a small bottle from inside the chest, held it up, and performed the rite as he described, "This is holy oil. With it I trace the sign of the cross of Jesus upon this woman, and now her sons. It will forever be a symbol of their new life as children of God." Next he picked up a pitcher of water, and Father Lezcano gestured for Taya to kneel down and bend her head forward. When she had obeyed Father Gamboa continued, quietly reciting the prescribed prayers, and then addressing the gathering in a compassionate voice as he placed a gentle hand on Taya's shoulder and poured a trickle of water over the front of her bowed head. "This woman will now be blessed by the waters of baptism in the name of our Heavenly Father, and of his Son, Jesus Christ, and of the Holy Spirit. This water, touched by God's grace, will rinse away any evil that has ever touched this woman. It will make her clean. In Christ's name, she will henceforth be known as Sarah."

He then turned to the boys. "Now, her children will also be baptized," he said, and at Taya's signal the boys knelt down beside her and followed her quiet example as the priest performed the rite twice more. He named the boys Marcos and Lucas, after the two disciples.

When the rite had concluded, Father Gamboa gestured for them to stand, smiled, and kept his eyes on Taya as he said loudly to the crowd, "By the blessings they have just received, all darkness has been removed from Sarah, whom you call Taya, and her sons. From this day forward they will be welcomed and honored among you. They will be taught many things, and they will show you the love of God by their kindness and goodness. In this way they will bring new light to your people."

Cabrillo had been watching Taya intently, had seen the tears form as she comprehended the priest's words, had sensed the depth of her elation that such things could be true, and he was moved by the desperation of her belief. When Father Gamboa saw the same emotions light her young face, his words dwindled. She smiled tenderly at the two priests, and her radiant face freed Father Gamboa's tongue enough to say, "May God always protect you, Sarah."

As the Chumash looked on uncertainly Taya took Father Gamboa's hand, then Father Lezcano's, and held them briefly to each cheek. She turned a gaze of profound appreciation toward Cabrillo, but before he could approach where she stood Matipuyaut strode forward and lightly took hold of her shoulders, studying her face as if for the first time. He glanced from the priests to Cabrillo, and back to his daughter, and gradually allowed his skepticism to be replaced by relieved acceptance. When he at last embraced her, his two small grandsons tentatively wrapped their arms around his legs. Soft exhales rose from the onlookers, and soon Taya and her boys were being hugged and greeted by many villagers. A few of the more daring sailors inched closer and would have joined in the clutching if Vargas hadn't growled them back to where they belonged.

Throughout the ritual Kipomo had kept a slight distance, and as the crowd made its way down the hillside he drew closer to and lingered at the base of the cross. When he was at last alone he reached out and touched the wood, gazed up at the sky, and softly sang a waving chant that was carried away by the wind. Glancing back up the hill, Father Lezcano saw the shaman's actions but could only guess his prayer's intentions.

It turned out that Cabrillo was among the last to offer his good wishes to Taya, and these congratulations were cut short by her father requesting his company. So he left her with a bow and walked with Matipuyaut toward the feasting grounds.

Well over an hour earlier Cabrillo had given the order for a dozen of his men to fish for the meal that was to follow the ceremonies. From all reports and from what he'd seen, no sooner had the sailors begun to set their hooks and cast their nets than some of the local men had pushed their canoes into the water and impressed the men of the fleet by displaying great skill in their own food-gathering techniques. Now, as the crowd made its way to a designated area of the beach, the smell of fish roasting on fire-heated rocks buried beneath the sand enticed the gatherers into close quarters to await the servers. Knowing it would be foolish to rely too heavily on so young and unproven an accord, the officers and boatswains locked attentive eyes upon their own men as well as the islanders and skillfully restricted the mingling between the two groups.

Not surprisingly, the horses were a powerful attraction to the natives, yet Cabrillo's men kept their equestrian treasures well guarded by strictly following the order to allow no more than two Indians at a time to approach and pet them. Young Mateo had been given the esteemed responsibility of helping watch over Viento, and this he did with the gravest dedication. When the feasting began and increased in liveliness as the few musicians of the fleet brought out their pipes and strings, Cabrillo's desire to check on Viento and the other horses grew. Promising to return shortly, he parted from Matipuyaut and made his way to the two crudely fashioned horse pens his men had hastily thrown together using little more than driftwood and boulders. It was beside Viento's pen that Taya and her twins found him, but before the first word could be exchanged between them, Father Lezcano appeared at his commander's side.

Taya turned a tender expression toward the priest, her appreciation to him and Father Gamboa still evident, but when she again faced Cabrillo she revealed an even stronger emotion. With hands and voice, she said, "You have given me and my sons a new life, a life with goodness. My people will love them now. What can I do to please you, Cabrillo?"

"Learn about our God from Father Lezcano," he replied. "Teach your sons and your people."

"This I will do," she promised and took a step closer. "Is there nothing more?"

With her so close, so undeniably and overpoweringly appealing, Cabrillo needed a breath before saying, "Nothing more." Her gaze fell in disappointment, so he hurried to add, "Today is for you and your sons, to bring you peace and happiness. Do what will bring you joy."

Before she could relay what might have made her happy, one of her boys tugged on her hand, shyly pointed to the horses, and asked, "Can we touch them, mother?"

Cabrillo chuckled at the child's wish, one he too would have made to capture the uniqueness of this day. "Yes, you shall all touch them."

He led the family to Luna's side and, with Mateo attending to her, held the boys up one at a time to pet her neck. Taya's hand joined theirs, and at the first touch she closed her eyes and inhaled deeply, taking in the scent and feel of this extraordinary animal. When her eyes opened they turned their glow upon Cabrillo. He smiled and asked, "Would you like to sit on her?"

Taya paused and asked, "Is she a mother?"

"She has delivered three young ones."

Finding comfort in this answer, reassured by the kindred nature of their positions, Taya moved to stand before the mare, looked into her eyes, and silently and respectfully asked permission. Only then did she say, "Yes."

Luna was led outside the corral, and it took little effort for Cabrillo to lift Taya's lithe form up and set her upon the smooth back. At this connection with the horse's body, Taya said, "So strong," in hushed wonder and held very still. Her sons, now shifting from side to side with excitement, were picked up, placed behind their mother, and each was shown how to wrap his arms around the waist in front of him. A small group of the feasters, all but forgotten by those near the mare, raised an approving buzz at the sight of their newly reclaimed family seated atop the horse. Cabrillo took the reins from Mateo as Taya and her boys clung tightly to their holds, and he walked the mare in a small oval with his nephew strolling at Luna's side. The exhilarated grins of the riders conveyed their feelings better than any words, and few who looked on could keep from smiling themselves. One lap of the oval was followed by three more and, as the riders grew more accustomed to the experience, each circuit was enjoyed more than the one before it.

As Cabrillo led them back toward the pen for the last time, a Chumash youth trotted up a little too close to Luna's rear, and she shot a hind foot out in his direction. Before any warning could have saved him from an injurious kick, the boy leaped agilely out of her range and saved himself from anything worse than a few moments of embarrassment amid the laughter from those near the scene. The mare had sidled slightly to recover from the kick but, again to Cabrillo's relief, Taya and her sons managed to hang on without mishap and seemingly without much effort. Mateo stared from the three riders to Cabrillo in astonishment, saying, "Why, sir, they ride almost as good as caballeros, and they have never ridden before."

Taya understood Mateo's tone and expression if not his words, and she sat a little taller upon the horse.

Sooner than they would have wished, Cabrillo brought the mare to the corral railing and Taya and her boys were lifted to the sand. All three thanked the mare with words and pats, and they left the pen walking at Cabrillo's side. When they reached Father Lezcano, the captain-general said, "I must talk with Matipuyaut, Father. Will you remain with this family and begin their instruction?"

"Gladly, sir."

Cabrillo bowed to Taya and went in search of his host.

In minutes the two commanders were sitting upon a long woven mat where Matipuyaut continued to give every indication that his ride aboard Viento had planted the fertile seeds of trust between them. They took their time as they talked and ate, relishing the bounty of the island, and the chief accepted with mixed reactions the samples of spices Cabrillo had had brought from the ship. When Matipuyaut peeled a roasted gulls egg and allowed Cabrillo to sprinkle it with a touch of black pepper, he took a bite and his face puckered with aversion. At his first taste of crushed cloves, however, he rolled it around on his tongue and nodded in fascinated approval. As if the food were unlocking reserves of promise seldom made available to a visitor, each new flavor seemed to increase Matipuyaut's comfort with Cabrillo. Even so, he remained sharply observant of every strange nuance being revealed.

When they'd finished their extensive meal, the two leaders called forth their trade goods and began to barter. Prices had more or less been established the day before and, again utilizing Father Lezcano's interpreting skills, the exchanges proceeded smoothly. When the trading of material goods concluded, information again became the chosen item of exchange. The ship's scribe sat not far from Cabrillo's elbow, recording what passed between the men just as he'd recorded the flow of trade goods. Captain Ferrelo, who had been allowed ashore to join them temporarily, sat beside Father Lezcano and attended closely to all that was signed and said.

Though the chief knew of no location where significant amounts of gold could be found, he had heard many times of a great river far up the mainland coast. He explained that neither he nor his islanders had traveled as far as this river. Since it was obvious to Cabrillo that these Chumash were men of the sea he questioned the chief at length about the winds and the tides that he might encounter as he sailed toward China. Captain Ferrelo was also encouraged to question the chief, and he did so at such a rate that the scribe could barely keep his quill scribbling fast enough to record the details of their discussion. The

209

captain-general occasionally took a moment to scan what had been written and to add a note or two of his own.

All too soon for his liking, Cabrillo realized that the hour had come for his landing party to return to the ships. He knew that the men still aboard needed a respite as badly as his horses had, and it was nearly time for the next watch to be relieved. Even the crew of the *San Miguel,* prior criminals and ruffians though they were, had been well behaved enough lately to earn a few hours away from their habitual confines. So Cabrillo bid farewell to Matipuyaut and was among the first of the feasted sailors to be rowed from the island, leaving Father Lezcano behind to act as one of the interpreters, to teach Taya, and to help the grooms watch over the horses. Captain Ferrelo followed his commander's example and soon reboarded *La Victoria,* leaving the shore parties under the command of Pilot San Remón, Vargas, and other thoughtfully chosen officers until Captain Correa could land.

Standing at the taffrail of his upper stern deck, Cabrillo gazed beyond the mouth of the harbor at the sky and the sea as he listened to a singing wind. *How long? How long will it blow?* This morning had done much to initiate ties with the islanders and heighten the promise of a relatively calm stay, but remaining here kept them away from their goal. They needed to conquer the coast with all haste, and haste was being denied them. *Curse this devilish wind!*

Then, there was the girl. She could too easily become an excuse to loiter here. Cabrillo was honest enough with himself to admit his attraction, and to know it should not be allowed to develop into more than that. And what about his men? They had been allowed ashore but ordered under threats of the harshest penalties to remain on the beach and within sight of the ships. And they had been strictly forbidden from interacting with the island's women. Their long restrained sexual hunger must be kept from igniting and resulting in actions that extended well beyond the hospitable offerings of the Chumash leader, or beyond the tolerance of the fleet's commander. Cabrillo and the other officers accepted the challenge of maintaining a balance between allowing their men enough freedom to remain hard-working and loyal yet restricting the opportunities that might entice disobedience. Beyond the fleet's leaders, the Chumash men of this island were powerfully built and vigilantly watchful, adding another influential deterrent to philandering.

Turning back toward shore, Cabrillo watched the outwardly peaceful scene of his men eating amongst the natives. Vargas and his guards stood in relaxed poses around the gathering, as did several Chumash warriors. So far, so good, but it might take little to stir contention.

As if to taunt him, a strong breeze found its way into the harbor and ruffled his long, curly hair. *Yes, I feel you, but you will not last forever.*

Three days aged into four and then seven, and Cabrillo began to pace the deck even when not on watch; his patience with the wind now all but spent. Two days earlier, just after most of them had celebrated Mass ashore, one of the usually well-behaved hands of *La Victoria* had been sent in chains to the *San Miguel* for a thankfully interrupted tryst with one of the Indian woman. Apologies, assurances, and trade goods were offered in an attempt to soothe the islanders, particularly the woman's husband, but these atonements proved to be only moderately effectively. Since then, shore leaves had been severely restricted, and Cabrillo knew that the innocent sailors felt their unearned confinements acutely. He and his officers kept them busy cleaning, repairing, and stocking, but the restlessness was growing.

He had also minimized his own visits to the island and had allowed Taya and her boys to come to the ship only once, and Father Lezcano was always with them. Matipuyaut came to each of the ships once and to the *San Salvador* twice, observing and questioning the purpose and workings of guns, riggings, cooking devices, nautical tools, and armaments until he was satisfied at last. Or so Cabrillo thought.

On the last visit, just as Matipuyaut was about to retake his canoe, Master Uribe sent a man aloft to grease the mainmast. The chief fastened his gaze on the sailor scaling the rigging with the agility of a spider climbing its webbing and proclaimed, "I wish to climb up."

Cabrillo's heart sank. Though he didn't surrender without a gallant effort, no amount of cajoling or persuading could change Matipuyaut's mind without offense. The determined chief even refused to wear a safety line. The only consolation allowed Cabrillo, and upon this he insisted, was that two sailors would accompany Matipuyaut as he climbed. Silently praying as he watched the first and every other grasp and foothold, the captain-general's stomach knotted but he managed to keep his face blank. When Matipuyaut made it to the crow's nest successfully more than a few sailors breathed sighs of relief. Cabrillo waited with hard fought patience for what he considered a gracious allotment of time and then invited the chief to rejoin him on deck, but it took a great deal more coaxing to convince the chief to finally leave his lofty vantage point and descend. When the chief once again planted his feet upon the *San Salvador*'s solid planking, Cabrillo ushered him politely to his canoe, immediately went to his cabin, filled and lifted a goblet of sherry to acknowledge the chief's survival, and kept his door closed for fifteen minutes of rare and much needed quiet that he shared only with his glass.

During the early evening of the seventh day in Isla de Posesión's harbor, Father Lezcano found Cabrillo and his pilot with their heads bent over several charts. He waited for a pause in their calculations and suppositions and then asked, "Do you intend to go ashore tomorrow, sir? If so, I would like to go along."

"Of course, Father. Tomorrow," he sighed broodingly. "We will have been anchored here twice as long as at any stop of our voyage." He glanced at the priest. "Can you offer a special prayer, something that will remind God of our need?"

"I have been praying most fervently, sir," he said gently, "in six languages. Perhaps if you and I were to pray together for awhile...?"

"Willingly. Say, some of Ignacio's prayers might be best. He is a Basque, is he not? He must have sympathies for men of the sea. There just might be something in his words that yield a little extra grace for us sailors."

Father Lezcano did not waste his breath muttering warnings about such a presumption. "Possibly so, sir. I brought his writings with me."

"Very well. Pilot, if you do not mind us continuing with the charts later...?"

"Of course not, sir."

Just as Pilot San Remón was about to withdraw, Cabrillo added pointedly, "Another voice surely would do no harm, eh, Father?" With little choice and no real reluctance, San Remón unloaded the rolled charts he'd just collected and went down on his knees between his commander and his priest. Their heads bowed low and Father Lezcano started reading aloud from the book in his hands. Later, they uttered together words of devotion that each had learned as young children. After the last prayers had been recited, Cabrillo rose and went to command his watch with a hopeful heart.

At the passage of midnight he returned to his cabin, fell into his bunk, and enjoyed the first sound sleep he'd known in a week.

The morning of October 25 was still cloaked in the deep darkness that lingers before dawn when Cabrillo bolted upright in his bunk and shouted a gruff, inaudible word. Manuel and Mateo scrambled into the cabin but the captain-general jerked out his arm in a silent command to keep still. His ears strained. Nothing. Nothing at all. Then he knew it had been the silence that had awakened him.

"Do you hear?" he asked, his eyes blinking the remaining lethargy away.

Manuel suddenly beamed with relief, "The wind. She stopped, sir. She stopped at last."

Throwing off his cover and scrambling for his clothes while Manuel lit a lamp, Cabrillo dressed so quickly that Paulo got to the cabin in time to do nothing more than ask peevishly what was wanted for breakfast. He was further put out when Cabrillo joyfully exclaimed, "Breakfast! No breakfast until the ships are underway. Who knows how long we have before the wind returns? Dear God bless Father Ignacio de Loyola and our own Father Lezcano!"

Whatever crewmembers still clung to their slumbers were immediately rousted and called to the capstans and lines. While the ships were being readied Cabrillo briefly considered going ashore to bid their host farewell, but in the end he sent Father Lezcano off in his stead with parting gifts and orders not to linger.

The breaking light quickened the hands of the crews, many of them as happy as their commander to be setting their sails again. Cabrillo, pacing the stern deck, studied the sky with a building hope that fueled his impatience to be off. The priest's boat rowed back to the flagship and was hurriedly secured as the bergantine began to maneuver into a position from which she could assist her flagship through the harbor's maze of rocks and reefs.

Father Lezcano had landed on deck wearing a broad smile, and he'd come directly to his captain-general. Although his expression made it evident that more could be shared, for now he said only, "They sent their farewells, sir." Whatever else he might have wished to convey he saved for a time when Cabrillo's attentions were not consumed by the need to safeguard his departing fleet. At times such as these, every one of his men knew enough to keep his silence and his distance unless life or limb was imminently imperiled.

At last, after all three ships had sailed to a safe distance from the reefs, Cabrillo relaxed his stance and expression, and thereby eased the tenseness of his men. They all welcomed the feel of their ships' keels slicing the sea beneath them and rejoiced at the now friendly breeze upon their faces. Arms reached energetically toward any task while backs welcomed the strain of muscle and sinew.

By noon, however, the lighthearted moods of the men and officers began to fade away with the continued slackening of the gentle gusts. They slowed, and slowed even more, and eventually floated to a near halt that left the ships within tantalizing view but beyond reach of the mainland. Hour followed hour but no amount of praying, wishing, or cursing was able to coax the advance of more than a few fathoms at a time from the whiffs of wind.

When Father Lezcano again made his way to the captain-general's side, Cabrillo stared at the beckoning land and said regretfully, "We asked that the wind take us from the island, rather than asking to be delivered to our next port. Next time we had better take more care with our prayers, eh Father?"

214

Chapter 18

LAND OF LUHUI

An hour before midnight the stillness was violently shattered by a squall so sudden and forceful that it threatened to drive the fleet onto the now looming shore. Cabrillo swiftly gauged their plight and swung the ships away, tacking farther out to sea where they could battle to round Cabo de Galera. As the wind whipped clothing against bodies with bruising strength and sails shrieked and masts groaned while straining to obey the commands of those at the lines, every man grittily bent to his work. Throughout the long night and into the next morning much was demanded in order to veer the ships back and forth at a safe distance from land, yet keep from surrendering precious miles. When even the laudable vigor of the crews began to ebb, finally, blessedly, a more cooperative breeze reached out from the south, huffing them around the cape and guiding them up an entirely new stretch of coastline.

Now, heartened by a warming sun, the weary yet grateful men of Cabrillo's fleet managed to sail on for twenty-five more miles. Their sustained ability to hug the shore lifted their spirits even higher and allowed them to admire the profuse flora and villages along the way. Manned canoes could be seen ashore, but none attempted to approach the ships. It may have been the anticipation of a new gale that kept the natives ashore, Cabrillo speculated, but whatever the reason he would not delay the voyage to meet with them. In the weeks to come he intended to take advantage of every favorable condition.

The weather, however, again foiled his hopes by loosing a volley of ferocious and fickle crosswinds that held them deadlocked for five days. From where they lay captive Cabrillo could see sure signs of a river, and he longed to put ashore to search its boundaries. But this

215

coastline was far too rocky to attempt an approach during such treacherous weather.

Though on the first morning of November Father Lezcano reminded Cabrillo that it was All Saints' Day, the captain-general saw no sign of heavenly benevolence in a dawning that brought a cold wind to bite at exposed skin and penetrate all but the heaviest clothing. He knew that their supply of firewood must be getting dangerously low, so he descended into the hold with his steward and took a cheerless inventory of the small pile left to them. His steward stared at the stack and shook his head as he stamped his chilled feet to encourage a warm flow of blood.

"That is it, then," said Cabrillo.

"Yes, all of it, sir."

Closing his eyes for a moment, Cabrillo pictured his men working in the cold all day and night without so much as a warm bowl of soup to comfort them. Even if they were willing to forego the solace of the heat, little of their consumables, mostly beans, rice, and salted meat and fish, could be made edible without the ability to boil it. Their dried biscuit was growing so populated with weevils that the men had taken to calling it weescuit.

As he climbed the steps out of the hold and those that led up to the main deck, he tried not to dwell on the quickening season and weather, or question for the hundredth time the location of the nearest Asian coast. Approaching Pilot San Remón, he buried his own disappointment as deeply as he could and said, "We are nearly out of firewood, pilot, and we dare not try to land here. We must ease the ships back and once again seek shelter behind Cabo de Galera."

Hard as it was to utter the words, the bitter wind made his commands easily acted upon and swiftly fulfilled. Within hours they had anchored near a large village that Father Gamboa named Galera Puerto de Todos Santos, and Cabrillo sent men ashore in search of wood and water. To his disheartened surprise the landing party returned empty handed, explaining that the villagers had little wood for their own use and could spare them none. The closest anchorage Cabrillo knew to have plenty of water and firewood was Pueblo de las Sardinas and, after a short conversation with his officers, he announced that they would set sails for that destination first thing in the morning.

Upon their arrival at the pueblo Cabrillo and his men had every reason to feel grateful that they had treated the natives so honorably during their visit two and a half weeks earlier. People from the villages on both sides of the river welcomed their return by providing enough wood to warm their food and chilled extremities for some time to come and enough fresh water to fill many empty barrels. In light of their congenial reception, Cabrillo decided to remain here a day or two so that his men could make ship repairs as well as sew stout clothing to protect them against the cold weather ahead.

The villagers were also covering their bodies more fittingly for the season, yet a number were willing to barter with some of their heavier furs and tanned leather. As Cabrillo strolled his deck during the first night watch at the pueblo, he smiled down at the large buff colored hides now covering several sleeping men. When the hour of midnight passed and he opened the door to his own cabin, he saw Paulo settling a beautiful blanket of sea otter fur atop his bunk.

Heartily pleased, Cabrillo opened his mouth to question its origin and express his thanks but Paulo merely smiled and said as he left the chamber, "Enjoy a good night's rest, sir."

Cabrillo undressed and slid into his bed with a moan of pleasure. Within moments he slipped into a sleep uncommonly free of hauntings.

The next morning he awoke to a gentle knocking at his door. "Yes, enter," he called, rising up on an elbow.

Pilot San Remón appeared at the door looking distinctly uncomfortable. "Forgive me, sir, but a woman has come aboard and she is demanding to see you."

"A woman?" Cabrillo asked as he reluctantly left his furs and pulled on his breeches. "A woman has made you so uneasy?"

"When you meet her, Captain-General, you will understand my, uh, my disquiet."

"Is she *that* beautiful?"

His pilot's expression revolted in protest. "Decidedly not, sir!"

Curious now, Cabrillo waved his pilot out, saying, "I will be on deck in a moment. Try to entertain her until then."

San Remón let a muffled whimper escape before he bowed and departed.

Emerging from his cabin and heading to the main deck, Cabrillo took one look at his latest guest and did indeed comprehend his pilot's behavior. Here stood a woman who had seen the passing of so many years that Cabrillo dared not even guess their number. Though stooped with age, there was unmistakable pride in the carriage of her tiny frame. Cabrillo couldn't help being appreciative that the nippy weather had enticed her to cover her body with furs that reached almost to her ankles, or for the expansive and intricate jewelry that hid most of her flagging chest. Her white hair was tied high atop her head and encircled by a masterful work of woven rushes and feathers that rose six inches above her forehead. Brawny guards hovered protectively behind and on both sides of her, further demonstrating her high status. She watched Cabrillo's approach with eyes still bright with keenness.

Noting that Father Lezcano already stood at her side, Cabrillo reached her and bowed deeply. "I welcome you to my ship."

She smiled with genuine warmth, revealing a gap where three top front teeth should have been. But Cabrillo was surprised to read a touch of mischief in the clever old face.

One of her guards announced and signed with great deference, "This is Luhui. She is the wise leader of all the villages in this region."

Cabrillo bowed as he said aside to Manuel, "Bring the chair from my cabin, and have Paulo gather some fitting gifts."

To Luhui, he said, "We are happy that you have come. Your people have been good to us. We wish to repay their kindness."

The aged woman's eyes shone with pleasure and in a wavering but authoritative voice, she said, "When you came before, I did not see you but I was told that you were generous with your gifts and that you shared many wonders with my people. All are glad you have returned. Now, I wish to learn about you and your ways."

The chair arrived and at Cabrillo's invitation she accepted her place of honor. Once seated, her feet dangling two inches off the floor, she ran her withered hands over the smoothness of the carved arms as she marveled at the comfort of such a contrivance. Paulo appeared with a small chest of goods, and Cabrillo drew out a six-foot length of crimson satin.

"Aaiio," breathed Luhui, as Cabrillo laid the cloth across her lap. She lifted it, admiring the play of light across its dramatic hue and the

218

feel of its silky surface. Next, after hesitating over its possible inappropriateness, he handed her a looking glass. When she caught the sight of her reflection, she started, held completely still for a moment, and then broke into an irresistible howl of laughter that carried not the slightest trace of vanity. Relieved and tickled by her reaction, Cabrillo lifted a lovely silver cup from the chest. Her eyes sparkled anew at its fascinating shape and delicately worked surface. She lowered her gifts to her lap and smiled upon Cabrillo as if he were a newly adopted son. "You are generous, Chief Cabrillo. You have already bestowed gifts to my chiefs and now you give these in exchange for wood and water."

"And kindness," he said.

If possible, the affection in her smile only deepened.

Handing her new treasures to the guard who had introduced her, she proclaimed happily to Cabrillo. "We will stay with you."

Although uncertain as to the intended scope of this statement, Cabrillo said what any good host would have, "You are welcome."

Little did he suspect that eleven hours would pass and Luhui and her guards would still be aboard the *San Salvador*, giving no indication of an intention to leave. After the first hour or so Cabrillo had left them in Father Lezcano's care, and they had proven to be amiable guests even while Luhui investigated every inch, tool, and sailor of the flagship. While overseeing the repair duties and keeping track of the progress of the clothing production, Cabrillo saw her frequently. Once he came across her patting the muscled bicep of a sailor who was trying to refit a pair of wheels to a cannon, and on another occasion he heard her praising a pair of soldiers who were polishing the ship's musketry. She also seemed captivated by Father Lezcano's instruction of the Christian faith and questioned him often about its origin and customs. The captain-general soon realized that, despite her willingness to answer every question posed to her, she was learning far more about them than the other way around.

When the time to dine arrived, Cabrillo entertained Luhui in the best manner their circumstances allowed. Considering the minuteness of her physique as well as the greatness of her social stature, he gave her only a sip of sherry with their meal while making only a small portion available to himself and the others at the table. As the dishes were being cleared Cabrillo invited his guests back out to the main deck, fully believing that they would choose to return to their homes at last. Luhui, however, went directly to the spot where her chair had previously rested and raised a questioning face to her host. A quick glance toward Manuel brought the chair back, and Luhui wasted no time in occupying it.

While her attention was momentarily captured by the old slave brand on Manuel's arm, Cabrillo drew Father Lezcano a couple of steps away. "Now what the devil do we do?"

Amused by his commander's consternation, the priest said, "Music, perhaps?"

"I do not appreciate your levity at the moment. How do we politely remove her from the ship?"

"My dear Captain-General, one does not politely remove a queen from one's ship if she does not wish to be removed."

Accepting the unwanted truth of these words, Cabrillo still cast his priest a scowl while surrendering with, "Very well, what music?"

"We can call on Father Gamboa. He is a most obliging piper, and Manuel can bring out his tambourine."

Cabrillo glanced at Luhui, now smiling up into Manuel's considerate face. "I will not let that woman take any closer notice of Manuel. She has been captivated by him all day, keeps eyeing him with that look of speculation. He may represent some kind of magic to her, and his banging on the tambourine could confirm it. Who knows what she may propose?"

The manner in which these last words were said made Father Lezcano's grin break free of its restraints. "Surely not that, sir. At her age?"

"Who knows?" he repeated. "I would not have the heart to order him to... entertain her."

"Very well, sir. Mateo can play the tambourine fairly well. The boy should be safe from such royal attentions."

Choosing to ignore his friend's impudence, Cabrillo said with a nod, "Please ask Master Uribe to have Father Gamboa brought over." Still chuckling inwardly, Father Lezcano left his side with a bow.

More surprised than anyone else, Cabrillo gradually found himself enjoying the evening. Captains Ferrelo and Correa accompanied Father Gamboa to the flagship to meet Luhui, and all three commanders displayed their best manners in her presence. Captain Ferrelo's natural grace and charm especially seemed to impress her, and she asked him to remain at her side, thereby relieving Manuel for a time. Without betraying the slightest trace of chagrin at being singled out by so ancient an admirer, Captain Ferrelo genially complied with her wishes.

Father Gamboa and Mateo soon settled into their positions and began to play a lively tune. With the first notes Luhui let out a mesmerized exclamation and the feet of the sailors began to tap the decking. At an acquiescing nod from Cabrillo, Master Uribe cried, "Dance before the mast if you wish, men."

Keeping a respectful distance between Luhui and the officers and themselves, several sailors immediately stepped forward to take advantage of this rare boon. They began with a few subtle movements to find the rhythm of the music, but things quickly evolved into a competition of sorts between several dancers, some performing steps known since childhood and others creating spins, capers, and leaps on the spot. To complement the soaring moods of the guests and dancers, Father Gamboa smoothly swung into an even faster second melody that was familiar to most. At this livelier pace more bodies began to turn and bounce, more hands to clap, and voices to sing. Out of exhilaration one of the sailors let out a high, piercing battle cry, and Luhui pulled in a breath and mimicked it beautifully, extracting an appreciative grin from the captain-general.

A pair of the more athletic men instigated an impromptu duel of flexibility by taking turns whirling around and then kicking their feet higher and higher into the air. To the delight of all, this continued until the taller of them was toeing the air inches above his head. As applause for the winner erupted and Father Gamboa broke into his next musical number, Luhui suddenly hopped down from her chair, tugged a chagrinned Manuel along with her, and joined in by kicking and tottering with abandon.

At first Cabrillo held his breath, fearful that the old lady would hurt herself, but for the moment she was maintaining her balance, and Manuel was staying close enough to catch her if she fell. When Father Gamboa spotted her he glanced at the captain-general, silently asking if he should continue. Cabrillo nodded guardedly. At the end of that tune, however, he signaled for a pause in the music that allowed Luhui to return to her chair, beaming but out of breath.

From that point on her spurts of activity were high-spirited but short-lived, and during her times of rest she sat in her chair and clapped delightedly along with the crew. A few of her own people, some needing a little encouragement from their leader, eventually joined the dancing crewmen and quickly picked up many of the maneuvers. The lantern-lit decks of the *San Salvador* bounced and echoed with stomping of feet, and the air around the flagship rang with music, merry shouts, and laughter.

All of the ruckus brought a dose of envy but much amusement to those aboard her sister ships, especially when Luhui's high, gleeful chortle could be heard above it all. The villagers ashore stood or sat by their fires and stared in wonder toward the huge, noisy canoe, a little apprehensive that a spell might have been cast upon their beloved chief.

The music went on for nearly an hour, but as the evening deepened Cabrillo grew more and more aware of how badly his men needed rest. It was time to bring the evening's entertainment to a close, and he pointedly but cordially extended parting words to his two captains. They took to their boats and pushed off toward the other ships, and Cabrillo approached Luhui's still occupied chair. Before he could offer to usher her to her canoe, she extinguished any hope of an immediate departure by saying. "I am tired, Chief Cabrillo. I wish to sleep here among your people."

Caught off guard, Cabrillo stood speechless for a moment but recovered quickly enough to hide all but a trace of frustration. Turning to Manuel, he said, "Chief Luhui is to be given my cabin. Have Paulo prepare it for her, and move a mattress for me into Pilot San Remón and Master Uribe's quarters. I will be joining them tonight."

He said to Luhui, "You are welcome to sleep in my lodgings."

Her eyes twinkled again and that perceptive look reappeared that told him she knew exactly what mischief she was causing. He couldn't keep from smiling at the old fox as he said, "I must watch over the ship now. Have a pleasant sleep."

That night the decks were so crowded with the bodies of Luhui's guards and his own sailors, even scattered around his usual sanctuary on the quarterdeck, that Cabrillo grumbled repeatedly as he sought safe places to set his restless feet. When at last midnight came and Master Uribe relieved him, rather than heading to his own well-padded bunk and private cabin Cabrillo made his way to a mattress wedged between his officers in their area of the main cabin. His disgruntled mutterings soon changed to snores that blended with those of the other two men.

Luhui awakened with the sun, as brightly curious as ever, and again indicated her desire to remain aboard the *San Salvador*. Since, try as he might, Cabrillo could come up with no delicate way to oust her on this early Sunday, Fathers Lezcano and Gamboa were asked to proceed with the celebration of Mass. She honored the gravity of the ceremony by maintaining a reverential demeanor throughout, showing an understanding of the existence of a higher authority, and she followed the signing, bowing, and kneeling practices right along with the Catholics. Afterward, as if during the service she'd received some assurance or answer she'd been awaiting, Luhui announced that she wished to board her canoe. Surrounded by her guards, she paused at the railing to say, "Cabrillo, come to my village to be my guest. You have been good to me."

An impulse seized Cabrillo to offer her something special, and the choice seemed obvious. Quietly, he gave the order to bring it from his cabin, and as he and Luhui waited he told himself that his carpenter could craft another chair without much trouble, not one so ornate perhaps, but perfectly adequate. When the chair appeared, he said to Luhui, "Take this gift, as a sign of my friendship."

The old woman, delighted beyond words, embraced Cabrillo with withered but surprisingly strong arms. Her eyes were wet when she released him and turned away, and she proudly signaled for her escort to bring the chair along. As her craft pushed off from the flagship, she gestured a renewed invitation for him to come ashore.

Late that afternoon Cabrillo accepted her summons with anticipation. He and his entourage made their way ashore and paused at the corner of the village square, where he and Father Lezcano gazed up at tall poles anchoring the fence that surrounded the central area. Each pole bore a variety of painted animals and astrological symbols. The captain-general found them fascinating, and he mused aloud, "What do you suppose they mean?"

Father Lezcano had shifted his attention to several fifteen-inch stone markers planted evenly along the outside of the enclosure. "The poles, sir? They may represent pagan sentinels of some kind. But these stones, now, I wonder if they serve as grave markers." They were allowed no more time for speculation when several of Luhui's lieutenants appeared from around the corner and led them to her house.

Inside this roomy Chumash structure they feasted on fresh clams, ground-baked maguey, hazelnuts, and acorn mush cakes. Cabrillo found this last dish to be so tasty that he decided he must trade for a few barrels of ground acorns before the fleet's departure. Luhui, surrounded by her family and trusted guards, ate sparingly but entertained all with colorful tales of the revelry that had taken place the previous night aboard the ship.

After the meal, Luhui announced to her guests, "This is a special day, and our ancestors must not be left out. A ceremony to honor them will soon begin. Cabrillo, just as we were allowed to join you as you spoke to your god, you and your men may join us today."

Cabrillo sensed that such an invitation was very infrequently made to strangers, and he was touched by the old woman's trust. He signaled his acceptance in a manner that he hoped conveyed his appreciation, and they soon joined a procession of hundreds of villagers to gather around what had been confirmed to be their cemetery. He saw that most of the locals carried arm-length canes with divided ends, the purpose of which Cabrillo could not guess. When he and his men were motioned to their places near a slight mound on the outside of the fence, one of these canes was placed in his hand, which heightened his curiosity.

Luhui waited for her new chair to be positioned on the raised earthen platform before taking up her position. She then motioned Cabrillo, his captains, and Fathers Gamboa and Lezcano to draw closer to her side.

The evening had turned so warm that the natives had left their clothing behind. Instead of furs, the Chumash of both sexes had covered their bodies with light dyes that circled and zigzagged the mounds and planes of their tawny forms, highlighting every feature. The provocative setting and inhabitants couldn't help but captivate Cabrillo, his priests, officers, soldiers, and sailors.

Now, two men and two women, evidently previously selected for the honor of dancing this evening, stepped from the crowd and faced one another. Each elaborately ornamented dancer stood tall and grave, and each held handfuls of brightly hued feathers. Moving to the music of bone flutes, they began to dance around the enclosure. The purpose of the long sticks became clear as the villagers began to strike them against the fence, the ground, or another cane, creating a rattling rhythm that matched each step of the unified dancers. Cabrillo replicated their beating motions with his own cane as all of the villagers, including Luhui, lifted eyes skyward and began to sing words that neither Cabrillo nor Father Lezcano could follow distinctly.

The two young couples danced like precisely mirrored waves, their bodies swaying as their arms lifted, bending as they lowered, and always to the tempo commanded by the canes and flutes. The intensity of their steps and gestures increased each time they neared one of the poles that dominated the fence line, giving dramatic recognition to these markers. Cabrillo found it hypnotizing, this flowing, pounding, chanting around him, the beautiful youthful bodies flowing before him, and he was glad to be witnessing it all. This, he would never forget.

The dancers didn't slow their steps until the entire enclosure had been circled, and then Luhui raised her arms and the music suddenly stilled. The dancers disappeared as quietly and deferentially as they had arrived, and with the withdrawal of the performers, the villagers also began to disperse.

Intending to return to his ship, Cabrillo turned to Luhui and bowed his thanks. She accepted them graciously, but when the captain-general wished her goodnight and started walking toward the beach, Luhui called for her guards and issued a few quick commands. They carefully lifted her in the chair and fell into step behind Cabrillo.

Glancing back, Father Lezcano said, "Uh, sir, you may have a cabin guest again tonight."

Cabrillo halted in his tracks, and when Luhui's litter came up, he said with feigned regret, "Luhui, my ships will depart with the rising of the sun. The night for us will be a short one."

"Since you are leaving," she said, "it is good that I will spend this last night near you."

Cabrillo held rigidly still as he bit his tongue, then bowed stiffly and continued walking, fortunately unaware of the bemused faces of Father Lezcano and his officers.

Aboard the peaceful *San Salvador*, Luhui slept the dark hours away in dreamless comfort upon Cabrillo's bunk while the captain-general tossed wakefully throughout the night.

Especially early the next morning Cabrillo at last met Luhui to bid her farewell, and as he did so he realized that during these past few days he'd grown genuinely fond of the aged Chumash leader. She parted from him with genuine warmth, saying, "You are a good man, Cabrillo, and a good leader." When her canoe landed she disembarked along with her much-loved chair, turned, and waved back at him. Many of her villagers joined in this salutation.

As anchors rose from the water, canoes arrived with a parting gift of three more barrels of prized and painstakingly prepared acorn flour, and her emissaries refused to accept anything in exchange. As the ships eased away, she remained on the beach, surrounded by her people. Raising her voice she called out, "Come back soon, Chief Cabrillo. I will dance again."

"If our God allows it, I will come!" he shouted, and watched for some time as her petite figure grew ever smaller.

Over the next few days the breeze was so light that their sails could extract very few miles, and Cabrillo began to fear that they'd be forced to return much sooner than he'd hoped. But when the fleet finally rounded Cabo de Galera for the second time and Luhui's lands vanished from his sight, he found himself shaking his head and smiling at the many memories she had created. He would enjoy telling Beatriz and his sons all about her. He and his family had been apart for nearly four and a half months now. During that length of time his letter writing had grown less frequent, and today he felt a sense of loss as he recognized that she held his thoughts less regularly, less intensely with each passing day. It was strange, he thought, how a man could come to long for his family more but need them less.

As he reflected anew on the lateness of the season and the unknown but seemingly endless distance that lay before him, he had no choice but to remember that it would be many, many more months before he and his wife could hold each other again. For now he must be content to be enfolded only by his good ship.

Chapter 19

ELEMENTAL FURY

Cabrillo lifted his face to the sun and closed his eyes, relishing what he suspected would be one of the last fair days before winter's grayness prevailed over the brilliance of autumn. During the past chilly nights his men had taken advantage of the heavier clothing they'd fashioned at Cabo de las Sardinas, and in another few hours they would most likely break out their jackets again, but for now they absorbed the benevolent warmth wearing nothing more than their linen shirts and breeches.

Just yesterday they'd retaken their northernmost latitude, the location they'd been forced to retreat from on All Saints' Day, and they'd made excellent progress since daybreak. The fifty miles or so had delivered them into a vastly wilder region than the lands to the south, with the coastline growing progressively rougher and the Indian villages dwindling until they disappeared entirely. High mountains that challenged the ocean for dominance had overtaken the lush beaches and harbors. Cabrillo had allowed Father Gamboa to name the mountains they'd been skirting, and the good priest had dubbed them the Sierra de San Martin range. When a little farther on these peaks ended before a small cape, it too was named after that saint, and Cabrillo was tempted to investigate what lay beyond its rocky coastal hills. Instead he pushed on while the weather demonstrated so favorable a mood.

Early twilight found him conversing with his pilot and his shipmaster at the stern railing. Somewhat doubtfully, he said, "38° north. I would feel better about our calculation if the only clouds of the day had not blocked the sun at noon. Perhaps we are not far off, however, and it is fitting that we recognize reaching something of a milestone. A thousand miles, gentlemen. A thousand miles along a coast previously unknown to our world." He gazed overhead at a small flock of passing gulls and said musingly, "And, if we could spread wings and fly due east from here, we would not miss Seville by many leagues to the north or south."

"Seville," muttered Master Uribe softly, "how different a place from this, how tame in comparison."

One by one they turned toward the rocky shore and wordlessly contrasted what they saw to the Spanish city they had known.

Shrugging off any inclination toward homesickness as he watched the waves crash and spray against the craggy cliffs dotted with trees, Cabrillo smiled and said, "It is magnificent in its wildness, is it not?"

"Indeed it is, sir," said his pilot.

"We have not yet found cities of gold or the Strait of Anián, but we have been blessed to look upon such lands as these."

"Not many men have, sir," said Pilot San Remón.

"And surely China can not lie far ahead."

"Surely not, sir," said his pilot, and Master Uribe nodded in agreement. "Perhaps tomorrow will give us some indication that we are close."

"Yes, pray we are granted a friendly omen. We shall remain under sail again tonight." When he went to his bunk after midnight, his faith helped calm his mind and quiet his dreams. Less than four hours passed before a sudden lurching of his ship, rising of the winds, and tromping of hurried feet woke him. Manuel was at his door in moments, holding a glowing lamp and declaring, "It is not bad yet, sir, but it's coming on fast."

Though it took only moments for Cabrillo to reach the main deck, Pilot San Remón had already called all hands to action and ordered the furling of most sails and the shortening of the foretopsail. One glance showed Cabrillo that the officers of the other two ships were responding just as readily to the danger at hand. The grumbling clouds suddenly loosed their rain so thickly that it stole the air from Cabrillo's lungs, and he gulped a breath before shouting over the first crack of thunder to his sailors, "Quickly, men!" To his shipmaster, he ordered, "No more than three feet of sail on our foremast, Master Uribe."

In seconds the decks were so drenched that they challenged every foot questing a hold, upending men as they bulled forward to reach the lines or rigging. They fought to gain and maintain their duty stations, where they hauled, tied, or furled with single-minded purpose.

Their efforts soon relieved the straining, flapping canvas, and left a foretopsail the width of a table runner to drive the ship before the vicious southwest wind.

As the *San Salvador* mounted a huge swell Cabrillo spun around and squinted through the punishing rain to see the *San Miguel's* hands battling to keep her close. He had to look a greater distance out to find *La Victoria*, and his heart fell. Despite the efforts of her crew, the heavier ship was lagging farther and farther behind the fleet. *Stay with us, Bartolomé*, he silently urged her captain before his own ship again seized his attention.

The waves were growing higher and more erratic and now conspired with the rain and wind by crashing over Cabrillo's decks, chilling him and his men to their bones and knocking many about while mighty gusts buffeted them from above. The captain-general shouted, "Secure lifelines!" and these soon cinched waists and anchored working bodies to cleats, yardarms, and masts. Furled sails snapped and clawed to loosen their tethers and sailors leapt to retie the few that succeeded.

As the ship rolled and pitched, Cabrillo heard the increasingly frightened screams of his horses. To Manuel, swaying at his side, he bellowed over the storm's howl, "See to Viento and Seguro!" Manuel nodded, slogged his way to the hatch, and disappeared.

Grabbing tightly to a handhold with each swinging step, Cabrillo directed himself to steerage. There, the swaying lantern cast an arcing ghostly glow over four men straining to control the whipstaff. Heaved by the current's assault on the rudder, the whipstaff tossed the men back and forth as if they were bags of grain. The forehead of one man bore a five-inch gash that had bloodied his collar and shoulder, and the eyelid of another had swollen almost shut. "Achabal! Lachiondo!" Cabrillo yelled to the nearest strong hands. "The tie-downs!" A pair of thick ropes appeared and each was quickly slipped around the whipstaff and into the grooved canals that encircled it. The captain-general took an instant to regauge the direction of the ship and the behavior of the wind and waves, and then grabbed onto the line several feet from the staff. Two men clasped the rope behind him as three others hurried to take up the other side. "Bring her a point to starboard, men." At these words the seamen braced feet, tightened their grips, and pulled. Weary as they were, those who'd already been contending with the whipstaff added their muscles to the heaving sailors. They all clenched and leaned and strained in a contest against the bucking staff while the last man on each line drew it tighter and tighter beneath the point of a wooden cleat, restricting its violent swaying by degrees. When the staff had been forced upright, quivering and groaning, Cabrillo said, "Tie her off and ease your holds." When the ends were snug the men gradually released their grasps and stood back panting as they stared at the humming lines. The oiled hemp vibrated so ominously that Cabrillo feared it was only a matter of time before its chords or his whipstaff burst.

"Stand well back, men." He wiped the water and sweat from his eyes and said with pride to those standing soaking wet, bloody, and bruised within the dimly lit chamber, "We have plenty of line and another whipstaff but, by God, not one of you is replaceable." To his helmsmen, he added, "Send me word of any change," and turned to leave.

Cabrillo took three such determined strides that he almost knocked Father Lezcano down, and it was only then that he realized the priest must have been working as the second man behind him in the near darkness. "Father!" he blurted but could utter no more before the priest took a firm hold of his arm, pulled him to just under the edge of the roof, and hissed as his chest heaved, "None of *us* is replaceable? What about *you*? *Just who would take your place?*" In the face of such extreme impudence Cabrillo's own anger would have flared if he had not immediately recognized the love and fear that had caused this. Father Lezcano's face was still livid as he demanded, "If that line had exploded in your hands, if that staff—"

Despite the fact that he was being scolded like a child on his own ship in the midst of a raging storm, Cabrillo said only, "It did not explode, my friend," and ducked out into the rain.

On the main deck, he grabbed a stair railing and barely managed to stay on his feet as the ship heeled wildly to starboard and the tip of her main yard almost sliced the peak of a colliding wave. With men sliding here and there, he hollered out an adjustment to the men at the whipstaff lines and studied the effect on the *San Salvador* as it was made. Master Uribe, God bless him, had the hands up in the next lightning flash to secure anything that needed tightening.

230

Pilot San Remón appeared before he could be summoned, and Cabrillo called out, "Take the helm, pilot. I am going below."

He had to veer around Vargas to reach the hatch. His sergeant major had planted himself just behind the mainmast next to the boatswain, where he was organizing his soldiers to assist the sailors working in turns at the pump lever and shifting them out before any collapsed. Giving them all a nod of approval as he stumbled past, Cabrillo descended to the stairs. He paused briefly near Manuel to reassure his horses, which were straining to find footing and often slipping into the support of their huge stall slings. He checked the fit and soundness of the slings and, satisfied, turned toward the main storage area.

As he'd suspected, anything that had not been tightly fastened down, which was thankfully little, now lay strewn about. Mateo was among the hands attempting to restore order as the ship rolled and bucked, and his uncle didn't distract him from his duties. Taking the lower flight of stairs downward and into the hold, Cabrillo paused to check the effectiveness of the pumping efforts on the main deck. For now, the water sloshed to and fro only a few inches higher than was usual. So far, so good, but it would get worse. His caulkers and their assistants were here too, holding lamps near the hull as they searched for potential breaches and putting their caulking cordage and blunted chisels to work wherever they found a leak. When they looked up and saw Cabrillo, he asked, "How is she bearing it, Señor Jimenez?"

"The best she can, sir, and that's better than most."

"Send me word at every rise of six-inches."

"Yes, Captain-General."

Making his way back to the main deck, he once again looked out to sea in search of his other ships. There, still, was the *San Miguel* close astern, and Cabrillo said a silent prayer of gratitude. He strained his eyes, scanning the mountainous waves all around, and then once again, but he looked in vain. *La Victoria* had disappeared.

His throat tightened at the thought of what this might mean, but with a great effort he shoved such a possibility out of acceptance. *La Victoria* and her men were safe. They had to be. He squeezed his eyes tightly shut and muttered into the storm, "Holy Father, please do not let her go down."

Throughout the night, helpless to aid his sister ship and nearly powerless to control his own, he did what he could by moving among the men with guidance and encouragement. Many hours after they'd met in steerage, he found Father Lezcano helping Dr. Fuentes treat a soldier whose arm had been badly broken in a fall. Cabrillo waited until the patient was bandaged, and then motioned the priest to his side. Cooler now, Father Lezcano had a hard time meeting his eyes, but Cabrillo asked quietly, "We have lost sight of *La Victoria*, Father. Will you pray for her, for all of us?"

"I have been, sir, and will continue to do so right here." He took a breath and engaged Cabrillo's gaze more squarely. "Sir, what I said, how I spoke to you…"

Cabrillo stopped him with a smile. "It is forgotten." He placed a hand on the priest's shoulder and squeezed, then left him without another word.

Through long hours of darkness they managed to resist the storm's unceasing attempts to crush them and send them to the ocean floor. They trusted in their God, their ship, and each other, but in the blackest hours many grew weary and afraid. Father Lezcano gathered those at rest and led them in prayers to the Blessed Mother, some saying the rosary and many promising to visit her shrine at the earliest opportunity. Cabrillo prayed with them, watched over them, and worked with them as commander, father, and brother. Although there had been little doubt of it before, he became convinced that, with the exception of very few, there had never been finer men on land or sea.

The *San Miguel* doggedly clung close by her flagship, and Cabrillo found comfort every time he looked back and spotted her lamps swaying madly from her stern. But nowhere in the tumultuous depths of the night could any sign of his third ship be discovered.

When the hour of dawn drew near, the captain-general took advantage of the spreading light to seek a glimpse of *La Victoria*, but his anxious search found nothing to prove she still existed. To his further concern, as the day gained maturity so did the ferocity of the storm, driving the already weary men even more viciously than it had the night before. The *San Salvador* and *San Miguel* had no choice but to fly northwestward before the gale, each with the aid of a sail shortened in size to little more than a handkerchief.

The tempest assailed the ships as if bent on their destruction but the crews threw themselves at the pumps until arm muscles gave out and legs buckled, and whenever a man tumbled onto the sodden deck, another always took his place. Cabrillo and his officers were every-where, navigating, heartening, and lending their own hands where needed, but after hour upon hour of battery by the unrelenting cold and wet and wind, the human energy was slowly draining. And yet it was the haunting absence of *La Victoria* that weighed most heavily on them all. The afternoon waned and darkness returned, and the storm still raged and howled about them as Father Lezcano located Cabrillo in steerage and asked. "May I speak with you, sir?"

With a gesture of agreement Cabrillo led the way to his cabin. Closing the door behind him, the priest wiped a hand across his face and said, "Forgive me, sir, but you are in great need of rest."

Cabrillo raised his own dripping face and red-rimmed eyes. "We all need rest, Father."

"You would not allow one of our men to go so long in this weather without food, warmth, and sleep, sir. They and your officers are bet-ter rested than you, and all have eaten full meals. They are capable men. If there is need, they will awaken you." When Cabrillo made no movement to comply, Father Lezcano said softly, "We dare not lose you, sir. Please, let Paulo bring you something to eat, and then rest."

"You, Father, are becoming a mother hen."

"I have been called worse things, sir."

With a weary twitch of his mouth that was meant to serve as a smile, Cabrillo tugged off his sodden jacket and let it fall to the floor with a heavy "plop." "Poor Paulo, he bears such a burden of useless-ness on my account. Very well then, please ask him to tend to me but have me wakened in two hours. And if *La Victoria* is spotted I am to be called at once."

The priest left him, and he stripped off the rest of his clothing, tow-eled himself dry, and was pulling on a clean shirt when Paulo entered with a tray of cold viands. With even more fastidiousness than usual, he served the sparse meal and poured a liberal tankard of sherry. His master thanked him before wolfing everything down, and then made his way to his bunk, let out a moaning sigh as he rolled under the furs, and began to dream before the table was fully cleared. In his dream the fleet was searching for *La Victoria* as the storm bucked and roared, the images around him diminishing and sharpening with each lightning flash. After what seemed like years of agonizing quest they suddenly came upon her, splintered and strewn along the rocky shore, her crew nowhere in sight. So a new search began for the men.

In utter disobedience to the orders Cabrillo had given him, Father Lezcano instructed Paulo not to waken his master until four hours had passed. When the captain-general was roused at that time, he surrendered the warmth of his furs with reluctance but his dreams with relief. He sat for a moment on the edge of his bunk, clearing away the demons of sleep and taking in reality. The storm's intensity had not diminished but he could tell by the movement of the ship that her pumps were keeping the sea at bay. Feeling somewhat more rested than he ought to have been, he became suspicious and asked Paulo the hour. Hearing the answer, he let out a muted growl and said to himself with little conviction, "That young pup. A single whipping must not have been enough." Once he was dressed and back on deck he wasted little time in finding his priest, again working at the side of a wounded man. Watching the concerned care with which Father Lezcano assisted Dr. Fuentes, Cabrillo felt his irritation draining away. Moments passed as they finished their work, and then Father Lezcano turned an exhausted smile up at his commander. Cabrillo's intended rebuke died away completely. Instead he gave several quiet words of consolation to the injured sailor and a few more in commendation to his caregivers. He then headed to steerage, telling himself he must be getting old or soft, or both.

Throughout the remainder of that night, into the feral morning, and well past noon of the next day the elements continued to pummel the fleet and her men to respond. At last, though the wind had not yet spent its fury, the rain began to slacken. The waves, as if grudgingly relinquishing their objective to overwhelm the ships, shrank by degrees and became more uniform in their direction. When the sky finally terminated its weeping and the ocean no longer slapped the decks, Cabrillo ordered his men to change into dry clothes.

The shroud of clouds slowly lifted, and a greater distance became visible. Since the mainmast still swayed like a reed in the wind Cabrillo called out to his gathered watch, "It is time to send a man aloft. Who is willing?" No one needed to be told what the lookout was to seek, and two men stepped forward at once, the oldest saying, "I'd be proud to go, sir."

This unhesitating courage after the men had endured so much made Cabrillo's throat tighten. He steadied his voice and said, "Not today, Paco. This is no job for a father of six. Let young Simon have a chance."

The sixteen-year-old lad stretched taller as he turned and made his way to the rigging, but Cabrillo called after him, "Bear a lifeline, Simon." The youth accepted a section of line from the outstretched hand of one of his shipmates, tied it around his waist, and began to climb the rigging. One tread at a time, securing his lifeline at intervals while scaling ropes that twisted and sang beneath his hands and feet and with the wind tearing at his hair and clothes, Simon ascended to the wooden platform. With his line he snugged himself to the pendulating mast and slowly brought his gaze in a full circle, intensely scanning the waters around the *San Salvador* and *San Miguel*. As those below waited anxiously he swept the sea again, and then again, but he saw only water and sky. In a voice that cracked with painful reluctance, he said, "All clear, sir."

The expression on every apprehensive, upturned face sagged, and each head lowered. The men silently resumed their duties, and eyes that had been so hopeful a moment before now refused to meet the gazes of their crewmates.

When the hour of vespers had passed, the wind eased and shifted to the west, and the ocean swells gradually diminished to a fraction of the former height. Cabrillo's officers gathered around him to receive new orders, though they had little doubt as to what these would be.

"We shall sail due east, gentlemen, and hold that course until we sight land. *La Victoria* will seek us out at the nearest bay. Hopefully, that will not be very distant."

Heads nodded and Master Uribe, who had just come on deck after a much needed rest, asked, "How's the *San Miguel* faring, sir?"

"Her pump is even busier than ours, but she has a worthy carpenter and caulker. She will bear up for a time."

Pilot San Remón asked, "Sir, how far north would you say the storm has thrown us?"

Staring northward, as if the answer would come from there, Cabrillo said, "With the sky clearing we might gain a reading at midnight, but my guess is near $39\frac{1}{2}°$, perhaps even higher."

"39½°, sir," his pilot mused. "Higher than we ever dreamed of finding China."

So softly that it was just audible, Cabrillo said, "Yes, much higher." He looked into each of their faces, seeing the mutual understanding that time was running out, and seeing the shared dread that if they left this area their fleet's number would be decreased by one vital ship. With an effort he straightened his shoulders and, turning toward his priest at the railing, he asked, "Father Lezcano, will you lead us all in another prayer for the safe deliverance of *La Victoria?*"

The priest readily agreed, the crew soon collected on the main deck, and the *San Miguel* hauled in close to leeward. Though these sailors and soldiers had been wrestling the storm to the point of collapse, these ragged men who had become brothers over the long months at sea, they now found strength enough to cry out "amen" with real enthusiasm as Father Lezcano pleaded to their Savior and his holy mother for the safety of their lost fellows. With the heads of the *San Salvador's* men bowed they did not see the lowered heads of Father Gamboa, the officers, and crewmembers of the *San Miguel* but now and again their words would reach them. As Father Lezcano's final prayer ended the men shifted, walked, or limped away, all wearing expressions of grim resolution. They must leave the fate of *La Victoria* and themselves in hands far more powerful than their own.

Cabrillo returned to steerage to adjust their course and then again found his well-worn planks on the stern deck. Midnight came and went, and though he ostensibly relinquished his watch at the appointed hour, he remained in the open air. Tonight, even Father Lezcano could not convince him to go inside and sleep.

The next morning's steely sky dawned hushed but brooding, and the captain-general at last went to his cabin but only to record their progress throughout the night. Master Uribe found him there, pouring over some notes on his writing desk, and he announced excitedly, "Captain-General, land lies to the northeast."

Cabrillo was surprised he hadn't heard a shout from the lookout, but he was on his feet and reaching for his jacket as he asked, "Any sign of her?"

"None, sir, but we may spot her when we round the arc of the point ahead. There appears to be a cove beyond."

They sailed on toward noon only to discover that the approaching coast rose steeply into a craggy mountain range, and the ocean still swelled much too violently to permit an anchorage near enough to shore for a landing. Before the sun's zenith could pass, Cabrillo and San Remón gauged its altitude and agreed on a measurement of 40° north. Not long afterward Master Uribe's earlier prediction came true, if a little farther up the coast than anticipated, in the form of a cape. As it opened before them all eyes sharpened their hunt for *La Victoria*, but to no avail. With heavy disappointment they anchored to rest muscle and will and to better bind the seeping wounds of their ships.

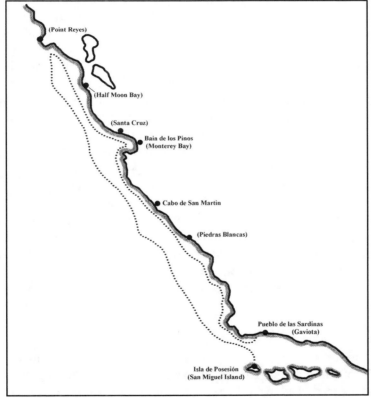

(Point Reyes)

(Half Moon Bay)

(Santa Cruz)

Baia de los Pinos
(Monterey Bay)

Cabo de San Martin

(Piedras Blancas)

Pueblo de las Sardinas
(Gaviota)

Isla de Posesión
(San Miguel Island)

Cabrillo could not fully appreciate the beauty of the high cliffs robed in a forest of pines. Instead, every color and dimension seemed sharpened by uneasiness for his ship; every breath of the pine-scented air seemed to carry the bite of potential tragedy. Even so, he was not

237

completely immune to this natural feast for the senses, and he recalled his previous burning desire to see the living trees that had provided the colossal driftwood they'd stumbled across on the island so far to the south. But that aspiration could not be fulfilled now, not with such imperative matters superceding it. Mustering the hope to one day return and wander these mountains and agreeing with Master Uribe's suggestion, he named the harbor Cabo de Pinos.

Each turning of the afternoon glass, each calling out of the half-hour, accentuated the heaviness of heart for the men yearning to spot a familiar sail on the horizon. Work went on and glances offshore became fewer. Eventually the hopes of even the most optimistic and those most determined to buoy the others began to falter. Light was fading when Cabrillo sent invitations to the officers of both ships to dine with him.

After a crowded supper marked by unfocused appetites and stilted conversations, Cabrillo sat amid the officers of the *San Miguel*, Pilot San Remón, Master Uribe, and Father Lezcano, while Paulo, Manuel, and Mateo attended to them. Captain Correa and the other visitors all suspected the basis for this meeting and despite several efforts to speak of other things the talk finally dwindled to an expectant hush. Correa cleared his throat and fixed his gaze on the lamp.

At last the captain-general stilled the fork he'd been teetering between his fingers, slowly set it down, and said gravely, "Gentlemen, our present situation must be faced and dealt with." Folding his hands together on the tabletop, he went on, saying, "There would be great risk in asking our ships to withstand the heavy storms of open sea without comprehensive repairs, which require an adequate harbor and significant time. Here, the weather is getting much colder and food sources are likely scarce and hard to obtain. Although wood surrounds us in abundance, gathering as much as would be necessary from those heights would expend much energy, and collecting enough water may also pose difficulties. For these reasons this harbor will not meet our needs for full repairs. We are left with the choice of turning back or pushing ahead. But even if every man of us was willing to accept the hazards of making hasty repairs and sailing on toward China, foremost among our reasons for yielding this position we have fought to reach is that there may be survivors behind us, men that we can aid. I will not abandon them without a thorough search."

Although everyone in the room had known these harsh truths and not one of them disagreed with their commander's intentions, hearing the words fall with such finality from his lips, understanding what surrendering this attempt meant to him, to all of them, was enough to cause sharp pain. Cabrillo gave them a minute: time to voice an objection. None came.

Their solidarity touched his battered spirit deeply, and his tone weakened as he said, "Our new course, to the south, is decided, then. Tomorrow, we will turn back." He briefly met their individual gazes. "For all that each of you has given to our mission thus far and to me, I am profoundly grateful."

At this last word his voice faltered and his gaze fell.

No one could speak, and as silence reigned over the group Mateo turned his face to the wall to hide his tears. It was Father Lezcano who dispelled the quiet by saying, "The captain-general has asked me to remain and pray with him, gentlemen. Will you kindly excuse us?" With a deliberation and deference that expressed what was left unsaid, the officers stood and bowed to their commander as they filed out, and as Pilot San Remón left the chamber he gently closed the door behind him.

Manuel went to Mateo and drew him to a far corner of the cabin. Paulo slowly rolled the cloth from the table and then stood with his back against the door, holding the bundle as if it were a swaddled baby, his head down and his eyes closed. Pulling one of the four holy books he possessed from his robe, Father Lezcano glanced at Cabrillo's drawn face and lowered eyelids, and began to read.

Chapter 20

HOPES SURRENDERED, HOPES FULFILLED

Wearing a weary expression that seemed almost calm, Cabrillo stood before the gathering men with his back turned to a golden sunrise. During the lengthy hours of the night he'd beaten back the personal demons that had still hovered after Father Lezcano's departure. Now the time had come to voice his decision to the crews, though word had undoubtedly spread to many of them already. The *San Miguel* floated close by, holding her position and awaiting the coming words from the fleet's commander.

"Men," he called out in a loud, clear voice, "during the storm you fought with the courage of lions, believing as you struggled that we would sail on to reach our goal in the East. But by every sign nature has given us, that end still lies far from our grasp, farther than we can hope to reach before the worst of winter arrives. For now, we must head for a warmer harbor and make repairs. This will postpone any reward for our labors but we *will* sail north again when the weather allows. Also, and certainly most important to us all, by retracing a portion of our previous route, we will seize the best chance of finding *La Victoria*."

Little more than a sigh was heard in reaction to his announcement. Though the expressions of a number of men showed relief, most faces reflected the same disappointment their leaders were trying to conceal. Only a few, a handful of rowers aboard the *San Miguel*, bent their heads together and muttered in disgust.

Cabrillo went on, his voice gaining power with each phrase. "As we sail southward each man and boy must keep a sharp watch. We must find that ship. Hear me, men! If she carries but a single survivor, we must find her!"

240

Shouts and raised fists demonstrated their willingness to accept Cabrillo's challenge, no matter how unlikely the prospects for success. One seaman stepped forward and avowed, "If she's still afloat, sir, we'll spy her out!"

Another cried, "Nary a floating stick will get by us, sir!"

Cabrillo watched them, silently praying their faith wouldn't be crushed.

As the crews retook their stations the captain-general called out the new course to his helmsman, and the two ships turned their bowsprits away from the land of their ambitions. Everyone on the decks glued his gaze to what lay before and around them in search of a sail, barrel, mast, or body.

Through the early hours they sailed swiftly on, covering many leagues along the coast. As the day aged, men who had strained their vision in the hope of being the first to notice anything unnatural now let their gazes stray. And they began to wonder, "Shouldn't we have seen something by now, some token of *La Victoria's* survival or destruction?" Many in the crew began to believe what they had refused to accept earlier; that the storm had overwhelmed *La Victoria* as it had countless other ships, and the sea had claimed those aboard for its own. When mile after additional mile revealed nothing they occasionally turned toward Cabrillo, attempting to guess his thoughts and anticipate his mood. Father Lezcano and Manuel kept a determined watch and prayed for an unlikely sighting, not only for the sakes of their sailing companions but also for the well-being of their captain-general.

Cabrillo would not leave the decks, not even to eat, and his probing glances swept the sea and shore with an intensity that only seemed to grow as the hours of remaining daylight diminished. Watching him, a few of his men wondered if he hoped to raise his lost ship from the depths by the sheer force of his will. The sun had been lowering for several hours, and its beams were breaking through a canopy of uneven clouds when Mateo approached Cabrillo with tentative steps. The captain-general did not stir, but Mateo said, "Sir?"

Cabrillo did not take his gaze from the sea.

"Sir," Mateo tried again, "Paulo asks that you come to your table. You have eaten nothing but a little cheese today, sir."

When no answer came Mateo was about to speak for the third time when Cabrillo said, "Tell Paulo I am not hungry, Mateo."

Sucking in a strengthening breath, Mateo said, "Sir, uncle, please."

"Uncle, is it?" At last Cabrillo looked at him and saw the worry and affection reflected there.

Momentarily stripped of a layer of emotional armor, Cabrillo allowed himself to feel his own exhaustion, his hunger, and even a small portion of his anguish. These sensations were not enough, however, to slacken his scrutiny while there was still sunlight. "Soon, Mateo," he gave the boy. "Tell Paulo I will come soon, and then I will eat my fill."

Mateo recognized this as a dismissal, but he could not bring himself to leave him yet. Cabrillo reached out and laid his hand on the boy's weather-tangled hair in a gesture that looked like a benediction. Father Lezcano, who had approached them quietly, stepped closer and said, "Come, Mateo."

As the boy reluctantly began to turn away his head lifted and his body went suddenly rigid. His eyes bulged, and he began to gasp, "Uh, uh, uh!" in such strident tones that many turned toward him. Cabrillo grabbed his shoulders, but Mateo jerked away and aimed a flailing arm toward the coast. Before the boy could utter an intelligible word the lookout screamed, "Captain-General, a sail ahead! A point off the port bow! A sail! A sail!"

Cabrillo's gaze flew in that direction, where it found and clung to white patches of canvas hugging the coast at least six miles ahead. Wild cheers burst from his men, and Cabrillo's haggard face shone with the overpowering sense of gratitude and relief that swept through him. She was safe. *La Victoria* was safe. After the initial moments of elation, however, Andrés de Urdaneta's cautioning words suddenly stung the captain-general's memory, and his expression abruptly wavered. Before their departure from Navidad his friend had said, "If you spot a Portuguese ship, beware." He had been advising Cabrillo to keep poison close at hand in the event he was captured during the voyage, a suggestion that had never been seriously considered. Now, with the ship ahead still too far away to clearly distinguish, he realized that she could be Portuguese, or even English. If so, given their weakened condition, what trials might await them?

The desperate hope that the ship within their sight was indeed *La Victoria* now tangled with the dread that it was an enemy vessel that could pose the worst kind of threat. With pumps and caulkers still working diligently to keep the *San Salvador* and *San Miguel* seaworthy, they could neither maneuver nor fight at their best. There might also be more ships in the vicinity beyond their view. A battle could swing against them. Still, he ordered no sails shortened. He must discover who she was as quickly yet as carefully as possible.

While his men watched him, most of them confused by his withheld joy, they began to understand his concern. Their boisterous mutterings died away, their apprehension building. The reason for their commander's disquiet was confirmed when he gave the order, "Prepare to engage, Master Uribe, and pass the word to the *San Miguel*." Men dispersed to their stations as officers barked to hurry and adjust them, guns and ammunition moved into position, and smaller weapons appeared on deck. Manuel brought Cabrillo's armor and strapped on the breastplate.

When all was ready the ship they pursued still lay too far ahead to recognize, yet a few of the fleet's men leaned out over the railing as if those few extra inches would help them confirm their hopes sooner. Every face was aimed at the waters ahead, searching the shape and movement of the masts, hull, and stern that slowly grew larger.

Cabrillo stared until his eyes burned, and it seemed to him that the ship, already running under full sails, was taking precautionary measures by keeping her distance, yet they were closing the gap with her. She was slower than they, which gave encouragement to the likelihood that she was his lost ship. If not, she might be less of a threat than he had feared. He knew every line and board of *La Victoria* and as moment after moment passed he began to allow himself to believe it was his beloved ship. When only two miles separated them, he did not need the lookout's shout to confirm his conclusion. *"La Victoria! La Victoria!* It's truly her, sir!"

Dozens of voices strengthened the cry, and Cabrillo took in her intact hull, unsplintered masts, and filled sails like a starving man gulps down his first bites of food. Although a joyful bedlam reigned over his men, at first Cabrillo whispered only, "Praise God, they are alive. And we need not fight today." His eyes continued to confirm beyond any doubt what he was beholding, and when the shouts from *La Victoria's* madly elated crew reached across the water to him, he let out an answering cry of his own. Exhibiting a profound lack of discipline,

Father Lezcano clasped the approaching Pilot San Remón by the upper arms and danced him around in a circle before the flustered officer could disengage himself. Cabrillo grabbed Mateo, lifted him to his chest, and nearly squeezed the life out of the happy boy. When he set him down, Mateo finally managed to declare, "I found her for you, sir."

"Indeed you did, nephew."

Cabrillo's brimming eyes met those of his priest. "After we clear these decks, a prayer of thanks would certainly be in order, eh, Father?"

The commands were given and weapons disappeared in record time. Sails were shortened for their approach to *La Victoria*, whose sails had already been struck, but well before the ships came together the captain-general and his men lowered themselves to their knees and bowed their heads. Father Lezcano's prayer was brief but abundantly heartfelt, and his words compelled tears to fall unashamedly from the eyes of a number of the men. Mateo knelt at Cabrillo's side, and as he prayed the captain-general's large, protective arm wrapped around the boy's shoulders.

The quiet offering of gratitude had just concluded when the attention of all was abruptly captured by a double roar from *La Victoria's* two swivel guns, causing the *San Salvador's* men to rush to the railing and renew their riotous salutations, waving, leaping, and pounding together hands and any other objects that made noise. Watching it all, Cabrillo shook his head and smiled from cheek to cheek.

Following form rather than necessity, he gave the order that adjusted their course to meet *La Victoria*. They would be side by side before the arrival of a quickly falling dusk.

Mateo beamed up at him. "Now, sir? Now will you come and eat the soup that Paulo has saved for you?"

Cabrillo actually laughed, provoking smiles from all who heard him. "I suddenly find myself famished." He glanced again at *La Victoria*, estimating that he had at least ten minutes to spare. "Pilot, will you take the watch?"

"With pleasure, sir. With immense pleasure. Uh, perhaps, sir, you would like the ship's priest to accompany you? A mere monk, one who never eats very much, might easily feel overcome by recent

244

events. His remaining on my, I mean, our quarterdeck might be ill-advised."

Feigning offense at this jesting by flashing a great scowl at the pilot, Father Lezcano nevertheless then turned a hopeful glance toward Cabrillo.

Again their commander laughed and gestured for the priest to follow him as he left for his cabin. Eat, they did, and they reveled in those quiet moments, but nothing could keep Cabrillo in the cabin for long.

As they sailed closer, he could see the pump handle being worked without stopping and other evidence of the battering the storm had inflicted. Unweathered sections of wood and unstained patches of sails revealed that Captain Ferrelo had already taken care of some of *La Victoria's* most desperate needs. And there was the good captain now, standing high on his stern deck, waving at Cabrillo and grinning as largely as any of his men. The captain-general returned his salute and a joyous clamor rose from the fleet yet again.

Even the sky seemed to rejoice at the reunion of the ships, dispatching its clouds to places far to the southwest and clearing the way for a brilliant sunset. When they had drawn as near as safety allowed, Cabrillo cupped his hands to his mouth and shouted across the gold-tinged water, "God bless the men of *La Victoria*!"

Echoes and answers burst out loud and strong and took awhile to settle down again. At last Cabrillo was able to ask, "How do you fare, Captain Ferrelo?"

"Not a man lost, sir! And we rejoice to see you all safe!"

At this distance Cabrillo could read the fatigue in the bodies of their men, but they were alive and whole. "And the ship?"

"Well enough, sir, though the storm took the cargo we had on deck, and the pump has never seen so much action. We will need to heal her soon."

This then clenched his resolve to continue southward. There was no wisdom in changing his earlier decision. His expression sobered slightly as he announced, "We will continue south day and night while weather permits, Captain. At the nearest bay possible we will make repairs and seek a warmer shelter for the winter."

While this news didn't appear to surprise Captain Ferrelo, his face showed resolve rather than relief, and his men accepted it almost as stoically as their leader. "We will follow you with as much speed as we can, captain-general. May God keep us together in the days to come!"

"Do you need a few more hands or any supplies?"

Ferrelo swung a questioning glance over his crew, who straightened and wiped the fatigue from their faces. Ferrelo answered with unveiled pride, "Not today, sir, but I thank you."

"Do not hesitate to signal us if assistance is needed, Captain."

"Very well, sir."

With her sails lifting, the *San Salvador* eased away and *La Victoria* turned to fall into position behind her. As the old formation became reestablished Cabrillo sensed that more than his fleet was again intact. His spirit, too, had been made whole once more.

For the first time since the storm had struck, the raw beauty of the coast could attract his attention, and it did so with insistence. Deep snow cloaked the peaks of the paralleling mountain range, sharpening the vividness of both sky above and slopes below. The land near shore was lavishly forested, though not a single inhabitant or puff of smoke appeared from amid the trees.

When the early stars began to emerge that evening, sails were shortened so that Captain Ferrelo and several of his men could take to their boat and be warmly welcomed aboard the *San Salvador*. In return, Cabrillo sent several of his stoutest men to *La Victoria* to help patch her seams and man her pump, providing a slight reprieve for the spent but stolid sailors. Though fresh provisions were awfully sparse and their future hopes and prospects were undeniably delayed and uncertain, the meal in Cabrillo's cabin was as festive as he could make it. This particular dinner was livened by the freedom with which the wine was encouraged to flow.

They sailed southeastward throughout the night, and daybreak delivered an expansive bay so tempting that despite the weakened condition of the ships Cabrillo ordered them in for a closer look. The rest of that day and part of the next were spent searching for a river and an anchorage that would allow a convenient access to shore, but not only did they fail to discover a means of filling their water barrels, they were also prevented from landing by the violence of the surf crashing against coast. Holding a steady position while performing the noontime calculation of the sun's elevation, Cabrillo and his pilot

soon agreed with their finding and the captain-general scratched 39°
into his record book. They both gazed at the number, thinking that
they still had many leagues to sail before attaining the warm latitude
they required.

Darkness threatened at an ever-earlier hour these days, and when
it did so tonight they lowered their anchors in unusually deep water.
From a safe distance offshore Cabrillo claimed this huge bay in the
name of God and king, again recognizing the abundance of trees by
calling it Baia de los Pinos.

Once more deprived by the waves and cliffs of the possibility of
gathering on shore, the higher officers were called to meet aboard the
flagship in order to discuss their needs and accept the prioritization of
the commander. Though the relief and joy roused by the reunion with
La Victoria had been intensely felt by all, the realities of relinquishing
any hope of reaching Asia this year had become increasingly burden-
some. Glumness was as visible on their faces as the redness branded
by the sun and wind. After their meal had been consumed and conditions of the ships and men had been shared, Cabrillo could do little to
lift the mood before dismissing them.

Dawn found him again evaluating the challenges of their surroundings only to affirm that no parties could be dispatched in search of
wood, food, or fresh water. These could wait for yet a little while,
but the most needed repairs to *La Victoria* could no longer be delayed. Many hands were set to work, and the temporary overhaul-
ing was completed efficiently enough to allow each man a few hours
of precious rest. As their crews relaxed, chatting in small groups or
napping, Cabrillo and Ferrelo were at liberty to enjoy an uncommon
hour of relative solitude in the captain-general's cabin, where they exchanged greater details about their experiences during the storm and
made plans for the days ahead. After spending some time bent over
Cabrillo's charts, discussing the currents and winds, speculating about
the predictability of these forces and how they might be harnessed during their return voyage in the spring, Cabrillo veered the discussion by
asking, "How are your men today, Bartolomé?"

Ferrelo set down his wine glass and stared into it. "Two more are
showing the early symptoms, sir; loose teeth, dark gums, purple spots
below the waist. The storm alone would have weakened them, but

without fresh food and water to help restore them, things are progressing quickly. And your crew? How many are suffering?"

"None severely, not yet, but perhaps five are losing strength."

Ferrelo lifted his glass and took another long sip before saying, "Things are a little worse aboard the *San Miguel*."

Cabrillo nodded.

"I heard, sir, that you lost a tooth today, a molar, I believe."

They exchanged a studied gaze into each other's lean faces, but neither man spoke another word about how exhaustion, dried food, and stale water were also taking their toll on the captains of their ships. Instead, Cabrillo said, "Let us discuss more fully which ports might offer the best refuge during an extended stay."

Captain Ferrelo refilled his glass and obliged.

At the sun's rising the growing need for fresh supplies induced the men of the fleet to fight through the mighty swells that met them near the southern rim of Baia de los Piños and helped them to seize the forceful breeze for their own purposes. As they rounded the tall rocky sentinel guarding the westernmost point of the bay, Cabrillo shivered against the chill as he took in the panorama of snow-dusted hills and chose to name this stretch of land Cabo de Nieve.

The dampness in the icy air made it painfully effective in gnawing through multiple layers of clothing and reaching deep into bones, and every man suffered. Glances inland seemed to heighten the chill as eyes fell upon white-clad mountains towering high enough to disappear into snow-heavy clouds. The peaks jogged along with them down the coast, acting as a constant reminder of how far winter's outstretched fingers had already reached, and how little time they had to outrun their continuing extension. At times massive waves broke against the bases of the frosty mountains with such roaring brutality that men crouched and threw their arm over their heads, reflexively protecting themselves in case the cliffs came crashing down. Even as Cabrillo pushed his men to sail beyond the potential danger represented by these mountains, he could not help marveling at their majesty, and he named them simply the Sierra Nevadas.

By the end of Cabrillo's night watch the fleet sailed well over sixty miles, yet in all that distance they'd seen no sign of humanity ashore. They found a little bay to shelter them through the hours of deepest darkness, naming it Cabo de San Martin, and by the North Star they

248

gauged their recent progress by calculating the latitude to be 37½°, but they dared not linger here. That day Cabrillo had watched with helpless dread as scurvy continued to spread its malice among his men. Another handful of his crewmembers now fought the telltale pain that was triggered at the slightest touch. One man's teeth were so loose that he could no longer eat anything that had not been ground to pulp or liquefied. The captain-general had seen this disease torture other men to death and he was grimly determined not to lose one of his.

The health of his crews had become a constant worry, but the next day another grave problem arose. The *San Miguel* had begun to leak profusely and the caulkers could do little but seal the ruptures for short periods. Their urgency to find a port was growing by the hour.

After valiantly managing to sail a little over forty miles, they at last beheld the welcome sight of smoke rising from manmade fires. Cabrillo drew the ships to a hasty anchorage and accompanied a landing party to the beach. With joy and gratitude he was able obtain some wood and water, and the natives were even willing to trade some of their own precious food supplies that included a little acorn meal and maize, but the manner of the Indians was noticeably guarded. The captain-general sensed that this limited willingness to interact was due to concern over their own limited winter stores. Troubled, he returned to his flagship.

That evening he met with his officers and, after much discussion, decided that the fleet's best choice for wintering now lay 130 miles southward on the island of Posesión, which had sheltered them once before.

When his companions had left, Cabrillo undressed wearily, crawled into his bunk, and pondered the choice that seemed to have been unanimously made by all gathered at his table. Now, however, he asked himself uneasily how much that decision might have been swayed by him, and by his memory of a dark-skinned woman with eyes as daring as any warrior's. He immediately chided himself for the thought, recalling the enthusiastic agreement of his officers, the protectiveness of the harbor, the cordiality of the chief, the adequacy of the water supply, and the abundance of sea life all around the island. It was the logical choice, the best choice. But later that night, while in sleep's deepest embrace, he awakened suddenly, muttering the name "Taya."

Chapter 21

POSESIÓN REVISITED

U nder long, gauzy clouds that were spreading a blush across the westward sky Cabrillo's ships entered the familiar harbor of Isla de Posesión only to face an unexpected and uneasy sight. Chumash warriors were drawn up on the beach as if they'd anticipated the fleet's arrival for days. The chief and his sons stood a little in front of the rest, their spears laid well within reach before them, their stillness revealing neither outright challenge nor welcome. As the ships maneuvered to a close-fitting anchorage, not one canoe came out to greet them.

"They look unwilling to accept us, sir," said Pilot San Remón with a scowl.

"The *San Miguel* can sail no farther," said Cabrillo. "We have little choice." He continued to watch them, weighing the risks of landing. "They are a wary people, and with reason. I must try to reassure them." He ordered the boatswain to ready his launch, sent word to the *San Miguel* and *La Victoria* for each to lower a boat, and signaled to the master gunner to prepare his weapons. "While I am ashore, pilot, keep to our plans."

Cabrillo, Father Lezcano, Manuel, and their contingent took to the boat as the fleet's guns were being primed and aimed where they could provide the best defense. A moment after his launch left the *San Salvador* his other ships' boats pushed off to join him.

As they rowed nearer, Cabrillo observed the natives' recently donned fur capes with interest. Even here, though the chill was much less severe than where they'd come from, late November made its presence felt. He wondered if beneath those capes the warriors were clasping bows, but as their space of separation diminished no weapons were lifted. When he was a few yards from the sand he leapt from the boat, waded out of the foam, waited for the others to land, and walked toward Matipuyaut, but the chief and his sons did not come to meet him. Cabrillo's guards formed a protective box around him, and he could sense Vargas' gauging the prospect of danger with each step they advanced. The captain-general halted several paces in front of Matipuyaut, who did not speak.

By signs and words that Cabrillo had learned over the past weeks, and for which Father Lezcano's assistance was no longer necessary, he hailed the chief. "It brings me joy to see you again, Chief Matipuyaut."

Now Matipuyaut spread his arms wide and said in a ringing voice. "I greet you, Cabrillo." In his tone less ceremonial, he added, "My people ask why you have returned."

From the corners of his eyes Cabrillo could see uneasiness, and in some cases resentment, on the faces of the Chumash men. "We did not look to return so soon. A storm at sea and the cold winds have forced us to return to your island. We wish to sail on to the distant shore as soon as the weather warms."

Matipuyaut considered for a moment. "That is a long time, Cabrillo, a long time. We must speak together of many things. For our talk, you are welcome in my lodge."

Acutely aware that leaving the beach meant relinquishing the security of the fleet's guns, Cabrillo nevertheless bowed in acceptance of the invitation. He gave no indication of disquiet as he and his small delegation followed the chief's group up the path toward the village.

Along the way he began to feel slightly reassured by the presence of more and more women and children, who paused in their work or play to stare at them as they passed. They showed less apprehension and mistrust than their men had, perhaps because they better recalled the peaceful nature of their prior visit. His covert glances repeatedly swept the gathering crowds but failed to locate the particular female face he sought.

When he reached Matipuyaut's lodge without having seen her, he told himself she would be inside. Upon entering, however, he found only the chief's wives, small children, and shaman. Kipomo, seated in front of the women, gave no greeting when Cabrillo entered, and he had barely had time to recognize this breach in manners when Taya appeared at the door of the house, stepped with a respectful nod in front of Father Lezcano, and approached Cabrillo. Ignoring the disap-

251

proving grumbles of the warriors as well as the stares of the soldiers, she came close, raised her face to him, and said, "I welcome you, my husband."

He took her hand. "Your welcome brings me pleasure, Taya."

A great harrumph from Matipuyaut recaptured Cabrillo's attention and sent Taya two steps backward. But rather than joining the other women at the edge of the round chamber, she seated herself not far behind Father Lezcano, who had settled down at Cabrillo's side. The scowl her father aimed at her caused no apparent discomfort and resulted in no alteration of her preferred perch.

Choosing to give her no more of his notice, Matipuyaut said, "You are thinner than when I saw you last, Cabrillo. Eat with us." Matipuyaut motioned to his wives, and they quickly added water and acorn flour to a hot fish soup cooking in the massive stone bowl over the fire. Matipuyaut seemed disinclined to start the discussion before his visitors had been served, so they exercised their patience until bowls of the thick, hot chowder were placed in the hands of Matipuyaut, his sons, and his guests. His warriors, though the soup could not stretch far enough to serve them as well, sat silent and stoic. While the fortunate ones ate the tasty meal, meaningful communication was limited to body language, and Cabrillo forced his face and posture to convey a level of confidence in the present congregation that was considerably higher than reality. As the bowls emptied Matipuyaut laid his aside and opened their conversation by asking, "Did you find signs of the land you sought, Cabrillo?"

"Not yet, Matipuyaut. We sailed far to the north, a land white with much snow, but winter sent us back to you. We will try again." He decided not to reveal the sad condition of the bergantine, at least not yet.

Matipuyaut nodded thoughtfully as his people exchanged speculative glances. Cabrillo continued, saying, "While we are here we will hunt in the seas for our food. We will trade for water and any other food you can spare. As before, we will help your people defend themselves against any attack from your enemies."

Glancing at each of his sons, reading their expressions, Matipuyaut said, "We have had many rains. Water is plentiful. The sea around our island yields much food even though fishing and hunting are harder in the cold times. I have seen that your men are hard workers, so there should be enough water, fish, and meat. We have not stored enough acorn flour or dried berries for my people and your men to have plenty, and we do not visit the main land to buy more after the winter storms come, but we can trade for a little of what we have."

"We will be happy with what you can spare."

The chief fixed his glance on Cabrillo and asked him searchingly, "What else will you wish of us while you are here?"

Cabrillo told him. "We must repair our ships, Matipuyaut. One, the smallest, must be brought ashore, but we will keep our men near the beach. We seek rest and shelter until the weather turns."

"And women?"

The abruptness of the question caught Cabrillo unprepared. He and his men had been offered women on the mainland, but he was still uncertain of acceptable customs. Judging from the unrest caused during their earlier stay, married women were forbidden from sharing favors other than those clearly granted by their husbands. Although it was true that Matipuyaut had given Taya to him, he was unsure of the permanence of even this arrangement. He feared that it would take little to raise trouble with these islanders, and he intended to avoid trouble like he would the plague. Cautiously, he answered, "Whatever pleases Matipuyaut and his people will please my men and me."

At this response, the shrewd eyes of the chief revealed curiosity. "One of our women is already yours, Cabrillo. Do you want more?"

"No, chief, no more."

Matipuyaut studied Cabrillo a moment longer and then turned his perusal to the soldiers. "A man is not happy for long without a woman to share his furs. If your ships stay until the warm days come, your men may grow uneasy."

What could Cabrillo say to this? They were already starved for sexual comfort. Before he could think of some reassuring reply, the chief said decisively, "We will allow your men to visit some of our unmarried women, but only those we choose and only at a house we make ready for them near the beach." He held up both hands and extended all of his fingers. "This many women will stay at the house, and this many of your men may come to the women each day, but they can not stay there. They must be back on the ships before the sun sleeps. Only you, your black friend, and your two holy men may remain among us when darkness comes."

253

Sensing the tightness that had seized Father Lezcano's body, for a split second he considered what refusing might trigger, and then he nodded appreciatively, but he was already feeling the weight of how such an arrangement could best be governed. "This is a fine gift, Matipuyaut. Your heart is big to share your people with mine. Now, tell me what you wish from us while we are here?"

"Keep all enemies from approaching our village, do not take food from our stores, and trade fairly with your goods."

The captain-general bowed over his crossed legs. Using words similar to those spoken earlier by Matipuyaut, he asked, "What else do you wish?"

"Cabrillo, I would also greet and sit upon your horse. And my sons and I wish to stay one day and one night aboard your great canoe."

At this, at last, Cabrillo allowed himself a smile. "You are most welcome, Matipuyaut. Is there anything more?"

The chief hesitated before making his final request. "I have seen your..." it took him an instant before he remembered the word he sought, "guns, and I have heard that you can make them roar like a whale and shoot fire like lightning. Will you show me this magic?"

"Yes, chief, I will show you how to make the guns roar. You will do this with your own hand, if you wish."

Surprised, a sudden anxiety mixing with his pleasure, the chief quickly recovered and bobbed his head once in confirmation.

Now that the initial terms of their stay had been agreed upon, Cabrillo, greatly relieved, steered the conversation toward lesser yet still practical matters such as how he and his men might interfere least with the daily practices of the islanders. He hoped that learning more about their ways would increase the chances for peace between their cultures, so he paid acute attention to all that was explained. Their talk lasted until the sunlight had faded and more wood was tossed onto the fire.

When Cabrillo finally left the chief in front of his house, he and his men made their way carefully along the dimly lit path and Taya fell into step beside him. These two walked slowly and spoke softly of small things, allowing the others to pass by. At last only Vargas, Father Lezcano, and Manuel lingered at the tail of the group, awaiting their commander.

Taya stopped and faced the man she claimed as her husband. "My house is very near. Will you stay with me tonight?"

Cabrillo glanced at his expectant men. "No, Taya, tonight I must go to my ships. I will try to come ashore again tomorrow."

She didn't try to hide her regret. "I am your woman, Cabrillo. I wish to please you." Taking a step nearer, so close that her breasts brushed against his chest, she asked, "Can you not find pleasure in a woman of my kind?"

With her body this temptingly and generously offered, it took a significant effort for Cabrillo to keep from responding with his own. Summoning a briskness he hoped would hide this inner struggle, he said, "I could find much pleasure, Taya, but I must leave you now." He sidestepped around her and led his men down the path at a pace not much slower than a trot.

In the later hours of evening the captains, pilots, and shipmasters gathered inside Cabrillo's cabin and conversed about Matipuyaut's offer of women until long after all trace of blue had leached from the sky. The fleet's two priests had not been invited to the assembly and their absence, conspicuous as it was, made the matter easier to discuss frankly. Even so, the logistics of safeguarding such a potentially explosive gift created a delicate challenge for the officers. Difficult questions sprouted like weeds, and one by one these were vigorously attacked. Should the women be available only to the officers? Should they be offered to some of the men as rewards for good behavior or performance? Should certain women be allotted for specific periods in a given day? How long an interlude should each man be allowed during a single shore leave? As these issues and others were posed and dissected the conversation rose and fell with extraordinary energy. At one point Captain Correa suggested that each captain should be allotted two women, the pilots each one, and the shipmasters could share a single female, leaving only one for all of the soldiers and low ranking sailors. This was met by a stone-cold silence from Cabrillo as well as the shipmasters, and it gave birth to a whole new round of conjecture.

When Cabrillo's patience had finally been consumed he placed his hands firmly on his table, stood up, and said, "Enough, gentlemen. Unless there are any overpowering objections," he cocked an eyebrow in warning at Correa, "this is how we will proceed. One woman will be chosen by Captain Ferrelo, and one by Captain Correa. Of the eight females remaining, three will be made available to the pilots and shipmasters, one to the boatswains, and the remaining four will be assigned to the men. The crewmen will be allowed to visit their women *only* as a special recompense for exemplary work and behavior, and no more than one man from *La Victoria,* one from the *San Miguel* per day may be rewarded. Because of her significantly larger crew, two men from the *San Salvador* may visit the women daily. Rotating men from a different watch each day might work best, but I leave that to you captains. Finally, no man is to be given leave to go ashore for pleasure until our repairs are well underway and our basic stores have been replenished. The *San Miguel* will be hauled ashore tomorrow, and until I give the word to the contrary none but those with special permission may leave the beach."

His glance swept the nodding heads, pausing pointedly at Correa until that officer closed his poised lips and smiled in angelic acquiescence. Cabrillo slapped the table decisively, substantiating the accord. "Good. There is but one more approval we need to obtain before we put our plan into action. Matipuyaut must agree that this will be workable for his people. If not, I will ask what might be more acceptable. Until I speak to the chief, there are to be no announcements made to the men. Is that understood, gentlemen?"

A muttered "Yes, sir," circled the group, and the meeting drew to an end at last.

Cabrillo warned them in parting, "Keep a vigilant watch, especially until dawn. I expect no trouble but each crew must be prepared for whatever comes. I wish you all a peaceful night."

Whether ears had been pressed to a wall or a keyhole, Cabrillo would never know, but he stepped from his cabin that night to be met by a distinctly more cheerful crew than the one he'd commanded before entering his chamber. As he moved about the decks, grins could not be fully erased from the younger men's faces. Knowing looks of anticipation shifted from station to station and deck to deck, though a measure of care was exerted to avoid being distinctly noticed by an officer. Seamen elbowed each other with a wink and a nod. Among even the oldest and crustiest of his sailors the captain-general perceived a new and benevolent sort of contentment, as if they'd just been assured of an open-armed greeting at the gates of heaven.

Accepting these proofs of the thinness of his cabin walls with neither wasted questions nor protestations, Cabrillo stood his watch in relative tranquility and kept his own anticipations and fears to himself. He reflected for a time on the fact that tomorrow had always been miserly about revealing her intentions to mortals, demanding instead that they await her actual arrival.

When the morning did appear Chief Matipuyaut wasted no daylight before visiting the *San Salvador*. A flustered Paulo wakened Cabrillo with, "Sir, that island king is approaching the ship." Much to Paulo's further discontentment, Cabrillo brushed him away and hurriedly dressed himself without choosing his newly washed breeches or fully taming his wild hair but finishing just in time to meet Matipuyaut's party as they set foot aboard.

Cabrillo had wished that the chief and his sons would accept his invitation to the ship after his crew had a chance to make her and themselves more presentable. Nevertheless, the men of the flagship did their best to receive them and their small cluster of guards with gracious hospitality. Shortly after formalities had been exchanged, Cabrillo took a moment to obtain the chief's permission to land the *San Miguel* and ordered that effort to proceed at once.

Once his men were in motion, Cabrillo led the islanders on Matipuyaut's second comprehensive tour of the flagship. He evidently found it even more fascinating than the first time, since he posed questions about everything from barrels and bunks to bridles and binnacles. Upon passing the below-deck quarters of the horses Matipuyaut shook his head in concern and asked, "Do they not wish to come ashore?"

"Yes, as badly as men do," Cabrillo answered.

Matipuyaut turned to one of his warriors and muttered a few short instructions, and the man quickly left them. "A place will be made ready where they stayed before, Cabrillo."

"I am grateful," he replied sincerely, though he had not forgotten Matipuyaut's request to ride Viento.

As they walked throughout the ship they conferred about the materials that might be available for repairs, as well as the terms of trade and the details for transporting goods from the island to their decks. When all preparations had been made, the party moved ashore to more closely observe the unloading and beaching of the bergantine. This process and every step of her initial repairs intrigued Matipuyaut

257

and his sons, down to scraping her hull, patching planking, caulking seams, and brewing pitch. Peering into the pitch pot, the chief asked a few questions and then offered insights into how his people concocted tar for sealing their own canoes, advice that Cabrillo and his caulkers noted closely since they had had only limited success in refining the *yop* they'd traded for on the mainland.

With the ships and the shore humming with activity, Cabrillo returned with Matipuyaut to the flagship to fulfill his promise of the evening before by demonstrating the mechanics of *San Salvador's* guns. Growing more comfortable and fascinated as the instructions progressed, the chief attended eagerly when Cabrillo ordered his master gunner to have one of the currently mounted bombardetas loaded and aimed. With swift precision the selected cannoneer slid a five-pound stone ball into the rear opening of the wrought-iron tube. He then grabbed up one of the gun's slightly conical-shaped and loop-handled iron powder chambers, and checked to see that his assistant had properly filled it with a cloth bag of gunpowder. Clapping the readied chamber in place at the butt of the bombardetta just behind the ball, he motioned for his assistant to ram a tapered breechblock between the powder chamber and the back brace of the wooden carriage, which he then gave a couple of sharp raps with his mallet to pound it snug. Finally, the gunner used his knife to quickly prick the chamber's powder bag through the touchhole, which worked to fill the small space with priming powder. It took only a moment longer to slightly reposition the loaded great gun to point at the spot Cabrillo had selected away from the people on shore.

When the loading was complete, the gunner turned toward the master gunner and the captain-general and waited with his slow twine fuse lit and handy. Cabrillo said "Master Uribe, have the men ashore warned of the blast." Uribe passed the order to the boatswain, who cried out, "Men on the beach, guns will be firing into the hillside to your north." The sailors paused long enough to understand the message, and while many stood still to watch the blast, many others returned to their tasks. Before giving the order to fire, Cabrillo cautioned their guests to stay clear of the gun and cover their ears. When he gave a nod and his master gunner ordered, "Fire!" the gunner brought his match cord to the touchhole and ignited the charge.

Although Matipuyaut and his men had obeyed Cabrillo's instructions to cover their ears, at the sudden roar that burst from the recoiling cannon nothing could have kept them from instinctively leaping backward. The blast sent the round stone crashing into the island's rocky cliff, scattering the sea lions below and setting off a barking uproar while chasing the terrified Chumash from the beach. Stunned for an instant, Matipuyaut turned his gaze from the hill, to the gun, to Cabrillo. His expression settled into a grave comprehension of the potential consequences foretold by the power he had just witnessed. Here was a might far beyond what his people possessed, a force equally capable of protection or conquest.

"The gods are watching what we do this day," he said reflectively.

He hesitated for a couple of seconds when Cabrillo asked if he'd like to fire the next round, and then walked up to the gun and accepted the match chord as another charge was loaded. Better prepared this time, he checked his emotions firmly, carefully lit the cannon's powder, and leaped beyond the reach of the recoil. When the ball exploded from the metal tube and smashed against the crag only three feet from the indentation caused by the first shot, the crewmen raised an approving cry that rivaled the roar of the weapon. When the cannon smoke cleared Matipuyaut stoically accepted the congratulations of the officers, but he and his warriors maintained a quiet reserve during the rest of their time aboard.

Word soon reached the ship through one of Matipuyaut's men that two corrals for the horses had been finished. Though Cabrillo silently questioned whether the bustle ashore was reaching too fevered a pitch for the Chumash to smoothly accept another foreign activity, he ultimately allowed the process of bringing his equine treasures ashore to commence. As he boarded his boat and watched his stallion descend into the water, he told himself that his accompanying Viento to the beach had nothing to do with a desire to see Taya. He would have done so anyway, but he *had* told her he'd come ashore today and during the brief landing this morning she had not appeared.

Viento was so eager to be off the ships that, much to Matipuyaut's astonishment, the stud hurried the rowers toward the sand rather than the other way around. Sitting near Cabrillo in the boat, hugely impressed by Viento's powerful strokes against the current, the chief uttered a continuous and excited string of encouragement to the swimming horses.

Once ashore, Father Lezcano quickly removed the lead lines, and Cabrillo slowly led Viento in a wide circle. After the first circuit, the captain-general invited Matipuyaut to walk with them, and Viento accepted his presence and his quiet, ongoing dialogue without protest. When Cabrillo felt that his stallion's muscles had been somewhat revived, he stopped, grabbed a handful of mane, and swung onto Viento's bare back.

Both man and horse reveled in this latest reunion of their bodies and hearts, and Cabrillo smiled as his stallion tossed his head and gently pranced in place. When Viento's legs had loosened a bit more, his master let him to walk in the ring they'd formed in the sand, his spirit soaring along with his pleasure.

Knowing that Cabrillo would relish a few moments of relative solitude with his horse, Father Lezcano escorted Matipuyaut back along the beach to where Seguro was now being landed. Cabrillo was parading around the circle, patting and talking to Viento, when he looked up and there on the hill above him stood Taya. Her hair, skirt, and fur cape danced lightly with the breeze, her two small boys at her sides. Cabrillo waved at them, and one of the boys waved back, and then Taya took hold of her sons' hands and headed toward the path that led down to the corral. Cabrillo and his stud arrived before them.

Surrendering Viento's reins to Mateo and noting that Matipuyaut was still occupied with Father Lezcano and Seguro, Cabrillo met Taya with a warm, "Taya, I am glad to see you." She smiled her greeting as her sons, half-hidden behind her, peered up at Cabrillo.

"Come," said Taya to her boys, gently inching them into full view. "This is Muhu," she said to Cabrillo, touching the head of the one on her left. With hand signals she indicated a bird and verbalized a low hooting sound.

"Ah, Muhu, owl," muttered Cabrillo.

The boy on her right, she introduced as "Alow" and pointed to a cloud overhead and another far to the east.

Nodding in understanding, Cabrillo repeated the name. Pointing to his chest, he said with authority, "Cabrillo."

Taya gently nudged them both, and they piped in unison, "Cabrillo!"

The captain-general chuckled at this, causing the two youngest members of his adopted family to break out in shy smiles.

Taya said, "I gathered prawns and a small squid this morning. Will you eat with us?"

Aware that more was being asked than these words indicated, he said, "Matipuyaut is my guest aboard the ship. I will try to come tomorrow."

Matipuyaut and Father Lezcano approached leading Seguro, giving Cabrillo little further opportunity to converse with Taya and her sons. While the priest led the gelding to the pen the chief came to a halt and shooed Taya away as if she were no older than her sons, and said, "I wish to ride upon Viento, Cabrillo. My daughter can watch from over there." Taya moved off but not quite as far as her father had indicated, and Father Lezcano came to stand beside her.

Cabrillo took the precaution of attaching a lead rope to his stud's bridle before giving Matipuyaut a brief lesson in how to hold and maneuver the reins and then relinquished control of the leather straps. Following his instructions, Matipuyaut gently signaled his wishes to Viento, though this was not really necessary with Cabrillo walking next to them as they advanced several times around the circle of sand. With every new circuit the chief grew more relaxed until he suddenly waved triumphantly to his people and let out a loud yip of delight. At the sudden cry, Viento shied sideways and Matipuyaut almost lost his seat despite Cabrillo's quick reaction to still his horse. After taking a moment to recover, the fact that he'd remained on his mount during this lurch pleased the chief greatly, and he rode about the ring for the last time sitting even taller and prouder than before. Returning to the corral, Matipuyaut dismounted with reluctance, ran his hand several times over Viento's neck and chest to show his appreciation, and announced to Cabrillo with wonderfully accurate pronunciation, "Now we go back to *San Salvador*." Within an hour of their landing the captain-general and the chief were rowed away from the island.

A few hours later, the fleet's guests sat down to dine with Cabrillo and their conversation turned to the near future dealings between the two cultures. Matipuyaut not only approved of Cabrillo's plan for the sailors' interactions with the ten native women, he informed him that the house was already available, complete with partitions, furnishings, and supplies. Ten women would be living there by this evening. Taya

261

was not mentioned, and Cabrillo understood the omission to imply that his visits with her were expected to take place at her home.

The evening was still relatively young when Matipuyaut rose from his bench and announced, "It is time for rest." With pleased anticipation, he proclaimed to his sons, "Tonight we sleep in the great canoe."

Cabrillo stood and bowed, "You are welcome to my cabin. Paulo will soon make it ready for the three of you."

At this, Matipuyaut looked deeply troubled. "Cabrillo must keep his own bed. We will sleep in a place that will not disturb you."

It did no good whatsoever to assure him that Cabrillo didn't mind sleeping elsewhere, and it was finally settled that the natives would spend the night in the officers' cabin, tightly snug though they would be. Giving his pilot and shipmaster a moment to gather their few things, Cabrillo led the way. Matipuyaut entered these less lavish quarters, which he'd already seen during his tours of the ship, and smiled with satisfaction. He cast his clothing aside, lay down on a sleeping pad, and drew the cover over him.

Standing at their cabin door, Cabrillo took in the look of profound repose that spread over Matipuyaut's face as he reclined on the thin mattress, relaxing fully under the influence of the gently rocking ship. The chief closed his eyes for a moment, sighed deeply as if about to fall asleep, and then abruptly propped himself up on his elbows, saying, "It feels as I hoped it would, Cabrillo. While I sleep upon the water tonight, perhaps I will have a rare dream."

Though their understanding of one another was still far from perfect, and the meanings of many words were yet assumed rather than known, at that moment Cabrillo felt an unexplainable kinship with the old chief, something that embodied the promise of real friendship. He stood aside to allow Matipuyaut's sons to enter and settle in around him.

"Sleep well," he said in the Chumash tongue, and left them so he could attend to the remainder of his night watch.

At the railing, listening to the barking and growling of the sea lions and the occasional whickering of his horses while he watched the sky for comets, he wondered what Matipuyaut was dreaming. Father Lezcano soon came to join him.

"You look especially thoughtful tonight, sir."

"Oh, I was just speculating that Matipuyaut might be dreaming about horses. It would be a fine dream, with him riding wild over his beloved island. Some day, there may be many horses on this mainland, but they would be difficult to raise here. We must be careful of our horses' feed even during this short stay."

Their talk moved to other things, both practical and philosophical, but they delicately avoided the subject of women. For this, Cabrillo was thankful. The female visitation agreement carried the potential for more mischief than either man's comfort allowed. He didn't want it adding the burden of hard feelings between the two of them.

Chapter 22

THE WARMTH OF TAYA'S LODGE

At the turning of the sandglass just after sunrise and shortly following the departure for shore by Matipuyaut's party, the *San Salvador's* boatswain lifted his voice in an official tone that halted the actions of every seaman and soldier. "Turn your attention here, men! Attention! Heed the words of our captain-general!"

Cabrillo stood on the quarterdeck with his back as lineal as the mast behind him, his chin high, and his countenance staid. "As each of your shipmasters has already informed you," he said, knowing full well the men had initially heard the news from each other, "Chief Matipuyaut has provided a house and a selected number of women for our benefit." Threatening glares from the shipmasters and boatswains kept the cheers clipped and muffled so Cabrillo could go on. "You have also been told that any man who has *unapproved* contact with a native woman will be dealt with harshly. The customs of these people will not allow unwanted advances to be made to their women, and *I* will not allow it. The penalty I would impose on any guilty man would be distinctly unforgettable." As Cabrillo's grave eyes swept the decks, the grinning faces before him sobered significantly. In the Spanish realm the sentence for the rape of a white woman varied little. Death. Lately, however, murmurings had circulated that some Spanish captains and magistrates had adopted the Moorish custom of castrating rapists. Though such defilement of the body was greatly frowned upon by the Church, something in Cabrillo's tone and gaze brought these rumors to the forefront of his crewmembers' supposition, and most understood the inference that this kind of sentence might be carried out in a tryst with an island woman.

Seeing that the men had grasped his meaning, Cabrillo continued. "We are here seeking shelter and replenishment. We must repay the granting of these by respectfully honoring their traditions and mandates, by trading fairly, and, if necessary, by defending their safety. Mark these words, men. I do not deliver them lightly."

Nods and muttered acquiescence climbed up to him.

"Work hard and step carefully, and our stay here may be both peaceful and agreeable. That is all, men. You may resume your duties."

Fully comprehending how his own manner and behavior set the expectations of the men, Cabrillo didn't go ashore until after his morning watch had been fulfilled. Efforts on the ships were progressing well: water barrels were full again and newly caught fish were being salted and stowed. Already, their sick men were responding to the food provided by the island or brought here through trade with the mainland Chumash.

When Cabrillo's launch slid onto the sandy beach, Viento lifted his muzzle and neighed in salutation. Approaching his horses with Vargas beside him, Cabrillo saw that Matipuyaut's second son was brushing his mare's coat with obvious gratification as Manuel stood attentively nearby. Although other Chumash warriors watched the advancement of Cabrillo and his Sergeant Major they showed no sign of aggression. The captain-general greeted the natives in their own language and went over to Mateo, who had taken up residence in the horse shelter along with Manuel. His nephew said, "Oh, sir, the horses are quite well. They love the island."

After enjoying several minutes among his equine soul mates, Cabrillo was interrupted when Matipuyaut's eldest son appeared with an invitation to come to the village, and they set off at once. Along the way they paused long enough to allow Cabrillo to inspect the house that had so recently been set up for the physical needs of his men. When he entered, six young women lowered their eyes respectfully. As he took in the well-ordered chamber, his eyes rested only momentarily on each of the maidens, none of whom appeared to be older than seventeen years, and he was impressed by Matipuyaut's munificence. They were all attractive. The other four of their number must be out attending to errands that would further feather this nest in preparation for the arrival of his men in a few days. Sensing the uneasiness caused by his unexpected arrival, he bid them a polite farewell and left.

It was clear that word of his coming had reached Taya since she was waiting for him at the edge of the village, her eyes eager and her mouth smiling. He had thought he'd been asked to the village to meet with Matipuyaut, but he now wondered if Taya's brother had escorted him here at her request. A glance at the young warrior's studied nonchalance was enough to strengthen this assumption, but when Cabrillo's eyes again found Taya his mind eased all other subjects to a more distant place.

The chief's son, noting the expression on Cabrillo's face, discreetly parted from them.

When Cabrillo and Taya had drawn close together, she said simply, "You have come."

"I can stay..." he struggled to communicate the passing of numbered hours to one unfamiliar with the concept, and he finished by pointing to the sky and saying, "until the sun reaches there."

She suppressed her dissatisfaction at so short a visit, turned, and led him to a small house not far from the dwelling of Matipuyaut. When Cabrillo entered, he saw Taya's sons sitting cross-legged before a young woman weaving a basket. At his arrival they all looked up, wide-eyed with curiosity and apprehension. He smiled to reassure them and said, "Greetings Muhu and Alow," and they returned the welcome courteously. Wanting to avoid confusing which boy was which, Cabrillo made a mental note of the short striped owl feather suspended from a thong and hanging down Muhu's small chest.

Taya introduced the young woman as her sister, and, after a subtle signal that Cabrillo didn't detect, the boys were gracefully ushered out of the house by their aunt.

"Do you wish to eat?" Taya asked.

Still standing, Cabrillo declined her offer as he took his time admiring the cleanliness and comfort of her home. He turned back to find that she now stood directly behind him. He hesitated, unsure of the next appropriate step, but Taya was looking meaningfully at his sword, and she said, "You may remove your weapon now, Cabrillo. There is no danger here."

Not altogether certain of the truth of this statement when all forms of danger were considered, he nevertheless unbuckled his belt and hung it from a wall peg. He then voiced something he'd wondered about many times. "Your name, Taya, what does it mean?"

266

"My full name is Tasin Taya." She thought for a moment, and then went to a deep narrow basket suspended by its handle from the wall and withdrew a small skin that had been painted with red angular markings. She pointed to several of these symbols, and then to the red garnet imbedded in an amulet he wore at his breast. "Tasin."

"Ah, red."

She then went to the cooking stone near her fire and brought back a bowl shaped from an abalone shell. Running her fingertips around the vessel, pointing out to sea, and then pantomiming how she'd pried the shell from a boulder, she again held it up and said, "Taya."

"Red abalone? Tasin Taya."

Gladdened by his comprehension, she replaced the bowl near the fire. She motioned for him to sit beside her on the furs, and when he had done so said with a slight hesitation, "Our elders say that the unions of our women and your men will bless the people of our island, because you are gods."

The shadow of a grin, insinuating that he was all too human, appeared at the corners of his mouth. "What do you say?"

Her eyes took him in, searching his face as if trying to discern the depth and texture of his soul. When she spoke it was with an intensity that moved him as much as her words. "I want a man." She placed her hand on his chest for a moment, and then continued to speak and gesture. "This man, not a god. You chose me over other women who were not marked by shame. You were not afraid of me or my sons. You and your holy men brought honor and safety to our lives." Dispelling the last of his unspoken questions, she said, "I want you, Cabrillo, only you."

She reached up and gently removed his flat, round-brimmed hat, and then started unfastening the buttons at the chest of his long-sleeved doublet. He did not still her hands. His mind surrendered and softened as his eyes took in every aspect of her hair, shoulders, and breasts, and his nose inhaled her sweet, smoky scent. His scarred, thin, weary body absorbed and anticipated her questing touches at each of his many fastenings. When he made a movement to help her, she shifted his hands away, determined to gain proficiency through practice at this new task. As she worked, her glances constantly returned to his, observing his reactions and emotions. From her tightening concentration Cabrillo began to perceive a suspended hunger not wholly unlike that

267

of a hunter nearing its prey, yet her agile fingers betrayed no outright sense of urgency as they moved steadily to his waist.

When the doublet was free she laid it aside and Cabrillo went to the bed of furs to remove his boots and hose. It didn't take him long. Standing once more, he would have untied his breeches, but here again Taya took over. She loosened the drawstring at his waist and her hands slid the breeches from his hips to the floor. His thigh-length shirt was now his only covering.

Casting one more glance at Taya, her beautiful features beckoning, he felt any lingering uncertainties crumble away. He pulled his shirt up and over his head with a single smooth motion. Under unabashed intensity he'd never before encountered in a woman, he held himself still as her eyes moved from his head to his feet, pausing where they would. Very soon, her fingers began to explore what her eyes had found.

His curiosity about what she was thinking and feeling quickly gave way to the hungers of his own body, and he pulled her nearer. Her cape and skirt fell away. Their bodies met in a feast of exploration and sensual acuteness that weakened their knees and lowered them to the bed.

The skilled workings of his mouth upon Taya's skin were new and enticing to her, and she responded with a fierceness of ardor that Cabrillo had not imagined possible. Here was neither the hesitant stranger giving her body in exchange for survival or reward, nor the virgin lady in love with him yet bound by doctrine and tradition to act chastely. No, Taya was different from any other woman he'd known.

As they moved upon the furs, as their bodies touched, and mingled, and tightened, Cabrillo vaguely sensed the depth of the emotion Taya was conveying with her body. She was offering herself freely, wildly, wholly, but this thought and every other was soon overtaken by the rising pitch of his passion. Neither of them uttered an intelligible word, and this only added force and intimacy as they reached and clung to the waves of their physical fulfillment.

In the first quiet moments that followed, as their bodies began to cool and their minds to calm, Taya lifted her head from where it rested upon his chest and said softly, "You are mine, Cabrillo, even if you have other women, even if you must go away. You are mine."

Gazing into her lovely, intense eyes, he realized somewhat to his own surprise that her words were neither inconsequential nor, in a sense, untrue. Despite his inevitable departure, despite the love he held for his wife, a share of his affection and spirit would remain with Taya when he sailed from this island, as hers would stay with him. And in the years to come, his memories would undoubtedly return to this courageous, tender, lovely native woman.

They spoke for a while about her sons, and then about his. But talking of his other family became difficult for both of them, so she asked about how far away his voyage would take him and when he might return. This subject too was soon abandoned, and when words seemed unable to bring them comfort Taya's hand began to glide gently across the hair of his chest. When she raised her lips to be kissed, inducing their lovemaking to commence again, Cabrillo's awareness of his own feelings gave his movements a heightened intensity and poignancy.

This second sharing of their bodies left them fully satisfied, and for a while they held each other without the need for words, listening to the sounds of the village. It was then, with painful clarity, that the image of Beatriz rose in Cabrillo's mind. He pictured her as she'd looked on the morning he'd left Santiago, standing before the window in her thin nightdress, and he remembered the words she'd uttered then. "I am not inexperienced enough to think there will be no other female to comfort you," she had said.

Now, he wondered if on that morning he'd truly intended to withhold his body and mind from every other woman, for two whole years and while so very far from everything he knew and loved. Such a thing would have been rare, if not unheard of, among his peers, but perhaps he had intended just that. If so, he'd failed. Would she, as her words implied, be able to forgive him? He prayed that she would, though he hoped she'd never know. He would not tell her. Confessing simply to try to cleanse himself of some of his own culpability would cause her much pain and cost them much affection. No, the guilt was his alone to bear.

He and Taya had shared little more than an hour together when she said with regret, "My sister and my sons will return soon." They rose and she led him to a large water basket, into which she dipped a cloth, and began to gently bathe him. When she had finished he took great pleasure in returning the kindness, so much so that his ministrations

269

threatened to carry them both back to the furs. Restraint managed to prevail, however, and they were soon fully dressed.

Perhaps it was the sobering effect of being clothed again that awakened the sudden realization in Cabrillo that his visits to this house could bring unwelcome consequences, and he cursed himself for thinking so little of it before. If Taya conceived a child, perhaps even twins again, it might result in serious hardship, especially since he would not be here to care for them. The islanders might even feel compelled to take drastic steps. There were many potions, he knew, that the native women had discovered to prevent or halt a pregnancy. Placing his hand upon her belly, he asked carefully, "Taya, what if a child comes?"

Concern and perhaps shame colored her cheeks, and she lowered her head, and Cabrillo guessed that she had already taken precautions to prevent such an outcome. He lifted her chin and said, "If you have done something to stop a child from coming, it is good. I cannot stay with you for long. A child could bring you much pain."

Her eyes shone with gratitude for his understanding. "If I had twins again, my people would be certain they, my sons, and I were cursed. We all might be killed."

"Yes. That must not happen." Cabrillo knew he spoke against the teachings of his faith, and that condoning the prevention of life was another sin he must shoulder, but he felt that God would rather a child not be conceived at all than be slain along with its family after its birth. He avoided dwelling on the obvious alternative of keeping his distance from Taya.

Much relieved now, she said, "You should eat."

Although he was not hungry, Cabrillo accepted the acorn cakes she offered with thanks. He'd grown quite fond of their flavor, as had his men, and he chewed them pensively, gradually letting his weightier thoughts drift away. When his hands were empty, Taya handed him another cake, which was indeed delicious. Having seen no oak trees on the island, he asked her, "What do your people trade in exchange for these acorns?"

"Many things." She walked to the edge of her bed, lifted a small woven pouch from a post, and brought the bag to him. Opening it, Cabrillo reached in and pulled out a handful of flat shell disks that were nearly uniform in size. A hole had been drilled into each so that they could be strung onto a chord. He had seen such shell beads several times on the mainland, and he understood them to be used as currency among the coastal Indians.

"My people make them from those shells," Taya said, pointing to a small basket of Olivella shells near the firestones.

Quite curious now, Cabrillo nodded and asked, "What else do you trade?"

Happy to share something of their ways with him, she said, "Tools, made from our island chert." She gathered up several items from around her home and brought him a knife artfully knapped from a piece of a lustrous gray stone, a scraper formed from chert of the same color as her otter skin cape, and a bead drill so white its source might be mistaken for polished ivory.

He nodded, admiring the translucency of the stones. "What else?"

She thought for a moment and then said, "We also trade baskets, bows and arrows, and otter skins."

He nodded again. "Your people are very…" he fought to remember a Chumash word for "resourceful" and finally offered, "clever."

"Acorn cakes are good to eat, and they help us through winters when fish and sea lions are scarce."

He would have questioned her further but they were then interrupted by the entrance of Taya's young boys, one of them cradling a small gray fox in his arms. When the animal spotted Cabrillo it let out a high-pitched yip and tucked its head into the crook of Alow's elbow.

Chuckling, Cabrillo said in Spanish, "So this is what's been making that sound in the night." He asked Taya, "Are there many of these animals on the island?"

"Yes, many."

Yet this was the first one Cabrillo had seen, so holding a tame one must be a rarity.

Seeming spellbound by Cabrillo's presence, and perhaps a little uneasy that their mother remained so close to the strange warrior from the sea, the boys didn't take their eyes from him as they and their aunt seated themselves several feet away.

Hoping to put them at ease, Cabrillo thought for a moment about what he possessed that might serve as gifts to two so young. Nothing came to mind and he was about to abandon the idea when he remembered the coins in the pouch at his belt, which he carried more out

271

of long habit than in anticipation of their usefulness here. Fingering through several of the small silver disks, he chose a couple of half-real pieces. Since being struck, these coins too had been drilled with holes, allowing their previous owners to string their wealth and keep it tucked into their shirts or breeches. Through gestures, the captain-general asked Taya to bring him two thin chords about eighteen inches in length. Once these thongs had been provided he made each boy a medallion necklace, handed them to Taya, and indicated that she was to give them to her sons.

Fascinated, she studied the side of a coin that bore the image of the late King Ferdinand II encircled by letters, and then the other showing the simple striped shield of Aragon. When her eyes lifted they held a thousand questions but, for now, she kept them to herself. She returned the necklaces to Cabrillo and in an earnest manner asked if he would bestow them himself.

Understanding now that the gifts would mean more if presented directly by him, he smiled and nodded. When Taya called Alow and Muhu nearer, Cabrillo said to the boys as he showed them each face of a coin, "These carry the marks of my king and my land. They are for you." He leaned forward, separately looped a necklace over each small head, and sat back to observe the looks of wonder on the enchantingly similar faces.

Taya said to them with a gravity that held their attention, "Wear these gifts with care, my sons. They carry much power."

Wide-eyed, the boys ran their fingers over the shiny metal with stamped images and raised edges, and looked up at the bearded man. Almost in unison, they gave him a sign that represented appreciation, and Cabrillo bowed his head in acknowledgment.

Suddenly restless, the boys asked their mother if they might show their new treasures to a friend and, receiving her permission, they scurried outside with their aunt close behind. Cabrillo smiled as he watched, then turned to their mother and said, "I must return to my duties, Taya."

She knew she had no choice but to accept this. "Will you come tomorrow?"

"I will try."

As he left her embrace and the warmth and relief she'd given him, he also relinquished the sense of family that he'd found for a few moments and with these surrenderings the feeling of guilt returned to steal much of the pleasure he'd known in her company. Yet as he walked away from her lodge he knew that he would return. He told himself that in the weeks to come the culpability that resulted from his weaknesses might grow easier to bear; no less damning, just less weighty.

He might even come to believe that God could forgive his frailties when he could not.

Chapter 23

THE BOY WHO DREAMED

Their days glided into an uneven pattern that ebbed and flowed with Cabrillo's visits to Taya and her family and his returns to the countless demands of the fleet. Wind and rain became familiar if unwelcome companions, but he didn't let weather forestall the work at hand. Food was caught in abundance and meted out with prudence, and there seemed more than enough fresh water to see them through their stay. Within the first two weeks, Cabrillo was pleased to see the ships sealed, scrubbed, and much closer to seaworthiness, especially the *San Miguel*. Men began to turn their free energies to trading for warmer clothing fashioned from the otter and sea lion skins harvested from around the island.

As intermittent winter storms broke out at sea and raged with fury, the harbor shielded them well. Cabrillo, his captains, and his pilots spent many hours studying the changes in the winds and reviewing the currents they'd charted, and they laid and relaid plans on how to seek the best route northeastward when the time came. With the days growing colder, winter delivered an occasional soft snow flurry to display the harbor in a picturesque whiteness.

Although squabbles inevitably broke out among the men over who was chosen to visit the "women's hut," as it was soon dubbed, nothing arose between Cabrillo's own men that couldn't be quelled by a couple of whacks from his boatswain's well-aimed billet. Not unusually, and despite Father Gamboa's unflagging efforts, tensions rose high aboard the *San Miguel* and the whip was called into action from time to time. Though Cabrillo was aware of these stirrings of discontent, he knew that Captain Correa and his officers made every effort to keep things controlled enough to avoid reporting their troubles.

What concerned Cabrillo even more than this was the growing strain between the fleet's men and the Chumash warriors. Fistfights had already taken place, and during the third altercation one of his men had been slashed by a stone knife. Fortunately the wound had not been serious and the responsible warrior, threatened by Matipuyaut with banishment if he did not offer adequate gifts for reconciliation, extended his olive branch. So things had settled into a delicately pendulating peace, but Cabrillo feared it would not last.

He did what he could to foster and maintain close ties with the island leaders, visiting them often, seldom empty-handed. In time the captain-general and his small group of close companions grew to be such a familiar sight that the natives began to lose some of their uneasiness around him. Much to the disquiet of Vargas, Cabrillo occasionally walked with only Taya, her father, or one of her brothers along various paths of Isla de Posesión, taking note of all he learned and working to improve his abilities with the Chumash language.

He soon discovered that the chert tools Taya had shown him on his first visit to her lodge represented only a small sample of the articles made from the local stone, and his interest in it often led him to the southeastern point of the island, where the natives conducted extensive mining activities. While either at the quarry or back among the knappers' lodges, Cabrillo enjoyed studying the methods of these artisans as they unearthed and shaped their points and edges. One of Taya's uncles even permitted the captain-general to try his hand at knapping, but this clumsy though concentrated endeavor created little more than a few minutes of amusement for the expert, several cuts to Cabrillo's fingers, and a distinct absence of interest in a second knapping attempt.

On other occasions, he and Taya walked to small quarries of another kind. He counted more than fifteen different sites where a type of volcanic rock could be extracted and worked to provide pestles, grinding stones, and huge oblong mortars. These pumice goods may have lacked the luminous beauty of the tools flaked from chert, but Taya informed him that they were highly prized by their mainland neighbors. During one of their first visits to a pumice works on a very early morning, he innocently asked if such heavy stones were difficult to transport in their small canoes.

Her expression became distant, and she said weakly, "Men can be lost. Good men." She started to turn away from him, but Cabrillo took her hand and drew her back.

In answer to his unspoken question, she said, "My husband was lost at sea." Showing grief that had lost much of its anguish but had not fully healed, she explained reluctantly, "He was a member of the Brotherhood-of-the-Canoe. Such men are much respected." She looked out at the ocean and let herself remember. "Nearly three years ago several canoes left our island to trade across the passage. One was his. A sudden storm came from the north and the waves took all but one of the canoes. My husband could not be saved."

Moments passed before Cabrillo asked, "Was he found?"

Uncertain of his meaning yet disinclined to further explanation, she said, "He is gone."

Deciding it would be best to learn about their beliefs in afterlife at another time, he let the matter rest. For a while they watched the waves slide onto the beach and away again, the earlier need for speech replaced by a desire for reflection. It was the kind of cloudy day that worked the sun's light mysteriously, making colors and contours exceedingly brilliant and rich, and for some time they stood in the breeze and let their eyes feast. In the same silent reverie they backed away from the view and allowed their steps to turn them toward the village.

But they had gone only a few dozen yards when a terrible wail burst from a hidden rocky outcropping behind them. As they pivoted and their gazes sought the source of the cry, it grew even louder with distress and helplessness. Suddenly a Chumash warrior appeared from behind the rocks, his face stricken with anguish as he struggled forward carrying the limp body of an adolescent boy.

At the sound of the first outburst Vargas and his handful of guards, standing watch on the plateau above, came rushing down the path toward Cabrillo, their hilts tightly gripped or their arrows at their strings. The captain-general waved to indicate there was no danger, and his men slowed but kept coming.

In his distress, the Chumash man saw Cabrillo not as a potential enemy but as someone who might have the power to save his unconscious son, and he called out to him for help. Cabrillo ran forward to support the boy's shoulders while the father took his knees. The young face was as still as death, his chest barely moving. The father was talking too excitedly for Cabrillo to grasp his words but Taya said, "We must take him home."

As Vargas and his soldiers scattered out of their way and they eased by with the boy, Cabrillo asked Taya, "What has happened to him?"

Quickly posing this question to the warrior, she then relayed his answer. "The boy was on his dream quest."

This helped Cabrillo not at all. "Did he fall?"

After exchanging a few more words with the father, Taya tried to explain by saying, "No, his vision holds him captive."

Again, Cabrillo was at a loss. "Has he eaten something that made him ill?"

She said quickly, "I have seen this once before. Another boy was overcome by *momoy*."

"What is *momoy*?"

"A drug, given by Kipomo to help a boy find his animal spirit."

At last, Cabrillo had something to work with. He turned back to Vargas and called out, "Send for Dr. Fuentes! And Father Lezcano!" Two of his men raced around them and back along the path. Vargas and the others kept coming, now trailing close behind their commander as more and more Chumash hurried toward the burdened group.

When Cabrillo and the father reached the plateau Vargas and his men flanked them and cleared the way toward the village. By the time they reached the boy's lodge Indians had surrounded them completely, but the father shouted them out of the way, and he and Cabrillo carried the youth inside. The mother rushed into the room and stumbled toward her son with an agonized cry of his name. Cabrillo helped lower the youth to a bed as other relatives entered the house more quietly.

The boy's breathing had grown so shallow it was hard to detect. His mother had begun to weep, his father to sway on his knees and mutter in lamentation.

Cabrillo searched his mind for anything he'd ever learned of physicians' remedies for such cases. He thought of the herbal curatives the natives of the south had recently taught him. A tea used as a purgative came to mind. He had no experience in its brewing or its outcome, but trying it was better than doing nothing. He glanced around the room in search of dried plants.

Taya had been watching him closely and, guessing his intention, she said under her breath, "Kipomo might not want your help, Cabrillo. Someone must have gone to tell him what has happened."

He had already considered this and its potential outcome. "Did the other boy live, the one who had taken *momoy*?"

She paused for an instant, and then said, "No."

"Then we must try to save this boy."

Cabrillo asked the mother to boil some water and bring him her herbs. She jumped to obey him, and he was quickly scrutinizing the small collection of dried plants as he prayed for Dr. Fuentes to hurry, but it was Kipomo who arrived first. The shaman nudged his way to the bedside and stared down at the youth. Reaching into his pouch, he produced a bundle of herbs and a small stone bowl. From a coal at the cooking fire, he lit the bundle and began to sing in a pitch so high and uneven that it made Cabrillo's tightened nerves stretch to a dangerous level. There was no time for this. Where was that damned physician!

Kipomo breathed smoke into the boy's face and began to chant once more. When this song ended, he looked again at the youth's face and placed his hand upon his chest. There was real concern written in his expression, maybe even regret. Perhaps he was remembering the first young man who had died. Suddenly, he seemed to reach a formidable conclusion. Turning to Cabrillo, Kipomo spoke the first words he'd ever delivered directly to him. "His spirit is leaving us. Can your god bring it back?"

Surprised by this willingness to put the boy's welfare over the sanctity of his own power, Cabrillo was about to offer his tea as a possible cure when he heard the pounding of running feet. *At last.* He answered Kipomo by saying, "My men are coming. They will try."

Father Lezcano appeared at the door, and Cabrillo waved him forward.

"I was at the beach, sir," he began, but then he spotted the boy. Kipomo moved aside and motioned for the priest to do what he could. Father Lezcano glanced at the unnaturally still face and asked Cabrillo, "Do you expect him to live, sir?"

"I know little of these things, but it looks grave. Where is the doctor?"

278

"He must be with the men I saw coming up from the beach behind me. He will be here very soon." He looked at the boy again and swallowed. "May I baptize him, sir?"

Cabrillo needed no more words. "Yes, Father."

"What is his name?"

Taya recognized the word and answered him. "He is Shuluwish."

At the priest's request, Taya brought him a bowl of water. He blessed the clear liquid and uttered the simple words, "I baptize you, Shuluwish, in the name of the Father, and of the Son, and of the Holy Spirit." He then traced the sign of the Christian cross upon the boy's forehead, lips, and chest, and the shortened baptism was complete. Father Lezcano then drew his rosary from his belt and placed its crucifix on the center of Shuluwish's chest. He began to pray, and Cabrillo and Vargas joined him. Taya had learned many of the words from her lessons with Father Lezcano, and where she could she added her soft voice to those of the men. In moments every person in the dwelling, even Kipomo, was kneeling on the floor and muttering intonations along with Father Lezcano, knowing none of the strange words but profoundly understanding the spirituality with which their mutual request was being made.

Dr. Fuentes found them just then. He entered respectfully but quickly, and they inched outward to make room for him near the patient. "He's been given a drug to help him dream," Cabrillo provided.

The physician lifted an eyelid and examined a reddened eye, and then he pressed his ear to the boy's ribcage. When he raised his head, his expression was grim. "What was the drug, sir? Was it Datura, the one the natives call *momoy*?"

"Yes."

"How long ago?"

Cabrillo and Taya translated this question to Kipomo, received an answer, and Cabrillo told the doctor, "It was given during a ceremony in the middle of the night."

This seemed to thin whatever optimism Dr. Fuentes had held, and he asked no more questions. "I will do what I can, sir, but I have little hope. Can these people be sent away?"

All of the villagers except the parents, Taya, and Kipomo were guided outside, many pausing at the entrance or in nearby houses. The doctor asked for water to be quickly heated as he pulled two bottles from his crowded pouch. Cabrillo, watching closely, was acutely aware of his good fortune at having a physician who understood the properties of herbs and who could mix his own medicines when an apothecary was not at hand.

In moments the water was hot enough, and Dr. Fuentes added a heavy dose of crushed dried roses, explaining to Cabrillo that he would attempt to induce vomiting. When the brew had steeped just long enough the physician hurriedly combined it with sugar syrup and then a measure of cooler water. At last Dr. Fuentes lifted Shuluwish's head, poured the concoction into the boy's mouth, and worked his jaw to ease it down his throat.

In hushed tones Father Lezcano and Kipomo continued to pray using their vastly different languages and methods.

The boy's mother and father sat quietly now, confused by these strange ministrations but desperately hoping their only son would not be taken from them.

As Cabrillo waited along with the others, willing the young stomach to rise up and expel the poison it had consumed, he watched the crucifix lift and fall with each weak breath. He again muttered the prayers of the rosary with his priest, but his mind melted the many words down to just one, and that single word surged repeatedly from his heart. "Please."

It seemed like a very long time had passed but in less than an hour, as they looked on, Shuluwish stirred a single forefinger. They all stilled in tense anticipation of another sign, but a moment later the crucifix stopped moving. Kipomo came close and called out the boy's name, then he shouted in a tone of terrible suffering.

From the other side of Shuluwish's bed Dr. Fuentes again placed his ear to the young chest. At the sadly conclusive shake of his head, Kipomo lowered his eyes in defeat and the boy's mother released a keening, heart-wrenching wail. The father, Taya, and many of those outside gave voice to their grief, and their mingling cries of woe circled the house like a newly abandoned wraith.

As the shaman and the doctor moved away, Father Lezcano approached Shuluwish's body, slowly picked up his rosary, and again made the sign of the cross.

Dr. Fuentes, saddened by so wasteful a death, muttered needlessly, "I was too late, Captain-General." Glancing at the heart-broken parents, he added, "I am sorry, sir."

At that moment Cabrillo saw Matipuyaut standing at the door, his arms crossed and his head bowed. When the chief's chin lifted and their eyes met, Cabrillo recognized the emotion carved upon Matipuyaut's face all too well. He knew it as he knew his own heart, for the same crushing sorrow had found him every time he'd lost a man, or a hundred men, in battle or in peace, and these glimpses into perdition had carved slices of him away whenever they'd come.

Heavily, he stood up and went to Matipuyaut. He took the chief's hand and clasped it briefly in both of his, and from the vice-like strength in the responding grip this seemed to have been enough to express what he felt. He motioned for Taya to stay with the family, and he and his men quietly left the village, allowing its residents to mourn according to their own customs.

To avoid intruding on the burial ceremonies of the natives, Cabrillo kept himself and his men from visiting the island for several days. When he finally came ashore again, Taya made him aware of how earnestly he'd been missed by showing him affectionate attentiveness as they ate with her sons and, as soon as they were alone, by giving her body with an enthusiasm that left him breathless.

After their lovemaking, with the sun still high and the boys due to return at any time, they left their sleeping furs and helped each other dress. With the lure of their bare skin now reduced, it was easier to concentrate on things beyond the two of them, and Cabrillo's thoughts drifted to the past few days. As she added wood to the fire he sat down beside her and asked, "Taya, will you tell me about the boy, about his burial?"

There was a moment of hesitation, of knowing such things were not meant for outsiders, but this was quickly replaced by resolve. "You are my husband and you have not learned such things, so I will tell you," she said, and yet she began slowly. "You know the place where our gods live."

Cabrillo nodded, having seen the cluster of idols made of stone, wood, and feathers during his walks, but he'd sensed its restricted nature and had never approached it closely.

"After the boy's spirit left him, Kipomo and a few followers wrapped his body in furs and carried him there. They built a fire so large we could see it from the village, and they stayed there all night to pray. In the morning most of the rest of us joined them."

From his ship Cabrillo had seen the red glow of fire reflected in the clouds. He nodded for her to go on.

"When we had gathered in a large ring around the boy, Kipomo lit his large stone pipe and smoked it as he chanted sacred words to help the soul's passage. He, and then his helpers, circled the body three times, and whenever he neared the boy's head he lifted the fur that covered his face and blew three breaths of purifying smoke upon it. And each time they neared his feet, the holy men cried out to ask the gods to watch over him. When these rites had been performed, the boy's relatives gave Kipomo strings of shell beads. As they stepped back from their son's body," her voice caught and her glance fell away from him, but she managed to say, "we all sang our grief."

Cabrillo had heard the mourning wails from his quarterdeck. "And was this the end of the ceremony?"

"Only in the ring of the gods. From there, Kipomo and his helpers carried the body to a place that had been prepared for the burial. We all followed, singing with great sadness because of his youth and his promise, that was now lost to us. When the body was lowered into the grave, the family encircled it with weapons, clothing, bowls, and many other things he would need in the next life. Our men covered him with earth and planted a spear upright above the spot where his head rested." When she lifted her eyes to Cabrillo, unshed tears shone in them. "He had been a fine fisherman for one so young, so his mother carefully laid his fishing tools on top of the grave. She bore a heavy heartache, the most dreadful kind that a mother can bear, yet she showed great courage, more courage than I could have shown if I had lost either of my sons."

Cabrillo placed his hand upon her knee and she covered it with her own, and they sat watching the embers and flames, lost in thought. After some time, he asked, "Taya, what do your people believe happened to the boy's soul?" When she did not answer, he said, "Can you tell me?"

Beginning slowly and in a hushed tone, she said, "A spirit remains near its earthly home for a while after a death. Food is set out for it so that it does not go hungry. Tomorrow will be the fifth day, and that is when it will travel to Humqaq."

She answered a few more of his queries, and Cabrillo came to understand that the Chumash considered Humqaq to lie northward across the channel at the place he had named Point Conception. "What happens at Humqaq?"

"There is a pool where the soul can bathe. As soon as it is cleansed, it paints itself with beautiful images depicting its life, and when all is ready a light appears in the west. The spirit rises into the air and follows the light to the gate that leads to Shimilaqsha, the heavenly land."

Very gently, he asked, "Then, your husband is in Shimilaqsha?"

She shook her head sadly and said with concern, "One who drowns is doomed to wander the seas forever. This is the main reason it takes great courage to be a man of the canoe." Her eyes begged him to take special care while sailing upon the water, for the sake of his soul as well as for himself and for her. Because of her apprehensions, he did not try to correct her beliefs. He merely said, "Tell me more about the gate."

"Before it are high walls of clashing rocks and two huge ravens, and each of these mighty birds pecks out an eye of the entering spirit."

Cabrillo frowned at this unpleasant image but didn't interrupt her.

"There are many beautiful poppies that grow there, and the spirit has only to pick two of these and place them where its eyes had been, and its sight returns. These new celestial eyes allow the spirit to travel the path of the dead to reach Shimilaqsha, where it is rewarded with brilliant eyes made from blue abalone. There are lights all along the pathway that a spirit travels, the same lights we see in the night sky that cluster close together to form a flattened ring."

"The Milky Way," murmured Cabrillo thoughtfully, "a pathway for the dead." He lay down and placed his head in her lap. "What does a spirit do then, Taya?"

"It visits all three lands of the world. The one beneath us, where two giant snakes hold up our earth, the world we live in, and the one above us that is held high up by the great eagle."

"It comes back to this world? Do you know when spirits come to visit?"

"No, Cabrillo. I have never been aware of one's return."

"I see. And once the spirit passes through all these lands, what happens?"

"It remains in Shimilaqsha being further cleansed and healed. When it is ready, it returns to the womb of a Chumash woman to be born again."

He took a moment to mull over these strange beliefs, and then he asked her, "So, the great eagle is also the sun and moon?"

A smile appeared, but she went on tolerantly, "No, the sun is a very old widower who carries his torch across the sky. The moon is a lovely female, and she has much power to heal and to bring forth children."

"Was it Kipomo who taught your people these things?"

Taya's brows knitted at the hint of scoffing behind the question. "These beliefs are different from those of your people, Cabrillo, but they are very old. And you should not doubt Kipomo's authority here, or his importance. He is needed."

"Very well, tell me how is he important?"

"He is wise in the ways of the stars. He reads their signs and chooses names for our children that will serve them throughout their lives. There was great sadness the other day, because the *momoy* was too strong for the boy who left us, but Kipomo has helped many boys reach manhood through their dream quests." She spoke faster and with more emotion as her defense mounted. "I have seen him heal souls that have been broken as well as bodies. Also, he will soon lead us in the sun prayers and dancing and feasting. He shows us where to place the sun sticks and poles so the sun will know of our watchfulness and will come back to earth."

Cabrillo well knew that the winter solstice was approaching, and he'd learned years ago of other native beliefs surrounding it. "Without Kipomo, the sun might continue to go away?"

"The days could grow shorter and shorter until there is only darkness."

He kept his voice as benign as possible but he had to ask, "Taya, do you believe that Kipomo has that kind of power, power to control the sun?"

She studied his face, her confusion clear. "Do you not believe that Father Lezcano can persuade God to send us fair weather, to heal us when we are sick, and to help all of us reach paradise? Are those powers not as strong?"

He had to silently admit that he could perceive her point, and he shook his head in surrender. "I see that Father Lezcano is the better man to speak of such things than I."

Heartened by this admission, Taya ran a finger over the arch of each of his eyebrows and let her gaze settle on his. "I am happy that you are with me, and I thank whatever god brought you here."

He pulled her closer and brushed his lips across hers.

Chapter 24

SNOW AND SWORD

W ith a fascination more readily found in a scientist than a sea captain, Cabrillo maintained a careful distance but close attention while observing the winter solstice rites Taya had described to him. Few of his men were quite as intrigued by the native dancing and praying or as watchfully studious of the movements of the shadows thrown by planted poles as the sun's distance from the earth expanded. During those few days that held such religious importance to the islanders, Cabrillo did his best to console Fathers Gamboa and Lezcano as they heard reports of these pagan practices from sailors who had gone ashore. As discouraging as it was to the priests that such native activities ignored the Christian teachings they'd been working to convey, they did their best to continue undauntedly on.

Winter's birth came and went, and the islanders rejoiced that Kipomo's guidance had convinced the sun to reverse its outward course and begin its journey back to them.

Perhaps because these heathen rituals had recently been conducted all around them, and even more because they were so far from their families and the pleasures of home, the Christians awaited the arrival of Christmas Day with great anticipation. This mood brought with it an unusual level of consideration from such roughened men. Many old affronts were forgiven or forgotten. Cursing fell to so low a level that the officers grew suspicious that some mischief must be afoot. Confessions were offered up to the priests in record numbers, keeping them happily busy throughout their days, and the plans for Christmas Mass and a feast ashore were being made with particular care.

When the glorious day arrived with an easing of the buffeting wind and a bright visit from the previously ineffusive sun, Cabrillo's men greeted each other with hearty voices and smiles. Some exchanged small gifts, half-embarrassed by the gratitude returned and insisting that the present was nothing at all. Others shared stories of Christmases past. All looked forward to the upcoming feast.

Once ashore men knelt for Mass and prayed with renewed hearts, minds, hopes, and intentions, and Father Gamboa blessed them in a tone that touched his flock with its deeply felt benevolence. Much to the happiness of both priests, many of the Chumash attended the rite as well, settling into an outer ring and standing, kneeling, and imitating the communal prayers in unison with the Christians. Beloved Christmas songs were sung with such gusto that even a few sea lions added their voices to the chorus.

Afterward, Cabrillo took pleasure in surveying the ongoing preparations for the feast. A handful of Vargas' soldiers and several islanders had killed, hauled ashore, and cleaned an elephant seal the previous evening, and its carcass had been roasting together with some of Cabrillo's precious spices in a stone-lined pit beneath the sand for more than fourteen hours. As both sailors and villagers began removing the layers of woven mats and leaves that protected this gastronomic treasure, Cabrillo inhaled the rich aroma, which triggered and outrageous growl from his empty stomach.

Taya, who had hurried back to her home after Mass, returned along with many other native women and their children. She carried a basket filled with acorn and seed cakes that would sweeten the special meal. The cooks from the *San Salvador* and *La Victoria* had been posted beside two huge iron pots, awaiting the signal to begin scooping mountains of steaming mussels and clams onto large woven mats before them, from which diners could serve themselves. Their massive cooking vessels were large enough to hold the flesh of a six-foot shark, and this was exactly what was cooking in the kettle overseen by the *San Miguel's* cook.

Captain Correa walked up to Cabrillo and grinned broadly at his commander. "It may not be home, sir, but we have been given a day to be grateful for, have we not?"

"All seems well, Captain, in heaven and on earth."

Correa slapped his stomach and smacked his lips. "It will be quite agreeable to fill this belly to near bursting. My clothes are hanging on mere bones."

287

It was true that they'd all lost weight, but Correa seemed to have lost less than anyone, so Cabrillo's eyebrow rose a bit at this proclamation.

His look of skepticism brought a bark of laughter from Correa. "Well, perhaps our men can use a fine meal as much as I."

Gaspar, one of Correa's more notoriously troublesome men, approached with a bowl tucked under his arm, bowed deeply, and said with deliberate care, "Pardon me, sirs, but I'm sent by Sergeant Major Vargas to respectfully ask when the meal is to commence. He fears the horde is showing, as he said, 'perilous signs of impatience.'"

Cabrillo glanced over at Matipuyaut, who appeared to be as anxious as everyone else to begin. "If all is ready, tell him the cooks may start dishing out."

"Thank you, Captain-General," said Gaspar, bowing again to each and departing at a trot.

As the two commanders walked back to the cook fires, Correa muttered in wonder, "I can scarcely believe the change in that man lately, sir. It must be the promise of women, but he's taken to his work with the diligence of a saint. He's not felt the whip in many a day."

"As I recall," said Cabrillo, "you wanted to throw him overboard a time or two while we were at sea, and I was hard pressed to think of a reason to forbid it."

"I did indeed, sir, but the man truly has done well lately. He's nearly convinced me he's worth his salt. I've told him he'll be allowed a visit to the women's hut tomorrow if he behaves 'til then." Chuckling low and rumbly, he said, "I've often thought it a fortunate thing that women fail to comprehend the power they have over us poor male creatures. If they only knew, they could govern every kingdom in the world."

Cabrillo grinned along with him. Then, thinking of Taya, he said to himself, "Perhaps, in a way, they do."

The two officers joined the crowd and soon had their wooden bowls and trenchers full. Cabrillo, sitting with Matipuyaut on one side, Father Lezcano on the other, and Taya and her boys in the ring of women and children not far behind, gazed between mouthfuls at those around him as they dove into their food. Sentimental on that Christmas day, the sailors laughed loudly and often as they ate, and their joviality during the feast helped fill homesick hearts as well as it did depleted bellies. Although Cabrillo had forbidden the consumption of anything stronger than spring water, the enforcement of this edict seemed to diminish none of the occasion's joy.

Before long Father Gamboa's bagpipe appeared and its hide bag quickly filled. A guitar and dozens of native flutes, rattles, and clacking sticks materialized as well. At the first clamorous notes of this colorfully assorted ensemble, much to the astonishment and amusement of the islanders, several sailors leaped up and began to perform various jigs, jotas, and less recognizable dances. While highly entertained by such exuberant and foreign movements on the sand, only a handful of Chumash could be convinced to try a few steps.

As Cabrillo watched the faces all around him, he contemplated the fact that the solitary emotional cloud appearing now and again came from the ever-present tensions between the Chumash men and sailors over the women. No amount of threats or punishments seemed able to keep some of the seamen from looking long and wistfully at particularly appealing females, and these glances were enough to cause the island men's faces to harden with jealousy. Fortunately, no smoking incident today had yet flared into an outright conflagration.

Though Matipuyaut sat very close throughout the festivities, Cabrillo could not help stealing glances at Taya, and when he did she would approach him to attend to his wishes, often letting a seemingly accidental touch remind him of their bond. He could see that she took pleasure in all she tasted, heard, and beheld, and he tucked these joy-filled images away in his memory, intending to keep them for a long, long time.

The feasting lasted until the munificent sun at last grew weary and began to descend toward its nightly repose. When the sated sailors at last returned to the ships after bidding Christmas farewells to the islanders, Cabrillo guessed that they would sleep with a peace few had known in many weeks.

Even after midnight he and Father Lezcano were in no hurry to seek their bunks, preferring to extend their stay outside on so fair a night, and when the watch was relieved they merely moved to the taffrail to allow the pilot to officiate over the ship from the front section of the quarterdeck. They watched the constellations and listened to the settling of the crew in friendly silence. After a while, Cabrillo gazed at the priest questioningly, but he did not ask.

Father Lezcano told him anyway, "I am thinking of my mother, sir."

"That is a proper thought on such a day. No doubt she was a good woman."

"A fine woman, sir." His voice grew wistful. "I was very young when my parents died, but I can clearly picture her praying at our Christmas table, her five children gathered around, my father sitting with unyielding severity in his tall chair." He looked at Cabrillo and confessed, "You are somewhat alike, you and she."

Surprised, Cabrillo asked, "I, like your mother?"

Almost regretting he'd started, Father Lezcano pushed on. "She had the same eyes, sir, and some of the same expressions. And she often thought far ahead, as you do, and..."

"And?"

"She too held inside the deep things that others would not understand." While Cabrillo considered this, Father Lezcano smiled and admitted, "I have often wondered if you might be a distant cousin of hers."

The captain-general liberated a smile of his own, one that was mellow and reflective. "If I ever found that to be true, I would be honored."

"It is a strange world, sir, is it not? Ten months ago I would never have imagined that today, Christmas Day, would find me grateful for the scars on my back, and for the man who had them put there."

They studiously looked at the sea rather than each other. Reflected there, the stars were numerous enough to do the speaking until they finally wished each other a good night.

Christmas had left them only hours earlier when a clap of thunder erupted like cannon fire and rolled toward them from the southwest, its echoing rumble strengthening as it came. Cabrillo yanked on his clothes while Paulo swiftly tied back his hair, and climbed to the quarterdeck to be met by the clout of an unusually warm wind and the first pellets of hail. Within moments men were pulling their jackets over their heads and sliding across the decks in search of shelter. Cabrillo found his own refuge in steerage.

"Double the anchors, Master Uribe," Cabrillo shouted as they huddled before the whipstaff. The hail pinged and pattered above their heads like the mad hammering of a hundred carpenters, yet the boat-swain somehow heard the shipmaster as he relayed Cabrillo's order, and then bellowed it out so loudly that it reverberated across to the other two ships. Anchormen danced and skidded to their stations upon the rolling decks while defending themselves against pelting ice balls the size of a four-real coin. After the additional anchors had been re-leased and their lines tightened, Pilot San Remón appeared in steerage sporting a grandly swelling right cheek. Resisting the temptation to rub the two lumps paining the back of his own head, Cabrillo said to his officers, "Post a man to watch each anchor line, gentlemen, and have them keep beneath a thick canvas or half-barrel for protection. I will not have the life beaten out of them by this cursed hail. While all is secure, let the other men stay under what cover they have found."

"Yes, sir."

Cabrillo stepped to the porthole, glanced at the white-speckled waves climbing and colliding near the beach, and knew that there was no hope of going ashore until this storm broke. As protective as their small bay had been, even it could not fully rebuff a wind that hound-ed them relentlessly. He peered through the white onslaught until he could see Manuel, Mateo, and two islanders struggling to drape the horses with what must have been their own blankets, and hurrying to shelter them up against the side of the cliff. They were all being cruelly pounded, and Cabrillo's heart ached as he helplessly watched.

Thankfully, the hail lasted only another ten minutes, but the wind grew colder with such speed and ferocity that it sent the bruised men scrambling for their warmest coverings. Within six hours the tem-perature had dropped thirty degrees, and by that evening snow was swirling around them. Whipped by the wind, the snowflakes found and clung to every board, brace, line, and body they touched. Before long the decks were slick with ice and the bobbing ships looked as if they'd been seized by a giant hand, inverted, and dipped in white paint. Though the sentries took advantage of what little cover they could find in the form of a mast, railing, or overhang, they stood their watches in frigid misery. Somehow, Manuel, Mateo and the two na-tive grooms managed to keep the horses covered and out of the worst of the wind.

An hour after midnight the clouds finally emptied of snow, and Cabrillo hoped the wind would concede an end to its assault. Instead it stubbornly screamed, whipped, and chilled for three more interminable days, and during that time not a soul could safely go ashore. Only Manuel and Mateo, emerging from their tiny shelter to care for the horses, and a very few islanders made appearances on the beach, and those emergences were fleeting. The storm held them all captive.

For Cabrillo the storm had made sleep an illusive visitor as well, and when the wind finally relented on the fourth night, he fell into a slumber so profound that it took a few moments for him to perceive that it was Captain Correa trying to wake him. On the second attempt, louder now, his words reached Cabrillo's groggy mind.

"Forgive me, Captain-General, but I said there's devilry afoot!"

Cabrillo sat up and blinked at Correa, trying to gather up full consciousness as he weighed the anger in his officer's tone and expression. From Paulo's outstretched hand he accepted his breeches and pulled them on, noting the bright light of a well risen sun, and asked, "Just what devilry, Captain?"

"That cursed Gaspar! He left the ship without my leave, sir, and he took that big Aztec and a handful of other men with him. I fear they've gone to the women."

This brought Cabrillo fully awake as he tugged on the rest of his clothes. "How long ago?"

"Just before dawn, sir. He told the men on watch he had orders to collect water, even loaded the launch with a few barrels, but I gave him no such orders. And if water was really what they sought, they would have been back by now."

It took but a glance outside for Cabrillo to know they'd been gone at least an hour. "Do you think they might harm the women?"

"Gaspar is a firebrand, sir, and he's owed a beating for more than one mischief done aboard the *San Miguel*, but even he's not that big a fool. He was promised leave days ago and was kept on the ship by the storm. He has doubtless gone to take what he feels he's owed, but by God, he knows what leaving without my order means, as do the others. I've been too light on them, and I intend to put an end to such insubordination once I get them back to my ship."

Holding a lesser degree of trust in Gaspar than Correa, Cabrillo asked, "Will you need assistance?"

"My men can handle this lot, sir. But perhaps I should take the war dogs, in case there is trouble with the natives."

"Definitely not, Captain. If there has been no difficulty, the dogs might create it, and if trouble starts, they will only make things worse."

"Then, sir, may I take Father Lezcano? He can speak to any islanders we encounter."

"If he accepts the request willingly, yes. I suggest taking a few of Vargas' soldiers also."

"Very well, sir."

"And, Captain, retrieve them as quietly as you can."

"I'll do that, Captain-General. Their hides won't bleed 'til they're back on my decks."

They quickly emerged from his cabin and within moments Correa, Father Lezcano, and enough armed men to fill Correa's two launches were heading toward the beach.

Watching them land, Cabrillo damned Gaspar under his breath. Things had been too tense with the natives even before this. He could only hope that the disobedient men would exercise better sense ashore than they'd used getting there. Intending to prepare for a case that proved otherwise, he turned to his shipmaster and said, "Lower both our boats, Master Uribe, and pray we do not need them right away."

"At once, sir."

"And, Master Uribe, please have Sergeant-Major Vargas sent to me."

"Yes, Captain-General."

Vargas soon appeared and Cabrillo had just begun discussing the situation when a shout from one of the *San Salvador's* lookouts brought their heads sharply around. Several of Correa's men were stumbling hurriedly backward toward their launches with swords drawn and muskets pointed back at the sand dune. Gaspar and his band of followers appeared, being driven ahead of Correa and his guards who had formed an arc behind them. An unseen archer fired an arrow from the direction of the dune, and it bit the sand two yards from Gaspar's feet. The next one imbedded into his thigh. A cry of pain rang out but Correa shouted for his men to hold their fire. The next arrow bounced off the leather vest worn by one of Gaspar's friends.

Viento reared and bucked in his corral, setting the other horses in motion as well. Manuel and Mateo appeared with ropes to secure Viento so he didn't break down the fence. The stunned island grooms, momentarily frozen in place, began to climb the hill behind the corral.

293

During these brief seconds Cabrillo had set his gunners in motion and waved for Vargas and his men to follow as he rushed toward his boat. He paused only long enough for their arms to be quickly loaded and to glance toward *La Victoria*. Captain Ferrelo stood waiting for his order: his face tight but otherwise calm. *La Victoria's* cannoneers were already working as busily as those aboard the flagship. Cabrillo called out, "Remain aboard and cover us, Captain." He knew that no additional orders were needed. His and every other gunner in the fleet would soon be ready, but they'd be held in check with the tightest restraint. Master Uribe was already overseeing their master gunner's preparations.

As Cabrillo reached his railing and was about to descend to his launch he turned and faced Pilot San Remón. In less than a breath, a year's worth of understanding passed between them, but Cabrillo said only, "Take the ship, Pilot."

While his rowers pulled frantically toward the beach, Cabrillo saw one of the deserters grab a musket from a guard and lift it, but Correa fiercely batted the gun away before it could discharge. The natives must have observed this because, though several more arrows flew into the air, they plummeted just behind the retreating men, aimed to warn rather than wound. Cabrillo leaned forward, silently willing his soldiers to cling to their discipline. *Hold your fire, men. By heaven, hold your fire!*

Now he could see the Chumash warriors emerging into the open, thirty or so, and he could hear the angry shouts hurled at the sailors. To his rowers he said, "Faster, men!"

They found more speed by pulling with all their strength. Vargas sat tense as a drum but steady as a rock beside him. They aimed for the shore on the side of the already beached launches that was away from the natives and Correa's party, but the sweeping tide brought Cabrillo's boats farther than intended to the northwest and nearly onto the rocks. Vargas and two other men leaped into the sea first and tried to angle the boat away from the water-slickened boulders. On the other side of the launch, Cabrillo jumped clear and fought a wave as he scrambled ashore. Manuel was there waiting, his crossbow at his back, his shield in one hand, and the other stretched out to help Cabrillo onto the sand. They exchanged grim smiles and began to move. Finding his footing, Cabrillo climbed to the top of a boulder and in the midst of his jostling men hurried toward Correa by leaping to another rock and another. As he advanced he glanced repeatedly at the pending battle, until the sand where the two cultures faced each other lay just yards away. On his final bound, he felt his falling foot slip from the wet rounded surface it sought, and he fell hard between two rocks. A grinding crack ignited his right leg and his growl of pain and frustration stopped Vargas and Manuel in their tracks. They pivoted and rushed back to his side.

Cabrillo struggled to free his leg as the pain shot all the way up his back. "Get me loose!"

They did so as gently as they could, but Vargas took one look at the crooked boot and said, "Sir, it's broken. We must take you back to the ship at once."

"No, damn you! Help me get to Captain Correa." At Vargas' hesitation, Cabrillo hissed, "At once, Sergeant-Major!"

So Vargas and Manuel each lifted an arm and placed it around their necks. As they lifted him, he bit back another cry of pain and they paused, but the captain-general shouted, "Move!" and they set out. When they reached the level sand Cabrillo's sailors formed a protective circle with their small round shields held before them.

Viento had seen his master's fall, had heard his cry, and he now neighed loudly over the din, rearing so wildly that he pulled Mateo off his feet.

Father Lezcano had spotted them too. He broke from Correa's ring and rushed to meet the three men, his worried glance darting to Cabrillo's leg. "Sir."

"Father, we must speak to the Chumash."

"I have tried, sir."

"Is Matipuyaut or his sons with them?"

"No, sir."

"Take me forward," he commanded, and his voice allowed no objection, but at Father Lezcano's insistence, Vargas gently surrendering his support of Cabrillo's right side so he could guard his commander with his own sword and shield.

The Chumash had also seen Cabrillo land, seen him slip, and now watched him draw fearlessly toward them. One of their leaders raised an arm and his men lowered their bows. Many infuriated warriors, however, kept their arrows nocked and ready.

When Cabrillo reached Correa, he ordered, "Get every man to the ships, Captain."

Correa's eyes fell to the captain-general's leg, but he held his tongue and moved at once to obey.

As his men eased away, Cabrillo had Manuel and Father Lezcano lower their holds on him to around his waist so he had use of his arms to communicate. Pale and sweating as he fought the pain, he faced the warriors and said, "Warriors, I wish to speak with you."

Their evident leader, a man Cabrillo knew only by sight, stepped forward. "That man," the native said, pointing to Gaspar, "he has defiled one of our married women, and the others have abused young women not given to them. We must have more than words."

"I understand your anger. I too am angry at these crimes. The men who have wronged your women will be punished."

This evoked stony expressions and grumblings of doubt, and the Chumash leader said, "Give them to us. We will punish them."

Cabrillo shifted slightly, and Manuel and Father Lezcano steadied him as he fought to keep his mind clear of the wisps of gray and sparks of silver that began to cloud his vision. He gulped a breath and said, "I ask you to come to the great ship and watch their punishment. You will see by what we do to them that they will not harm your women again. Nor will any of our other men."

The natives seemed to waver in their determination, but as Correa's crewmen began loading Gaspar and the others into the boat, bows swung in their direction and the island sub-chief took a step in their direction.

Intent on preventing bloodshed, Cabrillo called out, "Hold the boats, Captain Correa."

When even more Indians lifted their bows, and Cabrillo sensed that they would not be robbed of an immediate revenge, he decided to give it to them but only in the form of one man. He turned to Father Lezcano and said softly. "Go with Captain Correa, Father."

"I will not leave you, sir."

He firmed his tone and commanded. "I order you to go." Father Lezcano looked straight ahead and stood like a statue, his grip even tighter around his commander's waist, Cabrillo said in a low and urgent voice. "If you care for me, go now!"

His friend's gaze returned to him, holding tenderness more over-powering than his strength. *"Because* I care, I will not."

Glancing at Manuel and then Vargas, Cabrillo could see that they would obey this particular command no more willingly than Father Lezcano had. Against the growing agony of his leg, he stiffened his back and called out to the sub-chief, "I ask the brave Chumash to come and see these men punished for their wrongs. I ask them to take the word of one who has never lied to you."

Once more their leader hesitated. At last he scowled and said and signed a single word to Cabrillo, "When?"

"Today, when the sun is highest. I ask that Matipuyaut and his sons come also."

The slightest of nods from the warriors brought the bows down, some very grudgingly.

Vargas could no longer remain still. "Now, sir, we must return you to the *San Salvador*."

Manuel and Father Lezcano were already bending down to lift Ca-brillo, but he said through gritted teeth, "Not yet, please. Not until the rest of the men are away."

They knew no argument would supercede this wish, so Father Lez-cano prayed as Vargas ordered his guards to move off ahead of them, and all boats but Cabrillo's to push off.

This time, the warriors made no moves to stop the departing sailors, and after moments had passed with the slowness of decades, all three launches were rowing toward their ships.

Manuel and Father Lezcano slowly moved away from the clustered warriors. As they drew closer to the boat, which Correa's men had moved to within easier reach, Viento whinnied loud and long from where Mateo had staked him within the corral. Cabrillo looked that way and saw Mateo at the gate. "My nephew," he said before his voice faded away, and Vargas called out for the boy to join them.

The next time Cabrillo lifted his head, it was to gaze at his beloved horse, but it was now Father Lezcano's turn to insist. He gave Manuel a look, and they crossed the final distance to shoreline. When the captain-general tried to protest, the priest said, "There can be no more delays, sir. Not even for him."

"But, he knows..."

"I will come back for him, sir, for all of them. The Chumash will not harm your horses."

His bearers waded into the water and lifted him to the boat. As diligently as they tried, they could not keep from causing further misery as they loaded him, and he was panting heavily as the boat began to pull away. Through the curtain of pain he heard Viento call again. He told himself, and sincerely believed, that the natives honored the horses too highly to hurt them, but at this parting, this abandoning, he felt anguish strong enough to rival his physical pain.

Seeing his injured master being rowed away with Manuel and Mateo was too much for Viento to remain where he was. He bugled fiercely, lunged against his staked rope until it pulled free, and knocked the top railing off the fence as he leaped to freedom. With Seguro close behind Viento raced toward the water, the mares neighing and circling their separate and still intact coral in panic. Their equine cries brought the native grooms hurrying in the direction of the enclosure to calm them. Viento hit the water at a gallop, stumbled against the waves until he found his swimming legs and churned after Cabrillo's boat, his rope trailing behind. Seguro, more cautious but just as determined, came after him. Cabrillo watched them worriedly, but could see that their powerful legs and the relatively calm sea would allow them to reach the ship with little trouble. They would soon be harnessed by their best swimmers and hauled aboard.

A dreadful silence held his crew as Cabrillo was carefully lifted to his flagship. Captains Correa and Ferrelo were also there to meet him. All continued to hold their mouths tightly in check except young Mateo, who let out a single sob. Paulo quickly took the boy aside and assigned him a list of duties that would keep him busy for hours.

Once Cabrillo had been settled on his bunk, he spotted Captain Correa among the throng and said to him, "Return to your ship, Captain, and set the punishment for your men. It will be carried out on the *San Salvador* at noon. Several islanders will be here to witness it." He took a steadying breath, and said, "Captain Ferrelo, will you see to the mares. Bring them to *La Victoria* as soon as you deem it safe. Afterward, please return to me."

Both captains bowed and left him.

At Dr. Fuentes' insistence the crowded cabin was cleared of everyone else but Pilot San Remón, Master Uribe, Paulo, Manuel, and

Father Lezcano. The physician leaned over Cabrillo and asked, "Will you drink some brandy, sir?"

"Not yet."

Every eye moved to Cabrillo's leg as the doctor took a serrated knife from his chest and began to cut away the boot. As Dr. Fuentes eased the sliced footwear from the leg, blood spilled onto the bunk and decking, and he was forced to call upon every year he'd practiced medicine, every unwelcome diagnosis he'd had to make, in order to conceal his reaction from the patient. His effort to keep his face blank was wasted, however, since Cabrillo and every other soul in that chamber could see the damage for themselves. A couple of inches above the ankle the splintered shinbone protruded from the torn muscle and skin in three places. The unsupported foot would have twisted unnaturally inward if the doctor had not held it steady, quickly grabbed a roll of linen bandages, and braced it in place.

Standing back in the corner Paulo grew ashen and slid slowly into an awkward sitting position on the floor. For a moment, no one else moved. It was Cabrillo who spoke first, "What can you do, doctor?"

Dr. Fuentes said, "There are two choices, sir. I can reset the leg..."

"How?"

The physician was unable to evade a slight pause. "I can open the area around the break and move the bone sections into their proper placement, and then I would bind the muscles and skin around the bone."

"Or?"

"Or I can remove the leg, sir."

"Which do you recommend?"

"The chance of festering will be less if I take the leg, Captain-General."

Cabrillo closed his eyes for a moment, then, to the surprise of all except Manuel, he said, "I believe my left arm is also broken, just below the shoulder. Will you examine it now, doctor?"

Dr. Fuentes and Manuel removed Cabrillo's coat and shirt with great care, and it was now easy to see that his arm was already swollen and reddening. After the doctor had gently probed and maneuvered the elbow and shoulder, he concluded, "I can not tell with certainty, sir. It may indeed be broken or just badly bruised."

"And if it is broken?"

"It would be best to splint it, sir."

"Is there a chance it will fester also?"

After another unwilling hesitation, he said, "Yes, sir, a chance."

"Thank you, doctor."

"Sir, I should operate as soon as possible. The longer the wound remains open, the more blood will be lost and the greater the chance of corruption."

To his pilot, Cabrillo asked, "How long until noon?"

"About two hours, sir."

Cabrillo could hear horses' hooves upon the deck below, a reassuring sound. "If I choose to keep the leg, Dr. Fuentes, how long will the surgery take?"

"Sir, it would be preferable to—"

"How long?"

"The pain must first be dulled by spirits, sir, and then the surgery itself could take an hour or more." He couldn't keep from adding, "Amputation would be quicker, sir."

"And afterward I would be intoxicated or unconscious," Cabrillo muttered. "Then, doctor, wrap the leg to slow the flow of blood. The rest must wait until the Chumash have left."

"But, sir—" said the doctor, Father Lezcano, and Pilot San Remón almost at once.

Cabrillo weakly waved their concerns away with his right hand. "I have witnessed scores of surgeries, and I have seen men recover from worse injuries than these. Since it will be much more difficult to lead this fleet to Asia with only one leg, you must try to save the injured one. You may operate immediately after the punishment concludes." He kept to himself the awareness that he could die during any form of surgery, and this he could not risk until the Chumash had seen justice carried out, and his fleet was out of danger.

Dr. Fuentes bowed his head in submission and began to set out the wrappings and bindings he would need.

"You have been studying the cures of the Indians, doctor. I ask you to consider their methods of healing as well as ours."

"Yes, Captain-General."

Now Cabrillo, his words slowing at last under the weight of his torment, he said, "Manuel, I will take a glass of sherry while Dr. Fuentes gathers his supplies."

As the doctor studied the leg wound closely, Captain Ferrelo appeared at the cabin door and reported, "Viento and Seguro are safely aboard, sir. The mares are being transported now. There was no trouble bringing them off the island."

"Very good, Captain, very good." The first gulps of sherry were already warming his limbs but had done little to reduce the pain, and even the smallest movements made by Dr. Fuentes as he wiped the blood from around the wound required a clamping of Cabrillo's jaws to keep him from moaning. When the doctor reached for more bandages, Cabrillo said, "Master Uribe, Pilot San Remón, please prepare the ship for our visitors. The rest of you, I would like a moment alone with Captain Ferrelo." Dr. Fuentes was about to protest, but Cabrillo added, "Only a moment, doctor, and then you may finish."

When the door closed behind them, Captain Ferrelo faced Cabrillo squarely, forced himself to study the broken leg, and said, "I can guess why you wish to speak with me, sir. You want me to take command of the fleet in the event your death appears imminent. Do not ask me, sir. I have never disobeyed one of your orders, but I will refuse to accept your death or take command until I see the saints come down from heaven to carry you off."

Cabrillo could almost smile. "Heaven, eh? And the look of this leg does not discourage you?"

"As you told the doctor, sir, I have seen worse. Men without your strength and purpose have lived with little more than a limp after such a hurt. You survived the wounds you suffered while fighting with Cortés, and many battles since then. This is just one more."

"Very well, Bartolomé," he said, his tone heavy with affection, "I will do my best not to die. I hate to think of the fright you would endure if a horde of saints appeared on deck to carry me off. Now, attend to your duties and let my doctor return to his bandaging."

Chapter 25

A PRAYER WITH FATHER LEZCANO

After Captain Ferrelo departed, Dr. Fuentes did his best to stanch the blood still seeping from Cabrillo's elevated leg. With Manuel's help he padded it well with linen and wrapped it in several layers of bandages. When he'd finished, however, he could rally little faith that his ministrations would impede the flow for long. Cabrillo lay back and rested for a while, but then neither blood nor pain could stop him from calling Manuel to help him up and appearing on deck when Matipuyaut and his large party of warriors boarded the *San Salvador*. Although Father Lezcano, Dr. Fuentes, and Manuel remained watchfully at hand, Cabrillo had lost too much blood to trust his ability to brace himself upright for long, and he sat pale but relatively alert in his wooden chair. His stomach had managed to keep down the sherry, and he was hoping the liquor would help him endure his wounds until the punishments had been carried out.

Moments after Matipuyaut's arrival Captain Correa's launch came to the flagship, his accompanying prisoners grim in their chains. The shackled men needed assistance to board, which was given none too gently by the *San Salvador's* crew, and as they stood before the assembly Gaspar's face showed defiance but the others' eyes were unwilling to meet Cabrillo's.

The Captain-General asked, "What is the sentence, Captain Correa?"

"For Gaspar, Captain-General, sixty lashes and for the others, half that number. With your permission, sir, Gaspar will go last."

Cabrillo and several others had seen men die under such castigation, but the sailors had put the satisfaction of their own lust above the safety of the entire fleet, not to mention the injury they'd done to the

302

island women and their families, and such a penalty was not too harsh. He was not about to overrule Captain Correa's decision. Too much was at stake. "Father Lezcano," he said, "please translate the sentence for Matipuyaut and his people."

As he did so, the warriors shifted uncertainly, never having witnessed any kind of public physical punishment and not fully comprehending what was about to take place. They didn't have long to wait before becoming all too aware. The first of five men was led to the mainmast, his wrist shackles tied to a line, his arms hoisted high above his head, and his feet braced as far apart as the chains allowed. At Correa's signal the San Miguel's well-muscled boatswain stepped forward wearing an expression more fervent than reluctant and carrying his long-handled cat-of-nine-tails. Cabrillo never allowed a man to be flogged with a cat that had been made lethal by tying metal fragments to the ends of each leather strip, as many captains did, and even this occasion would be no exception. Even without the brutal enhancements, when the boatswain swept his arm back and then whipped it forward the nine knotted tentacles hit the bare back with a sharp "snap" that sliced into the flesh of the sailor. His piercing cry mingled with the stunned exclamations of the Chumash but the boatswain was already making his next swing. As the first few blows fell, most of the native faces showed satisfaction at the harshness with which their women were being avenged, but as the assault continued to rain down and thin crimson streams flowed in increasing number down the sailor's back, breeches, and legs, their expressions grew bleak. When the man was finally released, badly weakened but still able to stay upright on shaky legs as they hauled him away, Matipuyaut turned eyes on Cabrillo that mingled respect and abhorrence at what he'd just witnessed.

The next man was tied and the whippings began again, and this time the islanders did not utter a sound. It was the same with the two prisoners that followed. Only when Gaspar was brought forward did any of them mutter in anger and glare with a renewed hunger for retribution. But when the number of lashes that the others had received had been inflicted on Gaspar and still the blows continued, Matipuyaut glanced again at Cabrillo, questioning.

Gaspar had stopped slinging profanities and insults after twenty lashes, and had passed out at forty-three, but Captain Correa did not dismiss his boatswain until every prescribed lash of the whip had fallen. The boatswain, now dripping with sweat and swaying from exertion, stepped back so his shipmates could take what was left of Gaspar back to the *San Miguel*.

Father Lezcano, who'd been watching Cabrillo with concern during the entire process, saw now that he was losing his battle to remain attentive. As soon as Gaspar was released, the captain-general began to sag in his chair, and Manuel was there in an instant.

Addressing Matipuyaut loudly enough for his warriors to hear, Father Lezcano said, "Cabrillo is in need of care, but he would not be healed until he had avenged your people. You may go back to your village and tell your women that they will not be harmed again." Aside, he added, "We must take him to his cabin now, Matipuyaut. I will send you word of him."

As Manuel and another sailor lifted Cabrillo and carried him away, the Indian chief took from beneath his cape a leather pouch, which he handed to the priest. Aiming a look of genuine disquiet at the departing Cabrillo, he said, "This is from his woman, to make him well."

Father Lezcano listened keenly to the short instruction Matipuyaut relayed for the curative's preparation. He then offered his thanks and left the Indians to board their canoes.

Cabrillo had neither the strength nor will to object when they placed him on a wooden table already set up for his surgery. While his commander was being settled, Dr. Fuentes detained Pilot San Remón as he was about to leave and said softly, "Sir, will you send some men to collect any snow or ice they can find."

"Snow, doctor?"

The physician confessed, "I have read that a cold environment around a wound may help slow bleeding during surgery. Snow has never been at hand when I could have used it before, but it may help today."

"I will send men at once," the pilot said, already stepping away.

It was again necessary for the doctor to clear the captain-general's cabin of anyone not needed, leaving only Manuel and Father Lezcano to assist him. Paulo protested vehemently at being ordered away but Dr. Fuentes barked loudly, "I will not be distracted by a servant whose nerves are tempered with anything less rigid than steel, no matter how devoted he is. Out! Mateo, station yourself on the other side of the door and let no one come in."

Father Lezcano now showed Cabrillo and Dr. Fuentes the herbs that Taya had sent. Cabrillo eyed the pouch through a thickening haze and nodded, then he let his head fall back upon the table and asked in a whisper. "Do you know what it is, doctor?"

After examining the colors, textures, and smells of the contents and taking a tiny taste on the tip of his tongue, Dr. Fuentes frowned and said, "It seems to be a mixture of several ingredients, sir, only a few of which I recognize."

"I leave it to you, Dr. Fuentes, to use or not."

"Sir, I must ask you again if you—"

"Wasted breath, doctor. My decision is made. Put the leg back together. Please begin."

Begin. So simple a command. Dr. Fuentes knew his best chance of success was dependent on immobilizing his commander, but how does one adequately restrain a powerful man when his mangled leg is about to be restructured? Sherry was only minimally effective and frustratingly temporary when it came to killing pain and anesthetizing. Should he instead opt for native drugs with properties he could only imagine and which he'd never previously prepared or tested?

Father Lezcano saw Dr. Fuentes' mental struggle and asked, "What do you fear is in the herbs, doctor?"

"They may contain Datura."

"The drug that killed the Chumash boy? But why would Taya send that to us?"

Quietly, Cabrillo said, "She thought it would be useful."

Dr. Fuentes leaned over Cabrillo and said, "Matipuyaut explained how to prepare it, sir. But I am uneasy about what it might do, and for how long. Should I send for Taya?"

It took a moment before he said, "I doubt they would let her come, not after what has happened."

"Then, sir, may I send one of our men to her, so we can learn more?"

Cabrillo was about to say it was too dangerous but before he could utter a word Father Lezcano was already heading for the door. "I will go, sir," he said, and left without waiting for permission.

Dr. Fuentes gave Cabrillo another glass of sherry and, after he'd taken two large gulps, the drink seemed to help a bit as the doctor and Manuel removed clothing and loosened bandages from the wounded areas. Swallowing the last of the crimson liquid and waving the glass at Manuel, Cabrillo said in a manner meant to sound matter-of-fact, "Doctor, my personal papers are in a small chest inside that larger one there. In addition to my will and my letters, there is a document that confirms Manuel's freedom. Please see that it finds a safe home."

Manuel stared at him, unhappy at this turn of the conversation, but Cabrillo went on. "It would please me if you agree to make certain of that, and that my other documented wishes are carried out, Dr. Fuentes."

The physician paused as he laid out the last of his wooden and iron tools and said, "Forgive me, sir, but that is quite enough of such talk. Manuel and I will see you dancing again in Santiago and likely many other places besides. However, to put your mind at rest, if for whatever reason God grants me and Manuel a very old age that happens to extend beyond your own, I will honor your wishes."

"I thank you, doctor."

Dr. Fuentes had Manuel help him as he slid a square of canvas beneath Cabrillo's leg, and he was just rearranging his cleaning cloths, bandages, and splints, when Mateo stepped inside and announced the arrival of three sailors toting a small barrel filled with hard-packed snow and ice. They explained that they'd dug it from a deep crevice in the rocks and informed the doctor that there were three more barrels outside the cabin, which Mateo would watch over. Though it seemed much longer, Father Lezcano returned only minutes later and began to brew Taya's herbs just as she'd instructed him.

"Is she well?" Cabrillo asked.

"She is concerned for you, sir," he said, although this was an extreme understatement, "but she is otherwise well." He did not mention that she'd pleaded with Matipuyaut to allow her to come aboard the ship, or that her father had instead posted three men to guard her just before Father Lezcano had left the lodge. Though she neither screamed nor lashed out at those keeping her from Cabrillo, the emotional distress she was suffering was terrible to behold.

Although Taya had been very specific in her directions for the quantity of water and herbs to be used, under Dr. Fuentes' watchful eye, Father Lezcano took the precaution of adding a measure less of the potent plant mixture than she'd described. The priest didn't know how Cabrillo's body might react to a drug it had no resistance to, and he took the easy choice of erring on the side of pain versus possible death. He'd been allowed to question Taya only in the company of her father, Kipomo, and several other men, and he knew that it was forbidden for anyone to administer Datura but the shaman, so he dared not ask her if she'd added this plant to her mixture. Instead, he questioned her about its curative powers, how it was to be prepared, and how often it should be administered. Something in her manner told him that she was measuring her responses carefully, and when she held his gaze and said that her husband was to be held down tightly while his leg was treated, and that he must be watched closely during his recovery, the priest's suspicion that the hallucinogen was present in her medicine was strengthened.

The brew was soon ready, and Cabrillo emptied the cup in three swallows. Its strange tanginess hung at the back of his throat and almost made him cough, but he felt its first effects very quickly. Within minutes his eyes began to dull and his responses to slur.

Watching the patient intently, waiting just a little longer to allow the drug to gain its full power, Dr. Fuentes lay one end of a long leather strap across Cabrillo's waist, passed it under the table, and brought it up again, where he buckled both sides together, cinching his commander in place. He had Manuel and Father Lezcano lift Cabrillo's leg, quickly scooped snowy ice from the barrel onto the canvas, and placed a woolen blanket atop the snow before allowing the leg to be lowered. During these movements Cabrillo moaned loudly, and those tending to him heard Mateo's back bump in empathy against the cabin door. Dr. Fuentes then removed the bandages and dropped the blood-soaked strips on the floor.

Dr. Fuentes had boiled his instruments clean while he'd awaited the priest's return, a peculiar precaution he'd learned from a Moorish physician he'd met in many his travels, and he now took up a large glass syringe with which to purge the wound, and filled it with sherry. But before washing the torn flesh with the fortified wine, he turned to Father Lezcano and Manuel and said, "Hold him firmly."

Father Lezcano took a position that would provide him leverage and grasped the captain-general's shoulders well above his wounded arm as Manuel captured his thighs. Though the medication had allowed Cabrillo's mind to drift deeply into another realm, he could still feel too many of pain's sensations. His body tolerated Dr. Fuentes' cleaning without dangerous protest, but when this step was finished and the doctor lowered his knife and began to cut skin and muscle, the captain-general gave a sudden lurch in an attempt to shift out of reach, which might have done much damage if strong men hadn't restrained him. For some time afterward Manuel had to use much of his massive body to pin Cabrillo's legs to the table. Rather than crying out the patient muttered breathless, incomprehensible words as his semiconscious body rebelled with each new attack of the physician's tools.

Dr. Fuentes had worked carefully to wash the wound free of dirt, but his cleaning had set off a new surge of blood that he was forced to continually dab away. Soon the floor was strewn with sodden, red rags. Minutes trickled away as the doctor worked to remove what was irreparable and repeatedly tried to compress the useful pieces of shattered bone back into their proper positions. His fingers grew slick with blood, and every time he attempted to clear the sweat from his eyes he left another red streak across his face.

When Dr. Fuentes had nearly finished, he ordered Manuel to hold the set bone while he stitched the muscle and skin in place. At last he began to wind the bandages around the leg and splint it tightly to wooden slats. Exhausted, his shirt and face awash in sweat and blood, the doctor straightened his stiff back and lifted his head. Arching his back for a moment to relieve the muscles, he then sank into the nearby chair and let his chin sag to his chest. Manuel stayed at the table with his own bloody arms hanging heavily at his sides. He took a deep breath, and as he let it out he turned his head to stare out the portal toward the harbor's mouth. For a moment Father Lezcano seemed unwilling to release his hold of Cabrillo, not yet trusting that he would keep calm and still. He stared at Cabrillo's face, his closed eyes still pinched with pain, and marveled that his body, any body, could withstand such torture. Praise God and Taya for her medicine, which had surely eased the worst of it. At last the priest moved his hands away and walked slowly to the door. As he opened it, his eyes fell on the tear-streaked, fearful face of Mateo. Against every dictate chiseled through the ages by stalwart men of the sea, he bent down, picked up the child, and held him. "You may see him soon, my boy."

As Cabrillo slept fitfully during the hours that proceeded the surgery, the fleet seemed to be held in a hushed and anxious spell. Hasty movements were suspended and thoughts turned inward. The afternoon waned and still he did not awaken, and Dr. Fuentes began to recall again and again the death of the native boy. The physician's memories were not alone. Father Lezcano had also seen Shuluwish die, and that scene haunted him as he sat beside Cabrillo, now lying in his bunk.

The table and floors had been scrubbed clean, and all signs of the operation had been removed excepting the patient. Paulo hovered about looking so pathetically forlorn that he had been sent out to prepare a meal in case Cabrillo awoke hungry.

Manuel was lighting the lamps in the cabin when Father Lezcano smelled the aromas coming from Paulo's cooking pots and said to Pilot San Remón and Dr. Fuentes, "It smells like Paulo is preparing quite a dinner. Perhaps it will coax the captain-general to take some nourishment."

Their heads swung around as a voice cracked from the bunk, "I prefer wine first. My mouth feels as if it has eaten an island fox."

There he lay, pale and drawn but wearing a tremulous smile.

"Praise the Lord!" shouted Father Lezcano while Mateo let out a halloo of joy.

His pilot came to his side and said warmly, "Welcome back, Captain-General."

Cabrillo tried to shift his position and had to bite back a curse as the sudden pain raked him. "If I could erase the days until this leg firms up, Pilot," he said weakly, "I could accept your welcome with a little more grace."

"They will pass, sir, with many prayers to speed them along," said Father Lezcano.

Cabrillo muttered softly, "Thank you, Father." He accepted the glass Manuel held out to him, their eyes meeting meaningfully for a moment, and then he asked his pilot, "Any word or action from the islanders?"

"None, sir. All has been quite still, there and here."

"All but you, sir," said Dr. Fuentes, his expression more cautious in its optimism than those around him possessed. "Even after surgery you tried to speak to us, though we could not understand much of what you said."

Cabrillo paused, remembering. "Perhaps it was the concoction Taya sent, but I dreamed many strange things, far stranger than usual."

Resting his gaze on his physician, he said, "I am grateful to you, doctor."

"I will feel most appreciated, sir, if my patient obeys me well during his recovery."

At Cabrillo's feigned look of innocence, everyone in the room chuckled, their relief at last able to voice itself. These sounds and their implications traveled with the usual speed throughout the rest of the ship, as well as the two vessels floating nearby, and from Cabrillo's cabin those within could hear footfalls lighten and voices hearten.

Pilot San Remón smiled down at Cabrillo and said, "It seems less than necessary, sir, but I should go report your condition to the rest of the crew."

"Yes, Pilot. Tell them I look to the day when I shall again pace the stern deck."

"With pleasure, sir," he said as he left them.

Dr. Fuentes still eyed Cabrillo closely, noting how the drug's effects lingered. Cabrillo confirmed this when he said, "My head still swims a bit, and sleep wants to retake me. Perhaps I should eat something before my eyelids grow too heavy."

Paulo appeared even before he was summoned, his eyes brimming as he glanced toward Cabrillo. In a quavering voice he asked, "May I serve you now, sir?"

"Serve him at his bunk, Paulo," said the doctor authoritatively while carefully avoiding eye contact with the captain-general. "He is not to leave that bed for several days."

Paulo aimed questioning raised eyebrows at Cabrillo, received a nod, and left to prepare a plate holding three times the food that could be eaten. When he returned Cabrillo did manage to fill his stomach enough to stop its rumblings and please both his servant and his physician. Little coaxing was needed to get him to rest again, and those who cared for him now allowed themselves a meal of their own.

Cabrillo's sleep became so uneasy, his pain level rising so high, that by midnight Dr. Fuentes was sorely tempted to give him more of Taya's brew. Father Lezcano was in favor of this as well, but in the end the physician decided it would be taking too great a risk to give the second dose this soon after the first. The night was long and grueling for them all, and Father Lezcano's rosary was kept in constant use.

Daylight brought Cabrillo awake more fully, with his mind much clearer and the pain even worse. He opened his eyes to find Dr. Fuentes asleep, slumped in his own chair just three feet away. Father Lezcano, who was watching him, smiled tiredly and said, "May I wish you good health on this final day of the year, sir?"

"Indeed," said Cabrillo with as much normalcy as he could gather, "yes, a new year comes tomorrow."

"May 1543 bring us all to Asia, and the next year bring us home again."

Dr. Fuentes, wide awake now, bent close and asked what every physician through every age has asked on such occasions, "How do you feel, sir?"

"Hopeful, doctor, though this splint feels far too tight. The ache rivals any I have suffered before."

The doctor checked his bindings at once, loosening them slightly as he said, "The second day is always the worst, sir, and then improvement begins. We have been debating over whether to give you a little more of Taya's medicine. What do you advise?"

"The devil himself seems to have possessed this leg, and I would very much like him dispelled, but I am wary of how the potion overpowers my mind."

"Perhaps, sir," offered Father Lezcano, "a weaker dosage would be more suitable."

"Yes, but I will try some breakfast and sherry first."

The sherry helped very little even when dispensed in more and more generous quantities, and Cabrillo finally refused to drink another glass. Those who looked after him did what they could to distract him: Father Lezcano by reading, Mateo by describing every detail of Viento's grooming, and the officers of all three ships by appearing and reporting on any small thing that might cheer him. This continued until Dr. Fuentes called a halt to the visitors, declaring that the captain-general needed rest.

Throughout the day the doctor moved the onlookers aside to lift Cabrillo's covers and examine the bandages. Twice, he had changed the outermost layers when they'd become dampened by blood, gently shifting those securing the splints, but he'd dared not remove the inner bandages that held the bone segments in place.

Cabrillo chose to avoid mentioning the ache in his arm, which was far outweighed by the stabbing sensations in his leg and for which little could be done anyway. When Taya's medicine was offered a second time, he accepted it. Watched over attentively, he finally let slumber claim him, waking only in spurts throughout the night. He didn't stir with the rising sun.

Dr. Fuentes, attending in shifts with Manuel and Father Lezcano, had also managed to get some sleep. He was roused from his bed, however, in the light of early dawn.

"What is it, Father?"

There was no softening of the words he came to deliver, and his face told a great deal even before he said, "He has a fever, doctor. Please come at once."

Already dressed, the doctor threw back his bedcovers and hurried to Cabrillo's cabin. He touched the captain-general's cheeks and forehead and whispered, "How long?"

"His face began to redden just minutes ago. It was only then that I touched his skin and felt the heat."

Cabrillo opened his eyes halfway and turned his face to them. "I am not so bad yet, gentlemen, that I can not hear you. I am very thirsty." He took a drink from the glass Manuel placed in his hands and then said, "Please send for my officers."

They both stared, motionless.

"Please, gentlemen, do not make me ask again."

"But, sir," said the doctor, "this fever was to be expected with such a wound, with almost any wound. I see no need to…"

"I intend to hand over this command only temporarily, doctor, until I am well." When they still stood as if nailed to the decking, he turned a weak, beckoning gaze to Father Lezcano.

The priest's own stunned expression calmed, and he said, "I will tell Pilot San Remón to send for them, sir."

It took only a few minutes before every officer in the fleet crowded into his cabin. Cabrillo forced himself up on his bent elbows, Manuel helped brace him with a pillow, and he said to the glum faces before him, "Thank you, gentlemen. It seems providence has determined that we shall start this year with a temporary new commander. Until I am well, under the authority granted by my royal commission, I hereby name Captain Ferrelo as captain-general of our fleet. I know you will all serve him with the high loyalty you have shown me." Settling his eyes on Captain Ferrelo, he added, "You will be in excellent hands, gentlemen. He is as fine an officer as I have ever known."

Captain Ferrelo spoke up with such adamant sincerity that it made his tone sound harsh. "I am confident that I speak for us all, Captain-General Cabrillo, when I tell you that we all pray for your prompt recovery. And, sir, we want no commander but the one before us."

Cabrillo closed his eyes and took a moment to master his voice. "I thank you, gentlemen. Now, I wish to speak with Captain-General Ferrelo in private. Forgive me, Dr. Fuentes, but I ask that you leave us for a time as well."

They filed out bowing and muttering their good wishes until only Ferrelo remained behind with Cabrillo.

When the door closed, Ferrelo asked, "What do you wish to say to me, sir?"

"We have discussed the winds and currents often, Bartolomé. You are still the fleet's chief pilot. Describe to me, without our charts, how you would sail from this harbor to Asia."

Not wanting to pursue a conversation that implied what this one did, he nevertheless said, "If you insist, sir. I would, and *we* shall, sail clear of these reefs and obtain new supplies on the mainland before heading back up California's coast. Although we have calculated our present location to be roughly 625 miles east of the Moluccas, our orders are to follow the coastline, which cannot run much farther northward before we reach Asia." He speculated briefly on conditions they might encounter, speeds they might maintain, and several other matters Cabrillo might be concerned about. "Once we arrive in the East we will sail south toward the Spice or San Lázaro Islands. With luck, along the way we will discover the location of the Strait of Anián and claim its access to the Atlantic."

"Very good, Bartolomé."

Ferrelo could maintain his stiff compliance no longer. "Damn it all, sir, I may accept this command before the men, but, no. No, curse it! I will not recognize the possibility of your leaving us. You will get well!"

"I have already promised to do my best not to die, and I shall, but we must be prepared. All of us, Bartolomé."

313

With a stubbornness that could no longer be reasoned with, born of emotions stronger than logic, Ferrelo repeated, "No, sir. *Not* all of us." Then he took a long stride to reach Cabrillo's side, clasped his hand tightly as his eyes glared defiantly at the fever in his cheeks. "Tomorrow, sir, you shall be better."

Cabrillo smiled weakly up at him, his manner gently teasing as he said, "Yes, Captain-General, tomorrow. But now I must rest."

Seeing the energy it had cost Cabrillo to maintain even so short a conversation, Ferrelo repented instantly. "Of course, sir. Please forgive me. I will send for your physician."

"Bartolomé," Cabrillo said, forcing him to pause at the door, "I am very grateful my men have you to look after them for this short time."

"...I will speak with you in the morning, sir."

"Yes."

Cabrillo slept again, and for several hours his fever seemed to hold steady. His men moved around the ships quietly, keeping their hands busy with any activity they could find and repeating silent prayers as they worked.

That afternoon Cabrillo felt strong enough to ask Father Lezcano to pull his chair close and talk for a while. "Well, my dear friend," he said to the priest, "I find myself dwelling on questions I have never asked."

"About what, sir?"

"Well, you, for example." His words were a bit slow, his tongue heavy, but he was determined to discuss things other than his injuries. "I have always wondered why the viceroy sent you to join us, especially after the lashing I gave you. How you must have fought his order. Would he not listen?"

Father Lezcano glanced down at his hands. "The viceroy has never learned what took place in Santiago, sir."

Even through the fog of fever this surprised Cabrillo greatly. "You did not tell him?"

"I told no one."

They studied each other for a moment before Cabrillo said, "Then, when you received your orders, what reason did you give him for objecting?"

"Sir," said Father Lezcano, revealing the secret he'd held for so long, "he did not order me here. I requested to sail with you."

"You requested—"

"Yes, I did, sir." He smiled gently. "I wish I could say I had fore-seen or even guessed all that I would learn from you, how fond of you I would become, but I have never been that wise. Perhaps I wanted to see what you were really like. I had never met anyone like you."

Cabrillo shook his head slowly in wonder. After a thoughtful mo-ment, he turned his feverish eyes to Father Lezcano again and said, "I want you to know that the young man I have so often called father I would willingly and proudly call my son."

They let their gazes and the stillness hold them for a little longer, and then Father Lezcano leaned back in his chair and said, "There is something I have long wanted to ask you, sir. When and how did you learn to lead men?"

"I learned out of necessity, and the lessons took many years. It is a long story."

"If you feel able, I would love to hear it."

"Well then," Cabrillo said slowly, closing his eyes, "I suppose it started when I was a boy of twelve, when I came from Spain to Cuba. I served as a page for one of Narváez' officers." He sighed heavily. "Our commander's butchery of the natives horrified and sickened me: women, children, all slain without mercy. I was a boy, but I learned to use the sword and crossbow to survive." He tried not to remember those days as he went on. "Later, when I fought with Cortés, there was at least a measure of sanity in the slaughter; he had a goal beyond outright extermination. Before the battles at Tenochtitlán I was made captain of a small force of crossbowmen. Many smaller tribes of In-dians, who'd been brutalized by the Aztecs, joined us. We could have done little without them."

"I have heard, sir, that you were badly wounded during that fight-ing."

"Yes," Cabrillo said and then glanced at him searchingly. "Have you also heard of the orders I received before the final battle, orders to build the boats?"

Evasively, Father Lezcano answered, "Something, sir."

Cabrillo turned his gaze to the ceiling above his bunk. "We had been driven from the city, many of our men captured and sacrificed to their bloody gods. Cortés commanded me to build a fleet of small bergantines so we could cross the water surrounding the capital city and retake it. I soon discovered that we had nothing with which to seal the planking. Pine resin had been collected but we still needed animal fat to bind it, and we had none. It was our Indian allies who offered the solution. They were not squeamish about such things." He paused, recalling it all despite his efforts to block the images, and he needed another breath to go on. "They said their men would gather the dead bodies of our mutual enemies, and render the fat from them. Even after seeing the cruelty of the Aztecs first-hand, I shuddered at the thought of such use of their dead. But our allies' kinsmen had been taken by the Aztecs year after year, their hearts cut out and their bodies dumped down the sides of the pyramid to rot in heaps. They saw only justice in the use of Aztec bodies. In the end Cortés accepted no excuses. It was done. His ships were built. The capital was taken. But that is a sin that haunts me still."

Father Lezcano listened to every word the captain-general was willing to share with him.

Cabrillo sensed this and continued, "After that battle there were many more, most of them fought under Orozco and Alvarado. It is strange, but while I was fighting some tribes of Indians and making alliances with others, I came to respect many qualities of both. This respect, I believe, helped me as a commander, because I learned not to underestimate them. I began to appreciate them and my own men more."

"Sir, during our voyage you have avoided battles whenever possible, and we have not lost a single man."

"Perhaps, through so much warfare, learning to value life highly has been my most lasting lesson. A man should evade a fight if he can. People's lives should not be wasted, ours or theirs."

Father Lezcano said softly, "Thank you for telling me, sir. Would you like me to pray with you for awhile?"

"Please, Father."

Before the second decade of Father Lezcano's rosary had been touched, Cabrillo had drifted off to sleep again, and soon afterward Manuel and Mateo entered the cabin to join the priest in quiet prayer.

Chapter 26

A SMILE AT SUNSET

It was early evening when Dr. Fuentes returned to Cabrillo's cabin, nodded once in greeting to Father Lezcano, and walked toward Cabrillo's bunk. The priest and Manuel drew closer to observe as the physician lifted the covers from his patient's bandaged leg. The sign he'd been fearing most, the smell of rotting flesh, hit him like a blow. Cabrillo's fever had begun to rise during the last hour, but he still was able to focus well enough on the doctor's countenance to read his thoughts.

"Mateo," he said to his nephew, "go and help Paulo prepare my dinner. I wish to eat early today." When the boy left the room, he said hoarsely to Dr. Fuentes, "I smell it too."

The doctor could not speak, but he forced himself to look closely at blackening skin around the edge of the bandages and the red lines webbing out above and below them. It was spreading fast. At his slight touch, the flesh of the ruined leg gave out a crackling sound. At this evidence, he held no more than a grain of hope, but even that seed was blown away when Cabrillo told him, "I feel similar sensations in my arm as well."

Accepting the look of misery the physician could not completely conceal, Cabrillo said, "Dr. Fuentes, you have done all you could. I have sensed from the beginning that these would be my final wounds. During this voyage the sailors' sickness has weakened us all. It has stolen some of the strength I once had." Seeing that Dr. Fuentes was about to offer a comforting lie or voice his confidence in miracles, Cabrillo said gently, "The best of physicians cannot outmaneuver God's will. Take heart in my feeling as much at peace as a man can at such times. I am indebted to you for your care."

Father Lezcano fought to find the courage Cabrillo was demonstrating. He steadied his breathing and clamped his mouth, silently commanding the unvoiced cries of his protesting mind to silence, and the tears at the edges of his stinging eyes to remain unshed. He dared not look at Manuel, but he could feel him standing a few steps away, rigid as a stone tower.

Dr. Fuentes couldn't keep from saying, "I will drain the wound, sir. There is still hope."

Cabrillo dredged up the shadow of a smile as he shook his head. "Any remaining hope for me should be directed toward heaven. I will doubtless need more than the average number of prayers to reach so lofty a destination."

After a moment the doctor forced himself to nod. "How bad is the pain, sir?"

"It is terrible, and yet it seems to be coming from a distance that makes it bearable."

Dr. Fuentes had heard similar descriptions from other victims of corrupted injuries. "We will do whatever is possible to ease your suffering, sir. For now, will you drink some sherry before I change the outer bandages?"

Despite the doctor's obvious attempts at gentleness, at times this handling was excruciating for Cabrillo, and when his leg was finally at rest once more, his face was even redder than before. "How long, doctor, before the disease takes me?"

"Captain-General, it is progressing rapidly...No more than a few days, sir."

For several moments Cabrillo stared out at nothing. "Then, there are things that should be addressed without delay. I thank you for your frankness." At this the doctor stood and turned away, knowing that the toughness he'd managed to gain through years of living with pain and death would crumble if he did not.

Cabrillo said to his back, "Dr. Fuentes, please go and privately update Pilot San Remón on my condition." Before the physician left Cabrillo, he went to a cabinet, pulled out another bottle of the strongest fortified wine on the ship, and set it on the table.

Manuel still stood near the foot of the bunk, his face as unmoving as his body, his eyes now gazing unseeing straight ahead. Cabrillo said, "Manuel, we must talk."

318

The black face lifted, and when their eyes met it was Cabrillo's gaze that faltered. He strengthened his voice, however, and said, "When the voyage ends, you will have many choices as a free man. I ask that you do two things for me as my friend; first, visit Beatriz and our sons, and then take a wife of your own. You were meant to raise a family, Manuel."

The tightness around Manuel's heart and mind robbed him of every word, but he nodded, went to the table, and poured out a glass of sherry.

Taking it in a shaky hand, Cabrillo said in a diminishing voice, "Now, go and tell Mateo and Paulo. For them, this news should come from you. Keep them both with you in the open air for a while and talk with them. When they are calmer, and if they wish, they may be with me while I receive my last rites." He looked at his priest and said, "Until then, Father, I wish to offer my confession."

A quarter of an hour passed before the small group huddled together inside the cabin and the most final of Catholic sacraments began. While Cabrillo received blessings and the bread and wine of communion, each of his witnesses tried but failed to conceal his desolation at the thought of what he would soon be forced to surrender. Yet their prayers on his behalf were gravely sincere, and they even managed to sing a wavering, off-key hymn as the service concluded.

At Cabrillo's whispered request, Paulo ushered the others and himself out of the room so Cabrillo and Father Lezcano could be alone once more. Cabrillo accepted a drink of sherry that the priest offered, and said, "And now, is there anything else you wish to ask or tell me?"

With an openness that stripped his personal anguish bare, Father Lezcano said, "Sir, I am very afraid of losing you."

"You, my friend? You have a strength of spirit I have never seen in another man."

"I do not *want* to lose you."

"Nor I, you. But that choice is no longer ours."

With the ship's moaning, creaking murmurs all around them, they both struggled to submit to such a reality. At last Father Lezcano asked, "Are you afraid, sir?"

"I should be. I should tremble, given the life I have led, and yet I do not. I have seen death too many times, face to face, to be terrified of my own or of its consequences. I will be granted no more opportunities to attempt things a different way, to choose more wisely, so I must trust that, in time, God will forgive my wrongs. No, it is not so much dying I mind, as failing. I have real trust in Captain-General Ferrelo, but the ships will not last much longer without being rebuilt. If he does not reach Asia without great delay, if he does not find the strait or any other treasures, the voyage will have failed." He took another long drink, wanting to overpower the pain enough to voice his thoughts for as long as he could. "I had hoped for so much. Now, our efforts may deliver no riches beyond the knowledge of this land, its people, the winds, and the currents. I fear the viceroy and king will value these little."

Father Lezcano asked, "Would you blame yourself, sir, if it turns out that the river does not exist or that this coast does not touch upon Asia's shores?"

"I would not, and I believe there is much value in the knowledge we have gained. In the end, knowledge is the most valuable of God's gifts. But I am neither a viceroy nor a king."

The priest forced a smile. "I have always suspected you of being a scholar at heart, sir."

"You may be right. Many times through the years I have sensed that I should have been something other than a warrior, yet a warrior I became."

"And a captain, and then a captain-general."

"Yes." He sighed, and when he spoke again his words came even more slowly. "My greatest regret is that my lack of success will make life harder for my family. I pray that they will be treated fairly, and that they will not suffer harshly without me."

"With your permission, sir, I would like to visit your family. It would mean a great deal to me to know them."

Cabrillo's smile, feeble though it was, was laden with affection. "It is only right that you know them well, Julian, since you have become one of my sons. They will soon come to love you, as I do."

His voice faded, his eyes closed, and his breathing settled into a shallow rhythm. Father Lezcano took the cup that was about to fall from his slackened hand and set it on the table. He then knelt down on the decking and remained there in prayerful, anguished contemplation throughout the longest and darkest hours he'd ever known.

320

Deep in the night Cabrillo shifted his body and the merciless pain that struck him produced a shout of torment. Father Lezcano was quickly at his side, supporting his head and holding a full glass to his lips. After emptying it Cabrillo lay back, panting, his half-closed eyes unnaturally bright. When he had managed to steady his breathing somewhat, he said, "Please bring Mateo to me, Julian."

In moments the boy stood before him, his young face trying desperately to show nothing but courage. "Mateo," Cabrillo said, "I must leave you soon." The bravery on the young face wavered and his lips trembled. "Now, now, my dear nephew, it is a path we all must take." Cabrillo glanced at the priest and said, "Father Lezcano, I ask that you be Mateo's uncle as well as his priest. Mateo, honor this good man as you have honored me."

Mateo's wet, mournful eyes gazed up at Father Lezcano and back to Cabrillo. The boy wiped his dripping nose on his sleeve and nodded.

"When you reach home again," Cabrillo went on, "tell my family of my deep love for them." Again the boy nodded, and he could no longer hold back a sudden rush of tears. Reaching out a hand and clutching the blanket near Cabrillo's hand, Mateo sobbed, "I shall miss you, uncle." Father Lezcano gently took the boy by the shoulders and led him out the door.

When Father Lezcano returned to Cabrillo's side his face was pale, but he listened carefully as Cabrillo's voice fell to little more than a whisper. "I must ask one last thing, Julian. Taya..." his voice failed him completely and he closed his eyes for a moment, then he pushed on. "There is a ruby broach in my chest. Its color matches her name. Will you give it to her?"

"Of course, sir."

"And tell her...tell her I am sorry to leave her. Tell her I am grateful."

"I shall, sir, just as you ask. Now, you must rest."

Even faster that Dr. Fuentes had predicted, the disease spread through Cabrillo's body, as if hurrying to deplete so great a strength of will before it could rebuild itself. Since his caregivers could do heartbreakingly little else they gave him more of Taya's medical brew, but his fever and delirium steadily gained mastery. At times his mind pulled him into the violence of a battle fought long ago in his youth, and at others he was drawn back to the loving arms of his wife, and his painful cries would gradually die down to murmurs of longing and affection.

Unwilling to inflict further suffering, the doctor gave up his attempts to replace the bandages. At the end of the second day of high fever, as light faded from the cloudy evening sky, all of their prayers had evolved from beseeching God for a miraculous recovery to pleading that He end this misery as soon as possible.

Father Lezcano had also turned his prayers to the Blessed Virgin, whom he fervently believed would sympathize with the need to end a good man's intolerable suffering. At Manuel's request he began to softly pray aloud, "Hail Mary, full of grace, the Lord is with thee. Blessed art thou among women, and blessed is the fruit of thy womb, Jesus. Holy Mary, mother of God, pray for us sinners now and at the hour of our death. Amen." At these words, prayed by him innumerable times during his short tenure as a priest, he glanced up and by the gentle light of the oil lamps he saw that Cabrillo's eyes were open and focused on him. It was a sight he had not expected to behold again. No sound came from Cabrillo's lips, but his mouth formed the words, "Take care of them, my son," and his eyes closed very slowly.

Father Lezcano could not breathe. He stared at Cabrillo's face and then at his chest, watched him take one shallow inhale, one more, and then exhale and lay utterly still.

Manuel, who had shed not a tear through the interminable trial of watching Cabrillo die, fell to his knees and let out a roar of grief so deep and loud that it reverberated off the rafters and swept through the ship, to the other ships, and across the water to the island cliffs.

Captain-General Ferrelo burst into the cabin. He stared at the still form, the body of the man with whom he'd never again share trials, or joys, or theories. After one nearly strangling breath, he managed to contain his own grief only because he must, for the sake of the men he now commanded. His eyes found those of Father Lezcano, and the emotions of each was read by the other as clearly as if they'd been written with ink and paper. Ferrelo turned to Dr. Fuentes and said huskily, "Please prepare him, doctor. His services will be conducted as soon as arrangements can be made." His eyes returned to Cabrillo's face, and as if to himself, he muttered softly, "The third day of January. I shall never forget."

The man who now took up the burden of the fleet's leadership left them and went to the main deck to give the crews the official word of Cabrillo's death, but their mourning had begun the instant Manuel's great cry had reached them. While most stared off in heart-clenched silence or wept softly in as private a corner as they could find, some turned unashamedly into the arms of other crewmembers and surrendered to their tears. The *San Salvador's* two carpenters turned from the others and with unsteady voices began to plan as fine a coffin as their skills and materials could fashion.

On shore, only moments after Captain Ferrelo had made his announcement, woeful wails rose up from some of the islanders near shore who plainly understood what had come to pass. A native runner was sent to inform Matipuyaut, and within minutes he, his sons, and a grief-stricken Taya appeared at the water's edge. Matipuyaut would not permit any of them to board their canoes and approach the flagship. Just as Cabrillo had done when Shuluwish had left this world, he kept his people at a distance to allow the mourners privacy, but as the night deepened the Chumash built fires and Kipomo danced and chanted for the safe passage of Cabrillo's spirit.

The two groups remained apart. Hours slipped by, and the natives gradually made their way back to the village. Taya was the last to leave, and her departure was against her will. When beckoned away by Matipuyaut, she refused to move. Finally, as she protested with rising pleas, her brothers lifted her from the sand and carried her up the path.

Earlier that evening the new commander of the *San Salvador* had addressed his officers aboard *La Victoria*, saying, "I have been wrestling with our options for what must be done next, gentlemen. The simplest choice is to bury the captain-general near our harbor, but this could bring an outcome that *must* be avoided. I refuse to allow for the possibility that his body will not be left in peace. If he is buried anywhere on this island his remains could be disturbed. The natives might do so without meaning any disrespect, since the possession of body parts from their departed ones is meant to show homage. I have seen the bones of dead ancestors in several of their homes, and I shudder at the thought of such a thing happening to him. He must be protected, as decency and our church dictate."

"Absolutely, sir. What do you propose?" asked Captain Correa.

"We shall take him to the next island."

"Sir," Father Gamboa quietly pointed out, "that island is also inhabited."

"We will leave tonight, before the light returns. The *San Salvador* will be taken out very carefully until we are well clear of the rocks. I had thought of using the *San Miguel*, but it seems more fitting to use his ship and his crew. They will bear him to the other island, however, no one but the few men going ashore will know the exact location of his grave."

Every man present agreed with this plan. So, during the very depth of that night and well after the Chumash had left the beach, with clouds filtering much of the light shed by the moon and stars, the flagship alone quietly weighed anchor and left the harbor. She made her way to the nearby island they called San Lucas, and with hushed movements lowered two boats.

While the *San Salvador* lay in stillness offshore with her lamps extinguished, the landing party rowed away using oars muffled by rags. They pulled stealthily toward a well-chosen stretch of deserted shore and, reaching the sand, Father Lezcano, Manuel, Ferrelo, and three guards lifted the coffin from the boat. Followed by four more guards, and two men and Mateo bearing digging tools, they all headed up a narrow, climbing path that led inland. The group halted often to watch and listen for any sign that they'd been detected, but nothing around them stirred. When they reached level ground, an area was chosen for their purpose, the shovels and picks were handed out, and the work began. Arms moved rapidly to loosen and lift the dirt, digging deeper and deeper until Ferrelo said, "That will do, men. Climb on out." Father Lezcano was allowed only a few brief moments for prayer before Ferrelo ordered Cabrillo's coffin, bearing a likeness of his family's crest, to be lowered into its resting place.

The grave was quickly filled, and as the final few shovel loads were being placed, Mateo stepped forward and said to Ferrelo, "Please, sir, may I leave this with him?" He held out a flat, roughly rectangular piece of stone upon which he'd crudely scratched the joined letters of "JRC". Above this mark he'd carved a small cross, and beneath it, a headless stick figure. "It is a poor thing, sir," the boy said, "and I had no time to attempt his face, but… please, sir."

In a voice gone low with withheld emotion, Ferrelo said, "Of course, Mateo."

The boy placed his remembrance gently atop the loose soil, and then stood back and watched his stone disappear as the final few inches of dirt fell. In order to conceal the grave the burial crew now trod upon their work place, added a little more dirt, tamped it down again, and scattered the excess soil, swept the area with brush, and finally littered it with gathered sticks and stones. When every attempt had been made to disguise the location that cradled Cabrillo's body, Ferrelo said, "We must get back to the ship. Dawn is not far off." They moved away, and Father Lezcano, Mateo, and Manuel each glanced back and bid a final, silent farewell before their heavy feet took them from the island.

They made good time returning to Isla Posesión and a very dull gray light was all that revealed their return to the remainder of their anxious fleet. Men lined the railings of their sister ships, their faces weary, grave, and sorrowful, but also greatly relieved to have their flagship anchoring safely beside them once again.

Ferrelo could see no natives along the shore, but he had little doubt that the San Salvador's absence had been noted. Still, he'd done what he could for Cabrillo's honor, for the protection of his captain-general's body and soul, and for his own battered peace of mind.

When day broke more fully, every member of the fleet witnessed the ceremony held aboard the San Salvador to remember Juan Rodriguez Cabrillo. This time, Matipuyaut and a handful of his people had been asked to attend and they had accepted. Taya stood beside her father, her face lifeless and her body weak with grief. Father Gamboa, at Father Lezcano's request, presided over the service. While battling to keep his own bereavement in check, Father Lezcano kept close beside Mateo and Manuel.

When Father Gamboa concluded the religious rite, Captain-General Ferrelo lifted his voice and said, "Men, henceforth, this island will be called Isla Capitana de Juan Rodriguez in memory of the fine leader we have lost."

No cheers greeted this announcement, but many of the mourners nodded and muttered approvingly, finding a measure of comfort in the news.

The rest of that day men went about their duties in a listless state, finding it difficult to convince themselves that the captain-general was truly gone. When the turnings of the sandglass had run their regular course, though it felt like many more had been added, the sun began to set beneath a sky as heavily clouded as the hearts of Cabrillo's men.

Yet, as Father Lezcano stood alone at the stern rail, he lifted his eyes and watched the clouds at the farthest edge of the horizon begin to separate into layers. Their lower edges slowly curved and crested like inverted waves, and the underbelly of each swell gleamed with the brilliant orange-crimson of a fire's very last embers. Spellbound, he knew he'd never seen so magnificent a sight. And as the glory of the display held him, he suddenly understood. He was beholding a parting gift. When his tears came he let them fall, and smiled even as he wept.

Chapter 27

VIENTO'S RIDER

April 29, 1543

T he viceroy's official notary, Juan León, sat back in his wooden chair and pursed his lips thoughtfully as he gazed in turn at Captain-General Ferrelo, Captain Correa, Pilot San Remón, and Fathers Gamboa and Lezcano. They'd been called together at the home of Puerto de Navidad's alcalde, and now that most of their business had been completed León couldn't help but be somewhat moved by the evidence of deprivation and grief on the weathered faces seated around the table. Even so, a few points still needed to be confirmed.

"Then, Captain-General, on the second attempt to reach Asia you sailed only a hundred miles beyond the point reached under Captain-General Cabrillo?"

"That is correct, sir," said Ferrelo.

The notary glanced over his notes, furrowed his brows and said, "The viceroy had hoped for more."

Ferrelo's mouth tightened but he did not waste words on someone who couldn't empathize with the hardships they'd survived. To say that their own hopes had been disappointed would have been too ridiculous an understatement to voice. And yet, as Ferrelo's eyes now swept the men who shared this table, keen-eyed, thin, sunburned, and weakened, he felt a surge of love and dedication that he wouldn't have traded for great riches. This thought he also kept to himself. What he did say was, "If any man could have taken us to Asia under the conditions we faced, sir, Captain-General Cabrillo would have. His death was most grievous."

"Yes," said León, "of course." He cleared his throat, studied his notes again and, after posing a few additional clarifying questions, he concluded with, "Is there anything further you wish me to record, gentlemen?" When no one spoke, León said, "Then my orders from the Royal Audiencia and the viceroy have been fulfilled. Your testimonies and those of Cárdenas, Vargas, and the others will comprise the bulk of my report. Señor Urdaneta here," he nodded toward the slight man sitting to his left and reviewing his own set of newly written pages, "will help you complete your illustrations and charts. I thank you for your cooperation in providing so comprehensive an account of the voyage, gentlemen. You are now free to leave."

As they rose and began to make their way to the door, Urdaneta touched Father Lezcano's sleeve and asked softly, "Will you stay a moment, Father?"

Father Lezcano nodded and, lowering himself again into his seat, looked into the wise eyes of the man Cabrillo had repeatedly mentioned with admiration. Urdaneta did not speak until they were alone and the door had closed. "It was not difficult to discern that during the voyage you came to care a great deal for Captain-General Cabrillo."

Father Lezcano let his gaze soften. "He became a father to me, sir. The loss of him wounded deeply."

"He was a rare man. I liked him immensely. Encouraged by our last talk together, I have nearly decided to sail again one day. I had hoped to journey with him as our commander." Eyeing Father Lezcano, understanding his pain, he said, "Perhaps, instead, his *son* will sail by my side."

Father Lezcano gave him a sad, grateful smile. "I am honored by your words, sir, but I intend never to sail again."

"Ah, such an intention is to be expected, but you are very young, Father. Years ago when I sailed with Loaisa and Elcano, I never imagined being captured and held prisoner in the San Lázaros, and when I finally reached Spain again I intended to avoid ships for the rest of my days." He shook his head slowly. "But then I sailed here to Mexico. And now that I have seen the charts and log books from your voyage, I may even consider returning to the San Lázaros."

Father Lezcano looked at him in surprised wonder.

"Yes, my young priest, you, the notary, the viceroy, and perhaps even the captains of Cabrillo's fleet do not yet fully understand what you have delivered to the Spanish kingdom. With these charts," he swept his hand toward the large sheets of parchment, "our ships may soon be able to sail to the San Lázaro Islands and safely return to New Spain, something that has eluded us until now. Our lack of knowledge of the currents and winds has destroyed many ships and sent hundreds, or more likely thousands, of men to their deaths, as I have witnessed. Your voyage has done much to dispel our ignorance, and that will make it much easier to find the trade route. When we do, our ships will bring wealth to Spain in quantities large enough to impress even our king."

Seeing how Father Lezcano's amazement had grown, Urdaneta chuckled softly. "Seldom is new knowledge recognized for its true worth, but the future will show us the value of what you have paid for with your efforts and tears."

Father Lezcano stared at him, his thoughts grasping the repercussions of what such farsightedness foretold. "During one of our last discussions, Captain-General Cabrillo said that knowledge was one of God's greatest gifts."

"And so it is, Father, even if it produces something very different from gold and jewels." After a moment's reflection he said, "Who knows? One day California may even be prized as a place to settle. Based on these reports, it is beautiful."

"But, you, sir? Will you sail to the San Lázaros with our charts?"

"Perhaps, Father, but if not I, others will. More and more lately I feel called to a quiet religious life." Seeing that he had surprised Father Lezcano once more, he smiled and said, "Then again, perhaps I will take to the sea after I am ordained, just as you did."

Urdaneta began to rise, and Father Lezcano stood with him. "You must be very tired, and I will not delay you further, Father, but in the days to come I would very much like to discuss the possibility of my joining the Augustinians."

"It would be my pleasure, sir."

"Fine, fine. But for now, is there any service I can render you?"

Father Lezcano was about to decline his offer, but then he said, "There is something, sir, of a personal nature. You see, I wish very much to visit Señora Cabrillo, and it is appropriate that a letter precedes my arrival. I have tried several times to write to her only to stumble over my clumsiness with words. You were the captain-general's friend, so I hope it will not be too great an imposition to help me compose the message. It is said that you are a gifted writer."

329

"You honor me, Father. When do you wish to begin?"

"Do you have time now, sir? We have paper and ink before us."

"I do indeed."

In moments their heads were bent together over a sheet of parchment while Father Lezcano's quill carefully scratched words of introduction and condolence. When three pages had been filled, he closed his thoughts with the warmest of wishes, sanded the ink, rolled the letter inside an outer sheet, and sealed it with wax.

"There," he said with satisfaction. "I am in your debt, Señor Urdaneta."

"Not at all, Father. Will you let me know when you receive a reply?"

"Certainly, sir."

"Then I advise you to hurry if you intend to reach the post rider before he departs."

Father Lezcano bid him a hasty farewell and hurried out the door, waving his letter in a parting salute.

Not even a week had passed before the priest received his answering letter from Beatriz, inviting him to come to them as soon as he could leave Navidad. Now, after a few more weeks needed to complete the final duties to his commander and to recover his health, the priest was packing his few belongings into saddlebags slung across the top rail of the corral as Urdaneta stood patiently beside him.

"Well, sir, that is everything. I have only to saddle my horse."

"You need not hurry your preparations on my account, Father. I have had far too little of your company lately, and I am happy to see you off."

Father Lezcano strode into the stable and came out a few moments later leading his mount.

Rather than the dusty bay gelding the priest had ridden into Navidad nearly eleven months earlier, his horse was now a superbly appointed dappled gray Andalusian stud. The weeks since his return to Navidad had done the stallion as much good as it had his new owner, giving him back the tone to his muscles and gleam to his coat. Urdaneta's heart warmed as he watched the man and horse, their bond obvious in the way they moved comfortably in unison. Captain-General Ferrelo had told him of Cabrillo's leaving Viento to Father Lezcano in a written codicil, and now it was easier to understand why he had. As the two came nearer, Urdaneta noticed that the priest's brow had furrowed. After looping the reins over the fence, Father Lezcano lowered his eyes to the riding crop in his hand, staring at it as his expression clouded.

Observing the depth of the emotions crossing the young face, Urdaneta asked, "What is it, Father?"

As if speaking to the crop itself, he said softly, "Still hanging from a peg near my old saddle. I had forgotten I left it there before we sailed." Very slowly he tightened his fingers around the whip, silently recalling the details of a day that had altered his world. "It seems like ages ago. He told me a man's family could not always teach him what must be learned, that sometimes essential lessons are left to others." After a pause, he said, "So many lessons…" He looked up at Urdaneta, his eyes brightened by moisture. "How can one repay such things, especially when the teacher is no longer here?"

Urdaneta smiled with great gentleness. "The best way I have found is to share what we have learned with others, whenever we can."

"Yes, that I will try to do. Thank you, sir." Again glancing at the quirt, he asked, "Will you hold this for a moment?" Urdaneta accepted the whip and stood back while Father Lezcano saddled Viento and checked his hooves one more time, all the while talking to the horse in familiar, loving tones. At last, he said, "There now, Viento, all is ready."

Urdaneta patted Viento's neck and asked his master, "Are you still uneasy about meeting them, Father?"

"Perhaps a little, but, as you saw, her letter could not have been more welcoming."

"She will undoubtedly embrace you with affection."

"Mateo has been there with his family for some time, and I have missed him. I look forward to seeing Manuel at the Cabrillo encomienda as well, but it is Señora Cabrillo I long to meet. I have much to tell her, mostly words from him. Although they will be meant to comfort, I fear they will be difficult to hear. Her grief is very new."

"Then, for now, tell her only what she asks to know."

"Good advice, my wise friend. Take care of yourself while I am away."

Urdaneta's eyes shone fondly upon the priest, "I shall miss our talks. Until next month, farewell. Write to me if you find the time."

"I will make time." He gave Urdaneta a strong hug and then climbed into the saddle, and as he adjusted his tension on the reins to keep Viento in place Urdaneta handed him his quirt. He took and said with sudden intensity, "I have just decided what to do with this."

"Do with it, Father?"

After tucking the crop under the flap of a saddlebag, he said, "I will bury it along the way." The hint of a smile that had been too long absent came into his deep brown eyes. "And I know the perfect place for it to rest, a place I remember well." He extended a hand and clasped Urdaneta's. "God keep you well, sir."

He loosened the reins and let Viento walk away from the corral and onto the road that led eastward. Urdaneta watched him go, speculating on possible explanations behind the priest's strange intention to entomb the whip. At last he turned away, and with a shake of his head he muttered to himself, "Patience. He will tell the whole story when he finds the right time and place."

On the bowsprit of *Californian* while researching Cabrillo's voyage, Christine Echeverria Bender, a former resident of San Diego, California, now lives with her family in Boise, Idaho.

She may be contacted at www.christinebender.com.

For a free catalog of Caxton titles write to:

CAXTON PRESS
312 Main Street
Caldwell, ID 83605-3299

or

Visit our Internet website:

www.caxtonpress.com

Caxton Press is a division of The Caxton Printers, Ltd.